TO LOVE AGAIN

TO LOVE AGAIN

BL CLARK

SAPPHIRE BOOKS

SALINAS, CALIFORNIA

To Love Again
Copyright © 2015 by BL Clark. All rights reserved.

ISBN - 978-1-939062-99-4

Editor - Healther Flournoy
Book Design - LJ Reynolds
Cover Design - Michelle Brodeur

Sapphire Books
P.O. Box 8142
Salinas, CA 93912
www.sapphirebooks.com

Printed in the United States of America
First Edition – May 2015

This and other Sapphire Books titles can be found at
www.sapphirebooks.com

Dedication

This book is for my Grandma.
Thank you for always showing me unconditional love and
support.
I love you!

Acknowledgments

Chris and Schileen/Sapphire Books - Thank you for taking a risk and giving my writing a chance and me an opportunity to fulfill a dream that I have had since my early teens.

Heather Flournoy - Thank you for helping me to make this a better and stronger book. Also, thanks for trying not to scare me with the edits…I would love to say you didn't, but you did, and I am stronger for it.

Michelle Brodeur - Thank you for helping me to create an awesome cover.

Nicki Wachner and Tara Wentz - Thank you for your friendship and support. Both have made this process a whole lot less scary!

Teri Thomas - Hmmm, "thank you" doesn't really fit, but, we're going to work with that. It has been an honor working with you on our various writing adventures over the past couple of years. If you hadn't pushed me, I don't know that the idea of "To Love Again" would have fully formed, nor would it have been written. You have read everything, good and bad, that I have written since we met. I'm not sure what that says about you. I mean, I'm certain because it involves me, it says good things. Stop laughing; it could be true. Thanks for being a friend and an amazing writing partner. Oh, and thanks for helping to hide my comma phobia. Can you just imagine how embarrassing it would be if people truly knew?

Ashley Philmore - You are an amazing friend, and I feel very lucky to have met you. Thank you for helping to make my crudely drawn cover a reality.

Suzi Hautaniemi - Thank you for your support and help with hiding some of my writing flaws. You have been there driving and pushing me not to give up on myself when we all know I wanted to. Also, thanks for suggesting I submit my book to Sapphire Books. It appears to have worked out well for me.

Kristel Shaw - As one of my best friends - let me know if you see your influence in here. Thanks for the MANY years of support and kicks in the ass. Who would have pictured you and I would have become such good friends, even after I held your Tigger slippers for ransom?

Mom - Look what I did! Thank you for your love and support. We didn't always see eye to eye over the years, but we both grew from it. I love you!

Lexi Meyer - First off, you have no idea how hard it was not to list one of your various nicknames, you know like... What? I didn't write it. I'll attempt to behave - for once (it could happen). For a daughter, you were better than I deserved. As a friend, you are amazing. Your love and support over the years goes beyond words. Stop crying, sheesh. People are looking at us funny.

Kathy Meyer - My best friend, my partner, my soulmate… Anyone who really knows me knows that you have the patience of a saint. You have put up with me and my quirky ways for so many- Hey look, a chicken! Huh? Where was I? Oh yeah, you have put up with me and my quirky ways for so many years. How and why we won't say, but thank you! I love you!

Tony Clark - Meow!! You are the best, most opinionated and special cat. Even as an old fart, you rock, buddy. Your food is on the way, quit screaming.

Prologue

It was a crisp February afternoon as Jade sat outside the hospital chapel and thought back over the events of the last hour.

"Jade, I love you, always remember that," said the blond-haired woman from the hospital bed.

"You can't leave us. You need to fight this," cried Jade, looking at her frail, dying wife.

"We've been through this, sweetheart. That isn't what the fates want. I'm needed elsewhere. You are needed here to take care of our daughter."

"She needs you as much as she needs me. Please don't leave us, Amy."

"If there were any way that I could stay, I would, trust me. I love you both so much."

Amy started to cough and her oxygen monitor started to beep. Jade watched as the nurses and doctors piled into the room and worked to save her wife.

"Ma'am, you are going to have to step out of the room," said one of the nurses.

"That is my wife, she needs me here," said Jade.

"Jade, please, let them work. I won't leave you until I can say good-bye properly," said Amy, holding the oxygen mask away from her face and looking deep into her wife's blue eyes.

"Promise me," said Jade.

"I promise."

The doctors pulled the mask out of Amy's hand,

replaced it on her face, and told her if she wanted a chance to survive longer, she needed to leave it there. Jade took one last glance and headed toward the door.

"I know what she means to you, I have your number, and as soon as we are done or if something changes I will call you immediately," said the daytime nurse.

"Thank you, Cindy," said Jade, walking out into the hall. She wandered around the hospital lost in thought and memories before finding herself standing outside the hospital chapel. Jade wasn't a religious person, but then everyone tends to pick up some form of faith when their loved ones are seriously sick or dying. If she went in would it be pointless? What if there were others in there? Would she be disturbing them? Would she be taking away from them getting their prayers answered?

Jade slowly opened the door and saw that there was only one person in the room. She quietly made her way inside. Looking at the large crucifix at the front of the chapel made her feel small, almost insignificant.

Taking a seat at the end of the pew at the back, Jade folded her hands together and prayed.

"So, I don't know what is appropriate, but please help Amy. I know that she is in pain even if she doesn't say so. Our daughter needs her, I need her. I don't need the miracle of her being healthy right away, I just need more time with her." Jade looked up at the crucifix and stared, looking for a sign, something to give her hope.

Jade felt her phone vibrate and her heart sank. She rapidly exited the chapel to answer it out of respect to the person left in the sanctuary.

"Hello?"

"Hi Jade, it's Cindy," said the voice on the other

end.

"Is she…" started Jade, her voice shaking.

"She has been stabilized for now. Amy says she won't sleep until you see that she is okay. Are you still nearby?"

"I'm by the chapel, I will be there shortly," said Jade, and she hung up the phone and made her way up to Amy's room.

Slowly she opened the door and saw her wife lying there, watching for her. As she entered and allowed the door to close behind her, she saw her wife's frail hand rise and beckon her over.

"I love you," Jade said, taking her wife's outstretched hand and kissing it. Amy started to remove the oxygen mask and Jade stopped her. "Leave it on, you need it. Talk to me that way."

"It makes…it hard…to talk," Amy said, frowning.

"Tough, it keeps you alive, and I need that more than anything."

"Fine, you were always the stubborn one in this relationship." Amy smiled.

"One of us had to be, you are a pushover." Jade forced a smile as a tear rolled down the side of her face.

"Sweetheart, please, no tears," said Amy, reaching up and wiping away the tear and the one that fell to replace it.

"Easy for you to say, my love. You aren't the one that is going to be left here alone," said Jade as her breath hitched.

"You aren't alone, my love. You have our daughter who is going to need you more than ever."

"How do I explain this to her, Amy? She's only four. She has no understanding of any of this except that you can't be home and I cry a lot."

"You'll figure it out, Jade."

"Can I bring her to see you? Will you allow me to do that much?"

"You don't think all these wires and machines are going to scare the shit out of her?" asked Amy, a hint of anger in her voice.

"I don't have a clue, but she might understand more after seeing everything. Please...if you aren't going to come home she is going to need the closure and a chance to say good-bye," Jade said as another tear rolled down her face.

"All right, bring her in tomorrow. You have to be strong for us my love. Please," said Amy, holding her wife's hands. They sat together for a long time in silence before Amy fell asleep and Jade had to leave to go pick up their daughter.

Chapter One

Good-byes

All right sweetheart, we're going to go see Mommy. Remember she is very sick and has some wires and machines that are there to help her feel better."

"C-can I hug her?"

"Of course you can. I just don't want you to be scared when we go in the room."

"Will you be there, too?"

"Of course, I wouldn't make you go in alone. Come on baby, let's go." With that, they headed upstairs to the critical care unit. As they were walking down the hall, Jade saw Cindy coming out of Amy's room.

"Good morning, Jade," said Cindy. "And who is this little cutie?"

"Cindy, this is Brianna. Bri, this is Cindy, she is taking care of Mommy."

"Hi," said Brianna as she clung to her mother's leg.

"It's very nice to meet you."

"How is she doing?"

"She had a rough night, but she's excited to see you both."

"Thank you...for everything."

"It's a pleasure. Have a great visit," Cindy said as

she moved toward the nurses' station.

Jade picked up Brianna and they walked into Amy's room. They moved slowly to give Brianna time to absorb what she was seeing and to make sure she wasn't scared and overwhelmed by everything.

"Hey, Baby Girl," said Amy as she saw them enter. She went to remove the mask but chose to leave it on due to the darkening expression Jade could feel crossing her face. "Come give me a hug."

Jade walked them over and set their daughter up on the bed, and watched as Brianna quickly grabbed Amy and held her as tight as her little arms would let her.

"I miss you, Mommy. When are you coming home?" asked Brianna, a quiver in her voice.

"Baby, I'm not going to be able to come home."

"Why not?" her daughter asked. Tears started to well in her eyes and tears fell from Jade's.

"Mama told you I was sick, right?" asked Amy, and her daughter nodded. "Well this sickness is really bad."

"Like Mindy's Mommy?" Brianna asked, referring to her friend's mother that had passed away about two months prior.

"Exactly like Mindy's Mommy."

"But I don't want you to go to heaven. Mama and I need you here."

"I know, baby, but I'm afraid that isn't going to be able to happen. I will watch over both of you and will always, always love you," said Amy as she started to cry and pull her daughter closer, reaching her hand out for her wife's.

Jade took Amy's hand and then leaned in and hugged her wife and daughter. She knew deep in her heart that this was going to be the last time that they were together as a family. She could feel that Amy was too exhausted to keep fighting. The cancer was winning and going to claim another good soul.

They lay there together for a long time, until they heard Cindy come in to take Amy's vitals.

"I'm sorry to interrupt," Cindy said softly.

"It's okay," said Jade, taking Bri out of Amy's arms and feeling her turn and wrap her arms around her Mama's neck tightly.

"She isn't going to hurt Mommy, is she?" asked Brianna.

"No baby, she isn't going to hurt me."

"Would you like to help?" Cindy asked Bri.

"Can I, Mama?"

"Just listen to exactly what Cindy says," said Jade.

Cindy took Brianna from Jade's arms and set her on the bed and showed her which button to push to take Amy's blood pressure and temperature. She then showed her where to read how much medicine her Mommy was using. After Cindy was done she left Bri on the bed and smiled at Jade, and nodded for her to step out into the hall.

"I'll be right back. You take care of Mommy," said Jade, exiting the room.

"I just wanted to let you know that her stats are low, she is getting close. I know that isn't the news you wanted to hear, but I always try to be honest with my patients and their family." Cindy placed a caring hand on Jade's arm.

"I-I appreciate your honesty," Jade said as a tear rolled down her face.

"I wish I could have given you better news. The

doctor I'm sure will want to discuss things with you. Now, get back in there and spend as much time as you can together."

Jade entered the room and saw her wife looking at her with a concerned look. Their daughter had lain down and fallen asleep in Amy's arms.

"What did she say?"

"Your stats are down," said Jade, sitting down on the bed and taking her wife's hand.

"I love you so much, Jade," started Amy. "I don't want you to close yourself off because it hurts or because you don't want to move on."

"You can't ask either of those of me, dammit. I love you...you and Bri are my world," Jade said as tears streamed down her face.

"I know, and Bri will continue to be your world, but babe, you have a long life left to live yet. I don't expect you to be out dating the day after, but I do expect you to move on after you grieve for me."

"And if I don't want to move on?"

"Jade, you have to move on. You are going to find someone to make your life worth living again. You need to do that and be a happy influence for our daughter."

"I will promise you that I'll make sure our daughter has a good life, but that's the only thing I can promise," cried Jade.

Amy adjusted on the bed so she could sit up without disturbing their daughter, and wrapped her arms around her wife and held her close. They stayed that way for a long time, whispering words of love and devotion to one another until their daughter started to stir.

Jade composed herself as best she could and

quickly texted a friend to come and get Brianna so that she could spend more time with Amy. In her gut, she knew the time was short.

"Bri, I love you so much," said Amy, hugging her daughter close. "I want you to be the bestest girl you can for Mama."

"I love you, too, Mommy," said Bri as she hugged Amy tightly.

"Mama and Mommy have some talking to do so you are going to go spend the night at Aunt Kristel's tonight," Amy said. Kristel opened the door as if on cue, and Amy motioned for her to come in.

"Hey," said Kristel, walking over and hugging Jade, then going to hug Amy.

"Hi, Aunt Kristel," Brianna said. "Mommy said that I get to stay at your house tonight."

"Yep, and I think that Jake wanted pizza for dinner. You think that might be okay with you?"

"Can we get Canadian bacon for Mommy? It's her favorite," she asked.

"Anything you want," said Kristel, her voice breaking. She had known the two women for the past nine years and watched them fall in love, get married and bring this caring little girl into the world. She knew things were nearing the end, and had voiced she couldn't understand why it had to happen to such a great couple.

Jade filled Kristel in on things and Kristel said that Brianna could stay with them as long as needed. They hugged and then Jade said good-bye to her daughter as Kristel hugged Amy and promised her that she would look after them here if she promised to look after them from above.

After Brianna and Kristel left, Jade curled up on

the bed next to Amy and they held one another until the doctor came in. He told them that from the look of the stats it would be best to put their affairs in order as Amy had, at most, a day or two. They nodded and he left.

"Cindy was much easier to hear that from," Jade said softly.

"I didn't know there was an easy way to hear that."

"There isn't, but I knew she cared and understood what it was going to mean to me when she said it."

"So, do we have everything in place?"

"Yeah, we do. You made sure you had it all planned when we found out that you couldn't fight this anymore. I just really want more time with you. We aren't done yet," said Jade as Amy pulled her close.

"I just didn't want you to have to deal with anything other than Brianna. I love you, never forget that."

"I love you, too," Jade said before kissing her wife softly on the side of the head.

They lay together that night holding one another and enjoying the closeness and the privacy that they were given. Morning arrived and Amy went into distress. The doctors were able to stabilize her, but Jade knew that she didn't want to be kept alive on machines.

"We'll give you guys a few minutes," said Cindy.

"Thank you," said Jade as everyone left the room. It was just her and Amy. "I know you don't want to be kept alive on machines. I know I have to say good-bye...I'm not ready, though."

"You'll never...be...ready," Amy panted.

"And that's wrong?" asked Jade, brushing her

wife's hair out of her eyes.

"No, but...we have...to be...realistic."

"I know, but if you were saying good-bye to me you wouldn't be composed either."

"I *am* saying good-bye to you, though."

"You are, but..."

"No buts Jade. This is hard...for me as well. I don't...want to leave you two..."

They cried together and kissed for a few minutes before Amy told Jade she was ready. Jade went and got Cindy and held her wife's hand while they turned the machines off and they looked into one another's eyes as Amy passed.

Jade stayed there holding Amy's hand for a long time before they told her that they needed to take her. When she left, she called Kristel and told her the news and that she would be by in a couple of hours to get Brianna. She needed some time to process things.

Chapter Two

Acceptance

After Amy's funeral, Jade and Brianna tried to rebuild their life. Jade made sure that Brianna knew that her Mommy had loved her very much and that she wouldn't have left them by choice. After the first month, people started trying to get Jade to go out with them, but she wouldn't leave her daughter with a sitter or anyone.

"Jade, come on, you need to get out of the house," said Kristel.

"I do get out of the house. I go to work, and I take Brianna to the park," responded Jade.

"And that is fantastic, but you need to get out on your own, too."

"I can't, Kristel. I won't leave Brianna alone. She just lost her Mommy."

"I'm not asking you to leave her in the house by herself, I'm asking that you and I get a babysitter for Brianna and Jake, and for you and I to go out, get a cup of coffee or something."

"It's too soon," said Jade, starting to cry at the thought of Amy not being there. Kristel wrapped her friend in a hug and held her close.

"All right, but you are going to need to get out there eventually."

"I will, I just need time to grieve. We were

together for almost ten years, which should allot me some time."

"It does, I'm just doing what she asked of me."

"I know, and I appreciate it," said Jade.

Four months later

"Jade, you are leaving this house," stated Kristel.

"Kristel, I'm not ready."

"Jade, you aren't being asked to date, or anything, I just want us to go out for coffee. We can plan Brianna's birthday party."

"Fine," Jade said, exasperated. She knew there was no way she was going to win this one.

Jade called the babysitter she and Amy had used and the girl came right over. Angie sounded as though she had been surprised to get the call. Jade knew this was because she hadn't needed her since Amy was first hospitalized.

"Hi, Angie," said Jade, answering the door when the teen arrived and motioning for her to enter.

"Hi! How are you doing?" asked the teen nervously as she entered the house.

"I'm okay. Bri is going to be very excited to see you. Kristel is bringing Jake over shortly."

"Great. We'll have a fun time!"

"Mama, can you help me?" called Bri from the top of the stairs.

"Sure, sweetie," said Jade, heading towards the stairs and up to her daughter's room as Angie made herself comfortable in the living room. "Whatcha need, Baby Girl?"

"Is this okay to wear today?" Brianna asked, holding up a pair of shorts and a T-shirt that Jade knew Bri and Amy had bought together.

"Of course it is. Why wouldn't you think it was okay?"

"Because it was something that Mommy and I gotted together."

"Oh baby," said Jade, pulling her daughter into her arms. "Just because Mommy isn't here doesn't mean that you have to stop wearing the stuff you two bought together or stop playing with certain toys because they were ones you guys liked or she got you."

"Really? It won't upset you?"

"Really, it is perfectly okay."

"Mama, is Mommy really watching over us like she said she would be?"

"I believe she is, and I bet she will smile when she sees you wearing that outfit. Now, get changed and come downstairs. Angie is here, and Jake and Kristel will be here soon." Jade kissed the top of her daughter's head.

"Okay." Jade stepped out into the hall and composed herself enough to make it downstairs and she hoped she could maintain the strong façade until she was out of the house.

"I'm failing her and you," Jade whispered, looking up toward the sky.

❧❧❧❧

"Jade, are you okay?" Kristel asked as they drove away from the house.

"No," said Jade as a tear rolled down her face.

"What happened?"

"Bri asked me if it would be okay for her to wear some stuff that Amy bought her. She's been afraid to wear things and play with certain toys because Amy isn't here anymore."

"Jade, it'll be okay. You talked with her, right?"

"Yeah, I explained that it was okay. She then asked if I really thought that Amy was watching over us. She misses her so much."

"I'm guessing she isn't the only one," said Kristel, taking her friend's hand and squeezing it.

"I still wake up at night feeling her holding me. She's been gone almost six months, and I can't even start to let go yet."

"Jade, you two were so in love and worked so well together. It will take time. How about we get the coffee to go, and we find someplace to sit outside and enjoy the sun and no people?"

"I'd love that." Jade offered her friend a small smile.

Kristel went in and got their coffee, then they headed to an out of the way park that Kristel knew of and found a picnic table to sit at.

"So, what type of party are you thinking for Bri?" asked Kristel.

"She is really into that movie, *Frozen*. I was thinking something dealing with that."

"Jade, we are not renting a snow machine for your daughter's fifth birthday."

"I wasn't talking about renting a snow machine. I was just thinking the decorations." Jade rolled her eyes.

"Then, I think that would be great."

"Kristel, can you take Bri next Friday for the night?"

"Of course. Why?"

"It would have been our eighth wedding anniversary. I-I need a night alone," Jade said, staring down at the table.

"Oh Jade, I can't believe I forgot. Do you want me to take Bri for the weekend? Jakey and I were just going to be hanging around the house."

"No, she is going to be a big enough wreck just leaving me overnight. I just need to process things and come to grips with the fact that Amy is gone."

"Jade, have you thought about going to any of those group therapy things? I'm not saying you need to, but I hear they do help."

"I have looked into them, but I'm too scared to go," admitted Jade.

"Would it help if I went with? We can find one, and in a couple weeks, go together."

"I-I think that would help. I can't believe it has been almost six months that she has been gone."

"I know, and I know that you are still hurting, but given time, it will ease up."

"I hope so. Right now I'm still at the crawling-in-a-hole-and-waiting-out-life stage."

Kristel hugged Jade and they sat together in silence, just watching everyone at the park.

❧❧❧❧

"Bri, get your stuff packed. Kristel is going to be here soon," said Jade.

"I don't understand why I have to go over there. I don't like being away, Mama."

Jade knelt down and looked her daughter in the eyes and told her, "Today was Mommy's and my anniversary, and I need to work through things."

"But I can help you. Please don't send me away," Brianna said, starting to cry. They had only spent a couple of nights apart since Amy's death. Brianna had spent those nights with Amy's parents.

Jade pulled her daughter into her arms and held her close. "I'm not sending you away, Baby Girl. I just need some time to work it out in my head that Mommy isn't here anymore."

"I miss her, too, Mama," Brianna said into her mother's hair.

"I know you do. I love you so much," Jade said, hugging her daughter tighter.

"I love you, too, Mama!"

"All right, now I need you to get ready."

"All right," Brianna said, sniffling and grabbing her backpack, and starting to put her clothes into it.

Jade reached the bottom of the stairs just as Kristel knocked on the front door. Jade answered the door and motioned for her friend to come in.

"How are you doing?" asked Kristel as Jade closed the door behind her.

"I'm a wreck, but holding it together for Bri's sake."

"You mean until we leave," Kristel said, raising an eyebrow to her friend.

"Exactly."

Brianna came down the stairs and went over to her mom and motioned for Jade to bend down.

"What is it, sweetie?"

"Mr. Butters helps me when I get scared and miss Mommy. I want you to have Mr. Butters tonight to help you not be too sad." Brianna handed her yellow bunny to Jade.

"Thank you, sweetie," said Jade, hugging her daughter close and seeing Kristel wipe away a tear. "I will make sure to keep Mr. Butters with me tonight."

Jade said good-bye to her daughter and Kristel and after they left, she grabbed four photo albums and went into the living room and sat down on the couch. She propped Mr. Butters up next to her and opened the first album.

"Happy anniversary, my love," Jade said, running her fingers over the first picture of her and Amy ever taken. "I can feel you watching me. I can see you shaking your head at me for still holding on so tight to you. Deal with it. Bri misses you, and I miss you. I have no idea how I'm supposed to move on when my heart feels so empty with you gone. Kristel is taking me to some group therapy session next week. She's been our rock, just like you predicted."

Jade continued paging through the pictures. When she got to the wedding photos, she stopped and stared. "You were so beautiful that day. I still can't believe you wore a tux with tails just because you knew I loved the look. I have three happiest days. The first was the day you first kissed me, the second was the day we got married, and the third is the day Bri was born. How is it that you have been gone almost six months, my love? I feel like my heart stopped beating when you died...you were always the best part of me. Bri is growing up so fast. We're having a *Frozen* birthday party for her next weekend. I can't believe she is going to be five." Jade flipped through the pictures of Brianna's birth and them holding her while lying in the "family" room at the hospital. "She left Mr. Butters with me to help me get through tonight. Damn bunny reminds me of you and does make me feel closer to you. You couldn't have chosen a cuter stuffed animal?" Jade laughed, wiping more tears from her eyes.

Jade set the albums on the floor and grabbed the

yellow bunny. She hugged it close as she lay down on the couch and cried herself to sleep.

Morning came and Jade looked around the house, hearing the rain outside hitting the windows. She sighed. After taking some time to clear her head, she got up and put the albums away and went to shower before Kristel brought Brianna back.

❧❧❧❧

"Hey, Angie! Thanks again for babysitting Bri and Jake tonight," Jade said as the teen arrived.

"No problem. They are such great kids."

"I don't think that we will be too late, but if it gets to be later than, say, nine o'clock, I will give you a call."

"It's okay. I don't have school tomorrow, so please, stay out as late as you want."

"I appreciate the offer," said Jade, smiling.

Brianna and Jake entered the room and, each grabbing one of Angie's hands, led the teen into the living room where they had constructed a fort the size of the room.

Kristel and Jade headed out for the group Kristel had found.

❧❧❧❧

"I don't know that I can do this," Jade said as they pulled up outside the community center.

"I know it's scary, Jade, but you have to give it a try," said Kristel, pulling her friend from the car.

They walked inside and Kristel checked them in while Jade absently scanned the bulletin board.

"You know those flyers you are reading are at least ten years old," said the woman now standing next to her.

"Huh?" Jade said.

"Sorry. Those flyers you are pretending to read, they're at least ten years old."

"Oh, I was wondering about the pictures."

"Are you in the group?"

"Um, y-yeah."

"Well, I'm Rachel Cassidy and I lead the group. Welcome!"

"I'm Jade, and thank you."

Rachel took her coffee and headed into the room.

"Who was that?" Kristel asked.

"She said her name was Rachel. I guess she runs the group," said Jade.

"Oh that is her. I read her bio when I was doing research for the groups. She's had some tragedy in her life. Her wife was killed by a wolf while they were out hiking."

"Wow, that's horrible."

"We should probably get inside and get seats."

They entered the room and saw that there were about twelve people sitting in chairs set in a circle. Jade and Kristel chose two seats in the middle of an empty section, each hoping that nobody would sit next to them. As they looked around the room, they saw the same lost look in the eyes of the others who were there. Jade watched as Rachel closed the door to give them privacy in the room.

"All right, let's go over the group rules. First and foremost, be respectful of others. Everyone here has lost someone they loved and is trying to find a way to move on with life. Second, see rule one. Third, you don't have to speak unless there is something that you want to say. I do ask that you at least participate in the introductions. Lastly, please clean up after yourself before you leave. Are there any questions?" asked Rachel, looking around at everyone. "Great. I guess I'll start the introductions. I'm Rachel and I lost my wife and unborn daughter three years ago."

"I'm Doug, and I lost my husband three years ago," said the man to her left.

"I'm Sharon, and I lost my husband twenty-two months ago tomorrow. We have two kids together."

"I'm Carmen, and I lost my girlfriend nine months ago."

They continued around the room until they got to Jade.

"I'm Jade, and I lost my wife six months ago. We have a daughter who turns five on Saturday."

"I'm Kristel, and I'm here to support Jade. I lost one of my best friends when her wife died."

"Great, thank you everyone for sharing. I know how hard it is for some of you to come here. I think it is fantastic that you care enough, Kristel, to come and support Jade. Shall we get started? Does anyone want to share how your week has gone?"

"I was able to look at a picture of Diane for the first time without completely falling apart," said Carmen.

"That's great, Carmen," Rachel said, offering the woman a genuine smile.

"I saw my parents this week, and when they asked how I was doing, I was able to answer them without breaking into tears," said Sharon. "My kids even told me that they were proud of me."

"That's fantastic. I know that it was a huge step

for you and your children."

Jade raised her hand unsure what was compelling her to do so.

"Jade?"

"Friday would have been mine and Amy's eighth wedding anniversary. We were together almost ten years. I spent the night alone looking through our photo albums, talking to my wife, and holding a stuffed bunny my daughter gave me to help me not feel alone. It was the first time since she died that I let myself admit that she wasn't coming back."

Kristel put her arm around her friend, and two people passed her a tissue as she started to cry.

"We all have done that. I admit, I still find myself talking to my wife," said Rachel. "The important thing to remember is that you are always going to have that person as a part of your life and a part of you. Jade, you said that you have a daughter? Your daughter is always going to be a piece of you and your wife and as long as you hold on to that you will never be alone. I'm not saying pine for the loved one, but hold them in your heart and remember that you loved them and they loved you and it is okay to love others or love again."

"Have you moved on, Rachel?" asked the dark-haired man near Jade.

"I am not dating anyone, but I'm not opposed to the idea either."

The group continued to talk about their loved ones while Kristel and Jade listened. After two hours Rachel announced that they had to end the group for tonight, but she hoped everyone would be back next week.

"You ready to go?" Kristel asked Jade as soon as

the group ended.

"Yeah," nodded Jade.

"Um, Kristel? Jade?" called Rachel, walking over to them. "Thank you again for coming to group and sharing. I know that things are hard and feel impossible right now, but they will get easier. I wanted to give you each my card and number. I'm always available if things get too rough or if you need someone to talk to. I know that is cliché, but I also have been where you are and have some perspective on it."

"Thank you, Rachel," Jade said, offering a little smile.

"Thank you again for allowing me to sit in with Jade at the meeting," said Kristel.

"My pleasure, and you're both always welcome. I hope the meeting helped, and we see you next week," said Rachel, nodding to the women and heading over to some of the members who were waiting to speak with her.

"She's nice."

"Yeah, she is."

"Do you think you want to come back next week?"

"Yeah, I think I do, but will you come with me?"

"Of course. We'll have to make sure that Angie can babysit."

Chapter Three

Making It Work

M ama, what are you and Aunt Kristel planning for my birthday?"

"Well, if I told you that, then it wouldn't be a surprise now, would it?"

"I can still act surprised even if you tell me."

"Nice try, sweetie," said Jade, leaning down and kissing her daughter on the top of her head.

"Night, Mama."

"Good night, sweetie. I love you!"

Brianna snuggled with Mr. Butters and drifted off to sleep as Jade stood in the doorway watching her daughter.

Jade walked downstairs and pulled out her laptop. She started going through her checklist of things to get done for the party in a few days.

"You know, Amy, you were always better at this planning stuff than I am. I wish you were here to help," Jade said, losing herself in memories of planning parties with Amy.

"Jade, you can't just wing these things," said Amy.

"Well, unlike you, not all of us are anal enough to create spreadsheets and checklists with every detail in them. I bet you even have bathroom breaks in there," said Jade, sitting on Amy's lap and starting to scroll through the spreadsheet that was up on the laptop.

"Watch it, you," Amy said, pulling her wife close and kissing her deeply. "I may not have included bathroom breaks, but there might be a few make-out sessions in there.

"For us or for our three-year-old daughter?" Jade joked and started to squirm when Amy tickled her.

"I would hope for us, but if you would prefer her, I guess we could have Kristel send Jake over."

"No, I definitely prefer it being us," said Jade, looking deep into Amy's eyes before she kissed her, causing them both to groan as the lust inside them built.

Jade was brought back to reality when her phone started to buzz.

"H-Hello," she answered.

"Hello, is this Jade Donovan?" said the voice on the other end.

"Yes it is."

"Hi Mrs. Donovan. I'm Steve with The Party Shop and I was calling to verify that you were still having a party on Saturday and that you would like for us to come and set up."

"I'm sorry, how did you know about this?" asked Jade.

"An...Amy Donovan set this up a year ago it looks like. She has instructions to call you to verify the party and to get the theme details and for us to do the setup and the teardown so that you are free to enjoy your daughter's party."

"Amy," Jade said, shaking her head and looking up at the ceiling.

"Is this correct?"

"Yes, please, I need all the help I can get with this party."

"Well, what theme are you looking for?"

"Our daughter is obsessed with the movie *Frozen,* and I was hoping to do something along those lines. Is that workable?"

"It's a very popular one for us this year. I can promise you that we can accommodate what you need. Have you gotten a cake yet or would you like us to add that in as well?"

"If you can add that in, it will help me a great deal."

"That is not a problem, ma'am. What time is the party?"

"The invites went out for a party from eleven in the morning until two in the afternoon on Saturday. There are going to be six kids and four adults."

"Fantastic. Next, I need to find out if you want punch, juice, or if you are going to provide the drinks."

"I'm sorry, Steve. Did Amy leave a checklist with you to go through?" asked Jade, laughing.

"Yes, ma'am. She is very thorough. I would like to ask her if it would be okay if I borrowed this to help with my other planning."

"My wife passed away six months ago. I'm certain that she would be honored to have you use it."

"I'm sorry for your loss, ma'am, and I appreciate the authorization to borrow the list."

"She was an amazing woman. And I will provide the drinks. Thank you."

"Great. Do you have any questions for me?"

"I'm certain I know the answer to this, but did Amy set this up for an annual event?"

"She set it up for the next three years and has prepaid for the events."

"Thank you! I look forward to your assistance with making this a good memory for our daughter."

"It will be our pleasure. If you think of any questions, please just give us a call."

"Thank you. I will see you on Saturday."

"See you Saturday," said Steve as he hung up the phone.

Jade sat there and giggled. "You aren't even here, and you are still taking control. I know you are laughing at me up there and that isn't nice. I miss you, my love."

Jade sent a message to Kristel letting her know that Amy had already arranged for everything to be cared for before she passed away.

❧❧❧❧

Saturday arrived, and Brianna was up at seven in the morning, bouncing around the house.

"Mama, it's my birthday," exclaimed the pint-sized ball of energy as she entered her mother's room.

"Yes it is," said Jade, pulling her daughter into bed with her and holding her close. "Happy birthday!"

"Thank you, Mama!"

"So, what do you want for breakfast?"

"Can we have funny-shaped pancakes?" asked Brianna.

"You can have whatever you want. You're the birthday girl." Jade smiled before she kissed the tip of her daughter's nose.

Jade and Brianna went to the kitchen, and Jade made funny-shaped pancakes. After they ate together, she cleaned up the kitchen and went to shower and get ready for the day while Brianna took a bath.

After they were both ready, Jade heard a knock on her door, and she left Brianna in the living room watching cartoons.

"Hello," said Jade, answering the door to a tall, raven-haired man wearing a The Party Shop shirt.

"Hi, Mrs. Donovan?"

"Yes."

"Hi, I'm Steve. We spoke on the phone."

"Right, so are you here to set up?"

"We are and if you just point us to where the party is going to be I will have my team set up and get out of your way. We'll be back around 2:45 to clean up and tear down everything."

"Thank you. I truly appreciate this."

"It's what we do."

Jade showed Steve and his team to the backyard where they set up a *Frozen* theme complete with a talking Olaf statue. They had games and party favors for all the kids, and Steve placed a special gift on the gift table as well. He went and got Jade to show her what they had done.

"I just want to verify that everything meets your requirements," he said as they entered the backyard. Jade gasped.

"Steve this is amazing," said Jade. "I can't believe your team set this up in such a short time. Bri is going to love it."

"The Olaf statue talks and has been a favorite at our other parties."

"Thank you so much. Um, what is that on the gift table?" Jade asked.

"Another one of your wife's requests," said Steve softly.

"She truly thought of everything," Jade said as a tear rolled down her face. "Thank you again for all your help."

"It is our pleasure. Please enjoy your party and again we'll be back at 2:45 to do cleanup."

With that, Steve and his team left, and Jade went back inside.

"Mama, why are you crying?" said Bri as she rushed over to Jade's side as her mother wiped away a tear.

"Your Mommy made sure that everything for your party was taken care of."

"That made you sad?"

"No, it made me remember how well organized she always was and it made me miss her. I promise I'll be okay in a couple of minutes."

Jade sat down on the couch, and Brianna curled up on her lap and hugged her. They cuddled while Jade composed herself again.

Kristel and Jake arrived, and Jade told Kristel to go check out the backyard while she kept the kids inside until the party started.

"Jade, that is amazing," Kristel said when she came inside.

"I know. Amy set this all up, and the gift on the table is from her as well," gushed Jade.

"She was one of a kind."

The others arrived, and they took the kids out back and showed them the setup. Everyone was in awe of how the backyard had been transformed. The kids played and sung along with Olaf and played "Pin the tail on Sven." They had cake, and then it came time for the gifts. Brianna opened all but the one from Amy; she told everyone it was from her Mommy, and she wanted to open it later with just her Mama.

After everyone had left and the party had been cleaned up, Jade and Brianna sat in the living room and opened the gift from Amy. There was a stuffed animal and a chain with a locket on it. When Jade opened the locket there was a picture of the three of them and an inscription that read, *"Love Lives Forever."*

"Did you know that Mommy got this for me?" asked Brianna.

"I had no clue, Baby Girl. Just like I didn't know that she had arranged for your party. Your Mommy was pretty sneaky."

"She was?"

"She was. She loves you so very much," said Jade, hugging her daughter.

"I love her, too. I miss her, Mama."

"I know you do, but if you didn't believe it before, you should now. She is up there watching over us, and she's still taking care of us like she always did."

"Thank you, and I love you, Mommy," Brianna said, looking up beyond the ceiling and sky to Amy watching over them.

Chapter Four

Moving Forward

Hey, Jade," Rachel said as Jade entered the group room.

"Hi, Rachel," replied Jade, moving to help put the chairs out.

"How are you doing?"

"Thanks to you and these meetings, I've had more good days than bad over the past several weeks."

"I'm glad to hear that. I see Kristel isn't here tonight..."

"No, she wanted me to try this on my own tonight. I'm not sure I'm ready, though," admitted Jade.

"You know that you don't have to share if you aren't up to it. Just go with what feels natural. I'm going to be here so you're safe, or at least I hope you feel that way."

"I do, and thank you, Rachel. This group has helped me start to come to terms with Amy's death."

"I'm glad we're able to help," said Rachel as she set the last chair out. "How is Brianna doing?"

"Bri is coping. She's only five and Amy was, well, better prepared than we were for this. I still can't believe that she arranged to have Bri's parties taken care of for three years and she got her such an amazing gift."

"She got her a gift? I don't recall you mentioning that before," Rachel said, sitting down next to the shaken woman.

"She bought her a locket and had a picture of the three of us in it and she got it engraved. They delivered it when they set up the backyard for the party."

"Wow, she was really prepared. I'm amazed that she had such foresight."

"Amy was amazing at that." Jade took a deep breath to steady herself.

Rachel reached over and placed a comforting hand on Jade's. "It hasn't been a year yet, it'll take time."

"Part of me knows that it will get better, and part of me doesn't want it to because it means I have to accept she's truly gone forever."

"Do you have to get home right after group tonight?" asked Rachel.

"No, Bri is spending the night at Kristel's."

"Let's talk after the meeting." Rachel squeezed Jade's hand and smiled at her before standing as others started to enter the room and join the circle of chairs.

There weren't any new members in the group meeting so the night went smoothly. Jade sat and listened to stories, but refrained from participating, occasionally getting lost in her own thoughts. After the meeting ended, Rachel and Jade cleaned up the chairs.

"So, what's up?" Jade asked, putting the last chair away.

"You looked like you could use someone to talk to. A friend of mine owns a coffee bar nearby that is very quaint and private. Would you like to talk?"

"I would say no, but I know from the meetings

I should.”

"Great, the place is just down the street two blocks on the left.”

"I'll meet you there.”

When they entered, Jade noticed that the place was dimly lit and there were several areas that were private. Rachel waved to someone behind the counter who pointed to one of the alcove areas.

Once they were seated, they ordered some coffee and waited for it to arrive.

"This place is nice,” said Jade.

"Yeah, one of my previous group members owns it and she keeps an alcove for me should I need it.”

"That is a very good deal,” Jade said, taking a sip of her coffee.

"So, what has you troubled? Beyond the obvious,” asked Rachel.

"My birthday is next week. We celebrated last year just before Amy went into the hospital,” started Jade. "She went into the hospital for the first time two weeks later. She was home for Christmas and New Year's, but then went back in the hospital mid-January and passed away three weeks after that.”

"The adjustment to a birthday without her is definitely a tough situation. Are you up to talking in depth on it? We don't have to, but it may help.”

"I don't know what to say really.” Jade stared down at her cup.

"What's jumbled in your head?”

"How'd you know it was jumbled?”

"I've been there. Hell there are days I'm still there. Emily and I were together for five years before the accident. She was four months pregnant and, god, I don't think we could have been happier,” started

Rachel as she pulled a picture of them out of her purse and showed Jade.

"You two look happy together."

"We were." Rachel looked down, smiling at the picture.

"I'm finding it tiring some days to keep up the appearance that I'm doing well so that Brianna is happy and doesn't get brought down by my missing her Mommy."

"How do you think she would react if she knew you were sad?"

"Bri is very sensitive when it comes to feelings and if she knew that I was sad she would be sad herself and do what she could to make me feel better. I don't want my daughter sad. She is too young not to enjoy life."

"Yes, she's young, but I'm going to go out on a limb here and say so are you." Rachel raised her hand, stopping Jade as she was about to speak. "I'm not saying that you don't have a reason to still be grieving. Trust me, I'm not. I'm saying that you don't have to feel guilty for having a laugh or smiling. Would Amy want you to be sad and depressed?"

"No, she would be pissed that I'm still having a hard time dealing as it is."

"Well, she would be wrong to be pissed. As a therapist I can state that much as fact, but you need to allow yourself to live, too. Do you ever go out with friends?"

"No," said Jade, staring down at the table.

"Did you before Amy got sick?"

"I was always a bit of a recluse, but Amy, she was the most social person I knew, so we did go out quite a bit."

"Then try to go out once a week."

"I do." Jade smirked.

"As honored as I feel, my therapy session does not count as going out. It is nice to see you smile, though. How about this: one day per week you and I will go out for coffee or take Bri to the park, just something that gets you out into society again?"

"Why would you want to do that?" The question came out harsher than Jade had planned.

"Well, it would probably help us both. I need to get out, you need to get out, and your daughter would see you getting out and it would help her. It's just a suggestion. You don't have to take me up on it, but if you don't I want you to promise me that you will find someone to hang out with or something to do weekly outside the house and my therapy group."

"I just don't understand why you would be so kind to offer your time. I'm just someone in your group therapy session. You barely know me."

"Jade, I would offer this to anyone in my group session that I saw was struggling like you are. The core people that are in that group have found a semblance of life. You aren't ready to do that on your own so I'm offering to help," said Rachel.

"I'll think about it," Jade said, playing with her coffee cup.

"Thank you. Now, how are you doing?"

"My mind isn't as jumbled," said Jade, glancing up toward Rachel.

"Good, why don't you go home and try to think about what I suggested. You have my number if your mind gets too cluttered. And in case you are wondering, everyone in the group has my number and several of them have used it."

"Thank you, Rachel. I appreciate the time and the offer."

"Will I see you in group next week?"

"Actually you won't see me for the next couple of weeks. Kristel is taking Bri and me out for dinner and a movie for my birthday. The following week I have a business meeting out of town. I'll be back after that, though."

"Well, have a happy birthday," Rachel said, smiling.

"Thank you. Also, thanks for taking the time to talk with me. I really do appreciate it," said Jade.

❧❧❧❧

"Jade, it's your birthday. You could at least smile a little," said Kristel when she arrived to pick up Jade and Brianna.

"I'm trying," Jade said. "Bri, are you ready?"

"Coming, Mama," said Bri, bouncing down the stairs to meet them in the doorway. "Hi, Aunt Kristel. Hi, Jake."

"Hi, Bri," said Kristel and Jake in unison.

"Mama, I made you something," Brianna said, handing her mother a wrapped package.

Jade smiled and knelt down to be at her daughter's height as she opened the present. She opened the paper and saw it was a clay plaque that said, "World's Best Mama!" with some flowers painted on it.

"Sweetie, did you make this?" asked Jade, continuing to stare at the gift.

"Uh huh. Aunt Kristel and Jake had to help me some, though," Brianna said, looking down.

"Baby, I love it." Jade wrapped her arms around

her daughter, holding her close. "I love you so much!"

"I love you, too, Mama!"

The group went out to an early dinner, then to see a movie, and back to Jade's house for cake and ice cream. After a while the kids got tired. Brianna went to bed and Jake curled up on the little couch in her room.

"Thank you for helping her make the plaque," Jade said to Kristel.

"No problem. You seemed to get lost a lot tonight during dinner. Where did you go?"

"I was thinking about last year and the surprise party that Amy had for me."

"She went all-out on that. I can't believe she got you a limo to go bar hopping in."

"I think the limo was more for her than for me," said Jade, laughing.

"I think you're right. How did group go last week by yourself?"

"It was different but good. I didn't participate, but Rachel said that was okay. Afterward we went and had a coffee and talked."

"So, was this like a date?"

"No, as therapist/participant. I am not even close to being ready to thinking about dating. It hasn't even been a year."

"I know, but she's kind of cute…"

"I haven't noticed," said Jade.

"So, I have one last gift for you," Kristel said.

"Kristel, you didn't have to get me anything."

"I um, didn't…"

"Okay…then who's the gift from?" asked Jade, slightly agitated.

"Amy," whispered Kristel, handing Jade a small

box and a card.

"When? When did she give this to you?"

"When you were outside talking to the nurse. A couple of days before she passed away."

"You've had this since then and didn't tell me?"

"Yes. She made me promise, and in respect to her memory I did what she wished," Kristel defended.

"What were your instructions?" asked Jade in defeat.

"To give this to you at the end of the night and after Bri was in bed."

"You are a good friend," said Jade, leaning over and hugging her friend.

"Do you want me to stick around while you open it?"

"Thanks for the offer, but I think I need to do this on my own."

"All right. If you need to talk later, give me a call." Kristel headed out of the room to grab a sleeping Jake.

❧❧❧❧

Jade poured herself a glass of wine and settled onto the couch. She stared at the box and letter for a long time before she was able to open them. She started with the letter.

"Happy Birthday, My Love,

I wish it didn't have to be like this, but I am watching over you and loving you from afar. Today has to be a hard day for you; it wasn't easy for me writing this knowing that I wasn't going to be there for your birthday. I love you so much and want for you to have a perfect life."

"I had that and then you got sick. Why did you have to get sick? We were just getting started with our life together," mumbled Jade.

"I hope that you and Bri had a good night together. I know that Kristel was there for some of it since you are reading this. Please don't be mad that I asked her to hold this and give it to you. I'm also sorry if it doesn't help you get over me, but I love you and wanted to do this one last thing for you.

You are my forever and you will always be my forever, but I want you to move on and make a life with someone else who makes you happy. Stop glaring at the letter as if it were me. You aren't even thirty yet, Jade. You have a long life and I don't want you to spend it alone. I love you too much to be that selfish. I hope you have had a great birthday and I hope that you think about what I have said here.

All my love forever,

~ A"

Jade read the letter a couple more times before she put it down and looked at the package. Taking a deep breath, she picked up the package and held it in her hand trying to figure out if she really wanted to open it or not.

Jade opened the package and found a braided chain with a note saying *"For your wedding ring when you are ready to move on."* Next to the chain Jade saw a diamond band with another note. *"For you to wear to always remember that I love you!"*

Jade put the ring on, held the chain and letter close to her heart, and cried herself to sleep. That night she dreamed of what their future would have looked like had Amy not gotten sick.

Chapter Five

Reaching Out

As the holiday season approached, Kristel spent more time with Jade and Brianna. She joined Jade and Brianna in the annual holiday festivities with Amy's parents. Seeing Amy's parents appeared to help to keep Amy's memory alive for both Brianna and Jade, but Kristel knew it did little to keep the sadness and loneliness from threatening to overwhelm and overtake Jade.

After the new year arrived, Kristel noticed Jade's mood change and become darker. As the one-year anniversary of Amy's death approached, Jade had started to pull away from those around her. Kristel was concerned when Jade withdrew, and even more concerned as Jade continued to become more and more distant.

"Hello," Kristel said, answering the phone.

"Hi, Kristel?" said the female voice on the other end.

"Yes."

"Hi, this is Rachel Cassidy. The therapist from the group you and Jade were attending."

"Oh yes, Rachel. How are you doing?"

"I'm doing well. I'm calling because I am wondering how Jade is doing."

"What do you mean how Jade is doing?" asked

Kristel.

"Well, she hasn't been back to the group sessions since before her birthday, and she appeared to be conflicted at that time."

"I'm sorry; she hasn't been back to the group sessions?"

"No, and I just wanted to check to see how she was doing. I know she had told me she was doing better thanks to the group."

"She was. Although she has been rather distant lately, I am guessing it's because tomorrow is the anniversary of Amy's death. I'm supposed to take Brianna for the weekend."

"I knew it had to be close to when Amy died. I just wanted to verify that she was okay," said Rachel. "I've been through this and know how hard it can be."

"I wasn't aware that she wasn't still attending the group sessions. I appreciate the call and I'll make sure to check in on her."

"Great, thank you," Rachel said, hanging up the phone.

Kristel sat there for a moment reflecting on the call. She decided that it was time to pay Jade and Brianna a visit since Jake was still out with her mother. When Kristel pulled into the driveway, she saw Jade out in the backyard.

"Hey," said Kristel, walking through the fence gate.

"Oh hey, Kristel," said Jade, motioning for Kristel to join her on the deck.

"Where's Bri?"

"She is over at a friend's house," said Jade, sitting down in one of the lounge chairs.

"So, how are you doing?"

"I'm okay."

"What have you been up to lately? How is group going? It feels like forever since we last talked."

"I've been spending time with Brianna lately. Group is fine," answered Jade.

Kristel was well aware that Jade was avoiding making direct eye contact with her because it would give her away.

"Liar!"

"Excuse me?"

"Jade, Rachel called me today because she was worried about you and the fact that you haven't been back to the group sessions since before your birthday."

"Oh, I, er…" stammered Jade as her voice trailed off.

"What's going on? You're my best friend. Let me be here for you."

"After reading the letter from Amy I just haven't been able to bring myself to leave the house other than work or something for Bri. It hurts too much. I miss Amy too much."

"I wish you would have told me. I would have been here for you," said Kristel, taking Jade's hand in her own and squeezing it.

"Yeah, I know you would have and you have been amazing over the last year. I didn't want to be a burden on you anymore than I already have been."

"Jade Marie Donovan, you are not and will never be a burden," snapped Kristel. "I have an idea for you."

"I'm scared to hear this, but what is your idea?" Jade asked, smiling weakly.

"Call Rachel and see if she can meet with you either today or tomorrow."

"W-why?"

"Because, you need help. You can't make it through tomorrow alone. Rachel is a professional and she's been through what you are going through. Most importantly, she wants to help."

"You're right," Jade conceded. "I'll call her."

"Now?"

Jade sighed deeply and then nodded in agreement. She went into the kitchen to get Rachel's number and called her.

"Rachel's to going to come over in a couple hours. Happy?"

"Yep!" Kristel smiled.

Kristel hung out with Jade until Rachel arrived and then went to get Bri. Kristel said she would bring Brianna home in a couple of hours. She missed her niece and felt they needed some quality ice cream time.

❧❧❧❧

"So, what's been going on?" Rachel asked as soon as Kristel had left. Jade led them outside to the patio to sit.

Jade showed Rachel the letter and birthday presents from Amy.

"Well, I have to start by saying your wife has exquisite taste in jewelry," Rachel said, admiring the ring.

"Yeah, she did have a way of finding deals on the most amazing items," said Jade, smiling with pride.

"Emily did, too."

"You smile every time you mention her name. Would you tell me about what happened to her? If it isn't too painful."

"I'd be honored. I love talking about her and remembering my wife." Rachel smiled. "Emily was an elementary school teacher. She loved working with kids of all ages. She had some kids in her class who came from troubled homes. We sometimes would take a few of those kids out with us when we went to the trails for hiking. It was something to get them out of their home environment and to give them a change of scenery. Emily had heard of a new trail that was opening and so we were going to check it out. We hadn't read up on the area, but we figured if they were opening it to the public, it had to be safe. We were following the trail and found that it had a lot of wildlife along it. They seemed curious about us, not scared like most animals. We got to an area that was a bit rocky and Emily, being the athlete and adventurer that she was, decided to venture out on them. She got about halfway across the outcropping of rocks when she lost her grip and slipped down the rock face onto what we thought was just a ledge. I was trying to figure out how to get her out of there when she was attacked." Rachel grabbed a tissue and wiped her eyes to try to prevent the tears from falling.

Jade reached out and took Rachel's hand and squeezed it.

"Wolves are very sweet creatures, but they are very protective of their young and Emily happened to be at the entrance of a den with a very protective mother. I don't blame the wolf. If someone comes to my front door and pretty much barges in, I'm going to protect my kids as well. Emily was only bitten twice before she got out of there, but her leg got infected. Because of the baby Emily wouldn't allow them to give her certain antibiotics. She was afraid they would harm her or the baby. The infection got worse and by the time Emily was ready to let them treat her properly it was too late."

"I'm so sorry, Rachel." Jade knew in her heart that if she were faced with the decision that Emily had to make she would have done the same thing.

"It all happened so quickly that I don't know that I had time to process what was going on and what the implications were. After they were gone, that is when I hit some low times. I don't need to go into how low, I'm certain you have either been there or can imagine it. After that, anger hit hard. I was angry at the world that they were taken from me. I learned that I can be quite a bitch when I choose to be," said Rachel, looking toward Jade and saw her intently watching and listening. "Then the loneliness set in. When Emily's birthday came around all I could do that day was cry. Holidays, I was curled up on my couch crying and hugging a picture of her. My birthday—crying. The day our daughter would have been born was especially hard for me. I hit a new low that day. That was when I was dragged by Emily's sister to a group similar to the one I run now. Unlike you, it took me a good month before I could share anything other than my name. When I started to share, the pain inside that I had been suppressing came racing to the surface. I would love to tell you that after I started to share it got better, but it would be a lie. That was the first year. During the second year I led the group. I knew that Emily wouldn't want me feeling sorry for myself and the person that was running the group was moving, so I took over. This is where the healing started. It's been three years and I'm feeling pretty good about my state of mind. I still miss them both like crazy, but I'm not driving myself crazy about it anymore."

"I think the only thing that keeps me going some days is Bri. The knowledge that she needs me and that I promised that I would stay strong for her."

"Did you carry her or did Amy?"

"Amy did, my egg," said Jade.

"We were doing the same thing."

"She is a piece of both of us that way. Or at least that is how I feel."

"I agree. Do you have a picture of her? Of Amy that is?" asked Rachel.

Jade reached over to the picture frame on the end table and handed Rachel a copy of the picture that Amy had put in Bri's locket.

"Brianna looks like you and Amy. When was this taken?"

"Amy, I'm guessing, knew something was up. She insisted that we have family pictures taken a couple of days after Brianna's fourth birthday. So, about a year and a half ago." Jade sat there for a minute thinking about the day they had the pictures taken and how insistent Amy had been. "You know, that's the first time I've thought that she knew more than she told me. That she knew something was wrong."

"And not to go too cliché, but, how does that make you feel?" asked Rachel.

"Honestly, fucking pissed off and hurt. If she knew something was up she should have told me."

"What do you think her reasoning would be for not telling you?"

"She was protecting Bri and me. She would never ruin Bri's birthday or mine, and they are so close together. But this is—was—our life together, she should have told me." Jade was stunned by the realization that Amy had kept things from her. She felt as though her world was being turned upside down.

"Jade, did Amy tell you shortly after the picture was taken?" Rachel asked, as if sensing the inner turmoil playing out inside her mind.

"After my birthday she told me she'd been to the doctor…"

"All right, so it wasn't long. I'm not going to speak for Amy, because really, she is the only one that knows why she did things. But it sounds as though she indeed wanted you and Brianna to enjoy your birthdays. You stressing and fearing for the future would not have been a lasting positive memory for her to draw on when she needed the added strength."

"I still would have preferred to have known," Jade said, anger and hurt in her voice.

"I don't doubt that, but you need to somehow make it okay within yourself that Amy chose to wait to tell you, but when she did tell you, she hid nothing."

"How do I know that she hid nothing when she finally told me?"

"Did you attend the doctor's appointments?" Jade nodded slightly. "Were you allowed to ask questions in those appointments?" Again, Jade nodded. "Were you allowed a say in the decision-making process?"

"Yes," whispered Jade softly.

"Then I believe it's safe to say that she was hiding nothing else. Jade, it's more than obvious that she loved you and Brianna a great deal. Amy in my opinion made her decisions based on what was best for you and Brianna. She chose what was going to allow you both the opportunity to move forward with your lives. She wouldn't want you to be closed off and locked in this house forever."

"I'm still grieving, though. I need time for that… time to accept it…time to figure out who I am without her."

"Nobody is trying to take that away from you. I think most of what you have been doing is commendable. You are trying to mourn the loss of not only someone you loved a great deal, but someone with whom you also brought a beautiful little girl into this world. I don't doubt that you see Amy in Brianna daily."

"She has her smile and her ears," Jade stated, a tear rolling down her face.

"Amy is still alive in that little girl and in your heart. Your memories will keep her alive forever."

Rachel and Jade sat there for a while letting the words sink in. Jade wiped the tears off her face, but she couldn't bring herself to meet Rachel's gaze.

Chapter Six

Helpful Intentions

Jade hadn't heard the front door close, but she heard the footsteps of her daughter too late to pull herself together.

"Mama...Mama," called the little girl as she ran out of the back door stopping when she saw Jade and Rachel sitting there. Brianna was shocked to see Jade with tear streaks on her cheeks. "Mama?"

Jade reached out her arms and Brianna tentatively walked into them and hugged her. Jade pulled Brianna up on her lap and continued to hold her close.

"I love you, Bri. You know that right?"

"Uh huh. I love you, too, Mama," said Bri before turning to look at Rachel. "Why did you hurt my Mama and make her cry?"

Rachel's heart broke with the look that Brianna was giving her. It was a mix of hurt, anger, and bewilderment in her green eyes.

"She didn't, Bri. This is Rachel. She's the doctor that runs the group that Aunt Kristel and I were going to for a while."

"Why is she here? And why are you crying?"

"You remember what tomorrow is right?" Jade said, looking her daughter in the eyes.

"The day Mommy had to go to heaven…"

"That's right. I'm having a hard time with that

and Aunt Kristel brought Rachel over to see if she could help me."

"But Mommy said I was supposed to help and take care of you? That was supposed to be what I do," Brianna said, her voice cracking.

"Baby Girl, you are doing a great job of taking care of me and helping me," Jade said, holding her daughter closer.

"Brianna," started Rachel, feeling the name catch in her throat. "There are times that everyone needs a little extra help. More than what their loved ones can give them."

"And that's why I brought Rachel over," added Kristel, who was standing at the patio door watching the exchange.

"But she made Mama cry…"

"No, sweetie, she didn't." Jade kissed the side of her daughter's head. "Remembering and missing Mommy made me cry. Rachel was here to help me so that I could feel safe in remembering and missing her."

"She didn't upset you?" asked Brianna.

"No, Baby Girl, she didn't upset me."

"Mama, does she help kids, too?" she asked softly, taking Jade by surprise.

"I don't know, you would have to ask her."

"Um, R-Rachel, d-do you h-help kids, t-too?" stuttered Brianna, causing each woman's heart to catch.

"I do. Did you want to talk to me, too?"

"Is that okay, Mama?" asked Brianna, looking up at Jade.

"Of course it is. Do you want us out here or do you want to talk to Rachel alone?" Jade asked, completely taken aback by her daughter's question.

"Um, c-can I talk t-to her alone?"

"Certainly. Aunt Kristel and I will be inside." Jade sat her daughter on the chair she had been using and looked to Rachel who gave her a reassuring smile.

❧❧❧❧

"Kristel, what am I doing wrong?" asked a now-panicked Jade.

"Why do you think you are doing anything wrong?" Kristel led Jade away from the window and into another room to try to stop her friend from watching what was going on outside.

"I'm sorry, were you not out there? Did you not hear my daughter ask if she could speak to a therapist?"

"I was and I am very proud of your daughter for asking to speak to Rachel," started Kristel, receiving a pained look from her friend. "Jade, she's hurting, too. She lost her Mommy and she isn't old enough to understand why. She sees you hurting even if you try to hide it. She isn't dumb. My god, she is Amy's and your kid."

"I never…should I have taken her to see someone sooner?"

"Stop panicking. I think tomorrow is hitting you both harder than either of you anticipated it would. Let Bri talk to Rachel and then we'll see what Rachel has to say. She's obviously someone you trust if she was still here when we got back."

"I do trust her."

"Good, now make me some coffee and tell me about your talk with her." Kristel smiled as she sat down at the island in the kitchen and watched Jade make coffee for them.

☙☙☙☙☙

"So, you help people?" Brianna asked, looking over at Rachel.

"I do. I am a doctor and I run a group that helps people like your Mama deal with losing the people they love."

"Why?"

"Why what?"

"Why do you help people like Mama? That's a lot of sad."

"It is, but I don't think a person being sad is a way that they should live their life."

"Mama was doing better...then she got sad again," said Brianna, casting her eyes downward.

"How have you been doing?" asked Rachel.

"I try to be a good girl so that I don't upset Mama. I miss Mommy a lot and I know if I told Mama that it would hurt her feelings."

"Why do you think it would hurt her feelings?"

"Because she knew Mommy before me and so she hurts more than me and if she knew I was hurting then she would think she is doing something wrong because it's what Mama always does. If she thinks she was doing something wrong then she cries. I don't want to make Mama cry more so I don't tell her."

"Bri, honey, you need to tell her. Or we can tell her together. Would that help?" Rachel asked and received a nod from Brianna in response. "Was there anything that made you think it would be bad for you to tell your Mama?"

"One day I asked her if I could wear something that Mommy and I got together and she told me that I could and that Mommy would like to see me wearing the stuff she got me and playing with the toys she got me. Mama doesn't know that I heard her tell Mommy that she failed me. I know from school that failing isn't good. I don't want Mama to think she isn't doing good. She's the bestest Mama ever."

"Well, I can imagine that was hard for you to hear. I know your Mama a little bit, but you know her much better. Do you think that because your Mama hasn't gone through losing someone like your Mommy before that she just isn't sure what to do and what not to do?"

"Yeah."

"Do you think that maybe if you and I sat down with her and talked we could make it easier for you to tell her things and for her to not feel like she is doing things wrong or has to hide things from you?"

"Maybe. Mama is stubborn. Mommy used to say it all the time. I'm not allowed to say the whole thing because there's a naughty word in it."

"I know what phrase you are talking about. I think that you and I should sit your Mama down and the three of us should talk about how to make you two run better as a family. Then you can be open and honest with one another and not have to hide stuff. I am going to ask for your help with something I feel is important."

"M-my help?"

"Yep, I would like your Mama to try to come back to the meetings I run that help people like her. I don't know how to get her to do that, though. Do you think you can help me with that?"

"I can help you with that. Rachel, will I ever see you again? I don't mean just to talk. You're nice and don't make me feel like I'm not smart enough to understand things."

"I would like to see you again. I don't treat you like you aren't smart enough because I know you're smart enough," said Rachel, seeing her blush. "Should we go get your Mama and sit down and talk to her?"

"Yeah." Bri jumped off her chair and quickly made her way over to Rachel and hugged her, causing her eyes to tear up realizing that she would never have that with her own daughter.

⁂

"Jade, dammit, sit down," snapped Kristel as Jade paced the kitchen.

"Would you be able to sit still if Jake were out there talking to Rachel and you had no clue what the hell it was about?"

"I don't know, but what I do know is that if you keep pacing like that you are going to wear a hole in the floor. And as much as I think this is the most god-awful flooring around, I don't want to help you replace it."

"You think my flooring is ugly?" Jade stopped pacing to look at her best friend. "What the hell is wrong with you? I picked this out you know."

"Yes, I know and I asked Amy if you were hungover, still drunk, or going blind when she first showed it to me."

"Gee, thanks." Jade laughed, balling up a napkin and throwing it at her friend.

"What? If you can't be honest with your friends then who can you be honest with?"

"Uh huh. I'm going to remember what you

said about the flooring and make you help me when I redecorate," Jade said, admiring the tile she had chosen.

"Never going to happen, Donovan," said Kristel as their attention was quickly drawn to the sound of the sliding door closing.

❧❧❧❧

After they broke the hug, Rachel stood and Brianna took her hand and walked them inside. They heard Jade and Kristel laughing in the kitchen and made their way in.

"Mama, we need to talk," said Brianna, trying to be serious with her hands on her hips, but she gave herself away by smiling and giggling.

"Oh, we do, huh? And what do we need to talk about?" asked Jade, crouching down to her daughter's height.

"I'm going to leave you three to your chat. I have to pick Jake up from soccer at some point."

"He's with your mother. But subtle Kristel, very subtle." Jade laughed as she and Brianna hugged Kristel.

"Thank you, Rachel," Kristel said, turning to look at her.

"Thank you for getting her to call me and caring enough about these two to want to help them."

"They are more than worth it," Kristel said as she left the house.

"Coffee?" Jade offered Rachel.

"Please, thank you."

"Mama, can I have a juice box?"

"Of course." Jade smiled at her daughter as her

mind was still trying to figure out what they wanted to talk to her about.

After everyone had their drinks, Brianna took Jade's hand and led her into the living room where they all sat down to talk.

"So, you said you two wanted to talk to me." Jade addressed her daughter.

"Uh huh, but um, Rachel can you start?" Brianna said, giving Rachel a pleading expression.

"Of course," Rachel said, smiling at Bri and then meeting Jade's eyes.

"Does this have to do with what you two talked about outside?" asked Jade.

"Yeah, and I love you, Mama," said Bri, crawling up onto Jade's lap and hugging her tightly.

"Now you two are scaring me."

"Don't be. What we talked about was how Brianna feels and how she has been dealing with Amy's passing," Rachel started, smiling at the girl still curled up on Jade's lap. "Brianna has been afraid to tell you some things because—"

"I overheard you telling Mommy in heaven that you were failing us," interrupted Brianna.

"When?" asked Jade, directing her attention solely to her daughter.

"One day that Angie came over and you and Aunt Kristel went out. The day I asked about wearing something that Mommy and I got together."

"I remember that day. You weren't supposed to hear me say that," Jade said, shaking her head and mentally chastising herself.

"I didn't try to listen." Brianna seemed scared she was in trouble.

"I know you didn't, sweetie." Jade kissed her

daughter on the top of the head and then looked over at Rachel, her eyes asking for help.

"You have a very perceptive little girl there."

"That I definitely know."

"Mama, why don't you go to the meetings with Rachel anymore?"

"I don't have a good answer for that," Jade said honestly.

"Well, Rachel and I want you to go back to her meetings."

"Oh, you do?" asked Jade, looking between her daughter and the woman seated nearby.

"The meetings help," Rachel simply said.

"I understand that, but—"

"No buts, Mama. Don't be a stubborn naughty word like Mommy used to call you," Brianna said, giving her mother a stern look that told her she meant business.

"You aren't supposed to know that," said Jade, tickling her daughter. Jade could tell that Rachel wanted to talk to her more. "Why don't you go upstairs and get your stuff together for your bath, and then read. I'll be up shortly to help you."

"Okay Mama," Brianna said, kissing Jade on the cheek and scurrying over and hugging Rachel again before bounding upstairs.

"She's a pretty amazing kid," observed Rachel, a hint of sadness in her voice.

"That she is," said Jade, smiling and looking upstairs fondly.

"She's worried about you. She can tell that your mood has been getting worse and she's too young to understand or to know what to do. I really want you to think about coming back to the group. If it's too hard, then would you consider seeing either myself or someone privately?"

"I'll think about both. I just need to survive tomorrow."

"I'd like to help you both with that if you're willing to let me."

"I don't know how you can help…" Jade started.

"There are ways Jade, I've been working with grief for over three years. I've been a doctor for longer. I know what I'm doing."

"All right, Brianna trusts you, Kristel obviously trusts you, and you have never given me a reason not to trust you, so, please, help us survive tomorrow."

"I will," said Rachel, placing a hand on top of Jade's and giving it a small squeeze.

Rachel and Jade made plans for Rachel to come back over the following morning around eight o'clock to help Jade and Brianna get through the first anniversary of Amy's death.

After Rachel left, Jade went upstairs and helped Brianna with her bath, and then the two of them cuddled together in Jade's bed.

Chapter Seven

Surviving Hell

Jade slowly woke to find Brianna sleeping next to her and it made her smile. She knew that today was going to be a hard day for them both. Further, she was realizing that she couldn't survive this alone and was grateful that Rachel was going to be joining them.

"Morning, Mama."

"Morning, baby," Jade said, leaning forward and kissing her daughter on the top of her head. "What would you like for breakfast today?"

"Um, French toast?"

"Whatever you want I'll make. We need to get up and moving, though. Rachel will be here in about thirty minutes."

"Okay, Mama." Brianna hugged Jade and then went to her room to get dressed.

Jade watched as her daughter left and sighed to herself.

"Amy, I know you are watching over us. It hurts as much today as it did a year ago losing you. I am sure you saw us talking to Rachel, the group therapist. She is going to come and help me and Bri get through the day. I wish I were stronger. I love you, my wife," Jade said, waiting for the shower water to warm.

Jade quickly showered and got dressed in an old

pair of faded blue jeans and a navy blue V-neck T-shirt. She had decided to leave her hair down and let it air dry. Once she was done, she went into Brianna's room to make sure that she was ready. When she got to her daughter's room she could hear her daughter talking.

"Mr. Butters, you need to take care of Mama and me today. A year ago Mommy had to go to heaven and we don't get to see her anymore. Mama and I miss her lots and lots. This nice lady named Rachel is coming over today, too. You'd like her Mr. Butters. She's really nice and smart. I talked to her yesterday and she helped me. I think I was naughty, though. I made her sad both times when I hugged her. I'm scared that if Mama finds out I'm going to get in trouble," said Brianna to her stuffed bunny.

"Bri," Jade said from the doorway, causing her daughter's head to snap up.

"Mama...I um..."

Jade entered the room and sat down on the bed next to her daughter and pulled her onto her lap.

"You aren't in trouble. I always want you to tell me things you're thinking and feeling. As long as we're honest with each other we'll get through all of this sadness."

"I didn't mean to make Rachel sad."

"I know you didn't. Maybe you can talk to her about it while she is here."

"Do you think she'll talk to me? I mean if I made her sad I must have hurt her feelings and I didn't mean to," said Brianna, starting to bring herself into a mini panic.

"I know she will talk with you. And explain."

Jade kissed her daughter's head and told her that Rachel was going to be there soon so they should get downstairs so that she could get some coffee started and get some French toast made.

⚜ ⚜ ⚜ ⚜

Jade was in the kitchen when Rachel knocked on the door. Brianna answered it and escorted Rachel to the kitchen. When they entered Jade offered Rachel a small smile.

"Good morning, Rachel," smiled Brianna.

"Good morning, Brianna. How are you doing?" asked Rachel.

"I'm okay," Brianna said. The cheer that usually brightened her voice was noticeably absent.

"Good morning, Rachel. Would you like some coffee?" asked Jade with a smile.

"I'd love some, thank you," smiled Rachel.

"I'm about to make some French toast. Would you like some?"

"I don't want to be a bother," responded Rachel.

"Mama makes the bestest French toast. You have to try some," Brianna boasted.

"After that raving review, I would love some."

"Great, here is your coffee, and breakfast will be up in a few minutes."

The three talked and ate and after they were done, Jade quickly loaded the dishwasher and they moved into the living room.

"Mama, where did all of these photos come from?" asked Brianna, spotting the four large albums Jade had placed on the coffee table.

"Those were in the closet." Jade smiled at her daughter. "Didn't you have something you wanted to talk to Rachel about?"

Brianna's eyes bulged at Jade, and it was evident that she was nervous.

"What did you want to talk to me about, Brianna?" Rachel asked in a calm voice. "I promise that you can ask or tell me anything and it'll be okay."

"Mama heard me talking to Mr. Butters this morning," started Brianna, pulling the stuffed bunny up and showing him to Rachel. "I was telling him about you coming over today and that I was afraid to tell Mama that I thought I was naughty because I made you sad when I hugged you yesterday. I'm really, truly sorry for being naughty. I didn't mean it."

"Brianna, sweetie, relax and breathe," said Rachel, moving over to sit next to Brianna while Jade sat down on the other side of her daughter.

"But, but, I am really sorry."

"Bri, let Rachel speak."

"Brianna, the reason that I got sad wasn't your fault and I'm sorry you felt it was. Like your Mama, I lost someone I loved a whole lot."

"You were married like Mama and Mommy?"

"Yes I was. When Emily died, she was pregnant with our daughter."

"You mean her and your little girl both had to go to heaven?"

"Yep. So when you hugged me yesterday it made me sad because I won't ever get to hug my little girl."

"I-I know I'm n-not your daughter, but you can h-hug me when you n-need a hug from someone," said Brianna, causing Jade and Rachel to look at one another. "Mama said I'm good with hugs and if it will help, I wanna help."

"Thank you," Rachel managed to choke out before Bri threw herself into Rachel's arms and hugged her tightly.

※ ※ ※ ※

"Jacob, get your ass moving," yelled Kristel at the little boy who was playing with his cars rather than getting ready.

"Mom, my cars missed me," whined Jacob.

"You can play with them tonight. We have to stop by Jade and Brianna's on our way to school."

"YAY! I'll be ready real quick." Jake scrambled to put his cars away. Once his cars were packed up Jake put his socks and shoes on, brushed his teeth, and ran down the stairs. "I'm ready!"

"That was super quick, buddy. Thank you," said Kristel as her son smiled up at her.

"Why do we get to see Aunt Jade and Brianna before I go to school?"

"Today is going to be a hard day for them and we want to show them our love and support." Kristel and Jake made their way out of the house and into the car.

"Why is it a hard day, Mom?"

"Because one year ago today is when Aunt Amy went to heaven," said Kristel, her voice cracking.

"I miss Aunt Amy. She was nice," Jake said as he looked down at his hands.

"We all miss her, Jakey," Kristel said softly.

They drove in silence to Jade's house. When Kristel pulled into the driveway she saw that Rachel was already there. She was grateful that Jade had trusted Rachel enough to allow her to help them.

Kristel sat in the car for a minute thinking about her best friend. It was Jade's kindness and compassion that drew so many people in. The love she had to share with the world. How much she loved her family and those she surrounded herself with. Kristel knew that Jade would do anything for those she cared for. Why she had to suffer such tragedies Kristel couldn't understand. First her mother passing away, then her father and brother disowning her because she was gay, and to top it off, she lost her wife. It wasn't fair. Life is never fair, but this was more cruel than just unfair.

"Are we going inside?" asked Jake, bringing Kristel out of her thoughts and back to the present.

"We are, sorry I was lost in thought."

Kristel and Jake got out of the car, walked up to the front door, and knocked. Jade opened the door, smiled, and motioned for them to come in. They could hear voices coming from the living room so Kristel sent Jake in to talk to Brianna while she stayed with Jade for a moment.

"How are you holding up?" Kristel asked, hugging her best friend tight.

"I'm surviving," Jade managed to choke out. She squeezed Kristel tighter and tried to compose herself. "Thanks for stopping by."

As they pulled apart, their eyes met and the toll of Amy's loss on both of them was evident.

They made their way into the living room in time to see Jake shaking Rachel's hand after Brianna had introduced them.

"Hi, Kristel," said Rachel as the two women joined them.

"Good morning, Rachel."

"Mom, you already know Rachel?" asked Jake.

"Yes, I met her several months ago."

"Cool," said Jake as he and Brianna went to get

juice boxes.

"How are you doing today, Kristel?" asked Rachel.

"I'm sad, but I am processing and dealing with it. I hope we weren't interrupting anything."

"No, actually we were explaining to Brianna about Emily and the baby. She noticed some sadness on my part yesterday and was confused."

Jade saw Rachel starting to get choked up and took over.

"You know Bri. She told Rachel that she knew she wasn't Rachel's daughter, but if she needed a hug that she could come to her..." Jade said, her voice trailing off.

"That girl has your heart, Jade," said Kristel, shaking her head. "I also know she has Amy's insight and ability to read people. You're in trouble when she gets older." Kristel smirked.

"I'm afraid she's correct, Jade."

"I know. Trust me, I know."

Jake and Brianna came back into the room and after a few minutes, Kristel told them that they needed to get going so Jake wasn't late for school and she wasn't late for work. They hugged and said their good-byes. Kristel told Jade she would call her later, but if she needed anything not to hesitate in calling her. Jade thanked her and escorted them both out the door.

Chapter Eight

Pictures of the Past

After Kristel and Jake left, Jade took a moment to herself, leaning against the door. She took several deep breaths, preparing herself before slowly making her way back into the living room. She knew that now the hard part of the day was about to begin.

"You have a really great friend in Kristel," said Rachel as Jade sat down on the couch next to Brianna.

"I know. I'm very lucky to have her in my life. Jake has been a good friend to Bri as well."

"Jake's my best friend, Mama," corrected Brianna.

"I'm sorry. Jake is her best friend."

"Now do we get to look at the pictures?" asked Brianna.

"Rachel, I don't know what to do here," Jade admitted.

"Well, there is no right or wrong way to do this. Simply put it's what is easiest for you. Do you want to go through the albums and if there is a memory or a story that goes with the picture you can tell us? Or we can choose pictures at random."

"I think I'd like to just start at the beginning and go through them and if there is a story I'll tell you two, or Bri, honey, if you know a story about the picture you can share it with Rachel and me, too."

"Okay." Brianna crawled on Jade's lap and Rachel moved a little closer to be able to see the pictures, but did not encroach on their personal space.

Jade took a deep breath, grabbed the first photo album, and opened it to the first page. She saw a filmstrip of three pictures.

"You and Mommy look silly there."

"That was the first date that Mommy and I went on. We went to a carnival and they had this photo booth and somehow Amy talked me into going in with her."

"Oh come on, Jade. We are at this amazing carnival; you are on this amazing date with moi. You have to take a picture of the moment. Live and enjoy," Amy said, her smile lighting up the night.

"You are a corrupter, you know that?" Jade *laughed as she allowed herself to be pulled into the photo booth.*

"That's my job, and I do it well. Now smile." Amy *poked Jade in the ribs causing her to squeal and squirm just as the picture was taken.*

"That was unfair. Beware of paybacks." Jade gave *Amy a mock scowl as Amy feigned fright for the next picture.*

The final picture showed them looking into each other's eyes and smiling goofily.

"That was the day my life changed. We became inseparable after that."

"That sounds like an awesome start to a beautiful relationship," said Rachel "That sounds a lot like my first date with Emily."

They looked through a few more pages before Rachel pointed at a picture of Amy and Jade dressed for what looked like a toga party.

"Yeah, that story isn't for little ears, but sometime I'll tell you." Jade blushed, which made Rachel laugh.

"What is that a picture of Mama?" asked Brianna, pointing to one of Kristel, Amy, Jade, and someone the girl didn't know.

"This is from our one-year anniversary. We learned that eating mini donuts is not something to do just before going on a high-speed roller coaster."

"Jade, you have to live a little," said Amy, dragging the woman she loved toward the roller coaster.

"I do live. I live a lot actually," Jade said, pulling Amy into her arms and holding her close. "You make me feel more alive than anyone or anything ever has."

"Good, now go on the damn roller coaster with me," Amy said, laughing as she swatted Jade on the butt.

"This had better be true love…because I am totally going against my better judgment."

"It is true love. I love you," said Amy before kissing Jade quickly on the lips and dragging her to the front of the roller coaster line.

"Amy took the picture right after we got off the ride, just before I puked in that garbage can."

"Eww," said Brianna, wrinkling her nose.

"Yeah, but the guy running the game next to the ride was so impressed that I made it to the garbage can and was able to walk away that he gave us a huge teddy bear."

"You mean Timbear?"

"That's the one," Jade smiled as she kissed the side of her daughter's head just before Brianna jumped off her lap and went running upstairs.

"Interesting," giggled Rachel.

"Actually, the guy had been hitting on Amy every time we walked past. I think he thought it would win him points with her. Instead it has always been a reminder to me of that night. That was also the night she proposed to me."

"Wow, a bear and a ring. That sounds like a pretty nice anniversary." Rachel offered Jade a supportive smile. "Did she propose at the carnival?"

"Yeah, she did. Well, on the grounds. It wasn't like she did it on a ride or anything."

"Amy, where in the hell are we going?" Jade asked as she was pulled away from the crowds.

"Just shut up and come with me." Amy laughed, and headed for a grouping of trees.

"Mmmm, now that sounds fun," said Jade, halting their progress and pulling Amy to her and kissing her deeply.

"You kiss me like that again and I'm going to forget why I'm bringing you out here."

"I want to apologize, but then I want to kiss you again, too," Jade said, giving Amy a lopsided, sensual smile.

Amy let out a groan and wrapped her arms around Jade again and brushed their lips together several times, adding to the arousal they already felt. After several minutes of teasing one another they made their way to the trees.

"It's quiet out here," noticed Jade.

"Yeah, it is," agreed Amy as she played with Jade's fingers. "I was going to recite some romantic poem, or have something planned…but, it all comes down to I love you and want to spend the rest of my life falling asleep and waking up next to you. Will you marry me?"

"I love you, too! Yes, I will marry you," Jade said,

capturing Amy's lips and pressing her against the tree.

After kissing for several minutes Amy pulled a ring out of her pocket and put it on Jade's finger.

"There. You are officially mine."

"Forever," whispered Jade as she smiled at the glistening ring on her finger.

"Rachel, this is Timbear," said Brianna, carrying the brown stuffed bear in bright green lederhosen. The bear was almost as big as Brianna. "He sleeps at the end of my bed to scare away the monsters in the closet."

"He's very cute," Rachel said, smiling at Brianna who was already turning around and taking the bear back upstairs.

"You lie nicely." Jade smirked. "That bear is hideous, but she loves it and has since we brought her home from the hospital." Jade turned a few pages to a picture of Brianna leaning against Timbear. "That was the day we brought her home. She would cry nonstop unless she was either being held by us or leaned up against that damn bear. This one was taken after she had been home about a month."

"How did she get leaned up against the bear to begin with?" asked Rachel, intrigued by this story and the picture.

"Amy had run out to get some more diapers; the kid was a pooping machine. While she was gone I needed a minute to get her diaper and powder ready to change her and I leaned her up against him. She stopped crying and started to coo. I picked her up and set her in her bed and she started to scream. I brought her back out and leaned her up against the bear again and she was quiet and happy."

Brianna came back down the stairs and sat on

Jade's lap.

The three finished going through the first album. Jade had told them about the wedding, glossed over the honeymoon, and about buying the house. They started the next album and Jade made sure that Brianna saw that there was a section dedicated just to her.

"This is all about me?" Brianna asked, looking between the album and Jade.

"Yes it is," she said and looked over to Rachel. "I hope that this isn't too hard for you. If so, please just tell us and we'll move on."

"I appreciate the thought, but I am okay with it."

"Mama, why is this picture all smudgy blobby?"

"Sweetie, that is the very first picture ever taken of you," started Jade.

"It doesn't look like me…"

"Bri, that picture was taken while you were still inside Mommy's tummy."

"Whoa, you took a picture of me in Mommy's tummy? How? Can you tell if I'm smiling?"

"They use a special machine. Emily and I had one taken of our little girl, too," Rachel said, smiling and looking between Brianna and the photo.

"I bet she looked really pretty, just like you are," Brianna stated, causing Rachel to blush.

"Er, thank you," said Rachel, trying to hide her embarrassment.

"This is the first real picture we took as a family," Jade said, pointing at picture of her and Amy holding Brianna. They were all three in a hospital bed, but looked very cozy.

"Mama, what am I wearing in this picture?"

"That was your very first Halloween costume.

We dressed you up like a kitten and called you our Kitty Cutetastic."

"Amy, look at this outfit I got for Bri for Halloween," said Jade, rushing into the baby's room.

"That is so cute. Where did you find it?" asked Amy as she draped the costume across the squirming baby's body.

"I was at the mall and saw it. Let's put it on her now."

"Jade, tomorrow is Halloween. She can wait another day."

"She can, but I can't," pouted Jade, knowing her wife couldn't resist her pouts.

"That isn't fair," said Amy, trying to look away. Jade sniffled and Amy turned back to face her. "Fine, the pout wins...we'll put her in it now."

"You are the best wife a woman could ask for," Jade said, placing a kiss on her wife's lips.

"You can make it up to me later," Amy said, waggling her eyebrows.

Jade blushed at the memory of that day.

"Interesting blush you have going there," Rachel said, giving Jade a knowing smirk which only made her blush more.

"Shush, you," laughed Jade.

"Mama, do we get to add my pictures from this year into this album as well?"

"Yep, we will sit down and do that some night."

"Yay! Can I have another juice box?"

"Sure, sweetie," Jade said as the little girl hopped off her lap. "Can I get you anything to eat or drink?"

"I'm fine, thank you," said Rachel. "How does it feel going through these pictures and memories?"

"Painful, and oddly comforting. Does that even

make sense?"

"Yeah, it makes sense. You hurt because she isn't here, but you're comforted by the memories," started Rachel seeing a nod in agreement. "This date is going to be a hard one for you for years to come, you just have to remember that she is always looking down and watching over you."

"Is it easier for you yet?"

"No, Emily's birthday, the baby's due date, and the day they died are three days that haunt me still. I know how to deal with it, but that doesn't make it easier or less painful."

"Thank you for this, Rachel. I truly appreciate all of your support and help with Bri. I don't recall if I thanked you yesterday for taking the time to talk with her."

"I'm glad I could help and be here. Brianna is a really sweet little girl. It was my pleasure to help her."

"Well, you've made quite an impression on her. She is usually really shy and it takes time for her to warm up to people."

"I'm glad she's warmed up to me. It makes going through today easier for you both," Rachel said, smiling at Jade and then smiling at Brianna as she came into the room.

"Is it time for the next album?" asked Brianna.

"Yes it is. Maybe after that we can have lunch," Jade said, pulling her daughter close and holding her tight.

"Rachel, are you staying for lunch?"

"I'm not sure," Rachel answered.

"Please stay. The least I can do is make you something good for lunch for all your help yesterday and today," said Jade.

"If it isn't too much trouble," conceded Rachel.

"It will be my pleasure."

"Mama, can we have those muffin things?"

"Sure," she said to her daughter before turning to Rachel. "Any allergies I need to know about?" Rachel shook her head. "Good, well we'll be having corn bread muffins with corn, ham, and cheese mixed in."

"That sounds fantastic."

Jade made lunch for the three of them. Brianna told Rachel about school. After lunch they started to go through the albums again, and Brianna fell asleep and Jade moved her to the love seat.

"With Brianna asleep, are there pictures you would like to go through that you can't with her?" asked Rachel.

"Actually, I'd prefer to talk if that is okay with you," said Jade.

"Sure, whatever helps you the most."

"How do you do it? How do you move past your past?"

"Jade, this isn't the type of situation where things are just fixed overnight. You lost someone who you had given yourself to completely. There are going to be days where you feel like life is going pretty well, you will be happy, there are going to be low days. The goal is for more happy than sad days. I know the first time I found myself smiling and enjoying life, I felt so guilty after it. How could I be so insensitive? I went from enjoying the day to hating myself for a week. Why could my mind allow me to enjoy life? The truth is, you eventually will start to move on, and you will find happiness again. The hard part will be allowing yourself to enjoy the happiness and not shut it out."

"Have you done that? Found happiness again?"

"Yes and no. The first time I found myself attracted to someone else, I was shocked. I chastised myself for it. I thought 'how can I be attracted to her? Emily was my love' and then I pushed her away. I realized after that, Emily wouldn't want me sitting around sulking, so, instead of trying to date or anything like that, I made new friends, hung out with people from the support group. It helped. I've been on three dates, I don't know that I would classify them as successful, but I have attempted it at least."

"How long was it before you started to date?"

"The 'date' with the person I pushed away was close to a year after Emily passed away. The next one was about six months later. And remember, everyone's timeline is going to be different."

"Amy told me she wanted me to 'move on,' that I 'wasn't even thirty yet,' yadda, yadda, yadda. I just don't know how it would feel right."

"That's where it will take time. Get out with the group, Kristel, other friends, even if we hang out. You just need to start interacting with people," Rachel said.

"That sounds so much easier than it actually is," said Jade, laughing.

"Just promise me, or promise Brianna you will try. She's very perceptive and I'll give her my number to call if you don't make an effort," teased Rachel.

"You fight dirty, you know that?"

"Yeah, I do. So, will I start seeing you in group again?"

"Yes, I will be there next week as long as I can get a sitter for Bri." Jade glanced over at her daughter, who was still asleep.

"If you can't find a sitter, then bring her. There

is a playroom right off of the group meeting room. Some people have had to bring their kids in the past."

"Well, then I guess I have to show up no matter what." Jade laughed.

"Yep!"

"Rachel, honestly, thank you for coming over today and helping. I thought today was going to just be Brianna and me crying and missing Amy. It was nice to relive the happy memories."

"I'm glad it helped. I am going to head out, but if things get hard, call me. If I don't hear from you I'll see you in group next week."

Jade walked Rachel to the door and gave her a small hug and as she was saying good-bye Brianna came out of the living room.

"Are you leaving?" asked Brianna, rubbing her eyes.

"Yeah, you and your Mama need to spend some time together just the two of you."

"Thank you for helping my Mama," Bri said as Rachel knelt down and received a hug from her.

Rachel smiled and then said her good-byes and headed home. Jade and Brianna went back to finish going through the last album.

"Mama, I like Rachel. Can we spend the day with her again?" asked Brianna while getting ready for her bath.

"Maybe, sweetie," Jade said, smiling at her daughter.

Chapter Nine

Getting Out

A my, this is harder than I ever dreamed it would be...I don't know how to get out and about without you. I have been going to the meetings over the past few weeks like I promised Bri and Rachel I would. I just...I don't want for Brianna to feel like she is being neglected. Yes, I know that she doesn't in my heart, but right now my heart and my head aren't on speaking terms. I'm trying to do this; I just don't know how to live without you. I miss you my love," thought Jade, looking up to the sky as she waited for Kristel to meet her for coffee.

"You keep looking up like that and a bird is going to poop on your face," came a familiar voice from behind her. Jade turned to see Rachel standing there.

"And you would enjoy laughing at me wouldn't you," Jade said, turning to face Rachel.

"Well, for how my week has gone, yep," said Rachel, laughing. "How are you doing?"

"I'm..." started Jade before letting out a loud and long sigh. "I'm trying to get out like I promised you and Brianna I would, but dammit, it's hard."

"It has only been a few weeks since the anniversary. I told you it would be hard. If getting over the ones we have loved and lost were easy, I'd be out of a job. Seriously though, don't push yourself too hard, but just try to get out."

"I'm supposed to be meeting Kristel for coffee, but as usual, she's late."

"Well, if you don't mind I can keep you company until she arrives," suggested Rachel, pointing toward a table off to a side, but still within eyeshot of the door.

"Thank you, that sounds nice," Jade said.

The two women sat down and the waitress came over and got their orders and went to make their drinks.

"How is Brianna doing?" asked Rachel.

"She has her up and down days. She was having a bit of a down day yesterday. We stayed home last night, snuggled, had some hot chocolate and watched *Frozen*."

"That sounds like a good family night. Did she say what had her down?"

"Well, she heard me talking with the program facilitator of her after-school program," started Jade, the anger rising in her voice again.

"Not a good discussion?"

"Well, no, honestly. It was infuriating."

"Tell me about it," said Rachel, her therapist voice coming out.

"Well I drove to the school to pick Bri up. Once inside I waved at Brianna, she was at the other end of the room playing with some kids from her class. So as she was getting her stuff together I went to sign her out. Then Ms. Depew came over…"

"Hi Mrs. Donovan, I'm Denise Depew, the new program facilitator here at the school," started the woman.

"Hello," Jade said, shaking the woman's hand.

"I was wondering if we could talk for a moment," the woman continued.

"All right," Jade said, caution in her voice.

"I overheard Brianna saying that her Mommy is in heaven watching over her."

"And is there a problem with that?" asked Jade.

"Well, no disrespect, but you are standing here," said the woman.

"Yes, I am. If you had taken the time to look at our records, you would have also seen that my wife passed away a little over a year ago," Jade stated with both anger and sorrow.

"Hi, Mama." Brianna ran and leapt into Jade's arms.

"Hi, sweetie! Why don't you get your coat on while I finish talking to Ms. Depew," Jade said, smiling as she put her daughter down and Brianna moved to put her jacket on.

"I am sorry. I had no idea. I just overheard her and thought that it was something that you should be made aware of," stammered the young woman.

"Well, you brought it to my attention and you know now what the story is. Is there anything else?"

"No, ma'am. Again I am so sorry," said the woman.

"How long have you been the program facilitator here?"

"Three weeks. I just haven't taken the time to read through all of the student files."

"I would suggest making the time to go through the student files to make sure you are familiar with their history. Thankfully, Brianna doesn't have any medical concerns, but I am certain there are a few kids here who do," Jade said, taking Brianna's hand and *leaving the school.*

"Then on the way home Bri asked if she was in trouble," Jade said, shaking her head.

"What did you tell her?" asked Rachel.

"I said…"

"Not at all. Why would you think that? Should you be?" Jade teased, trying to ease Brianna's fears.

"Ms. Depew only talks to parents when the kids are in trouble…" Brianna said as her voice trailed off.

"Well, Ms. Depew made a mistake and made some assumptions that she shouldn't have. You have done nothing wrong."

"Mama, Ms. Depew made this a down day."

"Oh sweetie, how about we make the day better by putting in 'Frozen?' I'll make some hot chocolate…"

"With extra marshmallows?"

"Of course with extra marshmallows. How would it make the day better if there weren't extra marshmallows? Goofball," Jade said as they entered the house.

"You are an awesome mom. I hope you realize that." Rachel's words caused Jade to blush.

"I just love my daughter and want her to have the happiest life she can. She had to suffer loss so young; she doesn't need some dumb ass giving her bad days."

"Amen," said a voice from behind Rachel.

"You're late, Kristel," said Jade.

"I am, but it doesn't seem like you were missing me too much." Kristel laughed as she joined the two women.

"I just brought her in from taunting the birds." Rachel giggled, receiving a questioning look from Kristel and a groan from Jade.

"There's a story there, someone talk," demanded

Kristel.

"I was looking up to the sky talking to Amy and she told me if I kept that up a bird was going to poop on my face," answered Jade as both Kristel and Rachel started to laugh. "You are both evil."

"No, my good friend...well yeah, I am and you love me more for it," Kristel said, sticking her tongue out.

"I'm not going to get in the middle of this one," said Rachel.

"Oh crap." Jade looked at her watch. "We gotta go get Bri."

"Have a great day and I'll see you in group later," said Rachel as Kristel and Jade waved good-bye. "Jade, you forgot...your glasses."

Jade thought she heard Rachel call something to her about her glasses, but she was going to be late if she didn't hurry. Since Jade was going to see Rachel later, she would find out for certain what was said.

❧ ❧ ❧ ❧

"So, you and Rachel seemed to be getting along pretty well in there," Kristel said as she and Jade hurried to Jade's car to get to Brianna's school on time.

"We were talking about Bri having a sad day yesterday."

"What? Why did she have a sad day? Whose ass do I need to kick?"

"Oh, the After School lady made an ass out of herself. She overheard Bri talking about her Mommy in heaven. So, Ms. Depew decided to say something to me. To which I pointed out to her that my wife died a little over a year ago and maybe she should take the time to read her students' files. Then we left. On the way home, Bri told me the only time that Ms. Depew talks to people is when they are in trouble."

"Poor kid, I can't believe that the lady didn't bother to check her facts."

"I know. So we had a hot chocolate and *Frozen* night. I told her that I'd pick her up today so that she didn't have to bother going to After School."

"And that is what makes you such an extraordinary mother. You think about your daughter and things that will impact her negatively and you remove her from the equation."

"I do what's best for her," Jade said, looking over at her best friend.

"So back to Rachel…"

"What about her?" asked Jade as they stopped outside the school to wait for Brianna to exit.

"She's pretty attractive," Kristel said with a smile.

"Are you thinking of changing teams?" retorted Jade.

"No, but she would be someone that you could build something with," said Kristel.

"It is too soon for that. I can't do that yet. I'm barely making it with going to the meetings and out with you and some of the group people every now and then."

"All right, all right," said Kristel, raising her hands in defeat. "I'll back off, but you have to admit she is cute."

"I haven't noticed," Jade said just as Brianna opened the rear door.

"Hi, Mama. Hi, Aunt Kristel," Bri said as she got into the car.

"How's my favorite munchkin doing?" asked Kristel

"Good. Mama, I got all my letters and numbers right today," Brianna said giddily.

"That is fantastic. Ice cream or pizza?"

"Both!" exclaimed Brianna.

"Well, for that I am going to need some proof."

Brianna reached into her bag and pulled out two half-sheets of paper showing 100% and a large gold star on each page.

"See!"

"Pony up, Mama," Kristel snickered.

"Be nice or I won't let you and Jake stay for pizza and ice cream," threatened Jade.

"Do you have group tonight, Mama?"

"Yes, but if you need me I'll stay home."

"Will you say hi to Rachel for me and give her something I made her?"

"Yep, I will." Jade smiled as they pulled up outside Kristel's place.

Kristel jumped out to run and get Jake. After she was gone for a few minutes, Jade's phone rang. Kristel was calling to tell her that Jake was sick and that they couldn't make dinner tonight. She offered to have Bri stay so that Jade could go to group, but Jade told her it was okay, she didn't want to risk Brianna getting sick so she would just take her to group with her. Rachel had told her in the past that it was okay.

After getting home and eating, Jade and Brianna got some books and toys together to keep her entertained during group and they headed to the Community Center.

"Hi, Rachel," said Carmen as she entered the meeting room at the Community Center.

"Carmen, hello. How are you doing tonight?" asked Rachel.

"Good. Is there anything that you need help setting up?"

"If you would help me move the refreshment table over there that would be fantastic."

"Sure," Carmen said as the two women pulled the rectangle table from against the wall forward a few feet.

Rachel went about setting up the coffee and tea and the other snacks.

"Hi, Rachel," said Doug as he entered the room and headed for the coffee.

"Hi, Doug," she said as she finished putting the cups on the table.

"How was your day?" asked Doug.

"It was good. I'm glad it is my Friday, though," Rachel said.

"Me, too," said Sharon as she entered the room and joined Rachel and Doug.

Sharon and Carmen started talking about their weekend plans. Doug and another man that had just entered were discussing the latest cooking show they were watching.

Rachel was looking around; she knew that Jade hadn't called so she hoped she was still coming. There were three more people from the regular group who had yet to arrive or call. Rachel would wait a little bit longer before starting.

"Mama, are you sure that it is going to be okay for me to come to the group with you?" asked Brianna for the third time in their short drive.

"Yes, and like I told you the last two times, if you don't want to sit with me and the rest of the group, you can go into the playroom next door and read or color."

"Is Rachel going to be here tonight?"

"Yes, she runs the group. We can't have the group without her."

Jade pulled into a close parking spot, noting that there were only about seven cars there. She was thankful that this was going to be a small group. She hoped that they might get out early and she wouldn't have to disrupt her daughter's sleep schedule too much.

Brianna and Jade got out of the car. Bri put on her backpack containing her books and colors and then took her mother's hand. They walked into the Community Center and Brianna stopped and looked around. This was her first time being there in all the months that Jade had been coming to the support meetings.

"Mama, can I get a drink before we go in?" Brianna asked after spotting the water fountains.

"Sure," Jade said, smiling down at her daughter.

Brianna got a drink and then gave Jade a look that reminded her of Amy. Jade felt her insides catch and she wanted to laugh and cry at the same time.

"What's wrong, Mama?"

"You just looked so much like Mommy for a minute there," Jade said, leaning down and hugging her.

"I didn't mean to make you cry."

"You didn't. It was a surprise is all. Come on, let's get in the room before all the good seats are taken."

"Will we have to stand if they are all taken?" asked Brianna as they made their way toward the doors.

"No, we would just have to get some more chairs. There aren't a lot of people here today so it shouldn't be a problem."

As Jade and Brianna entered the room, Rachel glanced over and smiled and waved to them. Brianna dropped her mother's hand and quickly made her way over to Rachel. She stood there politely and let Rachel and Carmen finish their conversation before she spoke. Jade was just joining them as Rachel knelt down to hug Brianna.

"Hey there, Bri. How are you doing tonight?"

"I'm okay. I made you something in art class." Brianna opened her backpack, pulled out a picture that she had drawn, and handed it to Rachel. "See there is you, and me, and Mama, and Mommy watching from heaven, and Aunt Kristel and Jake are playing in the mud."

"This is a fantastic drawing. Why does it say thank you on it?" asked Carmen

"It says thank you because Rachel has helped me, and she helped Mama, and now we have more happy days than sad days."

Several group members in the room said, "Awwww."

Jade glanced over and saw Rachel wipe away a tear quickly. She offered her a knowing and comforting smile.

"Thank you for the wonderful picture. I'm going to put it up in my office when I get back there on Monday."

Rachel stood up and looked over at Jade.

"Jake is sick and I didn't want to expose her to it so I thought I would take you up on the 'if you are ever without a sitter just bring her,' statement," she said, laughing.

"Yeah, but I didn't realize that it would come with tears. This is really sweet. Did you help her with any of it?"

"Nope, she drew it in art class. She didn't even let me see it when we were home earlier. She can either sit with me or sit in the other room. She knows to be quiet during the meeting."

"Does anyone object to Jade's daughter Brianna sitting in on our meeting tonight?" Rachel asked, turning toward the rest of the group. Everyone smiled and shook their heads.

Jade and Brianna sat down and Brianna pulled out her book and started to read as everyone else took their seats and Rachel started the group.

"Well, shall we go around the room and everyone can talk if they want to about their week?" asked Rachel, looking to Doug to start.

"It was a good week. I went on a date on Wednesday," started Doug, and then paused for the congratulations that came from around the circle. "I'm not sure this is a long-term relationship, but we all have to start somewhere, right?"

"Today was an off day for me," said Sharon. "I think it was because my sister was in town and she never approved of my marriage. The rest of the week was good, though."

"The week was good. I used some of your techniques on remaining calm in stressful situations," Carmen said, looking toward Rachel and receiving a small smile.

"This was a pretty good week. I'm still working at getting out and either meeting people or just spending time away from the house. Brianna and I are planning to go to the zoo," said Jade. At the mention of her name, Brianna looked up from her book and smiled.

"Brianna, would you like to participate? You don't have to if you don't want to," said Rachel, offering the little girl a soft smile.

"Um, it was a good week except for yesterday when a mean lady at After School upset Mama and made me think I was in trouble...but Mama made it better."

"How'd she do that?" asked Doug.

"Mama made hot chocolate with extra marshmallows and we watched *Frozen*. It's my favorite movie," boasted Brianna, causing Jade to blush.

"You have a pretty amazing Mama," Doug said.

"Yep, she's the bestest." Brianna grinned as she crawled up into Jade's lap.

The others went through their week and Brianna eventually fell asleep in Jade's arms. At the end of the meeting, everyone quietly said their good-byes so as not to wake the little girl even though Jade had told them that she was a very sound sleeper.

"You have a pretty cute little girl," Doug said as he walked past and squeezed Jade's shoulder. She smiled back at him.

"I can't believe how much she looks like you," said Sharon.

"Well, just before we came in here she gave me

a look that was totally Amy. It made me laugh and cry at the same time."

"Kids can do that."

"So, what is up with Rachel and you?" asked Carmen bluntly after the others had left.

"I have no clue what you are talking about," Jade said, slightly offended by the woman's tone and accusation.

"Well, Rachel spent a good portion of the meeting watching your daughter. Brianna drew Rachel a picture…are you dating Rachel?"

"No, I'm not. She's been helping me, and my daughter, learn how to live again and get back out there now that Amy is gone. The same stuff she does for anyone else here."

"Hey, don't get all defensive. I was just checking. I didn't want to invade your territory if I were to ask her out."

"It isn't my territory so don't worry about invading anything," Jade said, standing up and balancing her daughter and her backpack. "I have to get Bri home."

"Well, see you next week," said Carmen as she went to fold some chairs.

As Jade and Brianna started walking toward the door, Rachel called for Jade to wait a minute.

"You forgot these at the coffee shop earlier," said Rachel, handing Jade her glasses.

"Oh, thank you. I thought I had lost those. I'll… um, see you next week," Jade said. "Thanks again for saving my glasses."

"You and Bri have a great weekend."

Jade left and carefully put her daughter into the booster seat and climbed into the car, letting out a deep breath. After composing herself, she started for home.

⁂

"Let me help you finish," said Carmen as she watched Rachel hand Jade something and then she and her daughter leave.

"Thanks," Rachel said, sighing.

"Long week?"

"What? Oh yeah. I am looking forward to shutting my mind off and relaxing."

"You seem pretty close with Jade and her daughter," said Carmen.

"Not really. I helped them through the one-year anniversary of Jade's wife's passing. Brianna was having a hard time as well so I took the time to work with her as well. She's a really great kid. She's what I had hoped Emily's and my daughter would have been like."

"I'm sorry. It has to be hard for you seeing Jade with her daughter."

"Actually it isn't. Brianna is a very rare kid. She has a heart of gold and she can read a person better than about anyone I know."

"Do you spend a lot of time with her?" asked Carmen.

"No, I've only spent time with her a few times. I was helping them through Amy's death. Why all the questions about Jade and Brianna? Are you interested in Jade? If so, be careful, I don't know that she is at a relationship stage yet."

"Actually, although Jade is very attractive and nice, I was wondering if you would like to go out sometime?"

"Wow, I'm flattered, but I don't date people from within my therapy groups."

"Oh," said Carmen, now very embarrassed.

"Please don't be embarrassed. You aren't the first to ask me out, I just have a personal rule to keep professional things at a platonic level."

Carmen helped Rachel finish cleaning up, but didn't say much and then left in a hurry. Rachel was indeed flattered, but she had to stick to her rules.

Chapter Ten

Admitting Fears

Jade was out shopping for clothes for Brianna on her lunch break. She knew that with Brianna going over to spend the weekend with Kristel and Jake at a water park, she was going to need several options.

"Rachel, hi," said Jade, coming out of the store and almost running into the woman.

"Hi," Rachel said, smiling at Jade. It had been a couple of weeks since they had seen one another outside of group and since Brianna had attended the group session. "How are you doing?"

"I'm good. Bri is going to a water park over the weekend with Kristel and Jake so I'm getting her some new stuff," Jade said, holding up the bags in her hand.

"Sounds like a fun weekend. So, what are you going to do with your free time?"

"I was actually going to um call you and well... the carnival that Amy and I used to go to every year is in town and I was wondering, if you didn't have plans, if you would like to go with me?" Jade asked cautiously.

"Are you sure you are ready to face that obstacle?"

"No, but I don't want to wait another year to face it either," Jade said bluntly. "I need to take this step for both myself and Brianna."

"Then I'd be happy to go and help you face it," Rachel said, smiling.

"Thank you! Oh, and I won't be at group this week."

"Okay. And it is my pleasure to help. I have to run, I have back-to-back sessions running right up to group."

"Thanks again, Rachel! I'll call you Friday and we can discuss it more," said Jade.

"Great," Rachel smiled before heading down the street.

Jade glanced at her watch and realized her lunch was almost over. She had just enough time to get back to work.

❧❧❧❧

"Mama, what are you going to do while I'm off with Aunt Kristel and Jake? I don't want you to be lonely," said Brianna Thursday night while Jade was helping her pack.

"Well, while you are off playing on all those waterslides, eating pizza, and staying up late, I'm going to be working with Rachel to overcome another obstacle."

"You're going to see Rachel?"

"Yeah. The carnival that Mommy and I used to go to is in town, so I am going to have Rachel go with me so that I'm not too scared or too sad to do it. That way next year you and I can go together."

"And Rachel is going to help you?"

"Yep. I told her I would call her tomorrow and we are going to make plans. Is it okay with you that Rachel and I do this?"

"I don't want you scared or sad. Do you want me to leave Mr. Butters home in case you are scared when you get home?"

"Thank you sweetie, but you take Mr. Butters. I'll be okay. Now, bedtime," said Jade as Brianna curled up in her bed and Jade tucked her in. "I love you!"

"I love you, too, Mama."

❧ ❧ ❧ ❧

Rachel finished her day with a smile having seen Jade and knowing that she and Jade were going to be spending time together that weekend.

Rachel quickly ran and got something to eat before heading to the community center. Rachel entered and unlocked the room and started to set up while she ate her lunch/dinner.

"Why don't you eat and I'll set up?" said a laughing voice from the doorway to the room. Rachel looked up to see Carmen standing there.

"I'll eat quickly."

"Take your time." Carmen put a chair out and pointed for Rachel to sit. She then went about setting up the chairs.

"Thanks."

"Busy day?" asked Carmen.

"Yeah. I had back-to-back appointments all afternoon," said Rachel as she finished her sandwich. "Thanks for giving me a minute to eat."

"No problem. I was hoping for a moment to talk with you anyway. I wanted to apologize for putting you in an awkward position a couple of weeks ago."

"It's okay, really," Rachel said, smiling at Carmen. "How have things been going for you?"

"Well, pretty good. I've been putting in a lot of hours at work."

"Well, don't overdo it or use it as an escape to not deal with things," Rachel said as they set the last of the chairs out and finished the setup.

"I won't. Do you think Jade is going to be here this week? I owe her a bit of an apology as well."

"She actually called and told me she wouldn't be here." Rachel hated to lie, but she didn't feel like her in-person encounter with Jade was any of Carmen's business.

"Oh, well, I hope everything is all right."

"She didn't say why, but I'm sure everything is fine. Shall we get started?" asked Rachel, hoping to get out of this conversation and moving forward to get the night over with.

Since only a few people made the meeting, they called it a night early. Everyone there helped clean up so that Rachel could get out of there quickly. The one thing that stood out to Rachel in the meeting was how much she missed having Jade there. She knew she shouldn't be getting attached to the woman; she had strict rules for a reason.

Rachel walked into her house and set the mail down on the table near the door. She looked around the empty space. She missed having someone there for her when she got home, someone to tell about her day. She didn't usually mind living alone, but some days were harder than others. Today was one of those harder days.

Rachel went upstairs and started a bubble bath. She went into her room and changed out of her work clothes and into a robe. She grabbed some clothes to put on after her bath and went into the bathroom. She shut the water off and slipped out of her robe, hanging it on the back of the door. Rachel eased into the tub and leaned back, closing her eyes and working to clear her mind.

"Emily, what am I doing? What in the hell is going on? Why can't I stop thinking about this woman? I set the rule of not getting involved with any current or prior member of my grief therapy group, or one of my clients. I need to find the strength to uphold that rule. But how?"

After her bath, Rachel went into her room and grabbed the book she had been reading off the nightstand and lay back to read until she would fall asleep. After reading the same page seven times, Rachel decided she was too distracted, so she put the book back on the nightstand and curled up under the covers, letting her mind drift while she tried to fall asleep.

❧❧❧❧

Jade had been awakened by an overly excited five-year-old bouncing on her bed. They had gotten ready and were headed over to Kristel's so that the kids could get to the water park early.

"Good morning," said Jade as Kristel opened the door and Jake pulled Brianna into the house.

"Good morning." Kristel laughed as Jade followed her into the kitchen.

"Are you sure you know what you are getting yourself into with that pair?" Jade asked, motioning toward Jake and Brianna who were now comparing their pool gear.

"No, but as long as we all return on Sunday I'll

call it a victory. What are you going to be doing this weekend?"

"Um, you know that the carnival that Amy and I always went to is in town," Jade said, receiving a nod from her best friend. "Well, I asked Rachel if she would go with me to get past another hurdle in this moving on thing."

"So, is this a date?" asked Kristel, trying to contain her excitement.

"No. This is me taking my therapist with me to a place that holds a lot of memories and trying to find a way to deal with them."

"Well, she's hot and you two look cute together. You can't blame me for trying." Kristel laughed. "I'm glad that you are working at getting past those demons, though. If you need to talk afterward call me…"

"I will. And you know if you keep stating how hot Rachel is I'm going to start wondering if you're changing teams," teased Jade.

"Very funny."

"Well, I have some errands to run. Bri, come give me a hug."

Brianna ran over and hugged and kissed Jade, and made her promise that if she got sad she would go lie in Bri's room and let the stuffed animals cheer her up. "I have already talked to them," she told Jade.

Jade left and instead of running her errands, went home to call Rachel. She knew she was going to be a wreck until she got things worked out with her.

❧ ❧ ❧ ❧

"Hello?" Rachel said, picking up her phone.

"Hey, Rachel. It's Jade."

"Jade. Hi! How are you doing this morning?"

"Good. How are you? Is this an okay time to talk?"

"Yeah, I was just having some coffee going over some notes. It's a great way to start the day," said Rachel, laughing.

"I bet it beats a five-year-old waking you up at six o'clock by bouncing on the bed asking if it is time to go yet." Jade laughed.

"Bri's a bit excited huh?"

"Yeah. I dropped her off about an hour ago. She's Kristel's issue now. I love my daughter, but sometimes she has too much of Amy in her."

"Oh yeah? How so?" Rachel asked, feeling a need to learn more about this woman and her life.

"Well, Amy was a big kid most of the time. She wasn't patient; it had to be now or she got cranky," Jade said, laughing. "But the reason I called was to see if you were still available tomorrow night to go to the carnival with me?"

"Of course. Do you have plans during the day tomorrow?"

"No, why? What's up?"

"I also have a demon I need to face and I was wondering if you might be willing to help me face it?" asked Rachel, trying to keep her breathing regulated.

"Of course."

"You should learn to ask for details before agreeing to things with me," giggled Rachel.

"Now I'm scared."

"I need to go take a hike on a nature trail. I haven't done it since the day of Emily's accident. The kids we used to take have been asking if I would take them again, and well, I need to make sure I can handle it before I agree."

"I'd love to help," said Jade.

"Really? Thank you!"

"You've done so much for Brianna and me, it's honestly the least I can do."

"Would it be all right if I picked you up around 10:30 and we can go for the hike, get lunch, and then go to the carnival?" suggested Rachel.

"Are you sure you don't mind picking me up?"

"Not at all. This way if you're too keyed up after the carnival I don't need to worry about you driving home."

"That sounds like a good idea. Um, what should I wear tomorrow?" Jade asked.

"Well, I suggest jeans, T-shirt, comfortable shoes...nothing special. The weather is supposed to be nice and the trail is an established one so there isn't any hiking over mysterious terrain."

"Great, I can handle that. I will see you tomorrow at 10:30 then."

"Sounds good."

Chapter Eleven

Facing Fears

Rachel got up and after making coffee, she sat out on the porch listening to the birds.

"My love, I'm going to give this hike thing another try. I know the kids have wanted to go out, but I just haven't been able to go. Jade and I are going to give it a try...today. I don't know if I am strong enough yet. I miss you still so much. Please help me get through the hike and the day. I love you."

Glancing at the clock, Rachel realized she had to get ready. After putting her coffee cup in the sink, she went to shower and get dressed.

Rachel opted for her light blue jeans and a green T-shirt with "I May Be Crazy But At Least I Have Each Other" printed in white letters. She wanted to feel as comfortable as she could, especially knowing the stress that today was going to put on her.

Checking the clock, Rachel grabbed her purse, a zip-up hoodie, and her keys and headed off to pick up Jade.

❧ ❧ ❧ ❧

Jade woke Saturday morning and saw that she had a text from Kristel asking her to call when she had a moment.

"Hey, Jade," said Kristel, answering the phone.

"Hey, Kristel. Is everything okay? Is Bri okay?"

"Yeah, everything is fine. Bri wanted to talk to you, though. One moment and I'll get her."

"Hi, Mama," said Bri.

"Hi, Baby Girl! How are you doing?"

"I'm having lots of fun!"

"That's good. What did you want to talk to me about?"

"I wanted to tell you to have a nice day at the carnival with Rachel. I know you can get over the sadness that it brings from remembering Mommy. Mommy will be proud of you, too."

"Thank you, sweetheart," Jade said, a little choked up. "I'm actually going to help Rachel with something today, too."

"Then you both can do it! Because I say so," Brianna stated confidently.

"I believe you," Jade said, smiling. "You have a great day with Kristel and Jake. I love you."

"I love you, too! Okay, here's Aunt Kristel again."

"Hey," said Kristel.

"Did you put her up to that?"

"Nope, that was all your kid. So, what's your plan today?"

"Well, Rachel is going to pick me up in about an hour and we're going to go for a hike so she can face one of her demons. After that we're going to grab lunch and head to the carnival."

"And you're sure this isn't a date?" asked Kristel.

"Yes I am sure. I'm not ready to date and she doesn't date people who are either her clients, or are or were in her groups."

"Bummer."

"Stop, I have to get going so I can be ready. Call me if you or Bri need me."

"Sounds good, try and have fun today."

"Bye," they both said and hung up the phone.

Jade sat there for a few minutes before getting up and getting ready for the day. She had opted for some light blue jeans and a blue shirt with a picture of a giraffe on it saying "Moo...I'm a goat." Jade looked through her closet and found a pair of comfortable shoes and went downstairs to wait for Rachel.

※ ※ ※ ※

Rachel pulled into Jade's driveway and turned off the car. She sat there for a minute, taking a deep breath before she opened the car door and headed up to the front door. Rachel rang the doorbell and waited for Jade.

Jade opened the door and smiled as she motioned for the newly arrived woman to enter.

"I love your shirt," Rachel said as she entered.

"Yours is pretty nifty, too," said Jade, amused. "I guess we were both thinking that quirky was the way to go today."

"Thanks. I have a whole drawer of T-shirts like this."

"Me, too!"

"Are you ready?"

"Lead the way," Jade said, grabbing her purse and a pullover hoodie.

Once they got on the road, Rachel started to relax.

"It's about a twenty-minute drive," Rachel advised Jade.

"So, where is it we're going?"

"We're going to the trail that was a favorite for Emily and me. It was the first one we ever went out on, and it's the kids' favorite. I'm hoping that if I can do this today that maybe in a few weeks I'll be ready to bring a few of the kids out."

"Tell me more about the kids?"

"Well, the two that always went with us were Connor and Lacey, but there were others. The kids were from single-parent or lower-income homes, or kids who just needed someone on their side. We would take them out to show them that there are options and people who care. Lacey was always told that she was dumb because she read slower than others. She takes a little bit longer to understand things. Lacey was really down on herself and Emily worked with her and made tweaks in her teaching style, and the girl went from getting failing grades to being a straight-A student. Her mom works three jobs to support the two of them so we used to spend a lot of time with her. Since Emily died, I've kept in touch with her, we go out once a month to either a movie or bowling, but she loved the hikes the most, so I want to be able to give that back to her."

"She is very lucky to have someone like you in her life, Rachel. I don't know of many people who would be willing to do what you and Emily were doing. Hell, and the fact that you still keep in touch with the kids shows how big your heart is," Jade said, causing Rachel to blush.

They parked near the entrance to the trails. Rachel pulled two bottles of water out of the cooler, attached belt clips to them and handed one to Jade.

"It just clips onto your belt loops. It makes it easier to carry," Rachel said as she clipped her own to her pants.

"That is an awesome idea," said Jade, clipping hers on. "Where did you find these, or is this a Rachel/Emily invention?"

"Emily found them online. I'd love to claim that they were my idea, but I believe people get in trouble for that sort of thing." Rachel laughed.

The two locked the car and headed down the trail.

"It is a beautiful day," said Jade as they walked along.

"Yeah, the temperature is perfect. Hey, look over there." Rachel pointed to their right. "There's a baby bunny."

"Aww, there are three of them. I think Mr. Butters is bigger than all of them combined!"

"I think you're right. How is Brianna doing?"

"She's good. I talked to her this morning. She gave me this adorable pep talk and told me that she was certain I could get over what I needed to for the carnival. I told her that I was helping you as well, and she said that she knew we could both get past these demons. 'Because I said so,' was how she put it."

"She is a rare kid. I think she's right, though. We can do this," Rachel said, smiling at Jade and receiving a smile in return.

They went along the trail for a while, Rachel pointing out the plants and them both pointing out the wildlife. They reached a hill and Rachel said that at the top was an amazing view. Jade followed her up the hill and when they reached the top, they could see the whole park area and the various trails all leading to where they were standing.

"Rachel, this is incredible," whispered Jade as she gaped at the beauty before her.

"This is why we do these hikes," Rachel told Jade before she unclipped her water and took a drink.

After taking some time to rest and enjoy the view they decided to head back to the car and go get some lunch.

The walk back seemed to take longer, but it was just as fascinating and enjoyable. Once they were back at the car they decided on salads for lunch since they would be going to a carnival and both knew that you had to get a funnel cake and mini donuts whenever you went. It was a requirement written somewhere.

"So, now that lunch is done, did you want to head to the carnival? Or there is a neat art gallery just down the road we could check out," Rachel posed.

"I haven't been to an art gallery to just look in years."

"Then to see the art it is," said Rachel as they walked down the street to the gallery.

Once they were inside the gallery, Jade took over and gave Rachel a mini history lesson on several of the paintings.

"Sorry, Amy always told me I got carried away when it came to my love of art and sharing the knowledge."

"Don't apologize. I think this is the best time I have ever had in an art gallery. We may have to do this more often," Rachel said, and Jade smiled back at her and nodded in agreement.

It had taken them two hours to get through the gallery, and the late afternoon had turned to early evening by the time they made their way to the carnival.

As it cooled down, Jade and Rachel both put on their hoodies and then started to laugh when they saw that they matched. Both hoodies had the picture of a unicorn on it with a caption that read, "Unicorns Are Just Horny Ponies."

"Amy would never be seen with me when I wore this." Jade laughed.

"Emily wouldn't either. Mrs. Donovan, you have exquisite taste in T-shirts and hoodies," said Rachel.

"So do you, Mrs. Cassidy."

❧❧❧❧

Jade and Rachel headed toward the entrance. They stopped at the ticket booth and Jade got them both unlimited ride passes.

As they were putting the wristbands on, Jade looked at Rachel and noticed the setting sun highlighting her red hair, and that she was a very beautiful woman. She wasn't sure what she had expected for today, but she was truly enjoying learning more about this caring woman.

"I suppose I should have checked to see how strong your stomach was," Jade said, looking sheepishly at Rachel.

"Oh, I can out-ride you…and that sounded better in my head," said Rachel as they both laughed. "How are you doing?"

"The smells remind me of her. There's the Tilt-A-Whirl. That was always our first ride," Jade said.

"Then, let's go," Rachel said as they made their way over to the line.

Within minutes they were in a car and the ride was starting.

"Oh shit," squeaked Rachel as the car they were in started to spin.

"Oh yeah, there is always one car that spins more than the others."

"Yeah, but did we need to get it?"

"Wimp," teased Jade as they continued to spin faster throughout the ride.

"All right, that does it. We're going to go on every ride and see who gives up first," said Rachel as they exited the ride.

"You're on. Beware, though. I have been doing this for years," Jade said, her competitive side coming out.

The pair moved to the next ride and decided that they were going to start there and work in a circle and hit every ride they passed.

"Do you want to share a car?" Jade asked as they came up to a ride called 'The Zipper'.

"Sure," said Rachel. The man running the ride opened the red car and both Rachel and Jade got in.

"It's a bit smaller than I remember," said Jade, feeling the warmth of Rachel's body against her own.

"Are you okay with this?"

"Yeah, I am. Are you?"

"Yep," said Rachel, and then she gasped as the ride started to move and the car started to flip. "Oh shit…"

Jade, hearing the panic in her voice, reached over and placed her hand over the top of Rachel's. Feeling Jade's hand on hers apparently helped Rachel ease her death grip. Glancing next to her, Jade offered Rachel a comforting smile as the ride ended and they waited to be let out.

"Are you okay?" Jade asked, noticing Rachel was a little paler than she was when they started the ride.

"Yeah, I just need a minute or two."

Jade saw an open table next to the concession stand. She took Rachel's hand and led her over.

"Here, rest for a minute. I'll be right back."

Jade went to the concession stand and got Rachel a drink to help calm her nerves and stomach.

"Here, drink this. Then, maybe we'll go through the Fun House instead of on another ride," Jade suggested, handing Rachel the soda.

"Thanks," Rachel said softly. "That was a ride I've never been on before."

"I gathered that, and I'm guessing it's one you may not go on again?"

"I might, but can we not do it again tonight?"

"No problem," said Jade, placing a comforting hand on Rachel's shoulder.

After Rachel finished her soda, they made their way to the Fun House. They entered and laughed at all of the odd stuff. They entered the "Hall of Mirrors" and giggled at what the different mirrors did to their image.

"Hey, look, let's go in here," said Rachel, taking Jade's hand and pulling her toward a door with a sign above it saying "Room of a Thousand Images."

The pair entered the room and suddenly they were surrounded by a thousand images of themselves. Jade let go of Rachel's hand and moved around the room, occasionally bumping into a mirror.

"This is surreal," said Jade.

"No kidding. I've never seen a room like this. Have you?" asked Rachel, leaning up against one of the mirrors.

"No, never," Jade said as the lights in the room dimmed slightly, changing the way the room looked and felt. "This appears to be something new within the

Fun House."

Rachel was trying to figure out which image in front of her was the real Jade and which was a mirror when Jade bumped into her. Well, more accurately, walked into her, pressing their bodies together.

"There you are," whispered Rachel. Her body was on fire everywhere that it met with Jade's.

"S-sorry," Jade said, taking a slight step backward.

She could still feel the heat coming off Rachel's body. The heat she felt was causing her core body temp to heat up as well. Jade felt her heart rate quicken. She wasn't sure why, but she moved forward again, pressing her body against Rachel's and then leaned her head down and softly brushed their lips together.

Feeling their lips touch caused their breath to catch. Jade couldn't explain how good it felt or the surge that exploded through the rest of her body. Rachel wrapped her arms around Jade's waist and pulled her closer. Jade leaned in and pressed their lips together again, instantly feeling the other woman responding. Their lips moved together, causing her to feel butterflies fluttering around her stomach. After a minute they broke apart and Jade took two steps backward.

"Wow," whispered Rachel.

"Yeah," Jade panted.

"I, er…"

"That…" started Jade before her voice faded away.

Rachel took Jade's hand in hers and they exited the Fun House, moving away from the crowd and over to a quiet area. They both sat down on the ground, needing to process what had just happened.

"Do you want to talk about what happened in there?" Rachel asked softly.

"Not yet. I don't regret it, though," said Jade, looking down at her hands in her lap.

"I don't either."

❧ ❧ ❧ ❧

Jade looked over at Rachel, who seemed deep in thought, but the scowl on her face told Jade it wasn't a pleasant one.

"Come on," said Jade, standing and extending her hand to Rachel.

"What?" asked the bewildered woman, being shaken from her thoughts.

"Please, come with me?" Jade asked sweetly, earning a soft smile from Rachel as she took the extended hand and allowed herself to be helped up. "We aren't helping ourselves sitting here. Would you join me please on another ride? I promise it will be tamer than The Zipper."

"Who's the therapist here?" Rachel laughed, bumping shoulders with Jade.

"Me, now move your ass," Jade said, laughing as they made their way over to one of the rides.

"Well, this appears to be adequately named," said Rachel after watching the ride called the Scrambler.

"Do you want to go on it?" asked Jade.

"Yep." Rachel smiled as they were let in to choose their seats. They sat in the middle of the seat, but as soon as the ride started they were pushed to the edge. Rachel found her body pressing against Jade's again. Although it was just side to side, she could still feel a surge inside her.

The ride ended and Jade helped Rachel out of the seat since they had been pressed against Jade's side of the car. They were both smiling as they moved to the bumper cars, then decided to play a couple of games.

"I'm horrible at all of these games," Jade said, looking around.

"Oh, I love this game," said Rachel, taking Jade by the hand and pulling her toward the game.

"Hello, ladies. Simple game, kids do it all the time. Get three balls in the fishbowls and win a fish. Get two in and I'll give you a fish sticker."

Rachel handed the man a dollar and he gave her three balls. She tossed the first one and it landed perfectly in the center fishbowl. She bounced the second one and it landed right next to the first ball. Rachel smiled at Jade and then turned back and bounced the last ball, which landed on the opposite side of the first ball.

"We have a winner," said the man running the game. He picked up a collection of fish in fishbowls and Rachel chose one. He put a cover over the bowl and handed it to her.

The two walked away, Rachel smiling at the fish that she had won and Jade smiling at Rachel.

"That was impressive," said Jade.

"Not really. It's just basic geometry," Rachel said offhandedly.

"It's just basic geometry? Are you telling me that you are a math whiz as well?"

"I was a nerd in school. I admit it and embrace it," Rachel said proudly.

"So, what are you going to name your new fish?"

"Well, I don't know. Would it be okay if I gave it to Brianna? You don't have to feel obligated to say yes. I didn't mean to put you on the spot or anything. Geez, I'm supposed to be a therapist. I must not be a very good one if I am here helping you try to overcome something and then I put you on the spot. I'm really sorry. I...I..." Rachel babbled until she saw Jade laughing. "You're laughing at me aren't you?"

"Hell yes I am," Jade said, trying to contain her laughter.

"That isn't very nice, you know," Rachel said, sticking her tongue out.

"Well, I'm sorry, but I have never heard anyone babble like that without passing out due to lack of oxygen."

"Well, now you see that in addition to being a nerd in school I can also do things for a long time without the need to stop for oxygen," said Rachel, who then blushed as did Jade, realizing how that could have been mistaken.

"Uh huh..."

"So, back to the original question before one of us, namely me, becomes more embarrassed. Would it be all right if I gave the fish to Brianna?"

"She'd love it. Thank you."

"It looks like they are starting to close down the rides," said Rachel.

"Wow, it's almost eleven o'clock already?" said Jade looking at her watch.

"Well, shall we head out then?"

"Sure," said Jade, absently taking Rachel's free hand as they walked toward the car.

Once they arrived at the car, Rachel handed Jade the tiny fishbowl and dug out her keys. They drove back to Jade's and she invited Rachel in, but Rachel declined, stating it was late. Rachel did however walk Jade to the door. They stepped inside so Jade could put the fish down.

"Thank you for going hiking with me today," said Rachel.

"Thank you for going to the carnival with me and for Brianna's new little friend. I had a good time today."

"Me, too."

They stood there staring into one another's eyes for a long moment before Rachel pulled Jade into a hug. Rachel found herself wrapping her arms around Jade's neck while Jade wrapped her arms around her waist. They held one another close. They started to pull back, and when their eyes met, Rachel leaned forward and pressed her lips to Jade's. After a moment she felt Jade responding to the kiss and pulling her body closer. Rachel ran her tongue along Jade's bottom lip, requesting access. She felt lips parting, and then their tongues were moving together. The feeling that was pulsing through Jade's body caused her to let out a small moan of enjoyment. They separated, both needing air, and pressed their foreheads together.

"Wow," Jade breathed.

"Breathtaking," whispered Rachel.

"Definitely…"

"I should, um, get going," Rachel said after they had both caught their breath and started to relax the hold they had on each other.

"Okay," Jade said. She leaned forward and gave Rachel a chaste kiss before they separated.

"I'll call you tomorrow," Rachel said as they made their way to the edge of the porch.

"I'd like that," Jade said, smiling at Rachel.

Jade watched as Rachel walked to her car and then pulled away. Jade wrapped her arms around herself and walked inside, closing the door and locking it.

Chapter Twelve

Aftershocks

Rachel drove home in a haze. She couldn't believe how the day had gone. She had survived the hiking trails, which felt phenomenal. She had helped Jade with her carnival demon. She had broken her rule of not getting involved with a past or present client or group member. What the hell was she doing? Once she got home, she got ready for bed and curled up under the covers and drifted off to sleep.

"Rachel, isn't it beautiful out here?" asked Emily as they started on the trail.

"Yeah, they said that it is supposed to be nice all day. Hopefully we'll see lots of wildlife," Rachel said, taking her wife's hand and entwining their fingers together.

The couple walked along the trail passing only a couple of people as they made their way to the top of the hill that overlooked the different trails.

"I packed a blanket in the bag for us to sit on when we get to the top of the hill," Emily informed her wife.

"That sounds nice," Rachel said, stopping and pulling her wife close and kissing her. "I love you."

"I love you too."

The couple took their time checking out the wildlife and the various plants along the trail until they made it up to the top of the hill. Emily opened her backpack and pulled out a special lightweight hiking blanket and laid it out under a tree, giving them shade but not compromising their view. The couple cuddled together and shared soft kisses.

"This is heaven," said Rachel, feeding her wife a piece of fruit.

"Anywhere with you is heaven," Emily said as she pulled the last grape out of the bin and teased Rachel's lips with it before allowing her to eat it.

As the afternoon came to an end and evening crept in, they packed up the blanket and the empty fruit container and headed back toward the car.

"Rachel, look." Emily pointed at a litter of baby foxes and their mother about twenty feet away.

"That is adorable, my love. Do you think we'll really have kids some day?"

"Well, I'm ready whenever you are."

"Emily, don't tease me," said Rachel, stopping them in the middle of the trail. "Are you really ready?"

"You know the deal. We can have kids as long as I can use your egg and carry your baby."

Rachel was in shock. She had wanted this for so long and Emily had always resisted the idea stating that they weren't ready. Now she was ready. Rachel pulled Emily into her arms and kissed her passionately.

"You are the most incredible woman in the world," Rachel said when they broke the kiss. "We need to get home soon so I can make love to the mother of my future children."

They hurried along the trail and quickly packed their stuff in the car and headed home.

"Rachel, who is this woman?" she heard Emily ask as Jade stood before them.

"She's one of my group members," said Rachel,

wrapping an arm around her wife's waist.

"Rachel, don't lie to her. Do not give her false hope. You know that being involved with someone you are professionally connected with ruins your objectivity," Emily stated. *"You aren't ready to let go of me yet."*

Rachel felt ropes tightening around her wrists. She had Jade pulling her on one side and Emily pulling her from the other. She felt like they were going to rip her or her soul in two.

Rachel jolted awake and sat up in bed. Her breathing was labored and she was covered in a light layer of sweat.

"Please…someone tell me what I'm supposed to do. Emily, my love, my wife, you aren't here. I miss you. God, do I miss you. I miss the life we had planned. I miss the children we were going to have. Oh, my baby girl, I miss getting to know you and seeing you grow into the amazing woman I know you would have become. I'll never get that with you…I'm alone here, trying to survive," cried Rachel. "I know I'm not supposed to get involved with anyone I'm working with professionally, but…I can't describe the feeling I get when Jade is around. The loneliness subsides, the fear of being alone dissipates, and the heartache eases. Baby, she isn't you, but she makes me smile. I kissed her and it felt good. I know it wasn't supposed to, but damn it, it did. I don't know what to do…Emily, help me."

Rachel lay back down, shaking from the emotions coursing through her body. She felt guilty, scared, and then there were the other unknown emotions. Her mind was racing. She was replaying the day, the kisses, and her life with Emily, what they had envisioned for their future, and then there was Brianna—the girl who had stolen her heart the moment she first saw her.

Rachel lay there shaking and crying until her body gave into the exhaustion and she fell into a dreamless and restless sleep.

❦❦❦❦

Jade made herself a cup of chamomile tea to help calm her mind. She really wanted to talk to Kristel, but she knew that it was late and she would have to wait until she brought the kids back on Sunday. Sipping the tea, Jade replayed the day in her mind. She couldn't believe how easy it was to be around Rachel. She felt comfortable, relaxed even. Jade had never felt that with anyone before. Even with Amy and Kristel, it had taken her a while to get comfortable. Yes, she had known Rachel for a while now through the weekly group sessions, but on a personal level, this was different.

Amy, what is going on? What is it about this woman that makes me feel comfortable? Safe even, thought Jade, finishing her tea and after putting the mug in the dishwasher, made her way upstairs and into bed.

Jade glanced at the clock and saw it was close to one in the morning. She knew she needed sleep. Brianna was going to be home soon and she would be full of energy and excitement from her weekend. Closing her eyes, Jade drifted off to sleep with visions of her daughter in her mind.

"Jade, come on," said Amy, pulling her wife with her. "There is nothing on this warning list that says if you are pregnant you can't go on it. I'm being careful."

"Amy, do you remember the wonderful bout of

morning sickness you had not thirty minutes ago? Babe, you got dizzy moving too quickly this morning," Jade *said as her wife pouted. "Argh, fine. You had damn well better not teach our children that pout."*

Amy smiled as she placed Jade's hand on her belly. She was only twelve weeks pregnant, but this was their baby, their creation.

"I love you," Amy said softly as she leaned forward and kissed Jade deeply in the middle of the carnival.

"I love you, too," said Jade as they broke apart. "Let's go get on the ride."

"You are the best wife and you are going to be the best mother."

"I already agreed to go on the ride. Although, if you want to make it up to me later, I won't object," Jade *whispered into Amy's ear, growling softly.*

Jade and Amy were walking through the Fun House when they got separated. Jade saw Rachel standing there...alone.

Jade pulled away from Amy. It was the weakened, cancer-ridden body that Jade had last seen in the hospital.

"Amy, I'm sorry. Please, forgive me..." Jade cried, reaching toward her wife. "You left me...you left Bri. It hurts so bad some days."

"I know I did. I wouldn't have chosen to leave... Jade, I want you to have a life again. You are young; you and Bri deserve that."

"But it's too soon. I need you...I still love you."

"You will always love me Jade. I will always love you. Do what's best for you and Bri..."

Jade woke up crying. Her pillow was wet and she knew she had been crying for a while. She was confused. She loved Amy beyond words, but she was gone and Rachel was here. Things felt different when she was with Rachel.

Glancing at the clock, Jade saw it was almost five. She knew she could and should try to go back to sleep, but she also knew she wasn't going to. She was going to have to wait until Kristel brought the kids home to talk with her. Jade got up and decided to do some laundry and cleaning while she waited.

❧❧❧❧

"All right, monsters, time to pack up," Kristel called as the two kids were running around the room.

"But, Mom," whined Jake.

"But, Jake," Kristel whined back at her son. "We need to check out and then go see Aunt Jade."

"Mama!" squealed Brianna at the mention of Jade's name.

"Yep, we need to get packed up and get going."

"Okay," said the two kids in unison as they started shoving their stuff into their bags.

After getting the kids packed up and surveying the room several times for left items, Kristel checked out and got them buckled into the car. Before leaving she sent a quick text message to Jade.

Kristel: We're leaving now. Be there in a couple of hours.

Jade: I can't wait to see Bri. Tell her I miss her. You and I need to talk...

Kristel: Are you okay?

Jade: Physically, yes...mentally, not sure. Mostly no...

Kristel: Is this because of yesterday with Rachel?

Jade: Yes!

Kristel: We'll be there as soon as I can safely get

us there.

Kristel turned and told Brianna that her Mama missed her. Brianna smiled and told Kristel she missed her Mama, too.

⚜ ⚜ ⚜ ⚜

Rachel woke and found her eyes hurt to open. She hazily looked at the clock and saw it was already 9:30. Rachel groaned, knowing she needed to get up, but after yesterday and her dream last night, she didn't know how she was going to make herself get out of bed.

Rachel heard her phone ringing and reached to answer it.

"Hello," she answered, her voice a bit scratchy.

"Hey, Rach! It's your favorite sister-in-law. How's it going?" asked the chipper voice on the other end of the phone.

"Skye?"

"Yeah, do you have another favorite sister-in-law?"

"No, sorry it was a rough night."

"You want some company to talk about it?"

"Yes, please."

"I'll be over in an hour," said Skye, and she hung up the phone.

Rachel smiled to herself. She was glad she hadn't lost touch with Skye after Emily died. Rachel showered and got dressed while she waited for her sister-in-law to arrive.

⚜ ⚜ ⚜ ⚜

Jade was pacing the house when she saw Kristel

pull into the driveway. She opened the door and stepped on the porch and saw Brianna bolt out of the car, running toward her.

"Mama," yelled Brianna as she ran toward the house.

Jade crouched down, scooped her daughter up in her arms and hugged her tightly.

"I missed you, Baby Girl."

"I missed you, too, Mama," Brianna said, squeezing her mother tighter.

"Did you have fun?"

"Yeah. Did you and Rachel have fun yesterday?" asked Brianna just as Kristel and Jake made their way up to the porch. Kristel was holding Bri's bag and looked at Jade's eyes. Jade knew that Kristel had received the true answer, the one that Jade wouldn't give her daughter.

"Yeah, we had a good time yesterday. Why don't you and Jake go and play in your room while Aunt Kristel and I chat?"

"Okay," said Brianna as Jade put her down.

Once they could tell the kids were upstairs, Kristel and Jade sat down on the porch swing.

"So, what's going on?" asked Kristel.

"I'm really confused…"

"I gathered that by the lack-of-sleep-look you're sporting today. Tell me about yesterday."

"Well, we went for a hike. It was gorgeous. The trail went through some amazing vegetation and there were some cute animals. We climbed up a hill where you could see the whole surrounding area. She told me about the kids that she and Emily used to take hiking. These were kids who really needed someone on their side. It was inspiring."

"Sounds like a good time."

"It was. We went and got lunch, checked out an art gallery, and then went to the carnival…" said Jade before bowing her head.

"Hey, this is me, Jade. Talk to me…let me help," Kristel said, wrapping an arm around her best friend.

"Things started out great. She has the same horny pony hoodie." Jade laughed and Kristel rolled her eyes and smiled. "We went on a couple of rides. The Zipper was one that she wasn't ready for. So, after resting and getting her something to drink we decided to walk through the Fun House…" Jade took a deep breath trying to center herself.

"What happened?" Kristel asked, feeling her friend shaking.

"We kissed…"

"What do you mean you kissed? Like you bumped into her cheek?"

"No. We were in this new area where you see yourself like a thousand times. Well, we got separated and she was leaning up against a mirror and I walked into her and then we pulled one another close and kissed."

"Wow. Did you talk about it?"

"No. We left the Fun House and sat outside for a while and then we went and played some games. She won Bri a fish."

"Aww, Bri will love that…but back to your story."

"Once we got back here she walked me in, we talked for a few minutes, mindless banter mostly, and then we kissed again. This time it was more intense."

"Whoa. What do you mean more intense?"

"Tongue…" Jade said and then looked down at the porch again.

"Jade, you have nothing to be ashamed about. Amy wanted you to live. She's been gone over a year."

"Yeah, the part that freaked me out was I dreamed about Amy and me at the carnival when she was pregnant with Bri. Then it morphed to Amy telling me what happened with Rachel was okay."

"That is a bit creepy. So, what has you more freaked, the dream or the kisses?"

"Both. When I'm with Rachel it feels different than it did with Amy."

"Jade, every relationship or friendship is going to feel different. If they all felt the same we'd be bored. You have grieved your wife, you will continue to grieve and miss her, but you can't stop your life either. Rachel isn't just some flake you picked up at a bar. She's hot, she's smart, and she understands what you are going through. Is she a good kisser?"

"You are so obsessed with her," smirked Jade. "I know she isn't just a flake or a rebound girl, but I don't want to hurt her either. I don't know if I'm ready for anything yet."

"Then talk to her. If you don't talk to her it's going to make it awkward for you going to group. And you are not getting out of doing that," Kristel said, giving her best friend a stern look. "You like her; she likes you. Just build from that. If it works out so that it's a relationship instead of just a friendship, that's fantastic. If not, then you still have a good, caring friend."

"When did you get so smart?" asked Jade, looking Kristel in the eyes for the first time since they had started talking.

"I used to hang around these two women who made me a better, smarter person."

"So, what do I do now? Oh wise one," Jade said,

giggling.

"Talk to her. How did you leave things?"

"She said she'd call me today."

"Invite her over and talk to her. Is she a better kisser than Amy?"

"How do you know how Amy kisses?" asked Jade.

"Remember that first New Year's Eve party we went to, the three of us…"

"Oh yeah," said Jade, laughing at her friend. "I'm still not telling you."

"Damn it. I have no man, at least I can live vicariously through you."

"Not going to happen!"

The two women got up to go inside and see what the kids were doing.

"You need to learn to kiss and tell, Donovan," Kristel said, bumping shoulders with her friend before pulling her into a hug and reassuring her that it would be okay and that she had done nothing wrong.

※ ※ ※ ※

"All right, Rach. What has you freaked out?" said Skye, having let herself in to the house.

"Dammit," said Rachel, jumping at the sound of her sister-in-law's voice behind her.

"If I apologize for scaring you, will you believe me?"

"No!"

"Good, because I am so not sorry," Skye said, sticking her tongue out.

"How is it that you are Emily's older sister? My god you have the maturity of a twelve-year-old."

"Bite me," teased Skye, seeing her sister-in-law

smile. "So give me coffee and talk to me."

Rachel poured them both some coffee and they went and sat out back on the deck.

"I kissed someone yesterday…" Rachel blurted out causing Skye to spit her coffee over the nearby railing.

"You what? Who? Where? What the hell, Rach? Details, now!"

"There's this woman that has been attending my grief support group. Her name is Jade. She's a single mom of this incredible little girl. She lost her wife a little over a year ago. We went for a hike yesterday," started Rachel.

"A hike? Have you done that since Emily died?" She saw Rachel shake her head. "Wow. Okay so you went for a hike, then?"

"That was her helping me. We then went to the carnival. That's something that Jade and her wife had done and so I helped her confront that demon. While we were there, we kissed. We were in the Fun House and she bumped into me…our bodies were so close and it just happened. Then when I dropped her off we kissed again. This time it was a deeper kiss."

Rachel set her coffee down and stood and leaned against the railing of the deck.

"Rachel, it's okay. Emily would want you to be happy, to find love again." Skye turned her sister-in-law around and put her hands on her shoulders. "You've done nothing wrong."

Rachel leaned her head on Skye's shoulder and cried for a few minutes.

"I have," said Rachel, pulling back and wiping the tears from her eyes.

"How?"

"Skye, you know the rule about not getting involved with a current or past client or group member. I'm her grief counselor."

"You are, Rachel, and from what you told me you didn't force yourself on her, she didn't tell you to go to hell or get away from her. You've done nothing wrong. But, you do need to talk to her. How did you end things? I mean besides the kiss."

"You are an ass, you know that?"

"What? Was it a good kiss?"

"I don't kiss and tell."

"My sister did," teased Skye, seeing Rachel turn the color of her red hair. "God you are more fun than Emily to tease. I love you, Rachel. Now how did you two leave things?"

"I told her I'd call her today."

"Then invite her over, go out for coffee, something, just get together and talk. I do however expect to meet this woman if you plan on dating her."

"Oh yeah, that won't be awkward. 'Jade, this is my sister-in-law Skye, she needs to check you out to make sure you are worthy of dating.'"

"I wouldn't put it that way, doofus. Emily may be gone, Rachel, but you are still and will always be family. When you married my sister you inherited us all."

"Someone should have told me that before. I might have thought twice," said Rachel, laughing.

"Yeah, that is our fun. Call the woman…and you can call me anytime day or night."

"Thanks, Skye."

Rachel hugged Skye, who gathered her things and left. Rachel continued to sit on the deck and think about her talk with Skye.

Chapter Thirteen

The Talk

Rachel went inside and got another cup of coffee and her cell phone before returning to the deck. She knew that it was mid-afternoon and she had told Jade that she would call her. That was easier said than done. She was afraid that Jade was going to regret what happened between them after having had time to think. Taking a deep breath, Rachel called her.

"Hello," said Brianna, answering Jade's cell phone.

"Hello, Brianna! This is Rachel."

"Hi, Rachel. Did you have fun with Mama yesterday?"

"Yes, I did. She helped me a lot."

"Mama is good at helping people."

"Did you have fun with Kristel and Jake?"

"Yeah, we went on lots of water slides and played in the wave pool. I went out further than Jake could and he's a little bit bigger than me."

"That is fantastic. It definitely sounds like you had a good time."

"Bri, who are you talking to on my phone?" Rachel heard Jade say in the background.

"It's Rachel," Brianna said.

"I see. Did she call to speak to you or me?"

"Rachel, did you call to talk to me or Mama?" asked Brianna.

Rachel could hear Jade laughing on the other end of the line and she loved the sound of the woman's laugh.

"Well, although it is good to hear your voice, I did call to talk to your Mama," Rachel said.

"She called to talk to you, Mama." Rachel heard Bri hand the phone over to Jade. "I'm going to play in the sandbox."

"Hello," Jade said.

"Hello," said Rachel. "How are you doing today?"

"I'm doing well. How are you?"

"I'm okay. It sounds like Brianna had a good weekend."

"I have a feeling she's going to sleep very well tonight," Jade said with amusement.

"Jade, can we get together sometime soon to talk about yesterday?"

"I'd like that. Would you like to come over and join Brianna and me for dinner tonight? If you have plans we can do it another time."

"If it isn't an imposition I'd love to see you and Bri tonight."

"Great. Why don't you come by around 5:30," said Jade.

"Is there anything that I can bring?"

"Nope. I have everything covered."

"All right. I will see you and Bri at 5:30 then."

"We'll see you then," Jade said with a smile on her face.

They hung up and Rachel knew she needed to tell Skye.

Rachel: I'm going over at 5:30 to have dinner with her and Bri and to talk.

Skye: Good! I'm glad you aren't putting this off.

Rachel: I'm nervous. What if she doesn't ever want to see me again?

Skye: Rach, the woman invited you over. You don't invite someone over if you never want to see them again.

Rachel: What if she wants to let me down easy?

Skye: You still don't invite someone over if you don't want to see them again. What are you going to wear?

Rachel: Huh? Do I have to wear something special? OMG, what am I going to wear?

Skye: LOL, relax Rach. I am just messing with you.

Rachel: That was mean, Skye.

Skye: Just wear some jeans and do you have a low-cut casual T-shirt? Wear something to make the ladies the center of attention?

Rachel: What ladies? What the hell are you talking about?

Skye: Your boobs, Rachel. My god, pick a T-shirt that is low cut so if you lean over she can see down your shirt and check out your boobs.

Rachel: I'll think about it. Did you give your sister this advice when she and I started dating?

Skye: Yep, and it worked like a charm. She told me how that first night she kept catching you checking out her boobs.

Rachel: I can't help that I like boobs.

Skye: We all know. Trust me. Emily told me how much you love them. Perv.

Rachel: And on that note, I'm going to get ready. I'll tell you how it goes.

Skye: Great. Love you, Rach. Let's do coffee tomorrow or dinner.

Rachel: Sounds good. Love you, too, Skye.

⚜

"Bri, we need to run to the store. Come wash your hands quick," Jade called after she hung up the phone with Rachel.

"Why are we going to the store, Mama?" asked the little girl.

"Rachel is coming over for dinner tonight."

"Really? She is?"

"Yep, so go get your hands washed and maybe comb your hair," said Jade.

"Okay, I'll be quick, Mama."

Brianna took care of the things Jade told her to do and then they headed to the store. Jade picked up some stuff to grill and when they got home she helped Bri unpack and she prepared dinner.

"Mama, can I set the table?"

Jade was about to answer when she heard the doorbell. Both she and Bri made their way to the door. Brianna opened the door and Rachel smiled seeing the excitement in her eyes.

"Hi, Rachel," said Brianna, smiling up at her.

"Hi, Brianna," Rachel said, hiding something behind her back.

"Come in, please." Jade smiled and saw the small package of fish food and a new, slightly larger fishbowl in Rachel's hand. Jade took it and quickly stepped into the kitchen and put the fish in the new bowl before following Rachel and Brianna into the living room.

"Bri, last night while Mama and I were at the carnival I got you something," Rachel said, glancing toward Jade and seeing her smile and setting the fishbowl out of sight.

"You got me a present? Wow, that's so cool." Her eyes fixated on the woman kneeling in front of her.

"Last night we got you a fish," Rachel said, pulling a little fishbowl from behind the small stack of books where Jade had set it.

"What's its name?"

"That is for you to decide," said Rachel.

"I'm going to name it Olaf," said Bri, taking the fish over to her coloring table in the corner of the room.

"I hope it was still okay that I gave her the fish. I know that we talked about it last night and that you were okay with it then. I probably should have checked with you that it was still okay, but seeing her face light up like that was so incredible. If you're mad about me giving her the fish I will get it back so that you don't have to be the bad person in this. I did bring the fish some food as well so that you wouldn't have to worry about getting any and...and...why are you laughing at me?"

"Your Rachel-babble is adorable. I am still very okay with Bri having the fish. I don't know about the name Olaf for it, but that was Bri's choice."

"She looks really happy over there. I've never seen a kid's face light up that way before. Is it always like that when they get excited?"

"Yeah, that is her normal excited face," Jade said, smiling in Brianna's direction.

"Mama, Olaf smiled at me. Rachel, come and see Olaf smile."

Rachel and Jade got up and joined Brianna, who pointed to the goldfish and showed them that it was smiling at her.

"That is pretty neat. I've never seen a fish smile before," said Rachel.

"Mama, have you seen a fish smile before?"

"No, Baby Girl, I haven't. You have a pretty special fish."

"Thank you so much, Rachel. I love my new fish," Brianna said, launching herself into Rachel's arms and hugging her tightly.

"You are very welcome. I'm glad you like the fish."

"I'm going to go start the grill. I'll be right back."

Jade left the room and went out to the back yard to take care of the grill, leaving Rachel and Brianna alone.

When she returned, Jade was accosted by her daughter. "Hi, Mama. I love you."

"I love you, too. What did I do to deserve such a fantastic hug?"

"Nothing."

"Well, thank you," Jade said, kissing her daughter on the top of her head.

"Welcome," said Brianna before running outside to play in her sandbox again.

"Let me help you." Rachel followed Jade into the kitchen.

"Thanks."

Jade handed Rachel the veggie tents to take out and she grabbed the chicken breasts that she had been marinating.

"Those aren't even cooked and they smell amazing," said Rachel.

"Thanks. Amy and I created the marinade recipe. It's a Caribbean jerk style."

"I've never had that before. If it tastes as good as it smells, I'm going to want the recipe."

"Sorry, we don't share the recipe. You may just have to come over for dinner again," Jade said, smiling over at Rachel.

Rachel smiled, giving Jade the impression that she didn't mind the idea of coming over for dinner again or at the idea of spending more time with them. Once Jade had the chicken and veggie tents on the grill, she handed Rachel a soda from the corner fridge.

"It's so peaceful here," commented Rachel as they watched Brianna play in the sandbox.

"It was one of the reasons we bought the house."

"Emily and I went for something that was close to our work," Rachel said with a laugh.

"Bri, time to wash up and then you can set the table," Jade said, checking on dinner and seeing that it was almost done.

"Rachel and I already set the table," Brianna said, running past Jade and Rachel and into the house to wash her hands.

"When did you two set the table?" Jade asked.

"We set it while you were out here starting the grill. I hope that is okay."

"That's fine. I just feel bad. I invited you over to have dinner with us and you brought a new fishbowl and food for the fish, you helped my daughter set the table, and you helped me carry dinner out."

"I like helping. You did the hard stuff anyway," Rachel said, smiling at Jade.

"Thank you. Let's head inside for dinner."

Rachel and Jade met Brianna in the dining room and the three of them ate dinner. Rachel complimented Jade on the chicken and Brianna told them in detail about her weekend with Kristel and Jake. After dinner the three of them cleared the table and loaded the dishwasher, and then Jade sent Brianna up to take a bath and get ready for bed.

"She'll be in the tub for thirty to forty-five minutes. I'm going to be in major trouble when she wants to start taking showers," said Jade as she and Rachel sat in the living room so that if Bri needed her she was close.

"Jade, do you have regrets about what happened last night?"

"No, d-d-do y-you?" said Jade, mentally berating herself for stuttering.

"No, absolutely not." Rachel took Jade's hand in her own. "I, um, actually had a dream last night with Emily in it. And then this morning I got a call out of the blue from Emily's sister, Skye. She came over and we talked about things."

"I had a dream with Amy in it last night...then when Kristel brought Bri home we went and talked about things as well," said Jade. "I can't imagine talking to one of Amy's family members about whatever is going on between us."

"Emily's family has made it clear that no matter what we are family. Skye and I have remained close after Emily's death. She's the one that made me start going to the meetings. I trust her to always be honest with me. She reminded me that Emily would want me to be happy and to not close myself off."

"Kristel told me the same thing. What are your expectations?" Jade asked bluntly.

"I have none. I'm not here to pressure you into anything you aren't ready for. That isn't what you need and honestly, neither do I. I won't deny that I feel a connection to you, but I know you are still in a pretty raw spot emotionally."

"I appreciate you not putting pressure on me." Jade started idly playing with Rachel's fingers. "I am still hurting over the loss of Amy, but I agree there is something between us. I just don't know if I'm ready for a relationship."

"Why don't we just see where things go? I would like to spend more time with you. Either just the two of us, or the three of us if you don't mind having Brianna around me."

"Brianna adores you Rachel. I'd like for us to take things slow and build from there."

"I'd like that as well. One of the things that bothered me was that I've always had a rule to not get involved with someone I'm connected professionally with."

"I understand that rule. I wouldn't like to let the others in group know about us at this point. I've always been a private person, and until I know what all is going on with us, I'd like to keep it between us. It saves on people interfering as well."

Brianna called from upstairs. Jade smiled and squeezed Rachel's hand before getting up and going to see what her daughter needed.

❧ ❧ ❧ ❧

"What's up?" Jade asked her daughter as she poked her head in the bathroom.

"I'm tired, so I'm done with my bath," said Brianna.

Jade helped her daughter out of the tub, with drying off, and then into her pajamas. The two then descended the stairs and returned to the living room.

"Why don't you pick a book and Rachel and I can read it to you. Then you can go upstairs to bed."

"Too tired, Mama."

"All right, give hugs and then it is time for bed."

"G'night, Rachel," said Brianna, giving Rachel a hug. "Thank you for Olaf!"

"Good night, Bri. I'm glad you like Olaf."

When their hug ended Brianna climbed into Jade's lap. Jade held her daughter for a minute then kissed the top of her head as she felt the little girl drifting toward sleep.

"I'll be right back. I think someone is very ready for bed," Jade told Rachel as she stood and carried her daughter upstairs and into her bedroom. Jade set her daughter down on the bed and covered her up. "Good night, my sweet girl."

"Night, Mama," said Bri as Jade leaned down and kissed her head before shutting the light off and heading back downstairs.

❧❧❧❧

Jade had taken Bri upstairs to go to bed and Rachel was looking around the room taking in the collection of books that filled the shelves. She saw that Jade owned several works by William Shakespeare. Pulling one of the books down, she smiled to herself.

Rachel was lost in thought, looking at one of the books when she heard a light cough bringing her attention back to the present. Jade moved closer and glanced at the book in Rachel's hands. Rachel was relieved to see Jade smile when she saw that it was her copy of *The Winter's Tale*.

"Sorry. This book brings back a lot of memories from my childhood," Rachel said, blushing.

"Mine, too," Jade said.

Rachel replaced the book and they sat back down on the couch.

"I was in the play when I was a kid," started Rachel. "My parents thought it would help me with my shyness."

"Did it?"

"Not a bit. I was terrified for the role I played in it."

"Which role?" asked Jade.

"I was a Jailer. I think I had ten lines in the whole play, but saying them in front of a crowd about killed me."

"Seriously? You played the Jailer?"

"Yeah, why?"

"I did, too. It was the first play I had ever done. I threw up twice before I went on stage," said Jade with an embarrassed laugh.

"Wow, that's funny. Well, not really funny that you threw up twice, but different and interesting. I mean I'm sure a lot of people have done the play and played the same characters as us. It was a long time ago and the book made me remember and now I'm babbling again and I can't..." Rachel was cut off by Jade's lips pressed against hers. They both responded to the kiss. It was a gentle kiss similar to their goodbye kiss the night before.

Rachel brought her hand to the back of Jade's neck pulling her closer. Jade moved her body closer to Rachel's. After a couple of minutes they broke apart naturally.

"Wow," whispered Rachel.

"That seems to be an effective way to stop your babbling."

"Definitely effective."

"I know I said I wanted to keep things slow, but you are a very good kisser…" Jade admitted and then tried to hide behind her hair to limit the amount of her obvious blushing.

"So are you," Rachel said, brushing Jade's hair behind her ear. "I should probably get going. I have an early meeting tomorrow morning. Will you go out on a date with me?"

"I'd love to go on a date with you," said Jade.

"I'll call you tomorrow and we can figure out when works. Thank you for an amazing weekend. I don't recall the last time I honestly enjoyed a real weekend."

"I know how you feel. It's been a long time since I felt like genuinely smiling."

Jade walked Rachel to the door and they shared another gentle kiss before Rachel left. Jade locked the door and shut down the lights and went up to bed to relax.

Chapter Fourteen

Moving Forward

Rachel woke up with a smile on her face. She knew that it was because she had hung out with Jade and Brianna the night before. Yes, they were going to take things slow, but it was a positive step forward for her. She still felt the guilt of breaking her one true rule since she became a therapist, but she needed to see where this went, if anywhere.

After getting showered and ready for work, Rachel went into the kitchen to make breakfast. Rachel heard her phone beep and saw she had a message from Skye saying "Call me!" After eating breakfast, Rachel grabbed her coffee and headed out the door. It was going to be a long day, but she was in a good mood so it was okay.

"Hello?" answered the voice on the other end of the phone.

"Hey, Skye," said Rachel, driving to work.

"What the fuck, Cassidy? What happened? Did you spend the night with her? Why didn't you message or call me? Details, now!"

"Geez, relax, Skye," said Rachel, laughing. "I went over, I gave Bri the goldfish."

"Did she like it?"

"What five-year-old isn't going to like a goldfish? She loved it. She named it Olaf."

"Olaf? You mean that goofy snowman from *Frozen*?"

"Yep!" laughed Rachel.

"All right, go on…"

"Jade made Caribbean jerk chicken and veggies for dinner. We talked while Bri was taking a bath. She wants to take things slow, but there is an interest there, so bonus for me."

"Did you do what I said and wear a low-cut shirt to show off your boobs?"

"No, I did not."

"Yeah, you're a bit boob deprived," teased Skye.

"HEY! Don't you dare try to tell me your sister told you that?"

"She didn't, but do you want to know what she told me about them?"

"What?" Rachel squeaked.

"Relax, Rach. I'm just messing with you. You make it too easy sometimes."

"You are rotten, Skye."

"I'm proud of it! So, you are going to take things slow. What does that mean?"

"It means we're going to try dating. I asked if she'd go out on a date with me sometime and she said yes."

"That's awesome, Rach. You know that if you take her on more than one date I get to meet her, right?"

"Skye," whined Rachel. "Why more than one date? You'll scare the crap out of her."

"I will not. I need to make sure that she's worthy of your heart."

"Give me more than a single date with her."

"No, Rachel, if you are going to go out with her

on a second date, we're going to dinner and I am going to meet her. This is not negotiable."

"Fine," Rachel said in defeat.

"You better not try to sneak more dates in without me meeting her. I'm serious, Rachel."

"I get it, Skye. I promise if Jade and I go on a second date it will involve you meeting her."

"Thank you. So, when are you going to go out with her?"

"I was thinking about seeing if she wants to go out this weekend. Maybe take Brianna to the zoo or something."

"That sounds nice. Call me if you need anything. I gotta run," said Skye.

"I will. Thanks for everything, Skye."

Rachel hung up with Skye just as she got to her office. Once she got to her office she pulled out her planner and noted toward at the end of her day to call Jade to schedule their date. Rachel went to get some more coffee and finish prepping for her meeting.

❧ ❧ ❧ ❧

Jade had woken up in a good mood that day. She and Brianna had gotten ready and were headed out the door for work and school.

"Mama," said Bri from her booster seat in the back.

"Yeah, sweetie," Jade said, glancing at her daughter in the rearview mirror.

"Will we really get to have Rachel over again for dinner?"

"Yeah, sweetie, I think we will. Why do you ask?"

"I like her. She's nice and funny and she doesn't

treat me like a little kid."

"She is very nice and funny."

Jade pulled up to Brianna's school and they walked together her to class. She then hurried back to the car and off to work.

"This is Jade," she said answering her desk phone.

"Hey, so, how'd it go last night?" asked Kristel.

"It was a nice night. Rachel came over, she gave Bri the goldfish she won for her at the carnival, we had dinner, talked, it was really nice," Jade said.

"So, what did you come to as a conclusion?"

"She asked if I'd go out on a date with her. I said yes, and she said she'd call me to set it up."

"Wow, there must really be something between you two. I'm happy for you, Jade. I like Rachel. She seems like a decent person."

"Gee, Mom, thanks for your approval," Jade said mockingly.

"Don't be an ass or I'll ground you," Kristel teased back. "Whatever night you need I'll watch Bri for you."

"Thank you! I gotta get back to work, but I'll let you know after Rachel calls."

"Sounds good. And Jade, I really am happy for you," Kristel said, and the sincerity in her voice rang through.

"Thanks!"

⁂

"Mrs. Donovan, I have a Rachel Cassidy asking for you," said Jade's assistant over the intercom.

"Great, put her through," said Jade, smiling to

herself.

"Yes, ma'am."

Jade sat back for a moment before the phone rang with the transfer from her assistant.

"Hello," said Jade, answering the call as it rang through.

"Hi, is this an okay time?"

"Yeah, it is a perfect time. How is your day going?"

"It's been a good day. I have one more appointment and then the day will be done."

"Must be nice." Jade sighed. "Mondays are my long days."

"So, what does Bri do then?" asked Rachel.

"Some weeks Kristel brings her down here; other weeks like today I go get her and then she hangs out with me until I get done. I feel bad, but it's how I'm able to be there for her Friday when she gets done with school at noon."

"That's nice that you are able to be home with her on Fridays," said Rachel.

"I try to be there as much as I can. I know it is cliché, but it really is hard being a single mom. Although I don't think that is why you called."

"I'm always here to listen and talk. I did call to see if you were still interested in going out on a date with me."

"I would love to," Jade said, smiling.

"Yay me! When works best for you?"

"Any night except for Thursday and Sunday works. Obviously Thursday because of group and Sunday because Bri has school the next day and I like to get her to bed early."

"Well, I was hoping that maybe Wednesday you

might be free for dinner and if that goes well, maybe Saturday, you, Bri, and I could go to the zoo?"

"I would love to go out with you on Wednesday and I know Bri would love to go to the zoo."

"Great!"

"Rachel, thanks for thinking about Bri. It really means a lot to me."

"She's a great kid. Jade, I know that being a part of your life in either a friendship or relationship capacity will always include Brianna. I also know that she is always the top priority."

"I know a lot of people who don't understand that, so thank you. I am sorry to cut this short, but I have to go get Bri from school."

"That's okay. My appointment should be here in about ten minutes. What time should I pick you up on Wednesday?"

"Does 6:30 work for you?"

"Perfect. I'll see you then."

"I'll see you then. Have a great night, Rachel."

"You, too, Jade."

Jade stared at the phone. She was in shock, and she was going out on a date on Wednesday. Jade sent a quick text message to Kristel to make sure that she could watch Brianna and then she headed out the door to get her daughter from school.

❧ ❧ ❧ ❧

Jade pulled up outside the school and went inside to pick up her daughter.

"Mama," called Brianna as she raced across the room and leapt into Jade's arms.

"Hi, sweetie," said Jade, hugging her daughter.

"Did you have a good day?"

"Yeah," nodded Brianna.

"Go clean up your spot and get your stuff so we can get back to the office," said Jade, setting her daughter down.

"Yes, ma'am."

"Hi, Jade," said the woman at the front of the class.

"Hi, Dawn. How was she today?"

"We had a great day. She drew this picture," said the teacher showing Jade a picture that had Brianna had drawn. The picture contained Jade, Brianna, and a red-haired woman playing on some swings. "Who is the redhead? I know Amy was a blond."

"That is the grief therapist from the group I am attending. We had her over for dinner last night. Bri really likes her."

"Just a therapist?" asked Dawn, smirking at Jade.

"And a friend. Fine, I have a date with her on Wednesday."

"I'm happy for you, Jade. I've known you for three years; the past year and a half have been the hardest to watch you survive. I just want you to be happy. If this woman makes you happy as a friend, or more, then I am all for it."

"Thanks, Dawn. Rachel and I are just going to take it slow. I don't know that I'm ready for a relationship yet, but she knows that and respects it," Jade said as Brianna joined them.

"Did you see my picture, Mama?"

"I did. Is that supposed to be Rachel?" Jade asked, bending down and pointing to the redhead that her daughter had drawn.

"Yep! I think we should go to the park together

sometime."

"Well, maybe we will," Jade said, hearing a giggle being stifled from the woman standing behind her.

"You two have a good night."

"Thank you, Ms. Lewis," said Brianna. "You, too."

"Thank you, Bri. I'll see you next week, Jade."

"See you next week, Dawn."

Brianna and Jade went back to the office and Jade finished her work while Brianna colored a new picture. After a couple of hours, Jade finally finished and she and Brianna packed up and went home. Jade made them dinner and then helped Brianna with her bath.

"Mama, do you think that Mommy will be mad that I didn't put her in the picture I drew?"

"No, I don't think that Mommy will be mad that you didn't put her in the picture," Jade said, tucking her daughter in bed. "Mommy is always a part of everything you do. Even when Mommy and I aren't physically with you, we are in your heart and that makes us a part of anything you put your heart into."

"Good. I love you, Mama," Brianna said, looking at Jade and then looking at the ceiling. "I love you, too, Mommy."

"We love you, too," said Jade as she leaned down and kissed her daughter on the head.

Jade left the room and went to take care of the dishes before getting ready for bed.

Chapter Fifteen

To Date or Not To Date

Work Tuesday and Wednesday flew by and Jade was now standing in front of the mirror in her bedroom in a pair of black jeans and a silk button-down blue shirt.

"Knock, knock," Kristel said, poking her head in the bedroom door.

"Hi, Kristel," Jade said, looking at the newly arrived woman in the mirror.

"How are you doing?"

"Do I look okay?"

"You look gorgeous." Kristel entered the bedroom and sat down on the bed. "I gather you're a bit nervous?"

"Yeah, it's only been, what, nine or ten years since I last went on a date."

"Things really haven't changed that much," joked Kristel, reaching into the jewelry box and pulling out a Celtic Mother's Knot necklace that Amy had given Jade for Mother's Day right after Brianna was born. Wear this," said Kristel, putting the necklace around Jade's neck. "It will give you strength and you look incredible in it."

"Thanks." Jade smiled, seeing the necklace Kristel had chosen.

"*Hello, my gorgeous and amazing wife. The*

mother of my child. I got you something," Amy said, coming up behind Jade and wrapping her arms around her wife's waist before producing a black velvet-covered box.

"I love the sounds of that. But, aren't you the mother of my child?" ask Jade, leaning into the embrace.

"We are the mother of each other's child. Now, open the damn box."

"You are going to have to learn some patience now that we have a newborn." Jade opened the box and pulled out the necklace. "Amy, it's gorgeous. What does it mean?"

"It is a Celtic Mother's Knot necklace. The holy trinity with a parent and child embrace, it is representative of the Madonna and child. Combined with a Celtic trinity knot, it is a testament to the enduring bond between a mother, her child, faith, and their Celtic heritage."

"You memorized the description from the website, didn't you?" Jade smirked as she turned in her wife's arms and saw her blushing.

"I may have, you will never know. Now, be nice or I'll have to find someone else to give the necklace to," said Amy, laughing as she took the necklace out of Jade's hand. "Do you want me to put it on you or not?"

"Yes, please." Jade turned to make it easier for Amy to put the necklace on.

"Oh, and you need to have a talk with Kristel."

"Why?" Jade asked, turning in her wife's arms.

"Oh, I asked her if she thought you'd like it. She called me a dumb ass and said you'd love it. I told her to bite me, she said she couldn't because, and I quote, 'I would bite you, but your wife told me to keep my lips to myself after that one New Year's where you got lippy

with me.' I tried to tell her that she got lippy with me but—"

"*It was your own fault, my love. You were the one that couldn't tell the difference between my masquerade costume and Kristel's. BUT, you are a very, very, good kisser, and now she knows one of the many reason that I am so lucky to be your wife.*" Jade kissed Amy deeply.

"Good memory?" Kristel put her hand on Jade's shoulder bringing her back from her thoughts.

"Yeah, I was just remembering the day Amy gave me the necklace."

Jade composed herself and then she and Kristel went downstairs to wait for Rachel.

❧❧❧❧

"Rachel, will you please sit still? How am I supposed to fix your hair if you keep moving around?"

"I'm sorry, I'm trying," Rachel said.

"Why are you so nervous?"

"This is the first date I have initiated since I first asked your sister out."

"Oh, that is so cute. Were you this nervous when you went out with my sister?"

"I think I was worse," Rachel said sheepishly.

"Is that why you almost missed when you tried to kiss her good night?"

"Oh god, she told you? Emily swore she wouldn't tell anyone."

"I told you my sister kissed and told. She did say that she thought it was very romantic that you kissed the tip of her nose before kissing her on the lips."

"Oh god, she really did kiss and tell." Rachel buried her face in her hands, trying to hide her embarrassment.

"Oh yeah, the things I know about you, Cassidy... you should be scared," said Skye. "Now let me finish or you are going to be late."

"Fine."

Skye finished doing Rachel's hair and then helped Rachel pick out what she was going to wear. They chose a pair of black jeans and a green silk button-down shirt.

"I bought you this when you and Emily first found out you were expecting. I wasn't sure when to give it to you, but for some reason I think now seems fitting." Skye opened a box to reveal a white-gold bracelet with "RDC" engraved on it.

"Skye, it's beautiful." Rachel put the bracelet on. "Thank you."

"It looks really good on you." Skye hugged her sister-in-law.

"Should I take her flowers?" asked Rachel as they exited her room and headed into the living room.

"Yeah, why not...go for the full wooing."

"All right. I need to get going then so I can stop to get some flowers," said Rachel.

"You'll be fine. Call me when you get home."

"Seriously?"

"It is either you promise to call me or I'll be here waiting when you get home. Your choice."

"Fine, I'll call you," said Rachel, grabbing her purse and keys and the two women exited the house.

ﷺﷺﷺ

Brianna was watching out the window when Rachel pulled in.

"She's here, she's here," squealed Brianna, running to the front door.

"Hi, Bri," said Rachel as the door opened.

"Hi, Rachel," grinned Brianna.

Rachel took one of the flowers she had brought for Jade and handed it to Brianna.

"That one is for you," Rachel said.

"Mama, look," said Brianna, turning to Jade and Kristel who had been standing behind her unnoticed by Rachel.

"That's beautiful," said Jade, smiling at Rachel.

"These are, um, for you," Rachel said nervously.

"Thank you," Jade said, taking and sniffing the flowers. "They're beautiful."

Rachel followed Jade and Brianna into the kitchen. Kristel was already there pulling two vases out for the flowers.

"Hi, Rachel," Kristel said, taking the flowers and putting them into the vases.

"Hi, Kristel." Rachel offered a nervous wave.

"Mama, can I talk to you before you leave?"

"Sure. I'll be right back," said Jade, offering Rachel a sympathetic smile.

"Relax, she is just as nervous as or maybe worse than you are."

"It's that obvious, huh?"

"Only if you haven't developed tremors since the last time I saw you," said Kristel, laughing and seeing Rachel relax a little.

"Thanks," Rachel smiled back at her.

"She likes you for who you are. Just keep being you and everything will be fine."

❦❦❦❦

"What's up?" Jade asked as she and Brianna entered her daughter's room.

"Mama, I want you to have fun tonight. Aunt Kristel and I talked about how this is a good thing for you. You smile when Rachel is around and I like it when you smile."

"Thank you, sweetheart."

Brianna hugged Jade and Jade kissed the side of her daughter's head.

They reentered the living room to see Kristel and Rachel sitting there waiting for their return.

"Sorry about that. Are you ready?" asked Jade as Bri went and sat on Kristel's lap.

"Yep," said Rachel, standing.

"You look really pretty, Rachel."

"Thanks, Brianna."

"You two have fun," said Kristel.

Rachel reached out toward Jade and when their hands met they entwined their fingers together as they left. Rachel opened the door for Jade.

"I hope Italian is okay," said Rachel as they drove to the restaurant.

"It's great." Jade glanced toward Rachel.

"I'm guessing you are as nervous as I am."

"Is it that obvious?"

"Kristel told me you were," Rachel said sheepishly.

"I'll kill her tonight when we get home," said Jade, laughing.

"Don't. If you would have come to my house Skye would have done something equally embarrassing."

"Skye is your sister-in-law, right?"

"Yeah, she claimed she came over to help me get ready. In reality I think it was to torment me. She loves to do that. I know that I'm lucky to have her in my life and I don't know how I would have gotten through the years without her, but sometimes I just don't understand the fun that she has making me blush and become uncomfortable. I can't imagine what it was like for Emily growing up with Skye as an older sister. I'm an only child so I don't understand having siblings and such, but she just…" babbled Rachel before they had stopped at a stoplight and Jade leaned over and kissed her.

"You can relax, I don't bite until at least the third date." Jade smiled as Rachel sat there, her mouth gaping open.

"Does this count as our first or second date?"

A car behind them honked their horn causing Rachel to look forward and start driving again. Jade chuckled to herself.

"Thank you," Rachel finally said as they pulled into the parking lot for the restaurant.

"I'm nervous, too. I haven't been on a date since Amy and I first went out like nine or ten years ago. Kristel told me that it hasn't changed much, but that doesn't make this any easier," Jade said, starting her own babble.

Rachel reached over and took Jade's hand and squeezed it, reassuring Jade with that gesture.

Rachel again opened Jade's door for her and they went into the restaurant. Rachel went to the hostess and checked in. They were taken back immediately. The table was in a dark corner secluded from the rest of the customers.

"Is this okay?" Rachel asked.

"It's great."

They looked over the menu and when the

waitress came back they each ordered a glass of wine and their meal. Once the waitress had left, Jade felt her nerves starting to kick in again.

"I should have said this earlier, but you look beautiful tonight," Rachel said, taking Jade's hand in hers.

"Thank you. You look beautiful, too. That is a really pretty bracelet."

"Thanks, Skye gave it to me. She thought having something personal like this might help with my nerves. She bought it for me right after Emily and I found out we were pregnant. I like your necklace."

"Amy gave it to me for my first Mother's Day after Bri was born. Kristel thought it would help with my nerves. Do you think they were trying to tell us something?"

"I'm not sure," said Rachel, amused by the gesture from their best friends.

The waitress brought their wine and some breadsticks.

"Thank you for understanding that I want to take this slow," Jade blurted out.

"Jade, I understand what it is like to start accepting that your spouse isn't coming back and that you have to try to learn to live life again. Wow, could that have sounded more clinical? Ugh, sometimes being a therapist isn't a good thing. Let me turn off my inner therapist and answer that again. You are worth taking it slow."

"Thank you," Jade said, blushing.

"How has your week been?"

"Not bad. My assistant is gone the rest of the week so it's going to be interesting. She's my right hand most days."

"At least there are just two days left in the week," said Rachel.

"I agree, I am looking forward to noon on Friday and the week being over." Jade laughed. "How has your week been?"

"Pretty uneventful, which, trust me, is a very good thing."

"I bet."

The waitress brought their food and they waited for her to leave before continuing their conversation.

"I love what I do and helping people, but the crisis situations are never fun."

"I don't know that I could do what you do, Rachel. I would have a hard time separating myself from those that I was helping." Jade smiled before taking another sip of her wine.

"I won't say that it isn't hard, but when you are able to help someone, it greatly outweighs the hard times."

"Is that why you have the grief therapy group?"

"Yeah, it is. And it gives me something to do on Thursday nights."

"Yes it does," agreed Jade. "Speaking of group, I never got a chance to really thank you for letting me bring Bri and for including her."

"She's a great kid, Jade. You've done an amazing job raising her and helping her transition. I loved having her there."

"I felt like most didn't mind her being there, but some…"

"Carmen?"

"Yeah, she didn't seem…I don't know, okay with the idea I guess is the best way to put it."

"It wasn't because of Brianna. Carmen asked me

out that night," Rachel said, blushing.

"Oh, wow, I had no idea," said Jade, her eyes widening.

"I told her I was flattered, but declined."

"You told her you don't date clients and group members and here we are out on a date," Jade said, bowing her head.

Rachel reached over and tilted Jade's head up and made sure they had eye contact before speaking.

"You were not the reason I declined. What I feel when we're together I cannot explain, but I know that where we are right now is the right place. I'm not pressuring you for anything, I just want a chance to get to know you and be a part of your life."

"Thank you. I feel a connection, too," Jade said softly.

"Good, now, let's finish eating and get out of here," Rachel said, smiling.

They finished their food, and they walked to Rachel's car close to one another, but not touching. Again Rachel opened the door for Jade, causing her date to chuckle.

"Are you laughing at my chivalry?" asked Rachel when she got in the car.

"No, but it is cute and I could get used to it," teased Jade. "So, now where are we headed?"

"I'm not telling," Rachel said with a mischievous grin.

They drove in silence, and after a couple of minutes Jade took Rachel's hand in hers. After about ten minutes Rachel pulled into the back lot of a building that Jade couldn't identify. Rachel picked up her cell phone and sent a quick message before getting out and opening Jade's door again.

"This way, m' lady," said Rachel, taking Jade's hand and walking toward the steel door. As they neared, the door opened and a tall, thin man stood there smiling.

"Dr. Cassidy, ma'am."

"Thank you," Rachel said, smiling back at the man.

They entered the building and went down a long corridor before they were met by another person. This man was dressed in a business suit.

"Hello, Rachel. How are you doing tonight?" asked the man.

"I'm doing great. How are you doing?"

"Fantastic, it has been a good month. Let me escort you and your date in."

Jade looked at Rachel questioningly.

"Give me two minutes and you'll understand," Rachel said, squeezing Jade's hand.

They followed the man to another door. He unlocked it and held it open for them.

"Thank you, Scott," said Rachel, leading Jade through the door and then hearing it close behind them.

"Where are we?" asked Jade, looking around at the mostly bare room.

"This way, please." Rachel grinned.

They walked through the room and then Rachel opened another door and Jade stepped through and started to smile.

"Art?"

"Scott is the curator of the gallery. I know how much you love art so I asked him if we could do an after-hours walk-through."

"Rachel, this is incredible. I've always wanted to come here, but never got around to it."

"Well then, shall we get started looking at some art?"

The women made their way to the front of the building and Rachel grabbed a map. They started their walk hand in hand through the art.

"I love this one," said Jade, pointing to a photograph of raindrops on a window distorting the lights and colors in the background.

"Me, too," said Rachel.

Jade looked closer at the photograph and the artist's name and turned to look at Rachel in shock. The name on the card was Rachel D. Cassidy.

"You're an artist as well?"

"No, I do amateur photography. This one was one of my better pictures. Scott saw it and asked if he could display it here in the local artist section. And no, I didn't bring you here to show it off."

"So, this wasn't a setup to woo me?" Jade joked.

"Not unless it's working," said Rachel, smiling.

"I am impressed," said Jade. "Raindrop images and the sound of thunderstorms are my favorite."

"I find both soothing, although lightning is not my friend."

"I'll protect you," Jade said as they moved on to look at more of the gallery.

"This area is a private collection, Scott said we could look, though," said Rachel as they came up to a roped-off, drape-covered corner.

Walking behind the curtain both girls stood in shock. There was a collection of prints and sculptures like nothing they had ever seen. Some paintings were eight feet high, others the size of a playing card. There were sculptures in abstract, and busts of people.

"This is incredible."

"Is this all the same artist?" asked Jade.

"Yes," said a male voice from the corner of the room, causing both women to jump a little. "Sorry, I didn't mean to startle you."

"Scott, this is amazing."

"Yeah, we just got it in about a week ago. I've been cataloging it and trying to come up with a theme for it."

"These are some stunning pieces," said Jade.

"I'm glad you like them. I'm going to be putting this on display in another week. You are the only two besides myself to have seen it."

"Thank you for letting us look," said Rachel. "And thank you for letting us go through the gallery tonight."

"Yes, thank you. It is an amazing gallery," Jade said.

"Thank you. And Rachel, you know you are always welcome," said Scott as he hugged Rachel.

The two women exited the gallery the way they came in. They noticed that the man that had let them in watched until they got in the car and pulled away.

"That was incredible, Rachel."

"Well, after learning how much you liked art, I thought it might be a nice place to go."

"So how do you know Scott?" asked Jade.

"Emily and I met him about five months before she died. He was out taking pictures on one of the trails and we just got to talking. After she died I hung up the camera, stopped the hikes, but he wouldn't let me stay away. About a year after Emily died Scott forced me to go out and take pictures one rainy day. That's where the photo came from."

"Well, hopefully you'll show me some of your

other pictures," said Jade, taking Rachel's hand in her own.

"I'd love to," Rachel said, smiling at Jade.

They pulled up to Jade's house. The living room curtains were closed, but the light was still on. Rachel got out and walked Jade to the door.

"I had a great night. Thank you," Jade said as they stood facing one another.

"I had a great night, too. Would you still like to go out again this weekend? Take Brianna to the zoo?"

"We're free on Saturday," Jade said coyly.

"Then it's a date," Rachel said, stepping closer. Jade wrapped her arms around Rachel's neck while Rachel put her hands on Jade's hips.

"It's a date," Jade said before they both leaned in for a gentle kiss.

Rachel pulled Jade closer and their lips moved together and then she felt Jade's tongue run across her lips, seeking entrance. Rachel opened her lips, granting access. Their tongues moved together in a slow but sensual kiss.

"I must say I do enjoy kissing you," Rachel said, blushing.

"I enjoy kissing you, too."

"Is anyone going to kiss me?" came a voice from inside the house.

Jade dropped her head to Rachel's shoulder and groaned.

"Nobody is going to kiss you, go away," said Jade.

"Amy kissed me." They heard Kristel's laugh as she walked away.

"I'm sorry about her."

"Don't be. That is something Skye would do. So, Amy kissed her?"

"We were drunk, it was a New Year's Eve masquerade party and Amy mixed up what I was wearing with what Kristel was wearing and well, I'm just grateful all she did was kiss her," said Jade, blushing. Rachel giggled in her arms. "I don't kiss and tell so Kristel has been trying to find out if you were a good kisser."

"I think she got her answer," said Rachel before leaning in and kissing Jade again.

"I think you're right," Jade said as they pulled apart.

"I should let you get in. Will you be at group tomorrow?"

"Yes, I'll be there."

"Great, and I'll call you Friday and we can figure out Saturday."

"Perfect," said Jade, giving Rachel a chaste kiss and then moving to the front door.

Rachel practically skipped to her car. She had survived their first date and had set up a second date.

Jade watched Rachel pull away before closing the front door and walking into the living room where Kristel was seated.

"So, she's a good kisser, huh?"

"Yes, fine," admitted Jade.

"Lucky! All right, I can see you are tired; I'll get the munchkin tomorrow from school so you just worry about getting to group. I'll hit you up for details when you pick Bri up tomorrow."

"Thanks," Jade said tiredly.

Kristel stood and hugged her best friend before leaving. Jade closed up the house and went upstairs and got ready for bed.

Chapter Sixteen

Discretion and Disclosure

Jade sat at her desk and stared at the papers in front of her. She looked to be working, but her mind had drifted to the night before and her date with Rachel. Is it okay for her to be this happy? Should she still be grieving her wife? If this keeps going, how is Brianna going to adjust?

"Knock, knock," came a voice from the doorway, bringing Jade back from her daydream.

"Kristel, hi."

"Your assistant wasn't at her desk."

"She has today and tomorrow off. What's up?"

"Well, I was wondering if you wanted to go to lunch with me," said Kristel.

"Sure, give me five minutes to finish this up," Jade said, smiling at her friend.

"Great."

While they waited for their food at the nearby deli, Kristel said, "So, do I need to ask who or what you were daydreaming about when I came in?" Jade blushed.

"Last night was really nice, but do I have the right to be happy yet? Is it too soon? What about Bri?"

"Whoa, you aren't marrying this woman. Jade, you are slowly getting back into the world. Yeah, you have a killer connection with Rachel, but that is it.

Don't rush things."

"You know how I love to overthink things."

"Yes, I do. So, tell me about last night…" Kristel said, grinning eagerly.

"Last night was incredible. We went to dinner at a little Italian restaurant, and then she took me to an art gallery for a private tour. I really liked one piece in particular and it turned out to be one of her photographs. Then we came home and you rudely interrupted our goodnight kiss."

"Back it up, Donovan. What do you mean you went to an art gallery for a private showing?"

"Rachel is friends with the owner of that gallery on the west side that we always say we want to check out. She knew I loved art, so she arranged for us to go in after hours to see the exhibits."

"Wow. That sounds amazing. How was the gallery in general?"

"I enjoyed it. There was a good flow between exhibits and we got to see an exhibit that was being prepped for showing."

"Advanced showing? Raw deal." Kristel pouted.

"We'll have to go when the exhibit opens."

"Great, I can't wait. It seems like you had a good night. Did you two make plans for another date?"

"Oh, you mean you weren't listening in at that point?" Jade said, sticking her tongue out at Kristel.

"No, I wasn't, smart-ass. So?"

"She wants to go out again on Saturday and take Bri to the zoo."

"Bri will love that. She and Jake have been begging me to go."

"I know that Bri likes Rachel. I just hope that she doesn't get hurt in all this."

"Jade, the only way she is going to get hurt is if you let her get more attached to Rachel than you are. Keep things friendly between you and Rachel in front of Bri, and when you two are certain about things, then let her in. That way if things don't work out romantically you still have that friendship working."

"You're right, that is a good way to do it."

"I know it will be hard because she is such a good kisser, but I truly think that you'll survive," Kristel teased. "How is it that you keep getting the good kissers? I don't get it."

"You're just jealous," taunted Jade.

"Maybe, maybe not. I need to get back to work and so do you. I'll pick Bri up and you can go enjoy your time at group."

"Thanks, Kristel!"

"That's what best friends are for," Kristel said, hugging Jade, and they both went back to work.

☙☙☙☙

Rachel finished with her last morning appointment, looked at her schedule, and saw she had two hours free. She thought about just going out and getting some air, but then she thought about Jade and the afternoon that she had bumped into her while she was shopping for Brianna.

"Hello?" said the voice on the other end of the line.

"Hey, Skye," said Rachel.

"Rach! What's up?"

"Will you have lunch with me? I'll even buy."

"Sure. Where do you want to go?"

"How about we get some subs and go to the park

and talk?" said Rachel.

"That works for me. Do you want to meet me there or pick me up?"

"I'll pick you up. I have a couple of hours before my next appointment."

"All right, I'll see you soon," said Skye.

Rachel hung up, grabbed her phone and keys, and headed out the door to pick up Skye.

"Hey lady, want a ride?" Rachel called out of the window of her car when she saw Skye sitting outside her house waiting.

"Do you have candy?" Skye asked as she walked toward the car.

"Nope," Rachel said, grinning.

"Go to hell then. The least you could do is be a good creepy stranger and have candy."

"Get in here," said Rachel, laughing as Skye opened the door and got in.

The two picked up their sandwiches from a sub shop and drove to the park. They found a private picnic table and sat down.

"So, what's up, Rach? You don't take lunch breaks," said Skye.

"And you know that being left alone with my own thoughts is dangerous to my health as well."

"Oh...my...god. You are trying to talk yourself out of this thing with Jade aren't you?"

Rachel didn't answer, but instead looked down intently at her sandwich.

"Rachel Danielle Cassidy, look at me!" Skye's tone caused Rachel's head to snap up. "You deserve to be happy. You deserve to have people in your life that make you happy. You're not a bad person because you broke some fucking rule you set for yourself before you knew you were going to meet a fantastic woman like Jade. Yeah, I haven't even met the woman and I know she's fantastic."

"How do you know?"

"I know because she makes you smile, she gives you that glint in your eye that has been absent since my sister died. Now, tell me what your fucked up little mind has you believing."

"You really are Emily's sister. The only time she used the F-word was when she was really mad at me."

"You're stalling. Talk!"

"Yes, I do enjoy spending time with Jade. What if I like her because of Brianna? What if I'm projecting the loss of the baby and Emily on her? What if things don't work out romantically between us? What if Brianna gets hurt in the aftermath? I don't think I can handle hurting her, not to mention hurting Jade."

"You really are a fucking idiot, you know that?" snapped Skye, looking Rachel dead in the eyes. "Who did you meet first, Jade or Brianna?"

"Jade."

"Who did you first take an interest in?"

"Jade."

"Do you think that Jade would let you near her or her daughter if she thought the only reason you wanted to be around them was because of Brianna?"

"No."

"If things don't work out romantically, do you want a friendship with Jade?"

"Of course! She is an amazing woman and if we were nothing more than friends I would be honored to have her in my life."

"Then stop being a jackass and open your fucking eyes. You just debunked your entire set of fears. What else do you got, Cassidy? I'm on a roll," said Skye, staring Rachel down.

"I, er, I got nothing else."

"Good, now that we have proved you are a huge idiot, tell me about your date."

Rachel told Skye about her date with Jade, where they went to eat, about the gallery, about kissing her outside and Kristel interrupting. She then told Skye about them wanting to go out again on Saturday to take Brianna to the zoo.

"So, when do I get to meet her? I also want to meet this Kristel person. She sounds like my kind of people."

"I'm supposed to call Jade tomorrow to set things up. I'll talk to her then."

"Great. Do you feel better?" asked Skye.

"Yes, thank you."

They finished their lunch and then Rachel dropped Skye back off at home. She returned to work to finish her write-ups and prep for her next client.

❧❧❧❧

Rachel was setting up the meeting room when people started to filter in and help with the setup. Jade came in, saw Doug struggling with a table, and went to help him.

"Thanks, Jade," said Doug. "How is Brianna doing?"

"She's great," Jade said, lighting up at the chance to talk about her daughter.

"Hey, Rachel," Doug called as people made their way over to the circle of chairs.

"Hey, Doug," Rachel said, smiling at the man.

"Did you have a hot lunch date today?" asked Doug in a singsong voice.

"Huh?" Rachel asked, looking at Doug. She saw Jade standing right behind him. Jade's eyes widened a little.

"I saw you at the park having lunch with some attractive woman and you two looked pretty close."

"Oh, that was my sister-in-law. I needed to get out of the office for a bit so I decided we needed to go to lunch," said Rachel, hoping that Jade was hearing the explanation.

"At one point it looked like she was yelling at you from where I was sitting."

"She was. I was being stupid about something and she needed to kick my head out of my ass," Rachel said bluntly.

"She sounds like a good person to have in your life," said Jade.

"She is. I don't know what I would do without her some days. Skye is the one that got me out of the house and brought me to my first grief group."

"Is she your wife's sister or is she married to one of your siblings?" asked Carmen.

"She is Emily's sister. When Emily died we stayed close and she has told me numerous times that we are family for life, and I believe her," Rachel said honestly. "So, shall we get started?"

They went around the room and everyone told how their week had been. Rachel was curious as to what Jade was going to say for her week when it was her turn.

"It has been a good week. Saturday I conquered one of my demons relating to my past with Amy. We used to go to the carnival every year, and this year, I didn't think I'd be able to do it, but I did."

"That's awesome!" "Congratulations." "Who'd you go with?" were responses called out by those in the circle.

"Seriously, though, who'd you go with?" asked Carmen.

"I went with a friend that I care a lot about and I'm learning cares a lot about me."

"Did Brianna go?" asked Doug.

"No, she was out of town with Kristel and her son."

"Well, I think that is a fantastic step forward in claiming a part of your life back," said Rachel.

They continued around to the other few remaining in the group before calling it a night.

"So, what is Brianna doing tonight?" Rachel asked Jade as they all walked out as a group.

"She's hanging out with Jake and Kristel. She likes to go see them on the nights I have group."

"Well, I think you should bring her once in a while," said Doug. "She was so cute and so good during the meeting. Is she always that well behaved?"

"Thank you, and yeah, she is a pretty terrific kid, although I may be biased."

"We'll see you next week," said Carmen.

"Good night, everyone," Jade said, getting into her car and heading off to pick up Brianna.

⚜ ⚜ ⚜ ⚜

Friday afternoon Jade and Brianna were playing outside when Jade heard her phone ring. She looked at the Caller ID and smiled when she saw it was Rachel.

"Hello," said Jade.

"Hey, Jade. It's Rachel."

"Hi Rachel. How are you doing today?"

"I'm doing well. How are you? Are you home with Bri yet?"

"Yeah, we got home a couple of hours ago. We were just outside playing," said Jade, Brianna giggling in the background.

"If this is a bad time I can call back," Rachel said quickly.

"No, now is perfect."

"I, um, wanted to see if you were okay with how, um, group started last night."

"You mean the part about you being on a date with an attractive woman yesterday?" teased Jade.

"It wasn't a date. Skye and I went to lunch because as she put it I was being a fucking idiot and she needed to get my head in the right place. I didn't mean for you to think that I was seeing someone else. You are the only one I am interested in seeing and I'm babbling and you are giggling at me."

"Yes, you were babbling and I was giggling. I appreciate the explanation, but you don't owe me one. I was surprised when Doug brought it up, but I trust you to be honest with me."

"I'm glad you trust me. I have to tell you that Skye really wants to meet you, Brianna, and Kristel. She made me promise that if we were going to go out on more than one date that I would introduce you to her," Rachel said.

"Well, why don't you invite her to come with us tomorrow and if you are okay with it we can invite Kristel and Jake, too."

"I think that is a great idea. One of the things that Skye and I talked about was about how we are presenting what we are to Brianna. I don't want anything to hurt her, Jade. I know how easy it is for kids to get lost in the shuffle of an adult relationship, and not that I think you would allow it to happen, but I want you to know that I take this seriously."

"I'm really happy to hear that. I was trying to figure out how to talk to you about this exact topic. I wanted to get your thoughts on whether we present just friendship in front of Bri until we know what is going on between us. When she isn't around we can be more...ugh, I am not wording or saying this correctly."

"I get it Jade. I was thinking the same thing. No hand-holding or kissing in front of her, but when she isn't around we can continue to see where this is going."

"Thank you for understanding," Jade said, sighing in relief.

"So, how would you like to work tomorrow?" asked Rachel.

"We could either have everyone meet here or at the zoo."

"What is going to be easiest for you and Kristel?" asked Rachel.

"Meeting here would probably be easiest."

"Great, what time should Skye and I meet you guys at your place?"

"How about you meet us here at ten? Is that too early?"

"That's perfect. I'm looking forward to seeing you again tomorrow."

"I'm looking forward to seeing you, too," said Jade, hoping the smile came through in her voice.

"Well, I'll let you get back to your time with Brianna, and Skye and I will see you tomorrow."

"I can't wait," said Jade before hanging up the phone.

"Who was that, Mama?" asked Brianna.

"That was Rachel. How would you like to go to the zoo tomorrow with Kristel, Jake, me, Rachel, and Rachel's sister-in-law Skye?"

"We get to go to the zoo!"

"Yep, I just need to call Kristel and see if they are free. Are you sure you want to go with us?"

"Please, please, please, pretty please," begged the five-year-old.

"Oh, all right," teased Jade as Brianna hugged her tight.

"You are the bestest Mama in the whole universe."

"Okay let me call Kristel and then we can go get a snack."

"Okay," said Brianna.

Jade called Kristel, who replied that she and Jake couldn't wait to spend time with Rachel and her sister-in-law.

Chapter Seventeen

Date Two at the Zoo

Jade had cleaned the house twice and changed her mind about what to wear three times before Kristel and Jake arrived.

"What the hell is wrong with you, Donovan?" Kristel laughed as she picked a pair of shorts and a T-shirt that said, "Dear Math, I'm not your therapist. Solve your own problems."

Jade looked at the T-shirt Kristel had chosen and started to laugh.

"Seriously?" asked Jade.

"You don't think she'll find the humor in that?"

"If she doesn't it is your fault," Jade said, raising an eyebrow at her friend.

"Fine, if she doesn't then it is my fault and I'll apologize. Why are you so nervous?"

"I don't know. I like Rachel. And no, not just because she is a good kisser. I like who she is. She's bringing her sister-in-law over. That is one step below meeting the parents, for crying out loud. What if Skye doesn't approve—"

"Stop, right there. You're an incredible woman. Rachel knows that, and Skye is going to see it. Just relax and be you. The one and only awesome Jade Donovan," said Kristel, trying to calm her friend down. "Now go get dressed before they get here and you have to answer the door in your underwear.”

“Thank you. For an asshole you make a good friend,” Jade said, smirking as she grabbed her clothes and ran into the bathroom.

“You’ll pay, Donovan. You’ll pay!”

* * *

“Hey, Rach,” called Skye as she walked into the house.

“Hey,” Rachel said as she came out of her room.

“Nice T-shirt, Rach.” Skye laughed as she read the text aloud. “On a scale of 1 to 10, what is your favorite color in the alphabet?”

“You love my T-shirt collection and you know it. Jade told me she has a collection of witty and cool shirts, too.”

“Geez, you two may be better matched than I thought.”

“Promise me you aren’t going to embarrass me today,” Rachel pleaded with Skye.

“Honey, there is no way in hell you will ever get me to make that promise.” Skye laughed as Rachel shook her head and groaned. “You already know these people, Rach. Just be you and I’ll just be me and it will be fine.”

“You being you is never fine,” mumbled Rachel.

“I heard that!”

“Nuh uh,” said Rachel, looking at the clock and seeing that it was time to leave.

“Come on, let’s go meet this new girl,” said Skye as they headed out of Rachel’s house.

* * *

Jade was sitting on the couch in the living room and looked at the clock to see it was almost ten. She glanced over at Kristel who offered her an encouraging smile. They could hear the laughter of Brianna and Jake playing in the backyard.

The sound of the doorbell ringing through the house caused Jade to jump a little and Kristel to laugh at her. They got up, and Jade glared at her best friend before heading to answer the door. Jade could see Rachel and Skye through the glass in the door and she could tell that Rachel was as nervous as she was.

"Hey," Jade said, smiling as she opened the door and saw Rachel look up and smile at her. Jade motioned for the women to enter.

"Hey," said Rachel softly.

"Hey, Rachel," said Kristel.

"Hi, Kristel," said Rachel. "Jade, Kristel, this is my sister-in-law, Skye. Skye, this is Jade and Kristel."

"Hi," Jade said as they shook hands. "It is nice to meet you."

"Hi, it's nice to meet you, too," said Skye.

"How are you doing?" asked Kristel as she shook hands with Skye.

"Good," she said as they both turned and smiled as they saw Rachel and Jade lost in one another.

Kristel motioned for Skye to follow her as they went around the corner.

Rachel reached her hand up and brushed a stray strand of hair behind Jade's ear. Rachel's hand cupped the side of Jade's face as she used the pad of her thumb to trace her jawline.

"You look beautiful," Jade said softly, giving a lopsided smirk. "And I love the T-shirt."

"Thank you," said Rachel. "You look gorgeous."

Jade's hands wrapped around Rachel's waist and moved them closer together. Jade's breath caught as she felt the heat emanating from Rachel's body. Finally, Rachel leaned forward and softly brushed their lips together, lingering for only a moment before pulling apart and resting their foreheads together.

"You take my breath away when you do that," whispered Jade.

"You take my breath away with your lopsided smile," Rachel said before leaning in and kissing her softly.

They stayed close for a few moments before pulling apart. It didn't take long for the privacy and intimacy they had just shared to be replaced by giggling and laughter from Kristel and Skye, causing both Rachel and Jade to blush and groan.

"That was so sweet and cute," Skye said, making her way over to Rachel and pinching her cheeks.

"She's right, you two. That was truly touching," said Kristel, in a tone dripping with sarcasm.

Jade looked at Rachel and they both sighed, knowing this was going to be a very long day.

"Go get the kids, smart-ass," Jade said, pushing Kristel's shoulder.

"Don't I get a snuggle or kiss?" teased Kristel.

"She told you the other night you don't get to learn how good a kisser I am," Rachel said, causing Jade to giggle and blush.

"Hey, my sister said you had some skills in that department."

"That she does, but of the four of us, those skills are going to remain between her and me," Jade said confidently as the room erupted in laughter.

"Fine, I'll go get the kids," said Kristel, leaving the room.

❧❧❧

Since Kristel had a van, she stated that she would drive. Jade and Rachel were seated in the very back so that they could keep an eye on Brianna and Jake who were so excited to be heading to the zoo. That left Skye in the passenger seat next to Kristel.

"You know it is probably dangerous having those two sitting together," Rachel said, looking up at Kristel and Skye.

"Yeah, but…" Jade casually took Rachel's hand in her own and smiled her lopsided smile as Rachel squeezed her hand.

"Mama, what are we going to do first when we get to the zoo?" asked Brianna.

"What would you like to do, sweetie?"

"Can we go to see the bears?"

"We sure can," said Jade.

"Aunty Jade?"

"What's up, Jake?" said Jade as she watched him try to turn in his booster seat.

"Will you go in the children's zoo with us? I mean in with the goats and stuff?"

"Sure, will you make sure they don't try to eat my hand?" Jade giggled.

"They eat hands?" exclaimed Jake in a shocked and questioning tone.

"Sometimes when they are eating the food out of your hand if you aren't careful they can nip at your fingers," said Kristel, seeing her son calm a little.

"I'm sorry Jakey. I didn't mean to make you

think that they would really eat my hand."

"It's okay, Aunt Jade. Them nipping at fingers is pretty close to eating your hand, but I'll still protect you."

"I'll protect you, Rachel, if you come in with us, too," said Brianna.

"Thank you. You are two pretty brave kids," Rachel said, smiling.

"Yeah, we are," agreed Jake proudly.

Kristel and Skye smiled at each other, obviously listening to the discussion going on behind them as they entered the zoo lot and found a good parking spot.

"You planned for Rachel to sit back there with you didn't you?" Kristel whispered to Jade once they had parked and were unloading the few things they had brought.

"Nope, but I am not going to complain either," Jade said, smirking at her friend.

"You're sneaky, Donovan."

Jade just smiled innocently and took Brianna's hand, and the group moved toward the entrance. Once they got inside they found a kiosk that had zoo maps and decided to plot a route to get them through to see all of the animals they wanted to.

"Um, Rachel, can I ask you a question?" Brianna asked just before they started toward the bears.

"Of course," said Rachel, crouching down to be at Brianna's level.

"If you and Skye are afraid of the wolves, we don't have to go to see them."

"Thank you. What makes you think we are afraid of the wolves?" asked Rachel.

"You both got really tense and you got a scared

and sad look on your face."

"Well, wolves don't scare me as much as they make me sad and think about my wife, who was Skye's sister."

"And your daughter?"

"Yep, and my daughter."

Rachel suddenly had little arms wrap around her neck and hug her tightly. Rachel hugged her back. After their hug Brianna went over and hugged Skye as well. This simple action by Brianna brought a tear to Skye's eyes.

"Where are your wife and daughter?" asked Jake, coming to stand by Rachel who was still crouched down.

"They're in heaven like my Mommy," said Brianna, letting go of Skye.

"Oh. I'm sorry," said Jake as he too hugged Rachel. "We won't go to the wolves. Today is a happy day."

Skye looked at both Jade and Kristel in amazement that these two kids were so perceptive and caring. Jade just smiled at the exchange. She was so proud to have such an amazing daughter and pseudo-nephew.

Once this exchange was over, Jade took both Brianna and Jake's hands and the three skipped toward the bears. Kristel hung back with Rachel and Skye.

"Did that really happen?" asked Skye.

"Yep," smiled Kristel.

"I told you she was a special one. Jake is equally as special," said Rachel.

The three exchanged a look of understanding that they had just taken part in a rare and special moment.

After seeing the bears, the penguins, the sea

otters, and the gorilla exhibit, Jade pulled out the map again and saw that they had to backtrack a little because Brianna and Jake insisted that they go nowhere near the wolves.

"Mama, my feet are getting tired," said Brianna.

"All right, sweetie," said Jade, who bent down and motioned for Brianna to get on her back. Once she was settled they continued on.

"Hey it's the giraffe," said Jake, watching him run ahead of them all.

"Do you think his name is Melman?" Rachel asked Jake when they all caught up to him.

"Probably," said Jake. "Mom, I'm hungry."

"Me, too. What do you say we go get some lunch and then go hang out at the children's zoo?"

"Yay!" squealed both kids.

The group made their way over to the Zoo Food Court and found an empty table. They sat down and everyone decided what they wanted. Jade offered to go get the food if the others wanted to guard the table. Rachel said she would help carry the food back. After getting everyone's orders, Jade left them with a map of the children's zoo and told the four of them to make plans and decide where they were going to start.

"Are you having a good day?" Jade asked while they got in line.

"Today is a great and amazing day," Rachel said, smiling.

"I really enjoy spending time with you," Jade said, glancing at the ground.

"I enjoy spending time with you, too. Brianna and Jake are such amazing kids. I've never met any kids like them."

"They are pretty special," Jade said, smiling.

They reached the front of the line and ordered the food. While Jade paid, Rachel got some napkins and condiments for the burgers and fries. They carried the two trays of food back and Jade made sure to sit down close to Rachel.

"So Jade, what do you do for a living?" asked Skye as they started to eat.

"I'm an art agent," Jade replied.

"What is an art agent?" asked Skye.

"I work with artists and help them get their art into galleries or showings. I have about twenty clients at the moment I'm working with."

"She's being modest," interrupted Kristel. "She may have twenty clients, but she has a wait list of at least forty or more."

"Wow. Why did I not know you were an art agent?" asked Rachel.

"Probably because you never asked what I did for a living." Jade laughed, taking a quick sip of her soda. "Until recently you only knew me in group. That isn't something that I have or would discuss in group. I told you last weekend that I liked art, I just never elaborated on how much or why."

"Mama, I gotta go potty," said Bri.

"I'll take her," said Kristel. "Do you need to go, too, Jake?"

They watched the three head toward the bathroom.

"So, Wednesday night when I took you to the gallery was that boring for you? I mean if it was, just tell me so that I know not to do that again. I would never want to take you someplace boring. I would hate to have you spend time either on a date or just hanging out doing something that was boring or that you didn't like. Wow, I was rude and should have asked…" babbled Rachel until Jade took Rachel's hand and brought it up to her lips and kissed it softly.

"I love art, Rachel. So there is no way that you would have bored me by taking me to an art gallery. Remember on Saturday when we went to that one gallery and I told you about all those works of art?" asked Jade, receiving a nod. "Well, I loved being there and sharing that with you. Wednesday, I got to see a new gallery, one I had never been to before. And it was with a beautiful woman that I am enjoying getting to know. If I don't like something I promise you I will let you know."

"Way to babble, Rach, and then pass it on," said Skye, laughing. Both Rachel and Jade had forgotten that Skye was even there.

"Shush, you."

Jade finished explaining what she did as Kristel returned with the kids and then they cleaned up and headed for the children's zoo. Once they got in, Jade bought each kid as well as herself and Rachel handfuls of feed for the goats. The four of them went into the pen while Kristel and Skye watched them and laughed.

"I can't believe they are in there letting those animals eat out of their hand," said Skye, wrinkling her nose up.

"I know. Can they get any more unsanitary and disgusting?" Kristel scrunched up her face as she saw two goats fighting for Jake's food-filled hand.

Rachel and Jade were having so much fun with the kids in the children's area that they almost forgot about Skye and Kristel. They had taken the kids to see the baby monkeys, the goats, the red pandas, and they had ridden the Merry-Go-Round three times before

Jake had suggested that they go for ice cream cones after seeing two other kids eating them. Jade told him that he could have whatever he wanted and he decided he wanted a chocolate ice cream cone with diced cherries sprinkled on it. Jade and Rachel agreed that his idea sounded awesome. Brianna asked if she could get hers without the cherries and instead get chocolate sprinkles. Jade agreed, and the four went to get the ice cream cones and were sitting at a table eating them when Kristel and Skye finally caught up with them.

"What, no ice cream for us?" asked Kristel.

"It's over there, Mom," Jake said, pointing to the ice cream stand to their left.

"Oh, really?"

"We're going to have to leave soon. The zoo is going to be closing," said Skye.

"Wow, it's almost seven," said Rachel, looking at her watch.

"Really? Wow." Jade seemed surprised that the day had gone by so fast.

They finished their cones and everyone got washed up and then headed to the van. Brianna and Jake were asleep before they even left the parking lot. The drive back to Jade's house was quiet, mostly so they wouldn't wake the kids.

"Just leave him, we'll take off in a minute and then he won't have to be crabby," said Kristel. "Today was a blast. We need to do it again."

Everyone agreed with Kristel and then Skye informed Rachel that Kristel was going to drop her off at home since it was on her way and that would give her and Jade some time together. They exchanged hugs and Jade carefully extracted Brianna from the van and carried her up to bed. She decided that sleeping in her undies and a T-shirt was fine for tonight, as it meant she disturbed her daughter less.

Rachel sat in the living room waiting for Jade while she put Brianna to bed. Rachel replayed the day in her head and knew that the pictures they had all taken were going to ensure they would have plenty of memories of their first outing together.

"Can I get you something to drink or eat?" Jade asked, entering the room.

"No, I'm fine." Rachel smiled at Jade who sat down next to her.

"Thank you for today," said Jade. "I don't remember the last time I had such a great day."

"I know how you feel. I loved today and hopefully we can do it again."

Jade smiled as they brought their lips together, feeling the surge of endorphins race through her body. Jade's fingers threaded through Rachel's hair coming to rest at the base of her skull as they encouraged her to move closer. Rachel deepened the kiss by opening her mouth and feeling Jade's tongue move with hers, learning what the other liked. Soft groans escaped both women's mouth as they continued kissing even when they felt their lungs start to burn from the lack of oxygen.

"I've wanted to do that all day," Jade said when they finally broke apart for air.

"I've wanted you to do that all day." Rachel licked her lips and stared intently at Jade's lips.

Jade placed soft kisses on Rachel's lips as her hand pulled the object of her affection closer. Rachel leaned her body into Jade's, feeling the heat from her skin against her own. Their breasts pressed together as their kisses became heated again. Rachel trailed a line of kisses along Jade's jawline and down her neck. She heard Jade's breathing quicken as she felt Jade's hand running along her back.

Rachel tilted her head slightly allowing Jade better access to her neck. Encouraged, Jade gently sucked on the pulse point feeling it flutter beneath her lips.

"That feels so good," moaned Rachel softly.

"I can feel your pulse speed up when I do this," said Jade, pressing her lips tightly to Rachel's neck.

Rachel brought Jade's lips up to hers and they allowed their tongues to fight for dominance until they couldn't take it any longer and needed to separate for air.

Jade tilted her forehead to meet Rachel's. They lay on the couch catching their breath and getting lost in each other's eyes.

"Would you like to come over for dinner Monday night?" Jade asked, interrupting the silence.

"I thought that was your long day?"

"It usually is, but Brianna is going to Amy's parents for the week. They are coming to pick her up Monday afternoon."

"In that case, I'd love to," said Rachel, gently kissing Jade again.

"I'll be getting done...with work...early that day...so what...mmmm...time would...you like to come over?" Jade asked in between kisses.

"My last client is done at five, I just have to swing home and change. I could be here by 5:45 or 6."

"Perfect," said Jade, kissing Rachel deeply, feeling the vibration from Rachel groaning into the kiss as their tongues responded together.

They kissed on the couch for another hour or so

before forcing themselves apart.

"I should get going," Rachel grudgingly said.

"Send me a message when you get home so I know you made it okay?"

"Of course," Rachel breathed before standing up and offering Jade her hand to help her up as well.

Jade walked Rachel to the door and they kissed again for several minutes before separating so that Rachel could leave.

Jade watched Rachel's taillights fade into the darkness before going back into the house and closing the door. She went upstairs and got ready for bed, and then lay in bed waiting for Rachel to message that she arrived.

Rachel: Hey, gorgeous. I am home safe.

Jade: Thank you again for today and tonight.

Rachel: You don't have to thank me for spending time with you, and kissing you is all my pleasure.

Jade: It is my pleasure as well, trust me!

Rachel: Get some sleep and I will see you Monday night.

Jade: Good night. I can't wait for Monday.

Rachel: Good night.

Chapter Eighteen

Baby Steps

Jade and Brianna spent Sunday doing laundry and getting the things together that Brianna was going to need when she went to stay with Amy's parents. Jade knew that she couldn't keep Brianna from Amy's parents, but the idea of a week, alone, in an empty house, felt intimidating. But the knowledge that Rachel would be coming over at least Monday night meant she wouldn't be alone all night. Jade smiled to herself as she thought about Rachel and their day together, and their heated session on the couch.

"Mama, can I take two of my stuffed animals to Grandma and Grandpa's?"

"Yep, you can. What two do you want to take?"

"Mr. Butters, and Captain Quackers," Brianna said proudly.

"Do you want me to leave them out or pack them tonight?" Jade asked while folding some of Brianna's clothes.

"You can pack them tonight. Mama, what are you going to do while I'm gone?"

Jade sat down on the bed and pulled her daughter onto her lap.

"I am going to have dinner with Rachel tomorrow night, then I am going to group on Thursday, and Aunt Kristel will be coming over at least one night during the week for dinner.”

“So, you won’t get lonely?”

“I will miss you like crazy, but I will find ways to keep myself busy. I don’t want you to worry about me. I want you to have fun at Grandma and Grandpa’s.”

“Will you call me every night?” asked Brianna.

“Don’t I always?” Jade said, smiling. “No matter what is going on here sweetie, you are most important and I always have time for you and will call you.”

“What if you and Rachel decide to go out?”

“Nope, I am making dinner and even if we went out, I would make time to call you,” Jade said, hugging her daughter.

“I love you, Mama.”

“I love you, too, Bri.”

❧ ❧ ❧

Rachel spent Sunday going through her case logs and cleaning the house. She lived alone, but with the hours she sometimes kept she didn’t always get around to do a full cleaning.

After she finished her work, Rachel decided it was time to relax. She made herself an early dinner and then sat down to watch a movie. As she lay on the couch, her mind drifted back to Saturday. The day had been one of the most enjoyable days she’d had in years. Spending time with Skye was something that she didn’t do as much anymore and she realized how much she truly missed it.

“Rach,” said Skye, answering the phone.

“Hi, Skye.”

“What’s going on?”

“I was just thinking about yesterday and what a

great day it was. I miss hanging out with you."

"I agree, yesterday was a great day. We should definitely hang out more often. How did things go with Jade after we left?"

"They went fine," Rachel said, knowing that Skye could tell she was blushing.

"So, still not kissing and telling?"

"Still not kissing and telling."

"Well, at least I know there was kissing," she said, laughing. "Did you make plans to get together again?"

"She invited me over for dinner tomorrow night."

"Go you. Just be careful. You don't want Brianna to start thinking you're around too much."

"Brianna won't be there, she's spending the week with Amy's parents. They're picking her up tomorrow afternoon."

"Well, in that case, go get her."

"We aren't at that stage yet. So I'm guessing she has your stamp of approval?"

"Yeah, she had my approval the moment I saw you two get lost in each other when we arrived. You looked happy, Rach. I can see that she makes you happy."

"She does, and I really enjoy spending time with her. And seeing her with Brianna is heartwarming."

"Watching you with Brianna and Jake was pretty special."

"I just followed Jade's lead," Rachel said modestly.

"Whatever. So, why don't you and I go out to dinner Tuesday night and you can tell me how Monday goes with Jade?"

"That sounds good."

"Great, I have to run. I will see you Tuesday night!"

"Later, Skye."

"Later, Rach."

After hanging up with Skye, Rachel decided that she needed to occupy her mind and the movie wasn't helping to do that. Rachel grabbed her laptop to surf the Internet for a bit.

❧❧❧❧

Jade had picked Brianna up from school and when they got home she made sure that everything was packed including Mr. Butters and Captain Quackers. She was just bringing the bags downstairs when she heard the doorbell ring followed by Brianna barreling toward the door. Brianna opened the door and squealed when she saw her grandparents standing there.

"Come in," Jade said, coming up behind Brianna. Jade motioned and everyone followed her into the living room.

After they all had made their rounds for hugs, Jade sat in the recliner and Amy's parents and Brianna sat on the couch.

"How are you doing?" asked Bo, Amy's father.

"I'm doing good. How are you two doing?" Jade said, hoping that they wouldn't want her to elaborate.

"We're doing good. We are looking forward to having this little one keeping us busy all week," said Alice, Amy's mom, tickling her granddaughter who was sitting on her lap.

"Well, she will definitely keep you busy," said Jade, laughing and looking at her daughter.

"Mama, can I take Olaf with me?"

"No, Olaf has to stay here. I promise to feed and talk to him every day, though."

"Who's Olaf?" asked Alice.

"Olaf is my goldfish." Brianna jumped up and grabbed the fish off the drawing table in the corner of the room. "Olaf, these are my grandparents. This is Olaf."

"Hi, Olaf," said Bo, waving to the fish. "When and where did you get Olaf?"

"Rachel gave him to me. Um, when was that again Mama?"

"She's had him a little over a week," Jade said, smiling at her daughter as she put the fish back on the table.

"Who's Rachel?" asked Alice, looking between Jade and Brianna.

"One of Mama's friends. She came over for dinner one night and gave him to me. Then we went to the zoo with her, Kristel, Jake, and Skye yesterday."

Jade saw both of Amy's parents look up at her questioningly and she groaned internally.

"Bri, why don't you go play upstairs for a few minutes while we talk with your Mama?"

"Okay, Grandma," said Brianna, jumping down and running upstairs to play.

"So, is this a new friend?" asked Bo, smirking as Jade tried to act indifferent.

"She's the grief counselor for the group I've been attending. Last Saturday the carnival was in town, and you both know how Amy and I loved to go. So, Rachel and I went to see if I could handle it, work through the demons that popped up so that in the future I can take Bri and show her the fun that Amy and I had when we went. I wanted to be able to do that with Brianna, and for Amy. While we were at the carnival, Rachel won Olaf playing one of those odd carnival games. She asked if I minded if she gave it to Bri. I knew she would love it so I said okay. The next day I invited Rachel over for dinner as a thank you and she gave Bri the fish and some food. It honestly wasn't a big deal."

"Was this the first time Brianna had met her?" asked Alice.

"No, Bri met Rachel the day before the one-year anniversary," Jade started as tears filled her eyes. She glanced over and saw Alice pat the spot between her and her husband, and Jade understood, moving over to the couch with them. She felt loved as they each wrapped an arm around her. "Kristel knew I was struggling and brought Rachel over. We talked for a long time and then when Bri got home she talked with Rachel as well. The next day Rachel came over and helped us celebrate Amy and her memory. We went through photos and told stories."

"That sounds like a wonderful tribute, honey," Alice said, squeezing Jade close.

"And then Bri went to group with me a few weeks ago as well. Jake was sick and I didn't want to send her over to Kristel's and risk her getting sick as well."

"You know you can always call us, Jade, if you need someone to watch her."

"I know, and I truly appreciate that, Bo. I may even take you up on it. I just…I'm doing the best I can. Thanks to the group I'm having a lot more good days."

"So, are you seeing Rachel professionally as well?" Alice asked.

"I see her in group, but not as a therapist if that is what you mean."

"I just...Jade, please don't take offense to this, and let me get this out before you react. You are an amazing mother; you and Amy were so good together. Amy told us repeatedly that she wanted you to move on and have a life, but I just worry about new people coming into Brianna's life. I don't want to see her get attached to someone who isn't going to be around in the future. This Rachel, yes, she is helping you both now, but does Brianna understand that? How is Brianna going to react if or when you feel strong enough to leave the group and Rachel isn't around?"

"You're worried about me parading dates in and out of Brianna's life? Is that what you're really asking?" Jade caught a hint of anger in her voice as she stood up and started to pace the room.

"Jade, you are a great mother and that girl is so lucky to have you. We just worry," said Bo, trying to help dig his wife out of the hole she had just put herself in.

"For the record, I am not parading anyone into Brianna's life that I don't feel will be there in the long run. Rachel, yes she is the therapist that has been helping us, but she is also a friend, just as Kristel is. And I always have that little girl's best interests in mind. I don't ever want her to experience another loss like she did when Amy died. I don't want her to learn what the emptiness feels like when after nine years the person you love more than your own life is ripped from your world and you can't do a damn thing about it. Our daughter is the only thing that keeps me going some days. I look at her, and I see Amy more than I see myself in her, especially now that she's getting older. In the past year, I have let exactly two people into my life and I have done that with extreme caution. I let

Rachel in because she knows what it's like to lose the woman you love more than life. Her wife, who was pregnant with their daughter, died due to an infection she got after being attacked by a wolf out on a hiking trail. Rachel and her wife were checking out a trail for the kids Emily taught who had absent parents or were at-risk kids. The other person is Skye, Emily's sister, Rachel's sister-in-law. Why? Because they understand love and loss. Even though her sister passed away, she's stayed close to Rachel because they are family. So, I'm not parading anyone through Brianna's life who isn't going to be around for a long time."

Jade was shaking and tears streamed down her face. She stopped behind the recliner and used it to stabilize herself.

"I'm sorry, Jade. I was out of line. I know that you wouldn't do anything to hurt Brianna," said Alice as her husband looked at Jade sympathetically.

"Not a day goes by that I don't miss Amy. Not a single one," Jade said, her voice shaking with pent up emotion.

"Mama, don't cry," said Brianna, clearly having heard Jade raise her voice earlier and made her way down the stairs to listen to what was going on.

Jade knelt down and Brianna ran into her arms, hugging her tight. Jade could feel Brianna shaking as she started to cry.

"Shh, it's okay, Baby Girl," Jade said, standing and picking her daughter up. She held her daughter close in her arms as Brianna wrapped her legs around Jade's waist.

"No! Grandma and Grandpa upset you and hurt your feelings. I know because you don't get upset like this unless your feelings are hurt or you are missing

Mommy."

"It'll be okay, though, sweetie," Jade said in a calming voice, kissing the side of her daughter's head.

"But they hurt you, and they want to make Rachel go away, and she is nice and you were smiling and... and...I like it when you smile, it makes me smile."

Jade glanced over Brianna's shoulder at Amy's parents and saw the regret and sadness in their eyes.

"Hey, look at me," Jade said, waiting for her daughter to look at her before continuing. "I don't want you upset. Rachel isn't going to go away. I promise. You know I don't make promises I'm not willing to keep."

Brianna nodded and then hugged Jade again. Jade set her daughter down and kissed the top of her head.

"Did you make sure you have everything?" Jade asked softly.

"I don't wanna go. I wanna stay here with you."

"Baby Girl, you love going over to stay with Grandma and Grandpa, right?" She saw Brianna nod slightly. "You know I'm going to call every night, right?" She received another nod. "You know I love you."

"Yes, I love you, too," Brianna said softly. "But you're upset..."

"Honey, you made me feel so much better by hugging me and telling me you love me. Knowing that is what I needed to feel better. And now I am doing better. You are what matters most to me."

"Brianna." Alice's voice caused both Brianna and Jade to turn and look at her. "It was my fault, and I'm sorry I upset your Mama. Jade, I am truly sorry."

"Thank you," said Jade, a hint of coldness still in her voice.

"Aaa, are you sure?"

"Yes, I am very sure. Now, you be a good girl while you are at Grandma and Grandpa's all right?" said Jade.

"Okay, and you are going to call me tonight?"

"Yes, I am. And every night that you're gone."

"Will you call me when you are at group on Thursday? That way I know Rachel isn't mad at us."

"Rachel and I will call you before group on Thursday."

"I love you, Mama."

"I love you, too, my sweet, sweet girl."

Jade hugged and kissed her daughter before grabbing her bags and handing them to Amy's parents. They had apologized again, but seemed to realize that it was going to take time to mend the relationship and trust they had broken today.

After they left, Jade's resolve broke and she started to cry. She was hurt by the accusations made by Amy's parents. She missed Amy. She felt so alone at that moment. She was trying to compose herself when her phone rang. She picked it up and answered without looking at who it was.

"Hello?" answered Jade, her voice shaky.

"Jade? Are you okay?" asked Rachel.

"Yeah, I, no, I'm not."

"Have Amy's parents come to get Bri yet?"

"They just left."

"Are you upset because Bri is gone or did something else happen?"

"Something happened. We can talk about it when you get here."

"Good, because I'm on my way now," Rachel said, and hung up before Jade could protest.

Chapter Nineteen

Disapproving Concerns

Fifteen minutes after hanging up the phone, Rachel found herself pulling into Jade's driveway. She parked the car and hurried toward the front door. When she got there, Rachel saw a note that said "in the living room" taped to the door. She let herself in and hurried into the living room and stopped cold when she saw Jade curled up in a ball on the couch, tears streaming down her face.

"Sweetie," Rachel said softly as she set her purse and keys on the coffee table and moved to the sofa and took Jade into her arms and held her close.

"I...I...I..." Jade tried to speak, but the tears came back.

"Shhh, just let me hold you. We'll talk about it later," said Rachel, kissing the side of Jade's head.

Rachel held Jade until she managed to calm herself down. Rachel's heart broke seeing this sweet caring woman cry. She couldn't imagine what could possibly have happened to upset her so much.

"Hey, beautiful," said Rachel as Jade pulled back a bit so that they could look into each other's eyes.

"I cannot be beautiful, Rachel," Jade said, softly wiping her eyes and tear-streaked face.

"You are very beautiful to me," said Rachel before leaning forward and softly kissing her.

"I can't believe you dropped everything to come over here."

"Well, I could tell this was where I was needed most."

"What about your patients?"

"I only had one appointment left, and I told my secretary to call and either reschedule or see if they would see one of the others in the practice if they were available."

"Thank you," Jade said, leaning forward and kissing her.

"Do you feel up to talking about it? We don't have to, but sometimes it helps."

"Amy's parents came to get Bri, and she mentioned you and the two of us spending time together. They sent Bri upstairs to play and then Amy's mom had the audacity to accuse me of parading dates and people into her life who would not be there in the long run and not having my daughter's best interests at heart. She essentially called me a bad mother."

"Seriously? I've only met a couple of people that care as much about their kids and what the repercussions of their actions could mean to their child as you do."

"I told them about all of the help that you have been and what we've done."

"You told them we kissed?" Rachel squeaked in surprise.

"Well, no, but I told them about how you helped Bri and I with Amy's anniversary and then the carnival. And that you and Skye were the only two people I have let into Brianna's and my life in the past year. And that a big part of that was because you both understand loss and pain."

"That sounds horrible. I can't believe they would do that to you."

"It gets worse," Jade said, seeing Rachel's eyes widen. "Brianna heard most of what I said."

"Oh no," said Rachel, the sadness evident in her eyes.

"Yeah. She came racing into the room and over to me crying and telling me not to cry. She's afraid that because of how Amy's parents reacted you will go away."

"What? I'm sorry, but you are stuck with me," Rachel said, smiling.

"I think I can handle that. And I sort of promised Bri that you weren't going away, and she knows I keep my promises. I also promised her that on Thursday before group you and I would call her so that she knows that you really aren't going away."

"Can I say hi to her when you call tonight? Unless, you want me to leave, and we can get together some other night if you don't feel up to it anymore."

"I definitely do not want you to leave," Jade said, looking deep into Rachel's eyes. "Did you want to leave?"

"Hell no." Rachel pulled Jade closer. "And for the record, you are an amazing mother."

"I should get dinner started," said Jade, glancing at the clock.

"Would you like some help?"

"That would be great."

The pair got up from the couch and Jade pulled Rachel into her arms and kissed her soundly.

The drive back to their house was a quiet one for Amy's parents and their granddaughter. They couldn't believe that the day had gone so badly so quickly. One minute they were happy and the next they had hurt their daughter-in-law and their granddaughter.

"What would you like for dinner tonight, Pumpkin? You can choose anything you want," said Bo.

"We can just have whatever is easy," Bri replied, sullen in the back seat.

"Brianna, honey, what's wrong?" asked Alice.

"Nothing."

"Brianna, please tell us what is going on."

"You made Mama cry. And I might lose a friend."

"What do you mean you might lose a friend?" asked her grandfather.

"Rachel. She helped me a lot and she is really nice. She made it okay for me to talk with Mama about being sad about missing Mommy. She makes Mama smile and Mama is really pretty when she smiles."

They pulled into the driveway and got Brianna out of the car and went inside before responding to her statement.

"Brianna, Grandma and I are sorry for upsetting your Mama. We didn't mean to do that. We apologized as well for hurting her. And Jade promised you that Rachel was not going anywhere and would still be part of your life. Now, we have missed you so much and we want to enjoy the week."

"Okay," Brianna pouted but hugged her grandparents.

"Now, what would you like for dinner?"

"Can we have burgers and sweet potato fries?" asked Brianna.

"You bet! You and Grandma get your stuff put

upstairs in your room and I'll go to the store and then we'll make dinner."

"Okay!"

Brianna grabbed her bag and dragged it on the floor toward the stairs.

"Let me take that, honey," said her grandma, taking the bag from her.

The two headed up the stairs to unpack.

❧❧❧❧

Jade led Rachel into the kitchen where she took a seat at the island while Jade started to gather the ingredients for dinner and set them on the island.

"So, what are we making for dinner?" asked Rachel.

"I was going to make pork tenderloin with green beans and couscous. Unless you would rather have something else. It will take about forty-five minutes for the tenderloin to cook."

"It sounds delicious and I think I know of a way we can pass the time," Rachel said, smiling.

"Coloring? Bri has some nifty coloring books," teased Jade as she put the tenderloin in the oven and set the timer. She then got the side items prepped so that they would only take a few minutes to cook once the meat was done.

"We could, or..." started Rachel before Jade took her hand and led her back into the living room and they lay very close together on the couch. "Aaa, are you sure?"

"I enjoy being with you. I enjoy feeling your body against mine. I really enjoy kissing you. I don't know that I am ready to move it past the teenage making out stage yet, if that is the d—" Jade said before she was cut off by Rachel leaning in and kissing her intently.

Their bodies melted into one as they lay together. Rachel could feel Jade's hands running down her back and tightly grasping her butt and massaging it as their tongues battled for dominance. They both moaned and groaned as their bodies moved together. Their hands were exploring each other's bodies, but cautiously avoiding intimate places.

"Oh god, that feels good," moaned Rachel as Jade started to tease the pulse point at the base of her neck.

Jade continued her assault on Rachel's neck before moving back to her lips. Their tongues battled until their breathing was labored. Jade couldn't remember feeling like this before, her senses were overloading with pleasure. As Rachel's hand cautiously made its way under Jade's shirt and rested on her stomach, she was exhilarated by the feel of skin on skin when the timer went off alerting them that dinner was almost done.

"You...weren't kidding...about...about the... teenage make out...session," panted Rachel.

"Mmmm, make out." Jade smiled at Rachel. "I should go check dinner."

"I guess that means I have to let you up huh?"

"For now. We can eat dinner, call Brianna, and then..." Jade said, winking at Rachel.

"Yes, ma'am," Rachel said, grudgingly rolling off the couch and standing to help Jade up.

They walked into the kitchen. Jade went about finishing the sides for dinner while the tenderloin rested. She glanced over and saw that Rachel was sitting on one of the stools at the island, looking as if she were lost in thought. Removing the food from the burners, Jade walked over and wrapped her arms around Rachel's waist from behind.

"Where'd you go?" Jade asked softly after kissing the side of Rachel's head.

"Sorry, my mind takes over sometimes. What'd you say?" asked Rachel, leaning back into Jade's embrace.

"I asked where you went. You looked so far away."

Rachel turned in Jade's arms and pulled her closer.

"Talk to me, beautiful," whispered Jade before kissing Rachel's forehead.

"Even if it's stupid?"

"No matter what, I always want you to talk to me."

"Being around you makes me feel incredible," said Rachel, her green eyes meeting Jade's blue ones. "When you touch me or kiss me, I can't even describe how that feels."

"But?"

"But, I don't want to push you into something you aren't ready for."

"You aren't. I know that I feel the same things you do when we're close or when we touch. Damn, it is amazing. I've never felt anything like this before, and I'll admit that does scare me. If you are afraid that you are a rebound or something, I can tell you for certain that you aren't."

"No, I'm not afraid of being a rebound. Not to put pressure, but are we dating? Are we a couple? Please, don't let this be a 'friends with benefits' situation," Rachel said, offering Jade a smirk.

"You aren't putting pressure on me. I would like

for us to be a couple, but if you are more comfortable with us just dating, I can manage that, too. I don't take relationships casually. I never have, and I especially can't now. I have to think about Brianna whenever I look at the bigger picture and make choices that are going to affect her."

"I'm not the casual dating type either...and when it comes to you, I have no desire to share you with anyone else. I like the idea of us being a couple." Rachel grinned.

"Rachel, was this your long-winded way of asking me to be your girlfriend?" teased Jade.

"I hadn't thought about it like that, but maybe."

They stared into one another's eyes for another long minute before they were drawn together in a kiss. This kiss was different, the emotion, and passion that passed through it they each felt deep inside. After a couple of moments Jade went back and finished making dinner. She plated dinner and lit a candle, dimmed the lights, and they sat at the island and had their first official meal as a couple.

⁂

"Jade, dinner was amazing," said Rachel as they cleaned up the dishes.

"I'm glad you liked it. I never enjoyed cooking for myself, but for people I care about, I love it."

"Maybe sometime you and I can make dinner together instead of me just watching you."

"You mean you watching the ladies? Yes, I saw you watching them quite intently."

"I'm a breast girl, what more can I say?" Rachel said, blushing.

"Let's go call Brianna," Jade said, trying to contain her laughter.

Rachel and Jade went into the living room and lay down on the couch spooning. Jade was in front of Rachel. Grabbing her phone off the coffee table Jade dialed her in-laws number and put the phone on speaker. Jade felt Rachel kiss her neck softly for support.

"Hello?" said a male voice.

"Hi, Bo. It's Jade."

"Hi, Jade." In the background she heard Brianna scream out "Mama" and then the sound of her running into the room. "Here's Bri."

"Hi, Mama," Brianna said breathlessly.

"Hey, sweetheart. How are you doing?"

"Good. Grandpa let me choose what I wanted for dinner."

"You didn't pick ice cream, did you?"

"Aww, I should have." She giggled. "We had burgers and sweet potato fries."

"That was going to be my second guess."

"Mama, did you talk to Rachel?" asked Brianna quietly into the phone.

"I did, and like I told you, she isn't going anywhere," Jade said, smiling as she looked at the woman leaning over her shoulder.

"Hey, kiddo," said Rachel.

"Hi," squeaked Brianna, realizing whom the voice belonged to.

"Your Mama is right, I'm not going anywhere."

"Yay! Thank you. Mama, Grandma wants to talk to you."

"Okay. I love you, Baby Girl. I'll talk to you tomorrow night."

"I love you, too!"

Jade took a deep breath as she heard Brianna handing the phone to Amy's mom. Rachel seemed to sense the tension in Jade's body and pulled her closer, whispering to her that it was going to be fine.

"Hello, Jade," said the woman on the other end of the phone.

"Hello, Alice," Jade said coldly.

"I want to again apologize for earlier. I was out of line and a blatant jackass. I had no right to question your parenting skills or who you are bringing into Brianna's life."

"What has changed in the last two-and-a-half hours?"

"A few things. Bo and I talked, and well, Amy chose you as her co-parent and I should have trusted in her...but I know you, Jade, and I know I even more so should have trusted in you. In all the years we've known you, I have never had a reason to question your integrity, your values, or your reasoning. I don't know what your friendship is or what the future holds for you and Rachel, but Bo and I would like to have you both over for dinner Saturday or Sunday, if you two can make it."

"I'll have to talk to Rachel. I don't know what her plans are."

"Of course. Jade, there is something else."

"Okay?" Jade said questioningly.

"I overheard Bri talking to Amy earlier."

"She and I both still do that," Jade said, taking Rachel's hand and squeezed it for support.

"She was telling Amy about a book you two made of things to do."

"Yeah, we called it our Family Bucket List. I

promised Amy before she died that Bri and I would still keep the list and check things off. Last weekend, Rachel and I went to the carnival. That was in preparation for one of the items on the list. It's to take Bri to the carnival and show her the fun that we found in it. Since I was able to do that this year, I am hoping to take Bri next year when they are in town."

"Well, it was what Bri said after that that proved to me what a fool I was, and what a wonderful, nurturing parent you are. She told Amy that she thinks if you two still do those things together with Amy watching over you, it's still you doing the list as a family."

"She really said that?" Jade said as tears sprung to her eyes and Rachel held her tighter.

"She wouldn't think or know that if you weren't supporting her and telling her about Amy and how much she was loved. Jade, I know I can't make up for what I said, but believe me when I say I know how wrong I was."

"Thank you," Jade said still in shock at her five-year-old's insight and wisdom.

"I won't keep you any longer, I just wanted to apologize and invite you and Rachel to dinner. Bo and I really would like to get to know her. She seems to have had quite an impact on Brianna."

"I'll talk to her, and let you know tomorrow night when I call Bri."

"Good night," both women said and hung up.

Rachel lay there holding Jade, allowing her time to process.

"You have an amazing daughter, you know that?" Rachel finally said.

"She never ceases to amaze me. She has so many of Amy's qualities in her. So, are you free for dinner with my in-laws?"

"She has you in her, too, Jade. What she said is completely something you would say and do. As for dinner with your in-laws, I'm yours whenever and wherever you want me."

"Really?" Jade said, cocking her eyebrow even though she knew Rachel couldn't see it, but she knew she could hear the tone.

"Oh yes," said Rachel, placing a kiss on Jade's neck causing her to shudder.

Jade turned in Rachel's arms to face her. Their eyes were darker, their need for intimacy growing. Jade captured Rachel's lips hungrily. Their bodies were humming as they touched.

Rachel and Jade were forced to break the kiss due to the lack of oxygen. Jade stood up and extended her hand to Rachel who took the offered hand and allowed herself to be pulled up.

"Will you stay tonight? I don't want to be alone after all that went on today," Jade said.

"Of course."

"Thank you."

Jade led Rachel out of the living room and up the stairs, past Brianna's room, down the hall and into her bedroom. Jade closed the door behind them and walked them over to the edge of the bed.

"I thought you weren't ready," said Rachel.

"I'm not, but I thought we'd be more comfortable up here."

"It does look more comfortable than the couch."

Jade crawled up the bed and lay on her side. Rachel stood there for a moment before joining her. They lay on their sides, facing each other.

"You are so beautiful," Jade said, running her

fingers along Rachel's jawline.

Rachel brushed her lips across Jade's.

Jade groaned and pulled Rachel closer. They lay there kissing and naturally broke apart, and Jade suggested that they get ready for bed. She pulled a T-shirt and boxers out for Rachel and a set for herself. They both changed and got into bed, and Rachel pulled Jade tight against her.

"Thank you," Jade said.

"Hey, I'm the lucky one. I get to fall asleep with a gorgeous lady in my arms," said Rachel, leaning down and kissing the top of Jade's head.

They lay there enjoying the closeness until they drifted off to sleep.

Chapter Twenty

Newly Familiar

Jade was slowly drawn out of her sleep by the feel of a warm body pressed against hers. She moved slightly and felt the arm around her waist tighten. It took her a moment to remember that it wasn't Amy. That it was Rachel.

"Good morning," Rachel said softly before running her tongue around Jade's ear and then nipping down her neck.

"Mmmm, good morning..."

Jade turned and softly kissed Rachel. Their lips touching was like a fire igniting. Their legs entwined together and they pulled each other as close as they could. Their kisses were becoming more heated and their breathing became more ragged.

"Oh, Rachel," moaned Jade as she pushed her onto her back and then rolled on top.

Their lower halves instinctually ground together, causing them both to let out a loud, frustrated moan. Jade felt the need that was growing deep within. She sucked on Rachel's pulse point at the base of her neck as Rachel's hands grasped at the thin material covering Jade's back. The T-shirt was old and thin. It allowed her to feel the heat coming from Rachel's body.

"Oh, that feels so good," moaned Rachel as Jade continued to lavish her neck with attention. After several more minutes Rachel pulled Jade away from her neck and captured her lips. They both moaned.

They continued to kiss for several more minutes before breaking apart, panting, desire oozing from every inch of them.

"I-I-I think w-we should..." started Jade, her eyes locked onto Rachel's.

"We should stop, before we both regret something," finished Rachel, seeing Jade nod in agreement.

Jade rolled off Rachel and they both lay on their backs trying to calm the raging fire inside. Neither was sure they were ready for the intensity of taking the relationship further...yet. Jade glanced at the clock and saw that it was still early.

"Thank you, for last night. For coming over when I needed you, for staying..."

"There's no place I would rather be," admitted Rachel. "I should get going so I can go home, take an ice-cold shower, and get ready for work."

"I need that same ice-cold shower."

"Oh, I think that if you were in there, it would definitely not be ice cold," Rachel said lustfully, causing them both to blush.

After several minutes they got up and Jade went downstairs to make some coffee while Rachel changed quickly. Just as Rachel was coming down the stairs Jade poured Rachel's coffee into a travel cup.

"I hope mocha is okay." Jade put the lid on the steaming cup.

"My favorite," Rachel said, smiling.

Rachel stepped closer, took the cup out of Jade's hand and set it on the island. Rachel pulled Jade close to her and just held her.

"Last night, and this morning, were amazing. I feel so connected when we're together," Rachel said into Jade's ear.

"I feel the connection, too. Will you call me later?"

"Of course. I'm having dinner with Skye, but if Amy's parent become turds again, or if you need me for anything, just call."

Jade nodded into Rachel's shoulder before pulling back and giving her a chaste kiss.

Rachel grabbed the cup of coffee Jade had made her, her purse, and keys, and after kissing Jade again, headed out the door and home. Jade watched as Rachel left, then grabbing her own coffee cup, went upstairs to get ready for work.

⁂

Jade had spent most of the day assisting one client with their collections and getting them into one of the galleries in town. She had skipped lunch and was getting ready to leave when her desk phone rang.

"Jade Donovan," she answered.

"Hey, Jade," said the voice on the other end.

"Kristel? Why are you calling my desk line?"

"Well, you haven't answered a single one of my text messages."

Jade pulled out her phone and realized it was on silent. She saw she had five messages from Kristel, and three from Rachel.

"Sorry, my phone was on silent. I spent the day working to get one artist a showing at a local gallery." Jade quickly read the messages from Kristel. "Dinner tonight would be awesome."

"Great. So, do you want to do this at your place

or mine? Or would you prefer dinner out?"

"I can come by your place. I'm too tired to go out," said Jade.

"How does an hour sound?"

"Sounds good, I'll see you then."

Jade hung up the phone and then read the messages from Rachel. The first one said, "Hey Beautiful, I hope you are having a good day. Don't forget to tell Bri 'hi' and Amy's parents we can make it whenever for dinner." Jade smiled at how sweet Rachel was. She read the second one. "Call me later tonight. I don't care what time; I just want to hear your voice." The third message came through just before Kristel called and said, "I hope I don't sound too needy..."

Jade quickly replied to Rachel's messages. "Hi, sweetie! Sorry, I had my phone on silent today. I miss your voice, too. I will call you after I talk to Bri, and have dinner with Kristel. Oh, and you don't sound too needy to me. :)"

Rachel replied with a smiley face which made Jade smile. She left work, and went home to change before heading over to Kristel's for dinner.

❧ ❧ ❧ ❧

Skye pulled up outside Rachel's house and smiled. She hadn't seen her sister-in-law happy in a long time, and she had forgotten how Rachel glowed when she was happy. Skye felt a little guilt that it wasn't still her sister that was making Rachel glow, but she told herself that Emily was watching over them, and happy that Rachel was finally healing from her loss.

Rachel met her at the door.

"Thanks for coming over," Rachel said, hugging

Skye.

"Hey, if you want to cook for me, who am I to complain?" laughed Skye as they made their way into the kitchen where Skye saw Rachel unpacking food from the Chinese restaurant down the street. "You bought dinner?"

"Yeah, well, I'll explain over dinner." Rachel blushed.

"Oh, this I can't wait to hear."

They made their plates and moved into the living room. Rachel curled up on her chaise lounge and Skye sat in the recliner.

"So, how was your day?" asked Rachel.

"Good, how was yours?" Skye sensed the hesitation and need to talk in her sister-in-law's tone.

"It was long. Well, work was long."

"Talk to me, Rach. You are horrible at avoidance, especially when you are stressed or confused. Does this have to do with Jade?"

"Dammit, how do you know me so well?" Rachel asked, shaking her head.

"I just do, now talk to me. What's going on?"

Rachel set her plate on the table next to the lounge and then looked over at Skye.

"You know that I was having dinner with her last night right?" asked Rachel, who received a nod of acknowledgment from her sister-in-law. "Well, I called to confirm what time worked for her, and she was in tears. I just dropped everything and went over there."

"Is she okay?"

"Yeah, Amy's parents had been over to pick up Brianna because she was spending the week with them. Well, the short story is that they accused her of being a bad parent and parading dates and people through Brianna's life that weren't going to be there in the long run and thus hurting the kid."

"What the hell? That is a crock of shit. Jade is an amazing mom and I've only met her once."

"Agreed. When I got there she was still in tears. Skye, it hurt so much to see her like that. I wrapped her in my arms and held her. After a while we talked, and we kissed."

"Really?" Skye sat up more and gave Rachel more of her attention. This was the most intimate details she had ever divulged.

"Yes, and in my fashion I sort of in a long, round-about way asked her...oh fuck it, we agreed we're a couple last night," said Rachel, blushing.

"It is about damn time. Kristel and I thought we were going to have to beat you two over the head or something."

"Gee, thanks."

"No problem!"

"I spent the night there," said Rachel.

"What!"

"Not like that. After what she had gone through with Amy's family, she didn't want to be alone. We wore pajamas, but I spent the night holding her."

"That isn't a bad thing, Rach."

"I just don't want to pressure her into something she isn't ready for..."

"Did she ask you to stay?" Skye asked.

"Yes."

"Then it isn't you pressuring her now is it?"

"No, but she was hurting. What if she thinks I was taking advantage of the situation?"

"Rachel Danielle Cassidy, you did NOT do

anything wrong or take advantage of anyone or anything. Dammit you need to let yourself live and love again, too. I know my sister; she would want you to be happy. Jade makes you happy. Honest and true happiness."

"She does. And it is so very different than it was with Emily, and so intense."

"I'm happy for you."

"There is one other thing…"

"What's that?" asked Skye.

"Amy's parents want Jade and me to come over for dinner this weekend."

"What? After they accused her and stuff? Talk about Jekyll and Hyde shit."

"Sorry, they apologized and said that if I was going to be a part of their life they wanted to meet and get to know me."

"So, are you going to go over there?"

"Yeah, we are," Rachel said.

"Wow, not even a week officially together and you are meeting her in-laws. When should I schedule the U-Haul?" teased Skye.

"Smart-ass." Rachel tossed a pillow and hit Skye directly in the face.

❧❧❧❧

Jade got home and changed into jeans and a T-shirt before sitting down to call her daughter.

"Hello?" said Alice as she answered the phone.

"Hi, Alice, it's Jade."

"Hi, Jade. How are you doing today?"

"Good. How are you doing?"

"I'm good. Bri has been waiting for you to call."

"Hi, Mama!"

"Hi, sweetheart! How are you doing? Did you have a good day?"

"I'm good. Today was fun. Grandpa and Grandma let me play with the sprinkler in the backyard. Then I got to help wash the car."

"That sounds like a lot of fun. Did you spray them with the hose like Mommy taught you?"

"Yep! I got Grandma really good like Mommy always said to. Does Olaf miss me?"

"Olaf does, but he had dinner and is relaxing now. Rachel told me to say hi to you."

"She did?"

"Yeah, she did, Baby Girl. We'll both call you on Thursday, too," Jade said, reminding her daughter.

"Yay! Mama, Grandma wants to talk to you again, and she says I need to go take my bath."

"Okay. Why don't you go take your bath, and I will call you tomorrow night? I love you!"

"I love you, too, Mama."

"Hi, again," said Alice.

"Hi," Jade said, still a little reserved.

"Did you get a chance to talk to Rachel about dinner this weekend?"

"I did and she said that she can make either night."

"Well, should we do Saturday since you were going to pick Brianna up that night anyway?"

"That sounds great. What time?"

"Why don't you come over around five o'clock? That will give us time to talk before dinner."

"Great, we will see you then. I'll call Bri again tomorrow night."

"All right. Have a good night," said Alice.

"You, too."

Jade hung up the phone and sat there for a minute before texting Rachel to let her know that dinner was on Saturday, and that they would need to leave by 4:15 to make it over to Amy's parents by five. Jade then headed out of the house and over to Kristel's.

⁂

Kristel opened the door. She waved her friend in and went back into the kitchen to finish dinner.

"Wow, home-cooked meal and everything," said Jade, entering the kitchen.

"Well, I figured with Bri gone you were eating take-out, ramen, or popcorn."

"You think you know me so well," Jade said, sticking her tongue out at her best friend. "I made pork tenderloin, couscous, and green beans last night."

"Oh right, Rachel came over," smirked Kristel seeing Jade blush. "How did that go?"

"I have lots to tell you about yesterday. Some is going to piss you off, though."

"Do I need to kick some redhead ass? You know I will, too."

"No, you leave her ass alone."

"Well, dinner is going to be ready in a little bit. Wine? Beer? Or would you like something else to drink?"

"Beer please," said Jade.

Kristel handed Jade a beer and grabbed one for herself, and they headed into the living room to talk.

"All right, talk to me."

"Amy's parents came over yesterday afternoon and Alice basically called me a bad parent."

"What? You are the best parent I know, and that

includes myself. Why would she say that?"

"Bri brought up Rachel. Bo and Alice asked me who she was. After that I explained about the group, what Rachel helped with for Amy's anniversary, and then us going to the zoo. Alice questioned me about parading people through Bri's life who weren't going to be there in the long run and not thinking of what introducing those people through could do to Bri mentally, not to mention physically, if I bring the wrong person home."

"Wait, are you telling me that she accused you of sleeping around?"

"Yes," Jade said before taking a large drink.

"Wow, I am going to go kick Alice's ass."

"Oh, it gets worse...Bri overheard..."

Kristel dropped her head. There was a mix of emotions running through her. She was sad that Brianna overheard what had transpired, she was angry that Alice would hurt Jade this way, and furious at the accusations made by Bo and Alice.

"After they left I broke down..."

"Why didn't you call me?"

"Rachel called right after. She could tell something was wrong and she dropped everything and came over. When she got there she just held me and let me cry."

"I like that woman more and more."

"Then we made dinner, she asked me to be her girlfriend, or more specifically, for us to be a couple, I said yes, we called and talked to Brianna. I guess Alice overheard Brianna talking to Amy and realized that she was an ass. Alice apologized to me and then invited Rachel and me over for dinner on Saturday. She said that she and Bo want to get to know Rachel because she is going to be a part of our lives."

"Back up there, Donovan." Kristel saw Jade avert her eyes. "Now, let's go back to the part of your little story where you said Rachel asked you to be her girlfriend."

"It seems fairly self-explanatory to me," Jade said, still not looking at Kristel.

"Very funny. So, you are seriously involved with the sexy redhead?"

"Yes," Jade said, blushing. "And you are going to have to get over your crush on her, too."

"Ha ha. There is more isn't there?"

"A heavy make-out session and she um, spent the night..."

"What? You slept with her?"

"No! Not in the way you're thinking. After everything that went on with Alice and Bo I didn't want to be alone. We wore pajamas and she held me."

"I thought I was going to have to kick her ass for taking advantage of you," Kristel said, relieved.

"She wouldn't do that. I will say that just kissing her is getting harder and harder each time."

"She's that good huh?" smirked Kristel as Jade turned a very dark shade of red.

"Good is not the appropriate word. Mind-blowing, breathtaking, those are closer."

"I'm happy for you Jade. Is it safe to assume that you are going to keep this between the four of us? And when I say the four of us, I mean you, Rachel, Skye, and myself. We all know that she is going to tell Skye just like you are telling me."

"Yeah. That's the plan," said Jade. "We also promised Bri that we would call her together before group on Thursday."

"Wow, very intense. Hopefully things go well on Saturday."

Jade nodded and Kristel looked at the clock and then went to get their plates. They ate and Kristel told Jade about her day.

⁂

Once Jade was home and curled up in bed, she cuddled with the pillow that Rachel had slept on the night before. The smell of the strawberry shampoo that Rachel used was embedded in the pillow.

"Hello, beautiful!" Rachel answered the phone.

"Hi, gorgeous! How was your day?"

"Well, waking up next to you started it out pretty damn good and I didn't let anything bring it down. How was your day?"

"It was good. I talked to Bri tonight. She says hi. I had dinner with Kristel, and told her about us," said Jade.

"I told Skye."

"And now I'm talking to this gorgeous woman and cuddling with the pillow she used last night because it still smells like her."

"What are your plans tomorrow night?"

"I don't have any plans," said Jade.

"Would you like to come over and have dinner with me?"

"That sounds fantastic."

Chapter Twenty-one

Firsts

Jade nervously arrived at Rachel's. She wasn't sure why she was nervous, but since this was the first time she had ever been there, she blamed that.

Jade walked up to the door. It was a nice ranch-style house, orange with green trim, conservatively landscaped. Jade rang the doorbell and waited for Rachel to answer.

"Hi," said Rachel, opening the door and allowing Jade in.

"Hi," Jade said, entering the house and kissing her softly.

Rachel led them out to the three-season porch at the back of the house.

"Can I get you something to drink?"

"Whatever you are having," Jade said, feeling comforted by Rachel's closeness.

Rachel went into the kitchen and grabbed two beers, and joined Jade on the sofa.

"How was your day?"

"Frustrating, but that improved when I got here," flirted Jade.

"Funny, my day improved as soon as you arrived here, too." Rachel moved to sit closer to Jade. "How is Brianna doing?"

"I haven't called her yet today. Would you mind

if we called her together?"

"I'd love that," Rachel beamed.

The couple cuddled up together and Jade dialed her in-laws and put it on speakerphone.

"Mama!" said Brianna as she answered the phone.

"There is my Baby Girl. I miss you so much." Jade sighed, relieved to hear her daughter's voice.

"I miss you, too, Mama. Today Grandpa took me out on a horse," Brianna said excitedly.

"Really," said Jade, feeling Rachel shudder next to her. "Did you have fun?"

"Yeah, he said that he taught Mommy to ride when she was my age."

"He did. Mommy used to love to go riding," Jade said, her voice shaking a little, but she stabilized it when she felt Rachel's arms pull her closer and hold her tighter.

"Did you ever go riding with her?"

"A few times. I wasn't very good at it, but we went a few times."

"Grandma got sad and cried because we went riding. Was I naughty?" Brianna's voice sounded as if she were on the verge of tears.

"No Baby Girl, you weren't naughty. Grandma just misses Mommy," Jade said, looking to Rachel for some help.

"Hi, Brianna," said Rachel before she softly kissed the top of Jade's head.

"Hi, Rachel."

"Remember when we were going through the pictures of your Mama and Mommy and talking about stories and memories?"

"Yes."

"Well, I imagine for your Grandma the memories of your Mommy at your age on the horses are a strong happy one."

"But she was sad…"

"Yes she was. Do you think that she might be sad because your Mommy isn't able to go riding with you? Or to teach you the stuff she knew?"

"Uh huh."

"Then that proves you didn't do anything wrong. Did you give your Grandma a big hug and tell her you loved her?"

"Kinda. I hugged her and told her not to be sad."

"I bet that helped her. Why don't you give her another big hug and tell her you love her when you get done talking to your Mama."

"Bri, honey, who are you talking to?" came a voice in the background.

"I'm talking to Mama," said Brianna, and then they heard her say, "I love you, Grandma."

Jade turned and smiled at Rachel. She was so grateful for her being a part of their life.

"Hello? Jade?"

"Hi, Alice," said Jade.

"I guess she told you about today. Was the hug her idea or yours? Because it helped." Alice chuckled.

"Actually it was Rachel's. Brianna was afraid that she had done something to upset you because of the riding. Rachel helped her understand that more likely you were sad that Amy isn't here to go riding with her or teach her."

"Rachel is correct," sighed Alice. "Is she still there so I might have a word with her?"

"Sure." Jade found herself amused that Alice didn't realize she was on speakerphone.

"Hello," said Rachel.

"Hello, Rachel, this is Alice, Amy's mother."

"Hi, Alice."

"Thank you for helping Brianna understand that it wasn't her. I tried to explain earlier, but she must have not understood."

"That's fine. She's a good kid, she's just hypersensitive to emotions. I don't know if that is an Amy or Jade trait, but I am sure she came by it honestly."

"I, um, also wanted to apologize to you for my words and accusations on Monday. I was out of line and I disrespected both you and Jade."

"Thank you, I appreciate that. I look forward to meeting and getting to know you and your husband on Saturday."

"Hello, Alice," Jade said, smiling back at Rachel.

"I won't keep you, but thank you for letting me apologize to her."

"No problem. Tell Bri I love her and will call her tomorrow."

"I will," Alice promised before they ended the call.

"Mmmm, thank you," said Jade before kissing Rachel firmly on the lips. She felt Rachel respond by deepening the kiss. Jade sucked Rachel's tongue into her own mouth, causing them both to moan.

"Oh...god...yes..." whimpered Rachel as they broke their kiss, and Jade's lips were instantly on Rachel's neck. Rachel brought her hand up and held Jade's lips to her neck.

Jade could feel her heart racing. She felt as if she were losing control, but she couldn't stop kissing and sucking on this woman's neck and lips. Jade allowed

Rachel to pull her back up and bring their lips together again. Jade adjusted Rachel so that she was straddling her lap. She could feel the heat from Rachel's body pressed against her own.

Rachel broke the kiss and moved to kiss along Jade's jawline and then she ran her tongue around the outside of Jade's ear causing Jade to moan. The sound of her own moan increased her own arousal, and she hoped that telegraphed to Rachel.

Jade couldn't believe the feelings she was having. She slid her hand underneath Rachel's shirt and then slowly moved her hand around Rachel's back and unhooked her bra. Once the fabric released, Jade moved her hand to cup one of Rachel's breasts. The sensation caused them both to gasp. The feeling of Rachel's erect nipple against the palm of Jade's hand made Jade dizzy with desire.

"Yes..." whispered Rachel, bringing her hands up and removing her shirt and bra.

"You are so beautiful," said Jade before leaning forward and sucking Rachel's other nipple into her mouth.

"Oooh," groaned Rachel, bringing a hand to the back of Jade's head to keep her head in place. Rachel arched into Jade's mouth as she used her tongue to tease the nipple in her mouth. Jade groaned and felt Rachel shudder.

"Your skin tastes so good," said Jade.

"Unless you want to stop here, we need to move to my room," said Rachel. "I don't want our first time to be on the couch."

Jade continued to run her hands up and down Rachel's back and sides their eyes locked together.

"Let's move to your room," Jade said, pulling

her lips away from the tantalizing nipples and offering a lopsided smile.

"Yes, please," said Rachel as the timer in the kitchen went off.

Rachel hurried in and put dinner in the refrigerator before leading Jade back to her room.

Rachel closed the door and wrapped her arms around Jade's neck. Rachel kissed her until she responded to the kiss and relaxed into the embrace at the feel of Rachel's lips on hers. Jade put her hands on Rachel's hips and eased her back toward the bed. After they reached the bed, Jade lay Rachel on her back and then hovered over her.

Jade leaned down and ran her tongue across Rachel's lips as Rachel slowly started to ease the hem of Jade's shirt up. Their eyes met and Jade nodded, knowing that Rachel was waiting for her approval to remove her shirt. Once Rachel had divested Jade of her shirt and bra she ran her hands up the front of Jade's body, cupping her breasts in her hands.

"Ohhh...Rachel," moaned Jade.

Rachel rolled them over so she was lying on top of Jade, their bodies pressed together as Rachel gently brushed her lips across Jade's. Rachel smiled at Jade before tilting her head to kiss down Jade's neck stopping to suck on her pulse point.

"Your pulse is racing," whispered Rachel.

"Oh, god that feels so good," said Jade.

Jade felt Rachel continue down to her collarbone, then slowly down until she felt her nipple slip into the warmth of Rachel's mouth.

"Ohhh, Rachel," moaned Jade. "Yes..."

Rachel continued her attention alternating between Jade's nipples. Jade brought her hands up and began to caress Rachel's breasts. Between what Rachel was doing to her, and the arousal from playing with Rachel's breasts, Jade wasn't sure how much longer she was going to be able to keep this up.

Rachel worked her way back up to Jade's lips. They rolled on their sides, facing the other, panting. Their eyes were still smoldering with desire.

"Tell me what you want," said Rachel.

"I-I want y-you to touch me, and allow me to touch you," said Jade nervously.

"Baby, if this is all you want to do, we don't have to go further."

"Thank you for understanding," Jade leaned in and kissed Rachel deeply.

They spent the rest of the night kissing, touching, and exploring one another. As exhaustion overtook them they drifted off to sleep holding one another. Jade hadn't planned on staying the full night, but she couldn't bring herself to leave.

※ ※ ※ ※

Rachel and Jade started to stir as the sun started to peek in the curtains. The previous night they had managed to divest all but their panties before falling asleep holding on to the other. If Rachel's breathing pattern change was any indication, Jade knew that they were both very aware of the lack of clothing separating their bodies.

Jade brought a hand up and cupped Rachel's face as she kissed her intently. They gasped as their breasts brushed together. Jade slid her hand down from Rachel's face to cup her breast. Rachel let out a groan that served as encouragement. Jade played with the taut nipple between her fingers and felt Rachel arch into her hand.

"Jade," whispered Rachel.

With their eyes locked together, and arousal pulsing through them. Jade rolled on her back and pulled Rachel on top of her. Jade allowed her hands to roam as Rachel began to lavish her neck with kisses. Jade's hands grabbed at Rachel's cloth-covered butt and pulled their hips together. They both shuddered as Jade started to ease Rachel's panties down. Rachel pulled back and looked deep into Jade's eyes. Jade knew that Rachel was seeing the raw lust, desire, and need burning within her.

Once Rachel was naked, Jade lay her back and began teasing her breasts. She ran the tip of her tongue around Rachel's erect nipple, feeling it harden. Jade moved to the other nipple and repeated the process. Jade began kneading one breast while teasing the other and alternating the ministrations. Rachel let out a moan and reached down and tugged at Jade's panties. Smiling to herself, Jade helped to remove her panties without stopping what she was doing. Rachel moaned again and bucked her hips. Jade knew that Rachel was looking for some contact, some friction, something more.

"Jade...touch me," moaned Rachel. Her words caused Jade to shudder with desire.

Jade stopped her teasing and began to kiss Rachel deeply as she ran her hand down her chest and stomach. She could sense how wet Rachel was before she even touched her.

"Oh, you are so wet," moaned Jade.

"Yes," said Rachel, her hips rising. Rachel lowered her hand and slowly started touching Jade.

"Oh...yes...Rachel," said Jade.

"That feels...mmmm...so...very amazing," panted Rachel.

They were moving their hips in a well-choreographed dance as they teased and pleasured one another.

As they neared their breaking point, Jade stretched up and kissed Rachel hard.

Jade pulled back from the kiss as they both climaxed. Jade felt alive.

Jade whispered Rachel's name as she felt an aftershock race through her. Jade looked at her lover and saw a sensual, yet mischievous grin play across the woman's features.

"Do you want me to take you again, slowly this time?" Rachel asked. All Jade could do was nod her response. "Lie back and enjoy."

"Oh Rachel...that...feels...oh don't stop," Jade said, feeling Rachel's hand and lips slowly moving all over her body.

Jade looked and saw Rachel smile as she ever so slightly started to move faster. Jade could tell that Rachel was very turned on just by how intently she was watching her reactions.

They continued until they both climaxed hard again, and then collapsed together, spent from their morning activities. Once they were able to move, Rachel turned and kissed Jade. As they kissed, Jade pulled Rachel's body as close to hers as she could.

"That was one hell of a way to wake up." Jade giggled.

"Yes, it was." Rachel nodded in agreement.

The women finally managed to shower and get dressed. It took them a while since their legs were boycotting the idea of moving.

"Thank you for last night, and this morning," said Jade as Rachel handed her a cup of coffee.

"Both were my pleasure so there is no need to thank me," Rachel said, taking a sip of her coffee.

"Oh, there was definitely enough pleasure to go around," said Jade, wrapping an arm around Rachel and pulling her close.

"Group is going to be hard tonight. I'm going to want to pull you close and kiss you the whole time," Rachel said before kissing Jade softly.

"I know, but for now I think it is best if we just keep this between us, Kristel, and Skye."

"I agree. Do you want to come over here before group to call Bri?"

"I'd love to," Jade smiled her lopsided smile, knowing the impact it had on her lover.

They finished their coffee and kissed for a few more minutes before Rachel left for work and Jade headed home to change before going to the office.

Chapter Twenty-two

Friends and Family Support

Jade arrived at work and saw Kristel sitting in her office.

"Good morning," said Jade, raising an eyebrow to the woman in her chair.

"Since when do you come in this late?" asked Kristel, glancing at the clock.

"Since today. I didn't have any clients scheduled so I took my time." Jade avoided direct eye contact.

"Liar!"

"Not entirely, and get the hell out of my chair." Jade playfully pushed Kristel and smiled as she moved to the other side of the desk.

"Seriously, are you okay?"

"I'm fine. I spent the night at Rachel's and we took our time going in to work since neither of us had anything going on right away."

"You two seem to be getting pretty close," Kristel questioned.

"Just ask what you are hinting at…"

"I'm just wondering where this is going. I know you both have strong feelings, but, I don't want you to get hurt."

"I understand, but right now, we're just seeing where this leads."

"And she is a good kisser so you are enjoying

that as well."

"That isn't all she is good at," mumbled Jade without thinking. She realized she had said it loud enough for Kristel to hear when she heard her friend choke on the drink of water she was taking.

"Care to explain that statement?" Kristel coughed.

"Not really," Jade said, not looking up, but turning a darker shade of red.

"You slept together?"

"Yeah, we slept in the same bed Monday night and last night. We discussed this already," said Jade, trying to semantically avoid Kristel's real meaning.

"Nuh uh, don't you go coy with me. You know damn well what I mean."

"Fine, yes..." said Jade, covering her face with her hands trying to hide the blush and smile that crept across her face as she remembered the start to the morning.

"And?"

"And, you know I don't kiss and tell."

"I know, but you already did by stating 'that isn't all she is good at' two minutes ago. Seriously, I just want to make sure you're okay with what happened."

"I am the one who started things last night, put the brakes on, and then started things this morning. I don't regret it, I feel some guilt, but I don't regret it."

"Why guilt?"

"She isn't Amy..."

"Jade, Amy died, you have to move on with your life. You're twenty-nine. You still have a long life ahead of you."

"I know, but..."

"But you and Amy were married and that was a lifelong commitment. Yes, I do listen to you when you speak to me. You are my best friend, and I love you. Rachel makes you happy, and you and Brianna deserve happiness. Amy wanted that for you both as well."

"Thank you. You never did tell me why you were here this morning."

"Something in my gut told me that my best friend needed me," Kristel said, smiling at Jade.

"I think I should buy your gut lunch or dinner soon."

"What are you doing tonight?" asked Kristel.

"Going to Rachel's to call Brianna and then we have group tonight."

"You two are still keeping the relationship private except for me and Skye, right?"

"Yeah, for now it seems best."

"Would you like some support to get through group tonight? I remember you and Amy at the mushy stage and you two couldn't keep your hands off one another."

"Support would be awesome. I'm afraid I am going to be fixated on her lips or something."

"Well, Jake is at his dad's tonight, so why don't you pick me up before group, and I'll help you and Rachel keep your little secret."

"Thank you!"

"Anytime. I have to run now, though. I have a meeting soon."

"Thank you, and I will see you tonight," said Jade, hugging her friend.

❧❧❧❧

"Hel—"

"Skye, help..." interrupted Rachel.

"Rach? What's wrong?"

"We slept together this morning...What if she regrets it? What if she blames me? What if she didn't enjoy it even though she said she did? Oh god, what if we can't hide it at group...will I lose respect from them? Skye, what am I going to do?"

"First, stop fucking freaking out and go back to the part where you said you slept together. I'm guessing that you don't just mean that as in the same bed sleeping together."

"Well, we did that Monday night. Last night we fooled around, but she stopped it..."

"And?"

"Then this morning she started and we did..."

"Are you okay with it? She's the first since my sister right?"

"Yes, she's the first since Emily. I don't regret it, but I've had almost four years Skye. For Jade it's only been about a year and a half."

"Rachel, you said she stopped it last night and started things this morning right?"

"Yeah."

"You didn't pressure her. You need to give yourself some breathing room around the guilt. I'm starting to wonder how it is that my sister ended up with someone as neurotic as you."

"Kiss my ass," scoffed Rachel.

"Nope, you have a girlfriend to do that now," Skye teased. "Honestly Rach, you can't take all of the pressure on yourself. There are two of you in this relationship and you both have the responsibility for what happens in it."

"There are technically three of us in this. Brianna's happiness is the most important thing for Jade."

"Right, and it should be, but what I'm saying is that you don't need to beat yourself up about the things that happen between you and Jade. Just keep the lines of communication open."

"When did you get so smart?"

"I've always been smart, you just never listened. So, group tonight. Just don't sit next to one another, and don't spend all of your time looking into one another's eyes."

Rachel's phone beeped and she saw it was a text from Jade.

"She just texted me…"

"Read it dumbass, and stop panicking. Better yet, just read the damn thing to me," said Skye.

"Hey Sexy. Kristel is going to come to group tonight to keep us from being obvious. I'll see you soon. xoxo -Jade"

"Yeah, that sounds horrible. You can just tell the lack of care and…"

"Shut up, you made your point" Rachel laughed even harder when she heard Skye's giggle.

"At least Kristel will be there. I was going to offer, but it would be weird for me to show up after all these years."

"Yeah, plus I would have to admit to knowing you in public and, ew," teased Rachel.

"Watch it, Cassidy! You keep that up and I may just show up to watch you blush."

"You wouldn't…"

"Oh, I would and you damn well know it."

"I know, I know," said Rachel, shaking her head. "I have to get to work. I'll talk to you later."

"Talk to you later."

"Hey, Skye, thanks."

"That is why I am here, Rachel."

⁂

The rest of the day passed in a blur for Rachel and Jade. They were both looking forward to seeing the other and dreading group.

"Hi, Beautiful," said Rachel as she opened the door when Jade arrived.

"Hey, Sexy," said Jade, entering.

Rachel closed the door and then wrapped her arms around Jade's waist as she felt Jade wrap her arms around her neck. They leaned together and kissed softly.

"How was your day?" asked Rachel, taking Jade's hand and leading her into the living room.

"Besides getting the third degree from Kristel? It was a good day. How was yours?" Jade sat down and pulled Rachel onto her lap.

"Definitely improving," Rachel said before pressing her torso against Jade's and kissing her sensually. Rachel brought her hand up and cupped Jade's face.

While their tongues danced together, Jade's hand started to wander. Jade cupped Rachel's butt and squeezed it, causing them both to groan.

"You keep that up and we aren't going to make it to group," growled Rachel.

"Fine, I'll try to behave, but you have to try to look less desirable."

"I'll do my best."

"Should we call Brianna to keep us behaving?" asked Jade.

"Yeah, we probably should."

Jade adjusted slightly so she could reach the phone in her back pocket.

"Oh, let me help," Rachel said with a mischievous grin on her face.

Jade, not thinking twice, allowed Rachel to help. Rachel adjusted so that she was straddling Jade as she had done on the couch the night before. Jade groaned in desire as Rachel's chest was thrust in her face as she leaned forward in order to reach behind Jade with both hands and grab the phone. Rachel slid the phone out of Jade's back pocket and continued to caress the flesh below her hands. Jade wrapped her arms around Rachel and mirrored what was being done to her. They both moaned.

Rachel tilted her head down and her lips met Jade's. They began to move slowly together. After several minutes, they separated.

"We should call her," said Jade, holding Rachel in place when she tried to move off her lap. "Please don't. It feels so nice with you right here." Rachel nodded as Jade dialed her in-laws' number.

"Hello."

"Hi, Bo, it's Jade."

"Hi, Jade. How are you doing today?"

"I'm good. How are you?"

"I'm wishing I had a little of Bri's energy. Hang on a sec, and I'll get her."

Jade muted her phone and leaned forward and started to kiss up and down Rachel's neck, paying extra attention to the pulse point. Rachel couldn't help but tilt her head allowing Jade more access, and as she did her hips started to rock slowly.

"Mmmm, Rachel," moaned Jade as felt Rachel's reaction to what she was doing.

"Hi, Mama," said Brianna, pulling Rachel and Jade out of their haze.

"Hi, sweetie," Jade said, blushing as she quickly un-muted her phone. She glanced at the woman sitting on her lap trying to contain her laughter.

"Hi, Bri," Rachel said, regaining composure.

"Hi, Rachel!"

"How was your day?" asked Jade.

"It was okay. I miss you lots, Mama."

"I miss you, too, Baby Girl. I'll be there Saturday to pick you up. Rachel and I are coming to have dinner with you, Grandma, and Grandpa."

"You are? Both of you?"

"Yep we are," Rachel said, smiling.

"Mommy heard me."

"What do you mean?" asked Jade, confused.

"I asked her to have Grandma and Grandpa stop being mean to you, and for her not to let Rachel go away."

"I guess your Mommy did hear you," said Rachel.

"You have to go to group, Mama."

Rachel and Jade glanced at the clock and saw that they did need to leave soon, but since Rachel lived closer they had a few minutes.

"Yes I do. I love you!"

"I love you, too! Bye, Rachel."

"Bye, Bri," said Rachel, and they hung up.

Jade set the phone on the couch and rested her hands on Rachel's hips before returning to her neck. Rachel's hand came up and threaded into Jade's hair.

"Do you...oh god...have any idea how...good you are at that?"

Jade smiled into Rachel's neck and allowed her hands to massage Rachel's butt. Rachel brought one hand up to hold Jade's head to her neck and used the other one to slip inside Jade's shirt and cup her breast. She could feel the nipple straining against the lacy fabric. Jade let out a soft moan as Rachel continued to tease her.

"We have to stop," whimpered Rachel.

"I know, but you're so responsive," said Jade, tilting her head before pulling Rachel into a powerful kiss.

"You need to go get Kristel, and I need to go set up...and maybe sit on a block of ice." Rachel laughed.

"I'm sorry." Jade knew that it wasn't nice of her to get them both so worked up before group, but after that morning she couldn't help herself.

"Don't be. Do you want to come back here after group?" asked Rachel with a seductive smile.

"I'd like that," Jade said.

They got up and straightened their clothes, kissed quickly, and then parted.

ﷺ

Jade pulled up to Kristel's house and honked the horn. Kristel skipped out and started to laugh as soon as she got in the car.

"What are you laughing at?"

"If you want to keep you and Rachel a secret, you might want to button your shirt correctly."

Jade looked down and saw she had missed a button and another was askew. Jade blushed and quickly fixed her shirt. "Shush, not another word on that."

"Oh, I intend on having a lot of fun with this. So, how's Rachel?"

"She's good," Jade said, blushing again.

"Uh huh. How's Bri?" asked Kristel.

"She's good. I think she's getting homesick."

"So, what's with the blushing?"

"Nothing." Jade turned red again. "I don't think that you are going to help me to not being obvious if you keep making me blush."

"Maybe you shouldn't have been making out with Rachel before coming to get me," she smirked.

"You are evil," Jade said as they pulled in the Community Center parking lot.

Kristel just sat there smugly. Jade parked the car next to Rachel's and the two headed inside.

≈≈≈≈

"Want some help?" said Skye, entering the Community Center room where Rachel, Doug, and Carmen were setting up.

Rachel looked up and turned a dark shade of red. Skye smiled, made her way over to the small group, and hugged Rachel.

"I thought you said you loved me," said Rachel, laughing nervously.

"I do, but there are days that I just can't pass up torturing and tormenting you."

"Doug, Carmen, this is my sister-in-law Skye. Skye, this is Doug and Carmen, two of my group members."

They exchanged hellos as Rachel glared at Skye.

"What? You sounded like you could use some extra support."

"Just behave, please?" pleaded Rachel.

"I'll try, but that is rarely any fun."

They finished setting up and were sitting around

talking when Kristel and Jade walked in.

"Oh shit, this cannot end well," whispered Jade as she started to turn to walk out the door she had just come in.

"What?" asked Kristel.

"Skye is here. You know damn well she is only here to torment Rachel and me," said Jade, nodding in the direction of the chairs. She saw Kristel smirk before looping arms and dragging Jade toward the circle.

"Hello Jade, Kristel," Rachel said trying not to make eye contact with either of them.

"Hi," the two women said.

"I hope you don't mind, but my sister-in-law will be joining the group tonight," Rachel said as Skye waved to them and smiled.

"Not at all." Jade casually turned and walked toward the refreshment table.

"I'm sorry, I would have warned you if I had had time," Rachel said quietly as she and Jade were alone at the table.

"I've met Skye. I know it wasn't your fault," said Jade, winking at Rachel, which helped to calm her nerves slightly.

Kristel and Jade found seats a few down from where Rachel and Skye were seated. They found that the seats were placed well so it wasn't easy for Rachel and Jade to see one another.

"So Skye, is Rachel different now than she was when you first met her?" asked Carmen.

"A little. She has been through a lot, and it changes you," answered Skye.

"You two seem close. Is it hard with your sister being gone?" asked Doug.

"We're very close," Skye said, smiling at Rachel.

"When she married Emily I told her that she was stuck with me as her sister for life. Just because Emily died doesn't mean that I stopped caring about Rachel. She has been a part of my life for several years, and she always will be."

"What if she gets involved with someone else?" asked Carmen, looking between Rachel and Jade.

Rachel and Jade exchanged a surreptitious glance. It was risky, but no one seemed to notice.

"Whomever Rachel chooses to date will have to get my approval. I won't let her be hurt if I can help it. She deserves happiness."

"What are your thoughts about having Skye in your life still, and about her having to approve who you date?" asked Kristel, causing Jade to groan internally.

Rachel blanched at the question for a moment before gathering her thoughts. "I love having Skye in my life. She is one of my best friends. And selfishly, it gives me a way to hold on to a piece of Emily. As for getting her approval for someone to date, I'm sure it is the same as with you and Jade. I know that she has my best interests at heart. She's seen me go through absolute hell and she doesn't want to see it happen again."

"Good point. And yeah, I've seen Jade hit the bottom, and I never want to see her hurt like that again."

The conversation switched gears, and the attendees started sharing about their week. When it came time for Jade to talk, she simply stated that Brianna had been at Amy's parents and she had been looking for creative ways to keep herself busy. The whole group turned and looked at her. Jade, realizing how her phrasing could have been taken, started to blush.

"Nice one Jade," Kristel teased as they were cleaning up after group.

"It sounded better in my head."

"I bet it did," said Skye, giving Jade a mischievous smile. "So, what creative ways have you found to keep busy?"

"Skye, behave," warned Rachel under her breath, glancing toward the door and seeing Carmen standing there.

Skye and Kristel followed her line of sight and saw Carmen watching them from the door. They got the hint.

The four walked out of the building and Rachel saw that Carmen's car was still in the lot.

"Carmen is still here," said Rachel, shaking Kristel's hand. Rachel also mentioned it to Skye as she hugged her and said that Jade was coming over after she dropped Kristel off. Rachel had noticed Carmen's car frequently in the same places as she was. She mentioned this to Skye, whose face showed her unease at hearing this information.

"Rach, you're going to Jade's tonight. Then, I'm calling my ex, and he is going to actually do something useful and find out what the hell is going on with Carmen," said Skye, and everyone agreed.

The group left and Carmen followed as they suspected. She followed Rachel to her house, and then Rachel saw Carmen watching the house. Rachel packed a bag as Skye had told her to do, and exited out the back of her house. Jade picked her up on the next street. Jade pulled into the garage to ensure that as they entered the house there was no chance of anyone seeing that Jade wasn't alone.

Chapter Twenty-three

Time Together

That was creepy," said Jade while she and Rachel made their way up to her bedroom.

"Yeah, it was. I wonder what her deal is."

"Sweetie," Jade said, wrapping her arms around Rachel's waist and pulling her against her body, their lips millimeters apart. "She likes you in a way in which I'm not willing to share you."

Rachel caught up to what Jade meant and smiled briefly before she felt Jade's lips on hers. They stood there kissing for a long minute before Jade broke the kiss and, taking Rachel's hand, walked them over to the bed. They changed into their pajamas and crawled into bed.

"Come here, sweetie," Jade said, opening her arms for Rachel to cuddle in.

Rachel swiftly moved into Jade's arms and felt them close around her. She enjoyed being held by her. Rachel wrapped an arm across Jade's waist and held on to her as well.

"Are you okay with me staying?" asked Rachel, breaking the silence.

"I wouldn't have agreed to Skye's idea if I wasn't, sweetie," said Jade, kissing the top of Rachel's head.

"I'm sorry I couldn't warn you that Skye was there. She blindsided me."

"Like I said at the meeting, I've met Skye, and I know it wasn't your fault. What's going through your mind, Rach?"

"I'm afraid I'm pushing you into something that you'll regret."

"You aren't. Do I feel some guilt? Yes. Is it your fault? No. Kristel pointed out to me earlier that it is going to take time for me to be one hundred percent okay with someone who isn't Amy. She was my wife. Do I want to risk losing you and what we have between us? Not at all. I can't explain how right it feels when we are together, it just feels right."

"I understand the feeling." Rachel's hand started to rub along Jade's stomach. "When I am with you it feels right. Is there something that I can do to help with the guilt?"

"Be patient with me," said Jade.

"Always. I can't say that I won't need you to be patient with me, too," Rachel said, lowering her eyes.

"Hey, look at me." Jade lifted Rachel's chin. "If this is going to work, we need be equals and supportive of one another."

"I agree, but baby, sometimes my mind goes into overdrive."

"And when it does, talk to me," said Jade, pulling Rachel's hand from her stomach and kissed the back of it.

"I promise," Rachel said, leaning up and kissing Jade.

"Rach, can you make me one more promise?"

"What's that?"

"The one thing I've missed since Amy died is cuddling. Can you promise me lots of cuddles?"

"You have my word. I promise you lots and lots

of cuddles for as long as you want me."

They lay down and kissed for a while before cuddling together and drifting off to sleep.

❧❧❧

Jade woke to the sound of her phone buzzing on the nightstand. She reached out and grabbed her phone and saw it was a message from Alice. When she opened the message she saw it contained a picture of Brianna on a horse. Jade smiled and placed the phone back on the nightstand before leaning back into Rachel's embrace.

"Are you okay?" asked Rachel.

"Yeah, Alice sent a picture of Bri on a horse and it reminded me of the first time Amy took me to the stables and convinced me to go riding."

"So, you aren't a regular rider?"

"No. That was Amy's thing. Are you a rider?" Jade turned in Rachel's arms to face her.

"Hell no! I avoid big arm- and finger-biting animals," said Rachel as Jade started to chuckle.

Rachel pouted and Jade's resolve crumble as she leaned forward, closing the distance between them and brushing their lips together. This sent shockwaves through Rachel's body and she moved closer to Jade and pressed their lips together again.

"You know that pout is unfair," Jade said.

Rachel smirked "It isn't that it's unfair, it's that you are powerless over it."

"What time do you have to be at work?"

"I don't. Fridays are my light days, and most of the time I don't see clients, I just work on paperwork. What about you?"

"Well, I was thinking of messaging my secretary and not going in today. The weather is supposed to be nice, so it might be a good day to just relax. If you don't have plans or a better offer would you care to join me?"

"Hmmm, going home and spending the day alone or doing paperwork, or, spending the day with a beautiful woman…"

"It's the paperwork isn't it?" teased Jade.

"How could you ever doubt that?" Rachel teased back and started to laugh.

Jade couldn't resist and rolled Rachel onto her back pinning her to the bed, lying on top of her lover.

"Now what are you going to do?" asked Jade, feeling the desire rising inside her.

"This," said Rachel, wrapping her arms around Jade's neck and pulling her into a deep, toe-curling kiss.

They continued to kiss and got lost in the feeling of their bodies molding together. It wasn't long before clothes were removed and playful noises were replaced with lust-filled moans.

❧❧❧

Rachel and Jade were cuddled together on a deck chair enjoying the quietness of the day and their time together.

"I could get use to this," said Jade.

"Me, too," Rachel said, smiling back. "Did you and Amy spend a lot of time out here?"

"We loved to be out here, especially with Brianna."

"I want to hear all about your life, and Brianna's,"

said Rachel. "I hope that didn't come across as too creepy."

"It didn't. And I want to hear all about your life, too." Jade kissed the top of Rachel's head.

"What were you like as a kid?"

"A lot like Brianna actually. I was curious and adventurous, but very sensitive to others' feelings. I remember my mother always telling me that she wished she could give me the world my heart was made for," started Jade, seeing a confused look on Rachel's face. "I could never understand why people had to be mean and cruel to others. Why they couldn't just respect individualism."

"That is pretty intense for a kid," smiled Rachel.

"Yeah, well, my brother and my father reminded me often that being mean and cruel were a part of the world and I needed to accept it. My mother did her best to shelter me from it, but like Bri, I was perceptive and knew the truth."

"I think this is the first time I've heard you mention your family."

"I don't associate with them anymore. My mother died when I was a teenager, and my brother and father want nothing to do with me because I'm gay. They phrase it with more ignorance, but that is the gist of it."

"I'm sorry to hear that," Rachel said, kissing Jade's cheek. "It's their loss."

"I'm grateful that I was able to come out to my mom before she passed away. She knew the real me."

"I'm glad you got to do that, too. Were you good in school or at sports?"

"I was quiet in school, but my grades were good. I went to college on a full academic scholarship. I got my BFA and then Amy encouraged me to continue on to get my MFA.”

“Wow, that is impressive. So, when you say you love art, you really mean it. When did you meet Amy?”

“In college. We knew each other casually in our first year, but we didn’t start dating until the middle of our second year. Amy for a long time just assumed I was innocent and naive.”

“You mean you aren’t?” teased Rachel.

Jade turned, and with her mouth millimeters from Rachel’s ear, lustfully said, “If I were, do you think we could have made one another feel so good the past two mornings?” Feeling Rachel shudder at the feel of Jade’s breath on her ear and hearing the groan she made from her words made Jade smile internally as she ran her tongue around the outside of her ear.

Rachel’s breathing became ragged and her eyes floated closed at the feel of Jade’s breath on her ear. Hearing the words Jade was saying made her heart speed up, and feeling Jade’s tongue tracing her ear was almost too much to handle. Rachel was helpless and could only whimper in response.

“You okay, sweetie?” Jade chuckled as she took Rachel’s earlobe between her teeth.

“You are anything but innocent and naive. Where did you learn to be such a tease?”

“Natural talent.”

They lay there sharing soft kisses for a bit before Jade got up to make them lunch. After eating they went inside and lay on the couch facing one another.

“What were you like as a kid?” Jade finally asked Rachel.

Rachel laughed. “I was a massive spazz.”

“So, the same as you are now,” teased Jade.

"Watch it, you." Rachel poked Jade in the side. "When I was really little I was similar to you and Brianna. I was inquisitive and always seeking to understand more than I needed to understand. My parents were always working and away. I was raised mostly by a nanny. You've seen those shows on television with the nanny from England that turns the troubled children into perfect angels? Well, that was what my nanny was like."

"I'm sorry, Rach. No kid should have to have absentee parents," said Jade, kissing Rachel's forehead.

"Nana, as I called her, always made me feel like I was her own kid and so loved. I never felt like I was missing out with my parents being away. That's bad to say, but true. Nana developed psychological issues as I got older which is why I went into the mental health field. As a teen, I was a computer geek. I was in all of the advanced and honors classes. I graduated from high school as valedictorian. My parents paid my full way through college. I guess it was their way of easing the guilt of not being in my life."

"That isn't right. They were missing out on such an amazing woman. I guess I shouldn't assume, but they still aren't a part of your life, are they?"

"I haven't talked to them since I was in my first year of college. They set up a trust fund and my schooling was paid through that. The deal was as long as I kept a straight-A or high-B average they would pay. I did receive a sympathy card from them when Emily died. I didn't even know they knew about her until Skye told me that Emily had sent them a wedding invitation and then a baby notice when we found out she was having a little girl."

"Well, at least they sent a card. Amy and I always

agreed that we were going to be hands-on parents, involved in our kids' lives whether they liked it or not."

"That's one of the things that make you such an incredible mother. You're always thinking about what is best for Brianna and how your choices affect her."

Rachel looked into Jade's eyes and saw tears form as she was speaking, and yet she was also blushing at the words.

"Rach, I have my flaws," said Jade.

"Who doesn't? One major flaw you have at the moment is you haven't kissed me in several minutes."

Jade smiled at the woman lying before her and brought their lips together. Jade gently pulled Rachel's lower lip between hers and sucked on it. She felt Rachel groan and move even closer. Their bodies were now pressed together and they enjoyed the feeling of contentment that came from their touching.

❧❧❧❧

After a lengthy and thorough make-out session on the couch, Rachel and Jade decided that they would go over to Rachel's and spend the night there before they headed to Amy's parents' house for dinner on Saturday. Jade insisted on getting cleaned up before they left.

While Jade showered and got ready, Rachel looked through one of the photo albums that they had started on the anniversary of Amy's passing. This album had mostly pictures of Brianna. Rachel smiled seeing the pictures of Amy pregnant and she thought of Emily and how she looked. They were both glowing while they were carrying their little girls. There was a page that showed Jade, Amy, and Brianna all when they each were first born. Rachel was surprised to see how much Brianna looked like Jade. She knew that they had used Jade's egg, but it was almost like looking at a mirror image. Rachel started to wonder if her daughter would have looked as much like her when she was born.

Jade entered the room and saw Rachel wiping away a stray tear before closing the album and pinching the bridge of her nose to try to stop the tears from flowing.

"What's going on in that pretty head?" Jade knelt in front of Rachel and moved the photo album out of their way.

"It's just a bunch of 'what ifs' and speculation," said Rachel, feeling Jade's hands rubbing up her thighs.

"Hey, sweetie. Talk to me," Jade said again. This time she leaned in and pressed her forehead to Rachel's.

"I was looking at the pictures of you, Amy, and Bri from when you were first born. Bri was a carbon copy of you. It got me wondering if my daughter would have looked that much like me if she had been born. Would she have had red hair or green eyes like me? Would she have had brown hair and blue eyes like Emily?"

"Aw, sweetie. I can tell you one thing for certain. She would have been beautiful."

Rachel let Jade hold her while she allowed herself this slight breakdown. Rachel hadn't truly realized how being around Jade and Brianna had affected her.

Once Rachel felt she had allowed herself enough time to dwell in her thoughts, she closed them up again and Jade put the album away before they got ready to leave. Before they walked out of the door, Jade pulled Rachel close and kissed her softly and reminded her of how much she truly cared for her and how grateful she was that she was a part of her life.

Rachel and Jade stopped to pick up something for dinner so that they didn't have to think about cooking. Rachel was happy to have Jade with her, holding her hand while they made their way to her house. She also knew that she was going to need some serious cuddles to get past the mind trip she had gone on with the "what ifs."

❧ ❧ ❧ ❧

As Rachel and Jade neared Rachel's house Jade noticed a familiar car parked in front of the house. She pulled onto a side street and answered Rachel's confused look by pointing toward the house. Rachel saw the car and groaned. She picked up her phone and messaged Skye. Within minutes Skye had messaged back telling Rachel and Jade to stay put, and that she and her ex were on their way. The pair watched the house and waited.

Rachel jumped when Skye knocked on her window, causing Skye to laugh.

"That wasn't funny," Rachel said, rolling down the window.

"Yeah it was," said Skye, smiling at Jade. "Hi, Jade."

"Hey, Skye," said Jade, as she squeezed Rachel's hand, offering her support. Jade received a weak smile from Rachel. She knew that her lover was still dealing with her emotions from the photo album.

"Dan and I are going to follow you over there,

and he's going to have a chat with Carmen."

"Okay." Jade watched Skye go back to her car and then the two cars proceeded down the road to Rachel's driveway. Jade and Rachel pulled in and Skye and her ex Dan pulled in behind them.

❧❧❧❧

"You don't have to get out until we've dealt with her," Rachel said, looking over at Jade.

"Rach, if we are portraying our relationship as only friends or if we allow people to see us as a couple, I'm standing by your side no matter what."

"I just don't want you or Brianna to have to deal with a psychopath because of me," said Rachel, averting her eyes.

Jade knew that Rachel was vulnerable right now and she needed to help her feel protected.

"Sweetie, I chose to be here and I choose to deal with her in any way that I need to." Jade leaned over and kissed Rachel softly. "Now let's go deal with Carmen so we can get inside, have dinner, and then I can have you wrapped in my arms."

"Thank you," said Rachel, offering Jade a warm smile.

❧❧❧❧

Rachel, Skye, and Dan exited the cars. Jade followed after a few seconds. Carmen walked up toward them.

"What the hell? I thought you didn't date people from your group," Carmen said, anger in her voice.

"What are you doing here, Carmen?" asked

Rachel tiredly.

"I wanted to talk. I was having some issues dealing with stuff."

"I don't appreciate you just showing up at my house."

"Well, Princess Jade is here at your house."

"I was invited," said Jade.

"Carmen, you already have restraining orders from three others, let's not make this an issue here," said Dan, speaking for the first time.

"How do you know that?" asked Carmen.

"I'm a police detective. I know that you followed Rachel last night, and you're waiting out here tonight. Not to mention that your car has been seen in several places that Rachel has been. And no, I don't believe in coincidence. Leave them alone, Carmen."

Skye was standing off to the side but was ready to step in front of her sister-in-law at a moment's notice. Jade, after speaking up, had stepped to Rachel's side, but was at a respectable distance.

"I-I-I'm sorry," said Carmen narrowing her eyes at Jade. "Better not break her heart, bitch."

Jade looked at Rachel and then stepped in front of her, squaring off with Carmen.

"You don't have to worry about her getting hurt by me. That's between Rachel and me."

"I...will make you regret it if you hurt her, remember that."

Jade took another step forward and was now within a foot of Carmen.

"Do not threaten me. First, it makes you look like an idiot because Dan already stated he's a cop and you have a history with restraining orders. Second, I can guarantee Rachel isn't the type to find that attractive.

Third, you have no clue what I am capable of, but I promise you that you do not scare me."

Carmen stood there in silence, staring Jade down. Skye was trying to contain her laughter. Dan was assessing the situation. And Rachel was becoming very turned on by Jade defending her, but she was also very concerned that something would happen to her girlfriend.

"Carmen, please, just leave," said Rachel, walking up and taking Jade's hand. Jade took the hint, backed up a step and wrapped an arm around Rachel's waist.

Carmen watched Rachel and Jade for another minute before turning and walking to her car and driving off.

"You okay?" asked Skye, putting a hand on Rachel's shoulder.

"Yeah, it's just been an emotional afternoon," Rachel said tiredly. Rachel turned and said thank you to Dan, smiled again at Skye, and reached out her hand for Jade.

"Go inside, I'll be there in a minute, sweetie," said Jade, kissing the side of Rachel's head and turned to Skye.

"Okay," said Rachel, grabbing the food and going inside.

Skye turned to Jade.

"She was looking at a photo album while I was getting ready and she started thinking about Emily and the baby."

"Do you want me to stay?"

"No, but thank you. Also, thank Dan for us. My gut tells me that we haven't seen the last of Carmen, but tonight I think we're okay."

"Rachel has amazing taste in women. First, she

gets my sister, and now you. Thank you, Jade."

"She is easy to care about." Jade looked toward the house. "I should get in there."

"Call if either of you need anything." Skye hugged Jade and then went and got in the car with Dan.

Jade looked to the door and took a deep breath and headed into the house to comfort her girlfriend.

Chapter Twenty-four

In-Laws

Once Jade went inside, the couple ate in silence, both processing what had gone on outside and what it could mean for the future and for them as a couple. Rachel cleaned up after dinner and Jade thought about what she could do to help Rachel.

They called Brianna quickly and told her that they were both looking forward to seeing her the next day, and that she would be coming home and Olaf missed her.

"Sweetie, what can I do to help?" Jade finally asked as Rachel came back into the living room after refreshing their drinks.

"Just be here and near me," said Rachel, allowing Jade to wrap her arms around her.

"I have an idea," said Jade, pulling away from Rachel for a moment. "If it's too much or a bad idea, just let me know, but I think it may help."

Rachel wasn't sure what Jade had in mind, but she was willing to do whatever she wanted. She felt so close and connected after all that had transpired over the past week, and especially the past couple of hours.

Jade led Rachel into her bedroom and sat her down on the bed. Grabbing two candles off the dresser, Jade disappeared into the bathroom. Rachel heard the water running in the tub and after several minutes,

Jade emerged.

Jade had a soft smile on her face as she walked over and slowly started to undress Rachel. She started by unbuttoning Rachel's shirt and easing it off her shoulders and down her arms. After setting the shirt on the bed, Jade moved to take Rachel's bra off. Seeing Rachel's eyes glisten told Jade this was what she needed. She needed to feel close and connected, Jade knelt down between Rachel's legs and carefully unbuttoned and unzipped Rachel's pants. She smiled when she saw Rachel lean back and lift her hips to allow her access to remove Rachel's pants and underwear. Jade slipped Rachel's socks off, and then with what was supposed to be a glance but turned into more of a leer, she looked up and down the now-naked body splayed out before her. Jade saw Rachel's eyes fixated on her, she carefully stood, and slowly removed her clothes until she too was naked. She heard Rachel's breath catch.

Reaching her hand out and feeling Rachel take it, Jade helped Rachel up and led her into the candlelit bathroom. Jade got into the tub and extended a hand as an invitation. Rachel took the invite and eased herself into the tub and leaned backward, feeling Jade's breasts make contact with her back. Jade wrapped her arms around Rachel's waist and while holding her close, gently pressed her lips to her neck and shoulder. Rachel couldn't stop as a moan of enjoyment escaped her lips.

"Relax and let me take care of you. The only thing that exists right now is us."

"Jade, this is amazing. I've never taken a romantic bath like this with someone before."

"Then I will make this extra special for you," Jade

said in a sultry voice as she felt Rachel give herself over to her touch.

Jade's lips returned to gently brushing across Rachel's skin. She kissed from Rachel's shoulder to the crook of her neck, lingering on the pulse point as she felt it speed up. Jade's lips slowly nipped up Rachel's neck and took her earlobe in her mouth and sucked on it.

"Ohhh," moaned Rachel as she leaned more into Jade's embrace.

Jade continued to lavish her lover's neck and earlobe with attention while she slowly brought a hand up to massage her pert breasts. Jade felt Rachel inhale deeply as her water-warmed hand came in contact with Rachel's very erect nipples. Jade could feel her own nipples harden as she touched Rachel. Jade groaned at the way that Rachel was responding to her touch.

Rachel adjusted to allow more access to her neck and breasts. Jade took advantage of the newly acquired room to drop the hand that had been around Rachel's waist to between her legs. With Jade's hand between her legs, Rachel seemed as though she couldn't resist any longer and turned her head and captured Jade's lips with her own as Jade was moving to nibble on her earlobe. Rachel brought a hand around to hold Jade's lips to her own as she felt one of Jade's fingers tease her by slipping inside her partially, and then back out slowly.

"Oh...baby..." moaned Rachel into Jade's lips. "Yessss."

Jade, encouraged by Rachel's hip movements, slid slowly inside her again. This time Jade didn't stop partway. She allowed Rachel to feel her delve inside.

Rachel moaned again. Jade stilled, halting while still deep inside Rachel. She used her other hand to tease Rachel's nipples again.

"Oh god...don't stop...please don't stop..." croaked Rachel, her voice becoming hoarse with lust and need.

"I...it feels too good...for me to stop," panted Jade as she eased a second finger inside Rachel and started to move them in and out, hitting Rachel's special spot each time she entered her. With each thrust Jade pinched Rachel's nipples and sucked on her lower lip.

"I...ohhhh...so...yes...Jade...close," panted Rachel as she allowed Jade to take her into oblivion.

Once Rachel's shudders stopped, she leaned limply against Jade.

"Wow. I can't say that I will ever think of a bath the same way again," giggled Rachel. "Thank you for being such an incredible woman."

Jade smiled as Rachel turned her head and kissed her.

"You are very special and mean a lot to me. I hope you know that."

Rachel smiled. "I not only know it, I feel it. I don't think I can walk back to bed, though."

Jade pulled the stopper with her foot and let the water out of the tub. As it was draining she slipped out of the tub and dried herself off. She bent over the edge of the tub and dried Rachel as best she could before picking her up and cradling her in her arms, walking them back to the bed.

"No need to walk," said Jade, pulling Rachel into her arms and kissed her softly.

They drifted off to sleep, both exhausted from the day, the wine, the bath, and the lovemaking.

ᔕ ᔕ ᔕ ᔕ

Rachel and Jade had slept in and spent the day cuddling, reading, and watching a romantic movie. Rachel was nervous about the dinner and Jade had been trying to convince her that there was nothing to be nervous about. They were going to continue to allow people to think that they were just friends for a while longer. They wanted to make sure that Brianna was okay with them being a couple before everyone else was brought into the loop.

Jade had showered first and had just finished getting dressed as Rachel exited the bathroom wearing just a towel.

"I know it was my idea for us to shower separately, but damn, you look sexy in that towel," said Jade, using the towel to pull Rachel closer so she could kiss her.

"Mmmm, if I look sexy in the towel, how do I look without it," teased Rachel, dropping the towel and stepping just outside of Jade's reach.

"Good enough to eat," Jade said, licking her lips sensually, causing Rachel to close her eyes and try to tame down her hormones.

"That was not fair," mumbled Rachel as Jade's phone rang. Jade answered and Rachel listened to Jade's side of the conversation.

"Hey Alice…Is Brianna okay?…When did this happen?…We'll meet you there. We are a little farther away, but yes, fine, I will have Rachel drive. I agree, we don't need an accident to go along with things. We'll be there as soon as we can."

By the time Jade hung up, Rachel was fully

dressed and had her hair pulled back, ready to leave.

"What's going on?" asked Rachel.

"Bri got stung by a bee earlier and is having an allergic reaction. Bo and Alice are taking her to the hospital," Jade said, shaking. Rachel hurried over to her and wrapped her into a hug.

"She is going to be fine, baby. I'll drive. What hospital?"

"The Children's Hospital on Lake. I'm glad they live close to it," said Jade as Rachel kissed the side of her head. They grabbed their stuff and got into Rachel's car. "Are you sure you want to take your car? What if she gets sick after we pick her up?"

"I'm positive, and if she gets sick I will get it detailed. I don't care about the car, Jade. I care about you and Brianna."

Jade smiled as Rachel pulled her hand up and kissed the back of it.

Rachel pulled up to the hospital entrance before going to find a spot in the ramp. She told Jade that it was more important that she get in and be with Brianna. Jade smiled at Rachel and then exited the car and went inside to find her daughter.

"Hi, my daughter was brought in a few minutes ago. Brianna Donovan," Jade said to the nurse working the emergency window.

"What for? Who brought her in?" asked the nurse.

"She was brought in by her grandparents for an allergic reaction to a bee sting," Jade said, starting to get frantic.

"Jade, let me," Rachel said as she arrived in the waiting room, placing a hand on Jade's lower back. "Her daughter..." started Rachel but was interrupted when she heard an older woman say Jade's name.

"Never mind, that's her mother-in-law."

Jade and Rachel raced over to Alice who had just come through a heavy looking set of doors.

"Alice, how is she?" asked Jade, her voice quivering.

"She's this way." Alice turned and led the two newly arrived women through the heavy doors and down a long corridor. Brianna's room was on the left. Since this was a children's hospital each room had a special theme. Brianna's room was a monkey theme.

"Mama?" Brianna said tiredly as they entered the room. Jade raced to her daughter's side and kissed her gently on the head.

"I'm right here, Baby Girl," Jade said, pulling her daughter into her arms while still being mindful of the tubes that were attached to her. Her nerves were shot from the shock of the ordeal and the memories of Amy being in the hospital. Jade let some tears roll down her face.

"Hi, I'm Dr. Ashe," said the woman as she entered the room. "How are you feeling Brianna?"

"Better."

"Hi, Rachel. Good to see you. And who do we have here?" asked the doctor as she looked at Jade after receiving a nod from Rachel.

"This is my Mama."

"Hi, I'm Jade Donovan," Jade said, extracting herself from Brianna and shook the doctors hand.

"It is nice to meet you. Brianna had a moderate to severe allergic reaction to a bee sting. We've given her some antihistamines and fluids through the IV. Her oxygen stats are improving and the swelling in her arm is going down. She is going to be fine. Has she ever had something like this happen before?"

"She's never been stung before," said Jade, shaking her head.

"Well, going forward I am going to prescribe an EpiPen just in case she gets stung again and there is a rapid onset of symptoms. It's strictly a precaution. She's going to need to be here a few more hours for observation."

"But she is and will be fine, right?" asked Jade as Rachel placed a hand on her back.

"Jade, why don't you let me talk to Dr. Ashe and you go hold Brianna? It'll make you feel better," Rachel said softly and received a smile from Jade.

"Rachel, you aren't leaving are you?" asked Brianna, seeing the doctor and Rachel turning toward the door.

"No, sweetie, I'm just going to step out with the doctor and talk to her while you and Mama cuddle," said Rachel, smiling at both Brianna and Jade.

⚶⚶⚶⚶

Rachel and Dr. Ashe exited the room to discuss Brianna's condition and the future possibilities of something like this happening again. During the discussion, Rachel frequently looked in the window at Jade and Brianna and smiled seeing Jade finally start to relax.

"I'm sorry what?" asked Rachel, realizing that she had missed the question.

"I asked if that was your girlfriend and daughter."

"No, Jade is in my grief support group. She lost her partner coming up on two years ago."

"She's a cute little girl," stated the doctor.

"She is, and she is very sweet."

"Well, I won't keep you. I'll be back to check on Brianna in about an hour. If you need anything before then just call the nurse."

Rachel thanked the doctor again and then quietly entered the room.

"What'd she say?" asked Jade, Brianna curled up in her arms.

"She'll be back in an hour to check on Bri, but if we need anything before then to just call the nurse."

"That's good, but I meant about the reaction," Jade said, smiling.

"She said that Bri is going to be fine and that she doesn't need the bubble you are already trying to figure out where to buy."

"Shush you," Jade said, sticking her tongue out at Rachel. "By the way, these are Amy's parents, Bo and Alice. If you two haven't guessed, this is Rachel."

Greetings were exchanged by all three adults.

"Rachel, if you don't mind me asking, how do you and Dr. Ashe know each other?" asked Alice.

"Sometimes being a therapist means that I have to come and meet with patients while they're in the hospital. I did my internship at a children's hospital and I affiliated myself with this one when Emily and I moved to town."

"So, does that mean you come and counsel kids?" asked Bo.

"Unfortunately, yes. And the hard part is that it happens more often than most people imagine," Rachel said, lowering her head and looked at her feet.

"Rachel, can you come here?" asked Brianna, sitting up from her mother's embrace.

Rachel walked over to the edge of the bed and Brianna hugged her. They stayed like that for a minute. When they broke the hug Brianna curled back up on Jade's lap, and Rachel sat on the edge of the bed as Brianna told her and Jade about her day. After Dr. Ashe came in for her next check on Brianna, the little girl had fallen asleep.

"Jade, can we talk to you in the hall for a moment?" asked Alice.

"Sure," said Jade, glancing at Rachel.

"I'll be here with her," Rachel said, comforting Jade with her words and tone. Once Jade got up, Rachel moved to lie next to Brianna so that she would still have the feel of someone next to her.

❧❧❧❧

Jade followed the older couple outside, but she wouldn't go farther than the window, wanting to keep an eye on her daughter. Bo and Alice were standing together and they both had a concerned look on their face.

"Jade, what is the real relationship between you and Rachel?" asked Alice.

"She's a friend of mine," Jade said dryly.

"You spent a lot of time together this week. It seemed like every time you called Brianna she was there," said Bo. "I don't recall you spending that much time with Kristel in the past."

"We did spend more time than we usually do because this was the first time since Amy died that Bri has been gone more than a night. Do either of you have any idea how big and lonely that house feels when you're there alone? When the love of your life isn't just working or taking your daughter to her parents'? She is gone, never coming back. I was accepting that and as Kristel put it when I had dinner with her, I was trying to move forward for the sake of our daughter. I'm not moving on and forgetting Amy, I'm moving forward to learn how not to spend every night grieving. I can't believe that either of you would choose now of all times to bring this up. Brianna is lying in that room after suffering what could have been a life-threatening bee sting."

"We are just looking out for our granddaughter," said Alice.

"And again you question my parenting skills, and my values and ethics. I'm going to say this once. That little girl in there is my world. If she told me to stay home and not associate with anyone I would do it to keep her happy, but she adores Rachel and wants her around."

"Jade, she's five years old. She isn't old enough to know better," Alice sneered.

"You are, so what's your excuse?"

"I don't understand what you're talking about."

"You seem to be under the delusion that I have forgotten my years with Amy, forgotten what it was like to love her, to be loved by her. I haven't, but unfortunately fate decided to rob me and Brianna of her and our future together as a family. If I could give you your daughter back I would. If I could trade places with Amy, I would, but I can't. I'm just trying to make the best of what I have left. And what I have left is Brianna. Now, if you'll excuse me, my daughter needs me."

With that Jade turned and walked back into the room, leaving the older couple standing there dumbfounded.

❧ ❧ ❧ ❧

"Jade?" asked Rachel when the woman entered severely upset.

"Monday revisited," was all Jade said. Rachel got up from beside Brianna and allowed Jade to take her spot back.

"I'll be right back," said Rachel as she left the room and Jade held her daughter close. "May I have a word with you two?"

"I'm not sure this is the right time," Alice said.

"I think it is the perfect time. You seemed to think that it was a fine time to pull Jade away from her daughter, I think you each owe me at least five or ten minutes," she snapped.

Rachel led the older couple to a consultation room so that she didn't have to worry about bothering any families.

"What is your issue with me?" Rachel asked bluntly.

"I don't understand why you think we have an issue with you," said Bo.

"Well, you have attacked Jade twice because of me. Have I done something that offended either of you?"

"We weren't attacking her," said Alice.

"Bullshit. I am a therapist and I can read lips. I know exactly what you said to her and what she said to you. Would you like to try answering my question again, truthfully?"

"We don't owe you anything," said Bo.

"You are correct, you don't owe me a damn thing, but you owe that woman and that little girl your love and trust. Jade has done nothing but love your daughter and work to keep her memory alive so that Brianna knows her Mommy loved her and wouldn't have left her if she had a choice. Jade has isolated herself most of the time since Amy's death. If it weren't for Kristel pushing her to come to my group, I don't know that Jade would still be here. Maybe that is what you want, but that is NOT what is best for Brianna. I also have no doubt in my mind that if Jade could trade places with Amy and give you your daughter back she would do it in a heartbeat. She loves Amy and she loves Brianna, but not a day goes by that she doesn't feel the guilt of being the one left alive. Would either of you trade places with Amy if you could?"

"Of course," the older couple said in unison.

"Then why is it so hard for you to believe that Jade wouldn't do the same? She has spent over a year and a half shouldering that guilt—alone. I was able to get through to her in the past couple of weeks and get her to see she doesn't have to be alone. There is no shame in letting someone else help you. I'm not trying to take your daughter's place; nobody can. I am trying to be a friend to those two because they not only deserve it, they need it."

"You seem to care more than professionalism should allow," commented Alice.

"That's because I do. Jade has become a friend of mine. How well did you know her before Amy got sick?"

"We knew her well. We were family. Why?" asked Bo.

"I was just curious because we see two different women and I was wondering why. I believe now that it is because you place blame on her for not being the one to get sick and die."

"I, we..." started Alice before she seemed to realize that what Rachel was saying was true. They did blame Jade.

"It's natural to blame the surviving spouse that is not your child. If Amy would have been the one to survive, you'd feel guilty for being thankful that it was Jade instead. Did you seek counseling after Amy's death?"

Bo's eyes welled with tears. "No."

"I think that it might be helpful, and I think that you might try talking to Jade after you've gotten some help to see if she will go to family counseling with you as well to help to quell this animosity that has built up," suggested Rachel.

"Would you consider seeing us?" asked Alice.

"No, but I can recommend a few people. My reasons are simply that Jade and I have a friendship and it would be a conflict of interest. I also would not see her professionally if she were to ask me to."

"Thank you," said Bo. "We'll apologize to Jade as well."

"Just have faith in her that she loves your daughter and there is no way that she is going to let Brianna forget about Amy and how much Amy loved her. Even if someday Jade meets someone and starts dating again, that isn't going to change how she feels about Amy or that she is Bri's Mommy. If the person she is involved with wants to replace Amy, then she is the wrong person for them," said Rachel.

"You are very good at your job," said Alice, embarrassed.

"Thank you, now please put pettiness aside, and let's go back and support Jade and Brianna. They need us all on their side."

"We agree and we're sorry we didn't give you a chance," said Bo, with genuine emotion.

The trio made their way back to Brianna's room just in time to see Dr. Ashe coming out.

"How is she?" asked Rachel.

"She should be ready to go home soon. I am going to get the prescriptions filled for Jade and then they'll be ready to go."

"Thank you," said Alice and Bo.

Chapter Twenty-five

Double Life

Rachel drove Jade and Brianna back to their house. They decided that Rachel would stay with them and then in the morning have either Kristel or Skye drive Jade's car back to her house. When they arrived at the house, Jade picked up Brianna and carried her up to her room to put her to bed. As Jade stood in the doorway she felt Rachel wrap her arms around her and rest her chin on Jade's shoulder.

"How are you holding up?" asked Rachel.

"I've never been as scared as I was tonight," Jade said, leaning into Rachel's embrace.

"It's understandable. Was this the first time she has been really sick or hurt?"

"Yeah," Jade said, her voice shaking with emotion.

Rachel turned Jade to face her and pulled her into an embrace as she started to cry. Rachel held her even closer.

"Shhh, it's okay. Let it out," said Rachel.

Jade cried on her shoulder for a few minutes before she heard Brianna stir and she didn't want her daughter to see her crying.

"Mama?" Brianna said in a scratchy voice.

"Yeah, sweetie," said Jade as she wiped her eyes quickly.

"When did we get home?"

Jade walked in and sat on the edge of the bed next to Brianna. She rubbed her daughter's back trying to convince herself that it was for her daughter's benefit, but knowing it was equally, or even more, for her own.

"A little while ago. How are you feeling?"

"My arm hurts a little, and I'm tired."

"That's from the medicine they gave you. You just need to sleep and you'll feel better in the morning."

"But I didn't get to see Rachel," said Brianna after yawning.

Jade glanced over to the doorway where Rachel was standing and motioned with her head for Rachel to join them.

Rachel crouched down next to the bed. "I'm right here, Bri. You rest now, and I'll be here in the morning to see you."

"Mama, will you make pancakes in the morning?"

"Whatever you want, I'll make." Jade smiled down at her daughter.

"You're the...best Mama," Brianna said around a yawn.

"I love you, Baby Girl. You go to sleep and I'll check on your later. If you need me I'll be just down the hall."

"I love you, too. Night, Mama. Night, Rachel."

"Good night, Brianna," said Rachel, kissing the top of her head.

Rachel and Jade retired to Jade's room. Rachel pulled Jade back into a hug and held her for a couple of minutes. After they broke apart they moved over to the bed and lay on their sides facing each other.

"Thank you for being here tonight," said Jade, gazing into Rachel's eyes.

"Baby, there is no other place that I could or would have been," said Rachel, leaning over and kissing Jade softly.

The two women kissed for a few minutes before changing for bed. Jade checked on Brianna one last time, and then they crawled into bed, cuddled together and drifted off to sleep.

❧❧❧❧

Jade woke up in the morning and started coffee before going to check on Brianna. She looked in the room and the little girl was still asleep. She went back down the hall to her room and saw Rachel was still asleep as well. Jade set the coffee on the nightstand and curled up next to Rachel and watched her sleep for a few minutes before she saw her start to wake up.

"I smell coffee," Rachel said before even opening her eyes.

"Well, it is good to know that your sense of smell works this morning."

Rachel reached over and pulled Jade close and kissed her softly.

"Good morning," said Rachel. "Sense of touch appears to be working as well."

"Good morning." Jade leaned forward and kissed Rachel again.

"How are you feeling?"

"Better. I know that Brianna is going to be okay and that is what truly matters. I don't know that I could have gotten through last night without you. Thank you."

"I'm glad I was able to be there for you. Have you looked in on Brianna? How is she doing this morning?"

"Yeah, I checked on her just before bringing the coffee in. We should get up and dressed, though. She should be waking up soon and if we are going to keep this between us for a bit yet..."

"Of course," said Rachel, leaning forward and kissing Jade again.

They got dressed and went downstairs to drink their coffee at the island. After about thirty minutes Brianna came down the stairs holding one of her stuffed animals since her two favorites were still at Amy's parents' house.

"Hi, baby," Jade said, walking over and picking her daughter up.

"Morning, Mama," said Brianna around a large yawn before laying her head on Jade's shoulder.

"Good morning, Bri. How are you feeling?" asked Rachel.

"Hi, Rachel. I'm tired, but I feel a lot better than I was at Grandma and Grandpa's."

"That's good."

Jade set Brianna down on the seat next to Rachel and she partially leaned against her. Rachel wrapped her arm around Brianna while Jade started making the pancakes.

"Do we get funny-shaped?"

"Well, do you want funny-shaped or boring rounds?" teased Jade.

Brianna giggled. "Funny-shaped, Mama."

Jade made them breakfast and they ate at the island. Rachel and Brianna watched cartoons while Jade called Kristel to see if she was able to bring her car back from Rachel's. Jade explained about the previous day and the scare that they had. Kristel was hurt that she wasn't notified sooner, but understood that there was a great deal of stress and not a lot of time. She said that she was going to drop Jake off at a sitter's house and then be over.

Jade lurked in the doorway watching Rachel and Brianna watching cartoons. They were sitting side by side on the couch. Brianna was wrapped in a blanket leaning against Rachel. Jade couldn't help but smile. She had seen Amy and Brianna sit like that so many times. Jade was sad that she would never see them like that again, but she was happy that Brianna trusted Rachel enough to allow her close. Through her time in the grief counseling group and then more recently Rachel helping with Amy's anniversary, Jade was pleased with the place Rachel held within their lives.

Rachel glanced over and saw Jade watching them, and smiled at her. Jade smiled back and then walked into the living room and sat down on the couch next to Bri.

"Mama, my arm hurts."

"I know sweetie. Do you want some medicine for it?"

"Um…"

"Brianna, the doctor said it was okay for you to have some. She even gave your Mama some pills for it," said Rachel.

"She did?"

"Yep, I have them in my purse. I'll go get you some." Jade retrieved Brianna's medicine and a juice box. When she returned she gave her daughter two pills to chew and the juice box to wash them down.

"Those didn't taste good Mama."

"I know, but they will help."

They watched television for a bit until Kristel

arrived. She quietly let herself in and saw the three of them in the living room looking cozy and it made her smile. Kristel knocked on the doorframe and Jade turned and smiled at her.

"Auntie Kristel," said Brianna tiredly.

"Hey, kiddo." Kristel cautiously hugged Brianna. "I hear you gave everyone a pretty good scare last night."

"I didn't mean to. A mean bee bit me."

"It was a very mean bee," Rachel said, smiling at Bri.

"Where's Jake?" asked Brianna.

"He's with a sitter. Your Mama left her car at Rachel's so I came to get her keys so I can drive it back here for her."

"Mama, why aren't you driving your own car?"

"Because I want to stay here and keep an eye on you," said Jade, kissing the top of her daughter's head.

"Why? Because of my arm?"

"Exactly."

The four of them sat watching TV for a little bit. Brianna had drifted off to sleep while leaning against Rachel. Jade smiled at the sight. "I'll take her upstairs."

When Jade returned to the living room, they decided that Rachel and Kristel would take Rachel's car to her house so Kristel could retrieve Jade's vehicle.

"Thank you again for last night," Jade said, wrapping her arms around Rachel's waist.

"My pleasure. I'll call you later to see how you and the munchkin are doing."

"Okay," said Jade, kissing Rachel before letting her go.

Kristel smiled. "You and Jade seem to be getting pretty close."

"She's an amazing woman." Rachel tried to hide the blush coloring her face.

"Oh, I know. It's nice to see her smiling again, too."

"Can I ask you a question?"

"What's up?" asked Kristel.

"Do you know Amy's parents at all?"

"A little, but I don't know them real well. Did something happen?"

"They attacked Jade about the status of our relationship, and they again questioned her as a parent."

"Son of a bitch! I need to go knock the shit out of them. When did this happen? Has it happened since Monday?"

"Last night at the hospital," said Rachel.

"Wow, they have incredible timing. Did they not realize that she might be under a bit of stress and worried about her daughter? Ugh!"

"Yeah, I recommended that they get some professional help and after a bit, talk to Jade about doing some group or family counseling."

"And they were okay with that?"

"They seemed open to the idea. We'll have to wait and see if they actually act on it or not."

"That's good. I'm tired of people making her life difficult. She's been through enough."

"I agree."

"So, what is going on with you and Jade? I mean, I know you're trying to build something, but, don't break her heart, please."

"I have no intention of breaking her heart."

"That is good. I like you and Skye, and I would hate to have to ruin both of your lives for hurting my best friend," Kristel said, smiling over at Rachel.

"I care a lot about Jade. I can honestly say I've never met anyone like her before. Well, Brianna is a lot like her, but that's just an added bonus."

"You really are good for them. I'm glad you found one another."

"Me, too."

"So, you don't have to answer this, but do you think you could fall in love with Jade?"

"Yeah, I do," Rachel answered honestly as they pulled into her driveway. "I won't rush anything for either of us, though. Brianna needs that stability and to trust that someone in her life isn't going to leave again."

"Thank you," Kristel said, leaning over and hugging Rachel.

❧❧❧❧

After retrieving Jade's car from Rachel's house, Kristel drove it back and found Jade seated in the living room.

"Hey."

"Hey," said Jade, smiling at her friend.

"Can we talk?"

"Should I be scared?"

"No. Rachel and I talked on the way over to her house and I want to know what your thoughts and feelings are about what's going on with you two," said Kristel.

"I care a lot about her, but honestly, Kristel, it

has only been like two weeks.”

“Yes and no. You may have only been physical or ‘dating’ for that timeframe, but you have been building this for several months.”

“True. I care about her. I’m happier when she is around than when she isn’t. I love watching her and Bri together. She is always so caring with her.”

“Do you think that’s because she is a therapist or because genuinely she cares?”

“Genuine. There is nothing clinical about how she interacts with Bri. I can tell that Brianna trusts her as well.”

“She trusts her now because she doesn’t know that you two are dating. That’s going to be different for her. She’s going to need to be reassured that Rachel isn’t here to replace Amy.”

“I know, and I would never want anyone to replace Amy. She will always have a part of my heart and be the one that gave me the most precious piece of my life. She gave me Brianna.”

“I’m happy for you, Jade.”

“You talked to Rachel about this didn’t you?” asked Jade, narrowing her eyes.

“Yes, and don’t worry, it was the same favorable feedback. She cares a lot about you and Brianna.”

Just as they were about to take the discussion deeper, they heard little feet coming down the stairs.

“Mama?”

“Over here, Baby Girl,” said Jade, opening her arms for Brianna to curl up in them. “How are you feeling?”

“I’m still tired, but I miss Mr. Butters and Captain Quackers.”

“Well, why don’t we call Grandma and Grandpa

and see if they would like to come over for dinner and if they will bring them home for you."

"Thank you, Mama," Brianna said, yawning.

"I'm going to take off. If you need anything, please let me know," said Kristel, hugging Brianna and Jade.

"Bye, Auntie Kristel."

"Thank you again, for everything."

"We're family, Jade, of course!"

Once Kristel was gone, Jade called and invited Bo and Alice over. They said they would love to come and they would bring Brianna's stuff with them. Jade pulled out Brianna's movie collection and Brianna predictably chose *Frozen* to watch while cuddled up to her Mama.

❧ ❧ ❧ ❧

Just as Rachel walked into the house her phone started to ring. She smiled when she saw the Caller ID and saw it was Skye.

"Hello?" answered Rachel as she set her keys and purse down on the table and curled up in her favorite chair in the living room.

"So? How'd it go?" asked Skye.

"Ugh," groaned Rachel.

"That good? Talk to me, Rachel."

"Amy's parents called as we were getting ready to leave and said that Bri had been stung by a bee, and they were taking her to the hospital."

"Oh no. Is she okay?" asked a concerned Skye.

"Yeah, but it was scary for a while."

"I bet. You got to spend time with Jade and Brianna, though. That had to be awesome."

"Oh, it was. Right up to the point where Amy's parents started grilling Jade about our relationship and insinuating that she is a bad mother."

"Wow, did you step in?"

"I had a chat with them and used a bit of my psychology mind tricks to help them realize that they were blaming Jade for being the one alive instead of Amy. I talked them into getting help."

"That's good," said Skye. "So, was Jade okay with what you did?"

"Yeah, she was fine with it. She was more concerned about Brianna, and that's how it should have been. I spent the night with her and I was just getting home when you called."

"So, does Brianna know that you're seeing her mother?"

"No, we're still playing the friends card there. I want to build a relationship with Brianna in addition to mine with Jade. I need to figure out something that we can do, so that I can spend time with them."

"Why not take them on a hike? You've been meaning to take the kids out again," suggested Skye.

"Hey, that is a great idea."

"I know, I thought of it. That makes it an awesome idea."

Rachel and Skye talked a little bit longer and when they were done Rachel started to look at trails that would be fun for Brianna.

Chapter Twenty-six

Pizza Night

Monday morning arrived and Jade walked Brianna into class.

"Good morning, Jade, Brianna," said Dawn Lewis, Brianna's teacher.

"Hi, Ms. Lewis," said Brianna, putting her stuff at her desk.

"Hi, Dawn," smiled Jade.

"So, what's up?"

"Well, I wanted to bring in Brianna's EpiPen."

"What happened?"

"Well, she got stung by a bee on Saturday afternoon and had a moderate reaction to it. The doctor gave her an EpiPen just in case she has another reaction," said Jade, handing Dawn the injector.

"Is this one for school or is she to bring it home?"

"This one is for school."

"I'll keep it in my desk. Thanks for bringing it in personally. A lot of parents just send a note."

"Well, I thought it would be better. I need to get to work. I'll be by to pick her up after school," said Jade, turning and waving to her daughter.

Brianna ran up and hugged her mother. "Bye, Mama."

"That's your mom?" asked one of the boys nearby. Brianna nodded. "She's pretty."

Jade overheard this as she was leaving and blushed as she walked out of the school.

⁂

Rachel arrived at work and looked at her schedule. She found that she had a couple of hours at lunch and then a light afternoon that would allow her the chance to talk with a few of the kids that she and Emily used to take hiking.

Rachel picked up the phone and dialed Jade's number.

"Hey cutie."

"Hey," said Rachel, blushing. "Did I call at an okay time?"

"Yeah, I was just reviewing a couple of contracts."

"That doesn't sound fun. How is Brianna doing?"

"She's doing a lot better. I took her to school and gave her EpiPen to her teacher Dawn."

"I'm glad she's doing better. I was wondering if you had lunch plans today?"

"Well, that depends on what time you were thinking. I have a meeting near your office. I could do a 12:30 lunch."

"That'd be perfect. Why don't you swing by the office after your meeting?"

"That sounds great. I will see you then."

⁂

Jade's morning went quickly. It always did when she had offsite meetings. Today she had expected it to go slow since she had lunch plans with Rachel, but it went remarkably fast. She pulled up outside Rachel's office building and began fixing her hair and checking her makeup.

What the hell am I doing? She's seen me in the morning. She's seen me naked, thought Jade, the last part bringing a smile to her face.

Jade got out of her car and went up to Rachel's office. Her secretary was at her desk and told Jade to have a seat and Rachel would be right with her. Jade waited for about five minutes before Rachel came out of her office.

"Hey," said Rachel, smiling at Jade. "Come on in."

"Hey."

The two women entered the office and Jade saw that Rachel had a small picnic set up in her office for them.

"This looks incredible, Rachel."

Rachel smiled. "I'm glad you like it. I wanted to do something special for you."

Jade took Rachel's hand and pulled her close so their bodies were flush together. "This is very, very, special." Jade punctuated each word with a kiss.

"You know, you kiss me and I forget everything around," Rachel said, causing Jade to blush.

"Well, that's twice today that someone has made me blush." Jade laughed as they sat down on the couch.

"Oh really? Do I have competition?"

"Yes, apparently a five-year-old boy in Brianna's class thinks I'm pretty. You had better step up your game, sweetie."

"Well, in that case..." Rachel cupped Jade's face with one hand and leaned in, sensually kissing her.

"Mmmm, wow," said Jade when they finally broke the kiss. "That was...wow."

"Very wow," agreed Rachel.

Jade looked over the spread. "Perhaps we should eat?" There was a small side salad for them each, half a turkey sandwich, and a fruit salad.

As they ate Jade told Rachel about the boy at school calling her pretty.

"That is amusing, but I think I am going to have to keep a closer eye on you."

"For some strange reason, I don't mind that idea at all," Jade said, giving Rachel a seductive smile.

"Do you and Brianna have plans on Saturday?" Jade shook her head. "Well, Skye and I were talking, and I was wondering if you two would like to go out for a hike with me. It would be an easier trail so that Brianna wouldn't get too tired. The trails are very safe and I was also thinking about maybe bringing a couple of the kids Emily and I used to take hiking with us. That is, if you are okay with it of course. You don't have to feel obligated to say yes, it's just something that I was thinking would be fun, and it would give Brianna a couple of people closer to her own age to interact with. They are both twelve."

"That sounds fantastic. I know Bri would love it. Plus I get to see 'Trail Master Rachel' in action."

"Really? Trail Master Rachel?"

"I like it, so you can deal with it," Jade said, and both women laughed.

After they finished lunch, Jade reluctantly told Rachel she had to get going, but that she would see her on Thursday at group. She also suggested that Rachel call her before then. Rachel promised and walked Jade to the door. Before opening the door Rachel pulled Jade close to her. They kissed for several minutes, each savoring the taste and the feel of each other.

Jade went back to her office and daydreamed

a bit about the sensual kiss that she had shared with Rachel. She realized she was becoming very used to kissing her and it was making her happy. She hoped that when they told Brianna that they were dating that she would take it well.

❧❧❧❧

Jade picked up Brianna and told her about the plans she had made with Rachel to go hiking on Saturday. Brianna was excited and full of questions. Jade told her that she would have to ask Rachel about those specifics. Brianna asked when she could call and ask Rachel. Jade explained to her that Rachel was supposed to call in the next couple of days and that Bri could ask her questions then. Bri whined that it was too long to wait, but Jade stood her ground. That night Jade and Brianna made dinner together and watched TV, and enjoyed their family time.

Tuesday went by quickly, and not long after Jade and Brianna had finished their dinner, Rachel called. Brianna finally got the opportunity to talk with Rachel. They talked for about fifteen minutes discussing all aspects of the hiking trail. Was it one Rachel had been on? Were there animals that she could pet? Were there flowers? Would those flowers have bees in them? Jade smiled as her daughter grilled Rachel. She was happy that Rachel was willing to talk to Brianna and answer her questions. When they finally got on the phone together, Brianna went to take her bath while the women talked.

"Thank you for talking with her," Jade said.

"My pleasure. She's a very bright little girl. A couple of her questions I hadn't even thought about.

How was your day?"

"It was a good day. How was yours?"

"Greatly improved, thanks to this call."

"That doesn't sound good," said Jade.

"I just had some rough clients today."

"Well, this doesn't help for tonight, but do you have plans tomorrow night?" asked Jade.

"None that I'm aware of."

"Great. Would you like to come and hang out with Bri and me? Tomorrow night is pizza night, so it's nothing fancy, but I'd love to see you."

"As long as I'm not invading something that is special for you two, I would love to hang with you and Bri."

"Great. How about six o'clock?"

"That works perfect for me."

The two women talked for bit longer and then Jade had to go extract Brianna from the tub, but told Rachel she'd see her the following night.

⚜ ⚜ ⚜ ⚜

"Mama? When is Rachel going to get here?" asked Brianna, staring out the front window.

"Soon, sweetie," Jade said, watching her daughter. She was a bit concerned at the attachment her daughter was forming with Rachel. She just wanted to make sure things with them were going to work out so that Brianna didn't get hurt.

It was another ten minutes and three questions later before Brianna announced that Rachel had finally arrived as she raced to the front door and opened it for her.

"Hi, Rachel."

"Hi, Brianna," said Rachel, smiling down at her.

"Hi," Jade said as she entered the room and smiled at Rachel.

"Hi," Rachel said, smiling at Jade.

"Mama already ordered dinner." Brianna pulled the two women into the living room with her.

"I hope you don't mind Hawaiian pizza. It is our favorite for pizza night," said Jade, tickling Brianna as they sat down in the living room.

"I happen to love Hawaiian pizza."

"On pizza night we get to play video games and eat pizza in the living room," Brianna stated as she went over to the shelf that had the games.

Rachel had a terrified look on her face that caused Jade to laugh.

"It isn't that bad." Jade put a hand on Rachel's arm. "Bri, why don't you put in bowling? That should be a safe one to start Rachel on."

"YAY!" squealed Brianna as she grabbed the game and set up the console.

"I'm not a good bowler," said Rachel softly to Jade.

"Neither am I, but video bowling is a whole lot easier and more fun. Trust me."

"I do. I completely trust you."

"Mama, can I build an av...av-...can I build Rachel into the system?"

"Why don't you ask Rachel if it is okay for you to build her an avatar? Maybe you two can do that while I get dinner together since it should be here any minute."

"Rachel, can we build you an av-avatar, too?"

"I'd like that." Rachel smiled as she saw Brianna's eyes light up.

Rachel and Brianna started to build her avatar while Jade went to the kitchen to get plates and drinks. As Jade was in the kitchen the doorbell rang, and she went to get the pizza and breadsticks she had ordered, grabbing plates and drinks as she made her way back into the living room just as Bri and Rachel were finishing up the avatar.

Brianna giggled, pointing at the television. "Mama, look at Rachel."

Jade looked and saw a slender, red-haired avatar with green eyes. She was wearing green and red striped socks, a pink tutu, and a green T-shirt with a peace sign on it. Jade couldn't help but laugh. She looked over to see Rachel's pout, and Jade's heart skipped a beat. She wanted to kiss the poor woman, but knew she couldn't with Bri right there.

"Very interesting," said Jade, smirking and trying not to laugh. "Bri, go wash your hands for dinner."

As soon as Jade heard Brianna on the stairs, she set the food down and leaned over to suck on Rachel's lower lip.

"I will make it up to you after she goes to bed," Jade whispered into Rachel's ear. She was so close to Rachel's ear that she felt the warmth of her breath and let out a soft groan as it stirred something inside her.

"I can't wait," Rachel said, offering Jade a look of desire.

As Jade stood to compose herself they heard Brianna bounding down the stairs. As she entered the room she showed Jade how clean her hands were. They each got a piece of pizza and a drink while Jade helped Rachel and Brianna finish Rachel's avatar. They changed the clothes so that she was now wearing black jeans, a red shirt, and a pair of red shoes. Jade started the game and showed Rachel how to play. The three of them ate, laughed, and bowled. After the first game Rachel had a pretty good handle of how the game worked and what to do. Brianna won the first game, Rachel won the second, and Jade the third. After the last game Jade sent Brianna to get ready for bed and told her they would be up to tuck her in.

"Thank you for including me," said Rachel as they cleaned up the living room and took the dishes into the kitchen.

"It was a lot of fun."

"I love the relationship you have with Brianna. She is so lucky to have you."

"I'm the lucky one to have her. I'm pretty lucky to have you as well," said Jade, hugging Rachel.

"The feeling is mutual."

The two women went upstairs and tucked Brianna in. They started to read a book to her, but she was asleep by the third page. Rachel and Jade headed back downstairs and lay down on the couch. Jade turned on a movie for background noise and covered them up with a light blanket. Rachel brought their lips together in a soft, sensual kiss. Jade groaned into the kiss as their lips started to move together. They took turns sucking on the other's lower lip. Jade had her hand on Rachel's hip and as their kissing heated up, she moved her hand down the back of Rachel's thigh until she neared her knee and encouraged Rachel's leg to rest on top of hers, allowing her thigh to press against Rachel's rapidly heating center. Rachel, feeling the desired pressure between her legs, slipped her hand under Jade's T-shirt and unhooked the front clasp of her bra. Rachel ran her fingers over Jade's breasts making sure to play with her nipples. Jade let out a satisfied moan as Rachel continued to massage her breasts. Jade's hand moved up Rachel's thigh to cup her butt and began squeezing and pulling her closer.

"Rachel," whispered Jade. "That feels so good."

"Mmmm, the way you touch me...drives me insane," panted Rachel, her arousal growing.

"I want you, but I'm scared because of Bri," Jade said, continuing to squeeze Rachel's ass and pull her closer.

"I know...oh god if you keep doing that...you are going to make me..." groaned Rachel as she moved her hips and rubbed against Jade's thigh.

Hearing that caused Jade to ease up a bit, so they could both calm down. She leaned her forehead against Rachel's.

"I'm sorry," Jade said, dropping her eyes.

"You have nothing to be sorry about. I know your daughter is upstairs and that we need to be cautious."

"Yeah, but again, I got you turned on only to hit the brakes. It isn't fair to you."

"Baby, look at me," said Rachel, waiting for Jade's eyes to meet hers before continuing. "Just being around you turns me on. I know that we have to be careful and that every time we want to be together we aren't going to be able to. It is just going to make the times we are able to be together that much more exciting."

"What did I do to deserve someone so understanding and wonderful?" asked Jade before leaning in and kissing Rachel softly.

"You were just you," Rachel said after their kiss ended.

"Rachel, if your hands keep that up, we're going out to your car and I'm taking you there so we can make noise," said Jade as Rachel's hands had never stopped playing with her breasts.

Rachel blushed. "Sorry. I told you I was a breast girl."

"You did and you are very, very, good at what you do with said breasts," said Jade, letting out a little whimper as Rachel moved her hands away.

"I should get going or I, er…" Rachel lost her train of thought as she saw Jade lick her lips. Jade realized what she had done and why Rachel had stopped talking. She smiled sheepishly.

"Sorry," said Jade.

"Uh huh," Rachel said, laughing.

The two women pulled apart. Jade fixed her bra and they sat up. Jade turned off the movie as Rachel stood up to leave.

Jade took Rachel's hand and walked her to the front door.

"Tonight was fantastic," said Rachel.

"Yes it was. Thank you for coming over, hanging with Bri and me, and for the need for a very cold shower."

"I need one of those, too. Tomorrow night is going to be hard. I enjoy kissing you a lot," admitted Rachel before she could stop herself.

"I enjoy kissing you a lot, too," Jade said with a wink.

"Goodnight, baby," said Rachel, giving Jade a chaste kiss before heading out the door.

Chapter Twenty-seven

Let's Go Hiking

Their group session went well. Carmen didn't show up and that alleviated a lot of stress from Rachel and Jade who were both apprehensive about what would happen if she did attend or start to cause trouble. After the meeting, Jade helped Rachel clean up and they agreed that Rachel would pick up Jade and Bri before going to get the other two kids. Rachel told Jade that she was borrowing a friend's SUV so that there would be more room for everyone. Jade offered to drive, but Rachel told her this gave them an excuse to spend more time together. Jade smiled at the idea that Rachel wanted to spend more time with them.

Saturday morning Brianna woke excited about the day.

"Mama, it's Saturday. Wake up! It's Saturday, we get to go hiking today," squealed Brianna, racing into Jade's room.

Jade opened one eye to see her daughter kneeling and bouncing on her bed. She smiled when she saw that Brianna was all dressed and ready to go. Jade quickly reached an arm out and pulled her daughter into a hug and kissed her, causing her to squeal again.

"Mama!" she giggled.

"What are you doing on my bed?" asked Jade,

tickling her daughter.

"It's time...time to get up." Brianna giggled as Jade continued to tickle and hug her.

"What if I don't want to get up?"

"You have to, Mama. We're going hiking today. You promised," said Brianna, barely able to contain her excitement.

"Oh yeah. I forgot about that. Do you really wanna go hiking?" teased Jade.

"You promised." Brianna crossed her arms and pouted.

"Yes I did. Now since you're all ready, I need to get ready. Go downstairs and watch television and I'll get us breakfast when I come down."

"Thank you, Mama," said the little girl, hugging her mother and kissing her cheek.

"I love you, Bri."

"I love you, too, Mama," Brianna said as she skipped out the door.

Jade smiled as her daughter left the room. Jade had chosen a pair of blue jeans and a green *Frozen* T-shirt for Brianna to wear. For herself she chose blue jeans and a light blue T-shirt with a cactus on it and the word "hugs?" underneath. Jade smiled to herself when she thought about hugging Rachel. She finished getting ready and headed downstairs to make breakfast.

After breakfast was cleaned up, Jade and Brianna sat in the living room reading and waiting for Rachel. Brianna was the first to hear the car pull into their driveway. She jumped up and ran to the door. By the time Rachel got to the house the little girl was bouncing up and down in excitement.

"Hey there, little jumping bean."

Brianna giggled. "Hi! I can't wait to go hiking."

"Bri, go put your books upstairs and get your shoes on," said Jade.

"Okay, Mama," said Brianna, racing into the living room, grabbed her books, and bolted up the stairs.

"Hi," said Jade as Rachel entered and closed the door.

"Hi. Nice shirt." Rachel smirked, and pulled Jade into a hug.

"It seemed safe for kids, and suggestive for you," Jade said, pushing Rachel back two steps so her back was against the door and their bodies leaned together.

Rachel groaned at the feeling of Jade's body pressed against her own. Jade then turned her head and kissed Rachel's neck several times before pulling back to kiss her lips.

"Mmmmm, thank you. I was afraid I was going to have to wait until later for a kiss."

"I wasn't willing to wait that long," Jade said with a smirk.

"Tease," said Rachel.

"Maybe." Jade kissed her again before pulling back and smiling.

"I'm hoping so," said Rachel, separating as they heard Brianna coming back down the stairs.

"I'm all ready to go."

"Well, then I guess we should get going," said Rachel.

Jade grabbed the small backpack she had put together and double checked that Brianna's EpiPen was in it. Just in case.

Rachel drove to the school where Emily used to teach to meet Connor and Lacey. Once the kids saw her pull up, they hurried toward the car. Rachel parked the car and got out quickly.

"Rachel!" screamed the two kids.

Rachel held out her arms as the two kids ran into them and hugged her close. Jade and Brianna got out of the car and watched the exchange.

"I've missed you two," said Rachel into the kids' hair. After several minutes of hugging the three grudgingly broke apart. "I have two people I want you to meet. They're going with us on the hike."

"Is she a new girlfriend?" asked Connor.

"I care about her and her daughter, but right now we're just close friends."

"You want her to be your girlfriend, though, don't you?" Lacey asked.

"Yes," Rachel admitted, blushing.

"She's really pretty," said Connor.

The three walked over to where Jade and Brianna were leaning against the car.

"Jade, Brianna, this is Connor and Lacey. Guys, this is Jade and her daughter Brianna."

"Hi."

They all got into the car and headed off to the trails.

❧❧❧❧

Connor, Lacey, and Rachel unpacked the stuff for the hike from the back of the car. Jade and Brianna watched. They could tell that they had done this several times before. Once they had the car unpacked, Rachel put together their backpacks. She added a couple of things to Jade's bag and even made a little one up for Brianna so she didn't feel left out. Jade caught Rachel's eye and mouthed "thank you" to her for including Brianna.

"All right. Connor, Lacey, you know the rules." Rachel looked at the two kids and saw them nod before she turned to Jade and Brianna. "Stay close, no wandering off, and no touching the animals, no matter how cute they are. Bri, honey, you need to keep a special eye on the flowers, too. We don't want any more bees to bite you."

"No bee bites," said Brianna, grabbing her arm where the bee had stung her the weekend prior.

"We'll help you watch out for them, too," said Connor, receiving an approving smile and wink from Rachel.

"Thank you," said Brianna.

"All right, let's head out," Rachel said.

Connor and Lacey took the lead while Jade and Rachel each took one of Brianna's hands and followed them. As they walked along the trail, Rachel pointed out some of the plants and flowers. Connor and Lacey added what they remembered about the plants as well. After about an hour Brianna felt comfortable with the two older kids and walked ahead with them, leaving Rachel and Jade behind.

"I see why you and Emily spent time with them. They are great kids," said Jade, walking close to Rachel.

"Yeah, and thanks to you, I can bring them out here again. I've missed them and hiking with them."

As they neared the rest area, Brianna had to use the restroom and Lacey offered to take her. Connor said he would escort them. Jade seemed okay as she saw how much fun her daughter was having with her new friends. Rachel realized it was a ploy for them to leave Rachel and Jade alone.

"Let me know if you think we're pushing Brianna

too much with the walking," said Rachel, taking Jade's hand and stopping just out of view of everyone there.

"She'll let us know. She seems to be having fun with her new friends."

"Well, since they are occupied, can I get another kiss?"

"You don't have to ask, goof." Jade brought their lips together.

The kiss allowed the two women the moment of closeness they had been craving. Jade's face reflected concern when they pulled apart.

"What's going on in there?" asked Rachel, seeing the pensive look on her girlfriend's face.

"Am I being unfair to you by keep our relationship essentially between us? Mainly because I'm afraid of how Brianna is going to react."

"No, you aren't," said Rachel. They started walking toward the rest area to meet the kids. "I agree that this is best for her. She needs to see and believe that I am going to be a stable, consistent part of her life before learning about us."

"I stand by my statement last night. I don't deserve you," Jade said, smiling.

"Remind me later and I'll prove to you how wrong that statement is," Rachel whispered in Jade's ear before quickly sucking on her earlobe.

❧ ❧ ❧ ❧

"So, do you spend a lot of time with Rachel?" Lacey asked as they walked to the bathrooms.

"More lately, she makes my Mama smile and laugh."

"Do you like spending time with Rachel?

"Yeah, she's really nice and funny. Mommy would have liked her if she would have gotten to meet her," Brianna said, her voice getting quiet. "Mommy is in heaven now."

"I'm sorry she isn't here anymore," Lacey said. "I'm glad that you got to know Rachel, though. That gave us a chance to meet you."

"I'm glad about that, too," said Brianna as the two girls walked up to where Connor was standing.

Connor motioned with his eyes for Lacey to look toward Rachel and Jade. She looked and happened to see Rachel pulling away from what looked like a private moment between her and Jade. Lacey knew from her short conversation with Brianna and from what she just witnessed that there was more going on than Rachel had told them.

Rachel and Jade started walking toward the kids when Rachel caught a look and a grin pass between Lacey and Connor, and she knew something was up.

"Mama," called Brianna as she sprinted towards Jade and launched into her arms.

"Hi, sweetie. Are you having fun?"

"Yeah, Lacey and Connor are really nice," Brianna said.

Rachel saw a smirk on Lacey's face and continued past Jade and Brianna to the two older kids. Connor continued toward Jade and Brianna while Rachel and Lacey stopped to talk.

"What's that look for?" Rachel asked Lacey.

"What look?" said Lacey.

"Lacey, you're twelve. You haven't mastered the art of hiding things. You had a smug smirk on your face. What's up?"

"You're already dating Jade, aren't you?"

"What? Why do you say that?" asked Rachel, unsuccessfully trying to hide the lump that just formed in her throat.

"I'm not blind. I see the way you look at her and the way she looks at you. You're happy and she is really nice and pretty. Brianna is great, too. That is all Connor and I have wanted for you since Emily died. We just want to see you happy. You just don't want her daughter to know because she's so young and won't understand."

Rachel pulled the girl into a hug and held her close for a minute.

"I am happy when I'm around Jade and I adore Brianna. I don't know what the future holds, but yeah, I'd like it to include them."

"Then let's get going. I want to get to know Jade better," Lacey said as they headed back to the others.

"Is everything okay?" Jade asked.

"Yep, I just needed some motherly advice from Rachel," said Lacey as Rachel wrapped an arm around the girls shoulder.

Jade raised an eyebrow slightly at Rachel and saw her avert her eyes.

"So, shall we get moving so that we can make it to the flats for lunch?" said Rachel in an attempt to get out of this situation.

Everyone agreed, and Brianna and Lacey started skipping down the path while Connor walked with them and Rachel and Jade brought up the back. Jade could tell that Rachel wasn't going to tell her what the conversation was about until later.

The group made it to the flats, as Rachel called it. What she had failed to mention was that it was at the top of a large hill that overlooked the trail area.

Rachel set out a blanket and the small lunch she had packed for them and they gathered around and ate. Brianna was mesmerized by the view. After they ate, Rachel took Brianna around the edge and pointed out plants and other landmarks. Brianna was in awe of it. While Rachel and Brianna were occupied, Connor and Lacey took the opportunity to get to know Jade. They asked about Amy, about her past, about what she did for a living, her hobbies and interests. Both kids were amazed at how much Rachel and Jade had in common.

On the walk back, Brianna got tired and Jade ended up carrying her daughter. Brianna tried her best to fight sleep, but once they got in the car she lost the battle and drifted to sleep.

Rachel pulled into the parking lot where they had picked Connor and Lacey up and everyone but Brianna got out of the car. Jade hugged the two kids and made sure they had her number. Lacey said she'd babysit Brianna whenever Jade needed. Connor reiterated his interest in art, so Jade said she'd bring him to her office someday and show him what she did.

After dropping off Connor and Lacey, Rachel and Jade drove back to Jade's house. Jade carried Brianna up to her room to let her rest.

"What was really going on when we were at the rest stop?" Jade sat facing Rachel on the couch.

"Those two are intuitive. Lacey told me she thought we were already dating." Rachel laughed. "And she understands about Bri being young, too."

"Wow, and is she okay with us dating?"

"Yeah, she said all she and Connor want is for me to be happy."

"And are you happy?"

"Oh god yes," said Rachel, pinning Jade

between the back of the couch and her own body and then capturing her lips in a searing kiss. The kiss transitioned into a heated make-out session, tongues fighting for dominance, hands roaming, hips rocking.

"Stay...tonight..." Jade panted when they broke for air.

"Are...you sure?"

"The other night I wanted you. Tonight I need you, but Bri will be waking up soon," said Jade, the lust in her eyes causing Rachel to let out a whimper.

"I need you, too."

They lay kissing for several minutes before they sat up and readjusted their clothes and fixed their hair. Shortly after, Brianna came shuffling down the stairs.

"Hi, Baby Girl."

"Hi, Mama. Hi, Rachel."

"Hi, Bri. Do you feel better after your nap?"

"Sort of. I'm still tired."

"Well, you can go to bed early tonight if you want," said Jade, looking over Brianna's head at Rachel, who looked back and licked her lips slowly, causing Jade to close her eyes to control her hyperactive hormones.

Jade made grilled cheese sandwiches for the three of them and it wasn't long after they ate that Brianna was ready to go upstairs to bed. Rachel and Jade tucked her in.

After getting her daughter settled, Jade took Rachel by the hand and led her into her bedroom. Jade stopped and locked the bedroom door before leading Rachel into the bathroom where she started the shower warming.

"This room is practically soundproof..." Jade looked at Rachel hungrily.

Rachel groaned at Jade's words. They quickly

undressed and stepped into the shower. As the water cascaded over them, Jade pressed Rachel against the wall and kissed her hard. Their bodies started to move together and lust and need took over, and they took each other hard and fast. They came together, calling out the other's name, then leaning together to hold themselves up.

"That..." panted Jade.

"Hot..." replied Rachel.

After washing one another in the shower, Rachel and Jade made their way to Jade's bed. Jade gently laid Rachel down on her back, gazed down at her, and felt the desire for this woman grow. Not in the animalistic way they took each other in the shower. No, she wanted to worship Rachel.

Jade positioned herself so that she was hovered over Rachel's upper body, her lower body pressed between Rachel's legs. Looking Rachel in the eyes, she leaned down and slowly kissed her, allowing the passion that she was feeling to transfer to Rachel. She heard Rachel moan into the kiss. Rachel threaded her fingers into Jade's hair pulling her closer. Rachel's other hand slid down her lover's back and encouraged her down so that their bodies were pressed together. Jade ground her hips as they both groaned. Jade pulled back from the kiss and worked her way along Rachel's jawline. When she reached Rachel's ear she ran her tongue around the edge of it, and when she reached the earlobe she sucked on it before whispering into Rachel's ear.

"I want to taste you."

"Oh...yes," said Rachel.

Jade kissed her way down to Rachel's breasts and began to tease her nipples with her tongue. After stimulating both breasts, Jade moved down her body.

"You make me feel things I've never felt before," groaned Rachel, giving herself over to her lover completely.

"Yes...like that...Yes!" Rachel breathlessly exclaimed. "Oh baby...Oh Jade...I love you...Yes..."

Jade wasn't sure if she heard Rachel right. Did she just tell her that she was in love with her? It was too soon. *Maybe she will think I didn't hear her if I just keep going.*

"You are amazing," said Jade, kissing Rachel deeply. "Thank you for a great day and an amazing night."

"Mmmm, thank you," Rachel said, looking sated from their adventure in the shower and then the attention she had just received. Jade was amused to see Rachel fighting to keep her eyes open.

"Sleep, sweetie."

"Your turn?"

"Wake me later once you've had some rest," said Jade, kissing Rachel.

"Yes, ma'am," said Rachel, cuddling into the embrace.

Jade lay there holding her lover and watching her sleep. *She said she loves me? How can she love me so quickly? Does she expect me to say it back? How do I feel about her? Could I love her?* thought Jade as she fell asleep.

❧❧❧❧

Rachel woke before Jade and she lay there watching the woman she knew she loved sleep. She was in awe of how beautiful Jade looked while she slept. Rachel's mind drifted back to the night before, how hot the sex was in the shower, how sensual it was here in bed. She groaned remembering how she told Jade she loved her. *What the hell? I told her I love her. Shit. Maybe she didn't hear me...but what if she did? Was she just being nice? It's too soon. Why did I say that?*

Jade started to stir and opened her eyes to see Rachel looking down at her.

"Morning, beautiful," said Rachel, leaning over and kissing Jade.

"Mmmmm, morning." Jade ran her hand up Rachel's naked body and cupped her breast. "I can't believe how responsive you are."

"It's your touch." Rachel arched into Jade's touch as she teased her nipple.

"Wanna fool around in the shower again?" asked Jade with a sultry smile.

"As long as I get to touch you all over, hell yes!"

Rachel leaned forward, captured Jade's lower lip in between her teeth, and tugged on it a little.

"Oh yes," moaned Jade.

The two women moved to the shower and Rachel firmly pressed Jade against the wall. Rachel sucked on Jade's nipples and ran her fingers through her lover's center as she rocked her hips.

"Oh yes...inside...please," panted Jade, pulling Rachel up and kissing her.

The two women rocked, teased, thrust, and kissed each other to climax. After they washed one another they went back into Jade's room. Jade quickly found Rachel something to wear since the overnight stay had not been planned.

After getting dressed Rachel and Jade went

downstairs, made coffee, and cuddled in the living room until they heard Brianna coming down the stairs.

"Morning," said Rachel, watching Brianna curl up on Jade's lap.

"Morning, Rachel. Morning, Mama."

"Good morning, sweetie. Did you sleep well?"

"Yeah. Can we go hiking again sometime?"

"We sure can," said Rachel. "I should get going, though. Skye and I are having lunch today."

"Good-bye," Brianna said, hugging Rachel.

"I'll see you soon," Rachel told her.

Jade told Brianna to go get dressed with the promise they could go out for breakfast after. Brianna ran up the stairs to get ready. Jade walked Rachel to the door and hugged her close.

"Thank you for taking us hiking with you yesterday, And thank you for last night and this morning," said Jade, leaning in and kissing Rachel.

"Call me later."

"I will," Jade said as they pulled apart, and Rachel waved and walked out the door. Jade watched her car pull away just as Brianna came in the room.

"What do you want for breakfast, sweetie?"

"Can we just stay home and have cereal?" asked Brianna softly.

"Um, sure. Are you feeling okay? Is something wrong?" Jade asked, putting her hand on her daughter's forehead to see if she had a fever.

"I'm fine. I just don't wanna go out for breakfast anymore. I just want to eat here and then color in my room."

"That sounds like a good plan. Let's make some cereal, then."

Chapter Twenty-eight

Down the Rabbit Hole

Jade hadn't seen or heard from Brianna in several hours. She went up to check on her and found her daughter in her room holding Mr. Butters and Captain Quackers. Her face was all red.

"Bri? Honey? What's wrong? Are you okay?"

"Fine," Brianna said coldly.

"You don't cry for no reason," said Jade, entering her daughter's room and sitting down on the bed next to her daughter. Jade was shocked when Brianna moved away from her. "Brianna, have I done something to upset you?"

"Just leave me alone," said Brianna, starting to cry again.

"Hey, don't talk to me like that. Now, why are you angry with me?"

"I saw you kiss Rachel..." Brianna said. It was like someone punched Jade in the stomach.

"When?"

"This morning, before she left, you two were hugging and you kissed her. You aren't supposed to kiss her. You're supposed to kiss Mommy, not Rachel."

"Bri..."

"I don't want her around anymore. I don't like her," she cried.

Jade's heart was breaking hearing Brianna's

harsh words and seeing her cry. She cared so much about Rachel. She felt alive with Rachel, but this was her daughter. Jade wiped a tear away from her face before scooping her daughter up in her arms and holding her close.

"Honey, please don't cry."

"You aren't supposed to kiss anyone but Mommy. Now Mommy isn't going to watch over us anymore. She's going to stop loving me…" Brianna cried.

"Brianna that is never going to happen. Your Mommy is always going to watch over us, and she is always, always, going to love you."

"No she isn't. You're going to stop loving her, and then she's going to be all alone in heaven. It's all Rachel's fault."

"Why do you think she is going to be alone in heaven?"

"Because, you will have Rachel instead, and when you go to heaven, you aren't going to want her anymore because you replaced her with Rachel. I hate Rachel!"

"Brianna Marie Donovan! We do not hate people. Hate is a very strong word and feeling. It's not something that can be taken lightly."

"I hate her," Brianna said again. "If you keep seeing her, I'm going to go live with Grandma and Grandpa."

"You can dislike her, but I do not ever want to hear you say you hate someone. Do I make myself clear?"

"It's what I feel. I don't like you much either. Are you going to replace me, too?"

"You are my daughter, and I love you no matter what. I don't know why you think I would replace you.

I want to talk about this."

"I don't want to. Get out of my room!" yelled Brianna. "I don't want to be around you or Rachel again."

"Brianna, don't yell at me. You know that you aren't supposed to yell at adults."

"I don't care! I want to go live with Grandma and Grandpa NOW! At least they love me."

Jade felt the words hit her like a slap in the face. "Brianna, either you stop yelling or you are grounded," she said sternly.

"No. I'll yell if I want to!"

"Fine, you are grounded until you stop yelling and are willing to apologize. That means no TV, no hanging out with friends or Jake, nothing other than staying here in your room except for school, eating, or bathroom time."

"So what?" snipped Brianna.

Jade stood up to leave. She unhooked Brianna's TV and removed it from the little girl's room. After putting the TV in her office, Jade went downstairs and curled up on the couch. Feeling the strain, she started to cry. A morning that had started so amazing, had given her so much hope and happiness, was now one of the worst days she could remember since losing Amy.

After a couple of hours, Brianna came down the stairs and saw Jade curled up on the couch crying and clutching a pillow tightly.

"Mama? Why are you crying?" asked Brianna, who was now standing next to the couch clutching Mr. Butters.

"I'm upset and sad," said Jade, reaching for a tissue on the end table.

"What made you upset and sad?"

"Hearing that you don't want to live here anymore with me hurt my feelings. Upsetting you made me sad. Hearing you say you hate someone upset me. There are a lot of things that made me sad today. Most of all, though, hearing you say that you don't think I love you."

"Do you like Rachel more than Mommy?"

"Sweetie, I love your Mommy so much. I miss her every day. I like Rachel, but it isn't the same as what I feel for your Mommy. If it wasn't for Mommy, I wouldn't have you. You are the most important person in my life."

"I am?" asked Brianna, surprised.

"Yeah, you are."

"I don't want Rachel around anymore. I don't like her."

"Bri, she isn't replacing Mommy. She doesn't want to replace Mommy. Nobody can ever replace Mommy."

"I don't like her anymore."

"What do you want me to do then?"

"Stop seeing her...or let me go live with Grandma and Grandpa so I don't have to see her."

Jade let out a defeated sigh. "I will make you a deal. If you will stop saying that you want to go live elsewhere and you stop using the word hate, I will tell Rachel that I can't see her anymore."

"Really?"

"Yes, really."

"What about group?" asked Brianna.

"I won't be going back there..."

"But it helped you..."

"Bri, you are more important than any of that

stuff. You are my daughter, the last piece of your Mommy that I get to hold onto. I'd give up everything for you."

"You promise you won't talk to Rachel anymore?"

"I promise," said Jade, feeling like her heart was being ripped in two.

"Then I don't want to go live with Grandma and Grandpa."

"Thank you," said Jade, picking up her cell phone and sending a text to Rachel that things were moving too fast, and she needed some time and space. She told Rachel that she would be in contact when she had a handle on her emotions. She also requested that Rachel not try to contact her. When Jade hit send, she felt a light go out inside her.

⁂

Rachel arrived home and lay on the couch daydreaming about the weekend. She couldn't imagine a better time than spending time with Jade, Brianna, Lacey, and Connor. The hike was incredible, and the romantic time and lovemaking with Jade was perfect. She was as happy as she had been since she was with Emily.

Skye called and Rachel invited her over for lunch and a talk. When Skye arrived, Rachel told her about the hike, about the hot and steamy sex in the shower, and then about saying "I love you" during the slow, passionate lovemaking. She explained to Skye that she didn't know if Jade heard her, but she partially hoped she hadn't. She didn't know if she was ready for love yet. Skye told Rachel not to be a fool and that anyone could see that she and Jade were falling in love.

It wasn't long after Rachel and Skye started talking about Jade and love when Rachel's phone beeped, and she smiled seeing it was a text from Jade. Rachel read the message and then dropped the phone and ran to the bathroom. Skye picked up the phone and read the message. She was shocked and appalled at what she read. She thought she had been a better judge about Jade's character. She did not think that Jade was going to use her sister-in-law, or at least treat her with such little respect.

Skye hurried to Rachel's side. She held Rachel while she threw up and cried. She held her sister-in-law while she tried to make sense of the text that Jade had sent. Both Rachel and Skye tried to call Jade back, but she didn't answer. Skye called Kristel to see if she knew what was going on. Kristel was as shocked as they were about the message. Kristel tried to call Jade, but didn't reach her. She drove over to talk to her friend, but nobody answered the door. Unsure of Jade's state of mind, Kristel used her key and entered the house. She found it empty. She checked Brianna's room and saw that the girls two favorite stuffed animals were missing, as was her suitcase. Kristel started to panic. She found the number to Amy's parents in the address book on Jade's desk. Kristel called them to see if they had heard from Jade. They told her that Jade had dropped Brianna off and requested that they watch her for the week. Jade had told them that she had an emergency business trip to go on. Kristel spoke to Brianna, who said she didn't know where Jade had gone, but she was sad and upset and was sorry for her part in it, but she wouldn't elaborate on her statements.

Out of ideas, Kristel went over to Rachel's to see how she was doing. When she arrived, she found that

Rachel and Skye were still very distraught.

"I had to have caused this by telling her I loved her," said Rachel. "It was too fast and she wasn't ready. It's all my fault."

"Bullshit, Rachel," Skye said.

"I agree with Skye," said Kristel. "Jade was falling for you hard. I don't know what happened today, but as soon as I track her ass down, I'm going to find out."

It was a week before Kristel heard from Jade. When she did, she was informed that Jade did not want to hear about Rachel, and that there would be no discussion further on that topic.

⁂

Rachel spent the week in a haze. How something that felt so right could go so wrong she didn't understand. She continued to blame herself for scaring Jade off. Kristel had called Rachel to let her know that Jade was safe, but that she didn't have any answers yet. Kristel promised to let Rachel know once she either found something out or cornered Jade.

Group on Thursday night was one of the hardest meetings Rachel had ever had including the ones when she first started going after Emily died. Not only was Jade not there, Carmen was back. The troubled woman kept her distance, but everyone could see that something was bothering their group leader. Several members tried to talk to her, but everything was still too raw. Rachel ended up cancelling the group and telling everyone she was sorry, but she just couldn't handle it right now.

⁂

When Jade returned to town from her week away, she picked up Brianna and they went home. Jade had refused to answer any calls except for the ones from Amy's parents while she was away. As the week progressed, Jade's mood didn't improve.

"Mama, are you still upset and sad?" Brianna asked as they entered the house Thursday night.

"Yes, but that is something I'm working on."

"Is this because of Rachel?" asked Brianna, confused about her mother's rapid mood change.

"It is an adult thing. I don't want to talk about it. And remember we aren't supposed to be discussing Rachel anymore. Now, go get washed up for dinner."

Brianna went upstairs and washed her hands while Jade made dinner. Brianna remembered after Amy died that Jade had been sad and upset. She remembered how Jade didn't leave the house; she didn't hang out with anyone other than Kristel. Now, she hadn't even seen Kristel or Jake in almost three weeks. Brianna knew she was grounded, but she still didn't like the dark mood Jade was in.

"Mama, can we see Aunt Kristel and Jake this weekend?" asked Brianna, entering the kitchen.

"I'll think about it."

"Are you going to group tonight?"

"I promised you I wasn't going back to that group, so no," said Jade, placing their dinner on the table. "Dinner is ready."

"Mama, are you sad like you were when Mommy died?"

"I'm fine Brianna. I love you, now eat your dinner, and maybe we can watch *Frozen* before your bath," offered Jade, trying to get away from the subject.

It had been almost two weeks since she had made the agreement with her daughter regarding Rachel. Two very long weeks. To make matters worse, Jade had a meeting that day with Scott at his gallery. It was the first time since her date with Rachel that she had been there. As they walked to Scott's office, they passed Rachel's photograph. Jade felt her stomach clench as she passed it. Jade thought she was going to be sick.

Jade and Brianna cleaned up dinner and cuddled on the couch and watched *Frozen*. Once the movie was over, Brianna went to take her bath. While she was in there, Jade went to her office and tried to work on some new contracts she had received.

"Amy, how did life get so messed up?" Jade said, looking at a picture of them after they first got engaged. "I love you. I miss you. I care a lot about Rachel, and I miss her in my life, but Bri...she is so sensitive, and all I want is for her to be happy. I feel so lost...and like I am just failing the world."

Jade heard her phone beep, and she looked and saw it was a message from Kristel.

Kristel: I get that something is going on, fine, but don't shut Jake and me out anymore. We miss you and Bri.

Jade: Bri was asking about seeing Jake this weekend.

Kristel: Great, how about Saturday?

Jade: Sounds good. Why don't you two come over here? We have the pool set up in the yard and we can grill out.

Kristel: We'll see you then. Maybe we can talk?

Jade: I have nothing to say on the subject. Please...I'm barely making it as it is.

Jade set the phone down again. She knew that Kristel wasn't going to let things go. After letting out an exasperated sigh, Jade went and got Brianna out of the tub.

"Kristel and Jake are coming over on Saturday," said Jade, handing Brianna her pajamas.

"Does that mean I'm not grounded anymore?"

"Yes, as of tomorrow, you are no longer grounded."

"Thank you, Mama," said Brianna, hugging Jade. "I love you!"

"I love you, too, Bri. More than anyone or anything in this whole universe," said Jade, picking up her daughter and walking them over to the little girl's bed.

After putting Brianna to sleep, Jade went into her room and got ready for bed. Jade grabbed a book and lay down to read. She had hoped to read, but instead her mind wandered to thoughts of Rachel. The guilt she felt for hurting her and being such a coward was overwhelming.

❧❧❧❧

Rachel had been spending a lot of time with Skye after everything that happened with Jade. Skye allowed her to function, or in the least, didn't allow her to shut down.

"Hey, Rach," said Skye, entering Rachel's office.

"Oh, hey. Why are you here?"

"I wanted to check on you and see if you would like some company at group tonight."

"Damn, today is Thursday, isn't it? This week has been a blur," said Rachel, running her hands through her hair.

"Well, it's almost over. This weekend I say we go out partying."

"I'm not up for partying, but we are definitely doing something," said Rachel.

Rachel had thrown herself into her work and her photography over the past two weeks. She was doing what she could to get by. She had only officially been with Jade for a couple of weeks, but when she thought about it, there was all that time in group that they had spent together, getting to know one another, building the foundation for what she thought was going to be a strong relationship. When she had opened herself up to Jade, she had no clue it would end up like this, and that she would be hurt so badly.

"Hey, you did nothing wrong," said Skye, seeing Rachel lose herself in thought.

"I wish I knew what went wrong." Rachel buried her head in her hands.

"Well, Kristel is going over there this weekend so hopefully she'll find something out."

"How do you know this?"

"Um, I was with her when she messaged Jade before I came to see you. Duh! We're both still hoping that you two get back together."

"I'm not sure that it will ever happen...She just shoved me away without really a word. I don't know that I want to let her in again. I don't know that I can handle the pain of allowing her in again."

"Don't say that, Rach. You two were good together and you will be again."

"I wish I had your optimism."

Saturday arrived and Jade was busy prepping for the day when Brianna came in and told her that Kristel and Jake were there.

Jade wiped her hands on a towel and greeted them. Jake and Brianna went outside to play while Kristel followed Jade back into the kitchen.

"You've lost weight. I mean a lot of weight," Kristel said.

"I haven't had an appetite lately," said Jade, turning her back to her friend.

"Talk to me, Jade. Let me help," said Kristel, hugging her from behind.

"There is nothing to talk about. I've just been stressed."

"Great, now that we've covered that subject, how about if we talk about Rachel?"

"I told you that subject was off limits," Jade said, raising her voice a little. "I can't go there—"

"Yeah, I know, but you see, when I see you hurting and miserable, I'm going to push for the answers. Tell me what's going on! I can help."

"No, you can't..." Jade said softly, through gritted teeth. "Just let it go Kristel...please."

"What happened, Jade? You were happy..." started Kristel, until she saw her friend turn and saw tears in her eyes, pain and anguish plastered across her face. Jade sat down at the island next to Kristel and prepared her thoughts to tell her what happened. She didn't have the strength to keep arguing with Kristel. She could barely function right now, let alone argue.

"I was very happy...but it all went to hell," started Jade, her eyes filling up with tears. "Here is the quick play-by-play. We went hiking, and it was amazing.

Connor and Lacey are fantastic kids. Bri had a lot of fun with them and with Rachel. When we came back here, Bri took a nap, Rachel and I made out on the couch. After Bri woke up, we had a quick dinner and she went to bed early. Rachel and I had some of the hottest sex I may have ever had in my life."

"So far I'm not seeing the issue here," said Kristel. "Hot sex is always a plus. I'm jealous."

"Yeah, well, I'm getting there. After the hot shower sex, we moved...what? Why do you have that look on your face?" Jade asked as her friend looked shocked.

"Shower sex? Really? I never pictured you as the shower sex type."

"Yeah, I prefer bath sex," said Jade, blushing at her admission. "Anyway, we moved from the shower to bed. We moved from hot to passionate sex, and she told me she loved me."

"What did you say?"

"I pretended I didn't hear her. It was said soft enough that I could have missed it."

"How did it make you feel?" asked Kristel.

"Confused," Jade answered honestly. "The next morning, we had some cuddle time. We hung with Bri for a bit. Rachel went to leave, we said good-bye at the door and I kissed her. After she left, Bri was distant. She went to her room to color for a bit. After I didn't see or hear from her for a couple of hours, I went to talk to her. Turns out, she saw me kissing Rachel."

"Oh boy."

"Yeah, so, she blew up. She told me I wasn't supposed to be kissing anyone but Amy, and now Amy wasn't going to watch over us or love us because I was kissing Rachel. She told me that she wanted to go live with Amy's parents and she hated Rachel."

"Hate is a strong word."

"Yeah, it is. I told her she can dislike someone but not hate them. She stood her ground. She insisted that she wanted to go live with Bo and Alice because they truly loved her and I didn't. She accused me of trying to replace Amy with Rachel and asked if I was going to replace her, too. She yelled at me and told me to get out of her room. I told her not to use that tone. She stood her ground, so I grounded her. She lost her TV and playtime with friends until last night."

"Wow. Okay, so, keep going…"

"After I took her TV away, I came down here and cried for a couple of hours. The morning had started so promising and then it just sucked. Brianna came down later and gave me the ultimatum of either I severed ties with Rachel, or she got to go live with Amy's parents."

"Wait, you called everything off because your kid threw a fucking tantrum about seeing you two kiss?"

"My daughter and her happiness come above everything else," Jade said sternly.

"No, she is a child. You are an adult…or at least you are old enough to be one," snapped Kristel.

"I am an adult and my daughter's happiness comes before anything else," Jade said with a thin edge in her voice.

"Fine, but you couldn't give Rachel the courtesy of telling her this shit? What the hell? Do you know that she has been blaming herself for all of this?" Kristel was severely annoyed. "She believes that it's because she said she loved you that you dumped her like she was trash."

"Since when are you all 'Team Rachel'?"

"Since she gave me the time of day and made my best friend, or who I thought was my best friend, happy. Why didn't you talk to me? Why did you push everyone away, and then run away? Where'd you go for that week?"

"You are really pissed, aren't you?"

"You bet I am fucking pissed. You devastated Rachel, screwed up something that made you extremely happy. And why? Because your daughter didn't like that you kissed someone else. She's a little kid. She doesn't understand that Amy isn't coming back. You do, or you should!" yelled Kristel. "Now, where the fuck did you go?"

"You want me to tell you after that little speech?"

"You owe me that much," Kristel said coldly.

"I don't owe you shit. After I dropped Bri at Amy's parents, I went to the cabin that Amy rented when she told me about the cancer. I sat on the porch, numb, and cried. After a few days there, I went and walked some of hiking trails Rachel had told me about."

"Alone?"

"Yeah, so what," said Jade, annoyed at the way Kristel was acting and talking to her.

"Nobody knew where you were. We were all worried about you. You could have been killed while you were out there and nobody would have known. That was stupid and really, really fucking selfish, Jade."

"Wow, you are just full of good words and warm fuzzy messages today, aren't you?"

"When you are stupid, I am going to tell you. This whole thing is a fucking mess," said Kristel, hanging her head in her hands. "So, are you just going to ignore how you feel about Rachel? How happy you two were? What future you could have had, because

Bri said so?"

"I don't know what else to do," Jade said, defeated. "It is over and done with and doesn't matter what I want or what I feel. Brianna's happiness is more important than my own."

"Mama?" said a little voice.

"Yes, Bri," Jade said without looking up, not wanting her daughter to see her crying.

"Why was Aunt Kristel yelling at you? Why are you crying?" she asked timidly.

"It's nothing for you to worry about."

"Bri, can I talk to you about something?" asked Kristel, receiving a tearful glare from Jade and a nod from Brianna.

"Don't," warned Jade, anger flashing in her eyes.

"Bri, let's go outside and talk," Kristel said, taking the little girl's hand.

"Kristel, I. Said. Don't," Jade said again, this time the anger coming through in her voice as well.

Kristel met Jade's glare and challenged it as she walked out of the room with Brianna. Jade moved quickly out of the kitchen and to the bathroom.

Jade sat up against the wall. Her body was shaking from throwing up. The thought of Kristel talking with and possibly upsetting Brianna made Jade sick to her stomach. She was already emotionally drained. Reliving even in generic terms what had happened with Kristel just reopened the wound and made the pain come back. Hearing Kristel state that she devastated Rachel, she knew that Rachel hadn't let anyone in until her. She broke the trust Rachel had in her. She broke her heart. Jade started to cry realizing how much she had hurt this woman she cared for and could have loved given a little more time.

Chapter Twenty-nine

Hope No More

Kristel and Brianna walked outside and sat down on the deck near Jake. Kristel knew that Jade was livid with her for doing this, but she also knew that Jade wouldn't and couldn't do it herself.

"Bri, you asked why I was yelling at your Mama," started Kristel seeing both Bri's and Jake's eyes watching her intently. "You know your Mama loves you more than anything, right?"

"Uh huh," answered Brianna softly.

"Because she loves you so much, she chose your happiness over her own. Has she seemed different the past two weeks?"

"Yeah. She's always sad, she cries a lot and throws up a lot, too. She doesn't know that I know, but I do."

"You know that your Mommy loved you tons and tons right?" Kristel said, seeing Brianna nod. "You know that she isn't coming back to be with you and Mama, right?"

"Cuz she's in heaven?" asked Jake.

"Exactly."

"This is about Mama kissing Rachel, isn't it?" Brianna asked, a hint of sadness and anger in her voice.

"Yeah, it is, Bri. Your Mommy is always going to be watching over you and loving you. You are her daughter, a piece of her."

"I'm part of Mama, too," added Brianna.

"Exactly, and when you saw your Mama kissing Rachel, that didn't change how your Mommy feels about you or how your Mama feels about you."

"It doesn't?"

"No. What it would have meant was that you had even more love coming your way because Rachel cared about you, too. She wasn't taking away from the love you already had, she was adding to it."

"Is that why Mama was happy then and isn't now?"

"Yeah. Your Mama cared a lot about Rachel, but she loves you more, so instead of upsetting you or making you unhappy, she chose to make herself unhappy."

"She was kissing Rachel and not Mommy, though," said Brianna as tears filled her eyes.

"Sweetie, your Mommy said it was okay for your Mama to love someone else so she wasn't alone."

"She did?"

"Yeah, she did. She told me to make sure your Mama didn't live her life alone…and right now she is very much alone."

"Aunt Jade isn't alone, Mom. She has us," Jake said.

"Yeah, she does, little man."

"She had Rachel, but now she doesn't," Brianna said, seeming to make the connection in her mind.

"Yeah, she loves you a lot," said Jake as Bri started to cry.

"Why? I made Rachel go away. And I told Mama I wanted to go live with Grandma and Grandpa."

"But your Mama knows you want her to be

happy." Jake looked at Brianna, then pointed toward the door.

Jade stood in the doorway. "Bri. Come here."

Brianna jumped up and ran over to Jade who scooped her up in her arms and hugged her close.

"I love you because you are my daughter. You were created from the love Mommy and I had for one another. You remind me so much of her."

"Did you really care about Rachel?" asked Brianna.

"Yeah, I did, but you are more important. You will always be more important to me than anyone else, even myself."

Jade hugged Brianna tight and then she felt Jake hugging her leg.

"I love you, Aunt Jade."

Jade bent down and pulled Jake into the hug with her and Brianna.

"I love you, too, Jakey."

"Mama, do you think Rachel still cares about us?"

"I don't know, baby. I think I screwed that up beyond repair," Jade said, her voice catching. "The way I handled things, I broke her trust and heart."

❦❦❦❦

Rachel was sitting in her home office working on some case files that she had brought home with her. Ever since Jade broke up with her she hadn't been able to focus on what she was doing. She spent hours trying to focus, but something said or something written always reminded her of Jade or Brianna.

Get a grip Cassidy, Rachel said to herself when

she noticed she was daydreaming again. *If she wanted you she would have called, sent you a text, or she would have found a way to reach you. More importantly, she wouldn't have done what she did.*

"Rachel, if you don't stop dreaming about her you are never going to get stuff done," said a voice from the doorway causing her to jump.

"Dammit, Skye," snapped Rachel a bit harsher than she had planned. "I'm going to take that damn key away from you."

"No, you aren't," Skye said smugly. "You still haven't heard from her?"

"At this point even if she called I wouldn't answer."

"You know that Kristel was going over there today don't you?"

"No, but I'm glad that Jade isn't shutting her out like she did me," said Rachel.

"Actually, she has been. Let's get out and do something Rachel. You have been cooped up in this place for too long. Let's go see a movie or just get out of town."

"I can't, I'm on call this weekend. I have to stay nearby in case one of the hospitals needs a psychologist."

"You are in a private practice. How the hell do you have to be on call?"

"When Emily and I moved here I affiliated myself with a few of the hospitals and a part of that affiliation is we rotate on-call duties. It is rare that we get called in, but if they need us we're there. I think I've been called to the Children's Hospital about four times over the past few years. That one always breaks my heart."

"You're a saint, Rachel. My sister was lucky to have you. Now, are you sure you don't have a twin brother or something?"

"Even if I did, I would never let him near you," teased Rachel. "Let's go get some coffee."

"Deal," said Skye, and the two women left the house headed for the coffee shop down the street from Rachel's house.

❧❧❧❧

Brianna and Jade were playing against Kristel and Jake in a game of badminton. Jade and Bri had the lead, but only by two. Kristel served the birdie and Brianna swung the racquet and launched it high in the air. When the birdie finally came down it hit Kristel on the head.

"Ow," said Kristel, rubbing the top of her head. "You did that on purpose didn't you?"

"No." Brianna giggled as Jake fell on the ground laughing.

"So, do I get to call you a bird brain now?" teased Jade.

"Watch it, Donovan," Kristel said, pointing the racquet and mock glaring at the woman.

They decided to end the game and Jake and Brianna played in her wading pool while Jade and Kristel made dinner. As dinner was finishing up, Kristel had Jake and Brianna go wash up. While they were inside Brianna grabbed Jade's phone off the table and found Rachel's number and called her. The phone just rang much to Brianna's dismay. She had hoped for a chance to talk to Rachel and maybe make things right.

After they ate dinner and kids helped clean up, they moved inside and watched a movie before Kristel and Jake had to leave. Jade promised not to be as distant and Kristel promised to be more annoying.

The rest of the weekend was quiet for Jade and Brianna. Sunday they wanted to go out for a walk, but a freak thunderstorm kept them inside. Jade and Brianna colored for most of the afternoon. That evening they made dinner together, and then Brianna took her bath and went to bed.

❧❧❧❧

Rachel spent the weekend doing notes for her cases and tending to the two calls she got from the hospital for patients in need of help. One was a little girl who was a little older than Brianna who came in with cigarette burns. Rachel worked with her and got her removed from her abusive home and into foster care. It broke her heart whenever she encountered an abused child. She knew that no matter how long she lived she would never understand how an adult could hurt a child.

The odd moment of Rachel's weekend happened while she was out having coffee with Skye. Her phone rang while they were talking and she saw that it was Jade's phone number. Rachel thought about answering, but then decided that she couldn't handle it. Skye commended her on not caving and told Rachel that she would be meeting Kristel for drinks on Tuesday night and she would find out then what she had learned.

❧❧❧❧

Jade had just arrived back from a meeting at Scott's gallery when her phone rang and she saw it was the school's number.

"Hello?" she answered.

"Jade? Hi, it's Dawn."

"Hi Dawn. What's wrong? Is Bri alright?"

"There was an accident on the playground and Bri fell and hurt her arm and hit her head. Jade, she was knocked out for several minutes. We called an ambulance and she is headed to the Children's Hospital now."

"How the hell did this happen?" asked a now frantic Jade as she scribbled a note to her assistant telling her to cancel her appointments for today and tomorrow and that Brianna was hurt.

"I am still trying to find out the details, but what I know is you need to get your butt moving and to the hospital. I'll stop by once school is over to see how Brianna is doing and tell you what I found out."

"Thanks Dawn. I'm getting in my car now."

Jade tried her best to remain calm as she drove the three miles in heavy traffic to the Children's Hospital. As Jade drove she called Kristel and told her what happened. Kristel said she would be there after she picked Jake up from school, but to let her know if there were any updates or if she needed anything.

⁂

Rachel was headed into the hospital through the ER entrance when an ambulance pulled up. She stepped out of the way letting the paramedics by and saw that they had a little girl on the gurney who was crying hard and looked petrified. "We have a five-year-old female with a possible broken arm and concussion. She was knocked out at the school and hasn't been able to help us identify if there is anything else wrong." An older gentleman followed behind looking lost.

"Dr. Cassidy, would you be able to help us try to calm the girl down? Her mother is on her way," asked the lead nurse when she saw Rachel in the ER. They had worked together before, and Rachel was always able to get through to the kids that were brought in.

"I'll do my best," said Rachel, following them into one of the private rooms. Rachel shuddered, remembering that it was just a short while ago that she was here with Brianna and Jade. That was one of the hardest nights for Jade, and Rachel was so happy to have been able to help her.

"Who are you?" asked the paramedic to the older man following them in and trying to stay close to the gurney.

"I'm the school's principal."

"Well, you need to wait outside. Do we know the girl's name?"

"Brianna, Brianna Donovan," said the principal, causing Rachel's heart to skip a couple of beats.

Rachel raced over to the bed and looked closely at the red-faced girl who was in hysterics by this point.

"Bri, honey?" Rachel said in a soothing voice, but the girl was too upset to respond. Rachel sat on the edge of the bed and waited for Brianna to look at her. When the girl turned and looked at her she could see her trying to place her. "Bri, it's Rachel. Honey, can you calm down for me?"

Once Brianna realized that it was Rachel talking to her, she started to calm down. Rachel reached over, brushed the hair out of her eyes, and smiled at her.

"Thank you for calming down. I'm going to stay right here with you until Mama gets here, okay?"

Brianna nodded. The doctor came over and startled her, causing her to scurry over to sit on Rachel's lap. As she moved she started to cry again.

"I need to check you over to see what's wrong," said the doctor in a gruff voice.

Brianna frantically shook her head and then her eyes rolled back in her head and her body went limp in Rachel's arms.

"I'm sorry, Dr. Hanson, but where the hell did you learn your bedside manners?" snapped Rachel.

"I'm sorry, but who are you?"

"She is the on-call psychologist who I asked to come in and help calm the patient. What happened?" asked the nurse, turning to Rachel.

"Brianna was starting to calm down when he rushed to the side of the bed and startled her. She ended up on my lap trying to get away from him. He said he needed to check her and she shook her head. I'm guessing with her concussion it was too much and she passed out."

"Do you think she's going to be okay with him looking her over?" the nurse asked Rachel as if the doctor wasn't standing right there.

"I don't believe that is a good idea. Is there someone else on staff?" asked Rachel. She started to feel Brianna waking up as the nurse dragged the doctor out and went to find another to check Brianna over.

"Rachel?" Brianna said in a groggy voice.

"I'm right here, honey. I'm not going to leave you alone," Rachel leaned down and kissed the top of Brianna's head.

"Where is Mama?" Brianna asked, sniffling.

"She's on her way. You're going to be okay."

Rachel held Brianna close trying to keep her calm and quiet. The nurse returned with a doctor who made sure that Brianna knew she was there before approaching the bed. The doctor tried to extract Brianna from Rachel, but she wouldn't budge.

"You are very good with her," said the nurse as the doctor moved around the bed to get a look at Brianna's head where she had hit the ground.

"I know her and her mother, so that makes it easier," Rachel said, smiling.

The doctor finished her exam and ordered an X-ray of Brianna's arm to confirm the break and a CAT scan to rule out any unforeseen trauma to the brain. The nurse and doctor left the room and Rachel adjusted.

"No," squealed the little girl as she started to cry again. "You promised you'd stay."

"I'm not leaving, I just want to get you into a better position," said Rachel.

The nurse brought a nervous Jade into the room where Brianna and Rachel were.

"Bri," called Jade as she entered the room and then stopped, seeing her daughter curled up in Rachel's arms.

"Mama," she sniffled.

"I'm right here, Baby Girl," said Jade, moving toward the bed. "Have they checked her yet?"

"Yeah, they ordered an X-ray of her arm to confirm that it is broken and a CAT scan to check to make sure there's no brain trauma," said Rachel as Jade sat on the bed near them.

"B-b-brain t-trauma?" stuttered Jade, looking

between Brianna and Rachel.

"She was knocked out. It's pretty standard and a great precautionary move. I was relieved when the doctor ordered it."

"How did you know she was here?"

"I was coming in to follow up with a patient I had over the weekend when she arrived. She was hysterical so they asked if I would help try to calm her down. It wasn't until we were in here that I heard her name."

"Thank you, Rachel," Jade said, hoping that she knew how sincerely she meant it.

"I'm glad I was here to help."

They managed to get Brianna moved to Jade's arms without hurting her. Rachel sat with them until the technician came to get them to go for the X-rays and CAT scan. Rachel told Brianna she would check in on her later and kissed her on the top of her head. Rachel turned without looking at Jade again and left the room.

While Brianna was getting her scans, Jade called Bo and Alice to tell them what happened. She told them not to come down yet. She was hoping that after Bri was done with the scans they would get to go home and if so, they could meet them there or come over following day. Jade then called Kristel and told her about how Brianna was doing and that when she got there, Rachel was holding Brianna.

❦ ❦ ❦ ❦

After exiting the room, Rachel leaned up against the wall to gain some composure. Her adrenaline had kicked in when she heard it was Brianna who was injured. Seeing Jade and not being able to comfort her was so hard. She just wanted to wrap her arms around Jade and kiss her and tell her it was going to be okay.

On the way up to the eighth floor to check on her patient, Rachel called Skye and filled her in on today's situation.

"Rach, you should go back down after your patient and see how Bri is doing," encouraged Skye.

"It hurts too much, Skye. I was ready to take that doctor's head off when he scared Bri. Then when Jade came in I just wanted to hold her, kiss her, and tell her it was going to be okay. I can look at Bri's files after they leave to see how she's doing."

"Rachel, just go check on them after you are done. For me?"

"Fine. For you," said Rachel before hanging up and going in to check on her patient.

The girl was responding to the medicine and the techniques Rachel had taught her to deal with the fear. Rachel was pleased with the progress and told her that once she was physically cleared, she would be able to leave and the state already had a foster family for her. The family was one that Rachel knew, and she told the girl that it was a good home. The girl visibly relaxed at Rachel's words.

After finishing with her patient, Rachel went back down to the ER to check on Brianna. When she reached the ER she saw Kristel at the front desk trying to find out any information she could.

"Kristel," said Rachel walking up to the desk.

"Rachel, thank god. Brianna is…"

"I know. I was arriving to visit a patient when she came in. I sat with her until Jade arrived."

"Is she okay?"

"She will be. They took her for X-rays and a CAT

scan just as a precaution. I was just about to check to see if there were any updates."

Just then a flustered brunette came up to the desk asking for Jade and Brianna.

"Dawn?" said Kristel.

"Oh thank god, Kristel. How is Bri?"

"I don't know yet. I just got here. Dawn, this is…"

"Dr. Cassidy," said the nurse coming up to the three women. "The little girl you helped with earlier."

"Brianna, yes. Is she okay?"

"She's upset again, and her mother asked if we could find you and to see if you would be willing to help."

"Of course, is she in the same room?" Rachel saw the nurse nod. "Okay, I'll be there in a minute."

"Rachel, what is wrong with her? Why would Brianna be upset again?" Kristel asked.

"Bri has a concussion, and being disoriented can be a side effect. I'll go make sure that she and Jade are okay. You are welcome to come with, but until Bri is calm, I don't want anyone else in the room."

"Thanks, Rachel. By the way, this is Dawn, Bri's teacher. Dawnie, this is Rachel, a very good friend of the family."

"It is nice to meet you," Dawn said, shaking Rachel's hand.

⁂

"Bri, Baby Girl, you need to calm down."

"I…didn't…like…t-that…m-machine," cried Brianna in Jade's arms.

Jade rocked her daughter, watching the door

and hoping that Rachel would be willing to help. She knew she didn't deserve her help or kindness, but Bri was just a kid and right now she was terrified.

Rachel entered the room and saw Brianna shaking, and the look of helplessness on Jade's face.

"Brianna?" said Rachel, entering. "Honey, remember earlier when I said you needed to calm down or you would make it hurt more?"

"Y-y-y-yeah."

"Crying like that isn't being calm. You're going to scare your Mama and make yourself sick." Rachel winked at her as she moved over next to them and saw Brianna calming.

"R-R-Rachel? Please don't hate Mama. It was my fault she broke up with you," Brianna said, starting to get worked up again.

"Bri, I don't hate your Mama," said Rachel, looking up at Jade. "I was hurt badly by what she did, but I don't hate her. If you can't stay calm, I can't bring Kristel and Dawn in."

"They're both here?" Jade asked, surprised.

"Yeah, but until Bri is calm, I'm not going to authorize them to come in. Did they tell you anything about the scans?"

"Her arm is broken, but it's a clean break so they'll be in to set it and put her in a cast shortly. As for the CAT scan, they said nothing," Jade said, a quiver in her voice.

Rachel reached over and squeezed Jade's hand for comfort and reassurance.

It wasn't long before Brianna was calm enough for Rachel to let Dawn and Kristel in. Brianna made Rachel promise to stay because she felt better with her there. When they came to put the cast on Brianna's forearm, she let Rachel pick the color of her cast. Rachel chose a blue one. After they put the cast on, the doctor came in and told them that the scan was negative as they suspected, but that Brianna would need to be on bed rest for the next two days and longer if the headache persisted. The doctor also told them that they would need to keep an eye on her for the next twenty-four hours, waking her every two hours to check on her. Rachel and Jade thanked the doctor, and they got their stuff together to leave.

"Jade, I'm so sorry Bri got hurt, but I'm glad she is going to be okay. I found out that there were some older kids fighting on the playground. One kid shoved the other and he knocked into Brianna. The police were notified and are going to receive a copy of the medical report. The boys will be held accountable," said Dawn. "Fighting isn't tolerated so they will either be suspended or expelled."

"Thank you for checking, Dawn," Jade said, hugging her.

Dawn moved over and kissed Bri on the head, and told her she would see her on Monday and no sooner. Kristel was next to say her good-byes. Rachel pulled her aside and told her about Brianna saying that Jade pulling away was her fault. Kristel confirmed it was true. Kristel then turned to Jade and told her to call if she needed anything, and if she didn't hear from her she would call around nine o'clock the following morning.

Rachel, Jade, and Brianna found themselves alone in the room. The level of discomfort was palpable.

"Thank you for everything today. I don't know what I would have done had you not been here," said

Jade.

"I'm glad I could be here. Brianna insists that she is the cause of what happened."

"She may have had the issue, but I made the choices that affected things. I won't let her take the blame for something that I did. I am sorry for hurting you. I owed you more respect than I showed you."

"Things are really broken and are going to take time to fix, if we can, but do you want me to help you get her situated at home? I can sleep on the couch."

"I'd love that, and you can sleep in my bed. I doubt I'll sleep tonight. Hell, I doubt I'll leave her side."

Once they received the discharge papers and instructions, Rachel headed to her car and told Jade she was going to stop at home to get a change of clothes and then she would be over. Jade and Brianna headed home. Once they arrived, Jade helped Bri get changed into her pajamas and was helping her get into bed when Rachel arrived. Rachel assisted in getting Brianna's arm into a comfortable position. It was just a matter of minutes before she drifted off to sleep.

Chapter Thirty

Is There A Future?

Rachel watched as Jade watched Brianna sleeping. She wasn't sure what to do, but being there with the two of them still felt right.

"Jade," started Rachel softly. "I'll watch her, you go get comfortable."

"But…" started Jade turning toward Rachel.

"I'll be here with her; you know I won't let anything happen to her."

"Okay, but I'll be really quick," said Jade, moving out of the room to change.

Rachel thought about the past couple of weeks, the pain of how Jade had left things, and the fact that she did it via text. She hadn't had the courtesy to talk to her, explain to her that it was because of Brianna. No, Jade just texted that she needed some space and time and then disappeared. Rachel watched Brianna sleeping. She thought about how scared she was and how she calmed with Rachel's presence. It made Rachel smile.

"How is she doing?" asked Jade, entering Brianna's room while putting her hair into a ponytail and wearing an old pair of grey sweatpants and a burgundy T-shirt that said "Easily distracted by shiny objects."

"She's fine," said Rachel, stifling a gulp at how

gorgeous her ex-lover looked. "She's probably going to sleep for a while. We should wake her up in about an hour and a half."

"I'm glad you're here. Do you want something to drink? I could make something to eat?"

"Jade, relax. Something to drink would be nice," Rachel said.

Jade and Rachel headed downstairs to the kitchen and Jade got them each a soda. They moved into the living room and sat at opposite ends of the couch. Jade seemed uncomfortable.

"I know I have already said this, but thank you for helping Bri, and for being here tonight." Jade was unable to look at Rachel and stared at her hands.

"What went wrong with us? I know this is a shitty time to ask, but I want to understand."

"What went wrong with us? Me, it was my fault. I am so sorry, Rachel. I know that doesn't really mean anything, but I am sorry, and I want you to know it was never my intention to hurt you."

"Tell me what I did wrong? Was it because I told you I loved you?"

"You did nothing wrong. And no, it wasn't because you told me you loved me. I guess I just need to tell you the full story. That is, if you want to know."

"Of course I want to know."

"I was so...god, that Sunday when you left I can't explain how happy I was. It all went south after that. Brianna saw us kissing."

"When?"

"At the door, she must have come down quicker than we knew. She was distant for part of the day, and then she told me why. She told me that I wasn't supposed to be kissing you, that I was only supposed to be kissing Amy. She screamed, and she knew what to say to hurt me," started Jade. She finished recapping the events that caused Brianna to be grounded and how she took the TV to her office before coming down to the living room to cry.

"Wow," said Rachel.

"Yeah, Bri came down a while later and saw me crying," continued Jade explaining the agreement that she made with Brianna to get her to stop trying to move away. "Kristel ripped me a new ass for agreeing with a five-year-old's demands, but at that point, I was so beaten down and confused. I agreed, and that's when I sent you the text. After I sent it I...I felt like something inside me died."

"Yeah, I know that feeling," Rachel said softly.

"I can imagine you do...I was so sick to my stomach at that point. I told Brianna to go pack for the week and I called Bo and Alice and told them that I had an emergency business trip. They said they'd love to watch her. I dropped her off, and I left. When I got back, all the joy for life was gone. I think I was more depressed than I have ever been. I knew that I had betrayed you and the trust you put in me, in us. I knew that I had hurt you and I was disgusted with myself for it. Kristel came over Saturday, which was the first day that Brianna wasn't grounded. She told me how I had lost weight and looked like crap. I eventually told her what happened. She yelled at me...a lot. She told me how stupid I was and how wrong it was that I accepted a five-year-old's demands. She told me that you blamed yourself...and that reopened the wounds and guilt to a raw state. Then she talked with Brianna. I don't know what was said, but when they were done Bri asked if I really liked you. I told her I did, and that you made me happy. She apologized and said she now understood that I could still love Amy and have you in my life and that you weren't trying to replace her Mommy. Then today…at the hospital…you have to hate me, but you still looked after Brianna. You are here. I don't know why…I don't deserve you in my life. I'm too messed up." Tears ran down Jade's face.

"For the record, Kristel was wrong. Yes, you do look thin, but you could never look like crap. I'm glad Bri doesn't hate me anymore. I wish you would have told me this before. You are right. I did let you in and put my guard down for the first time really since Emily died. I knew saying I loved you would seem too soon and may have scared you, but damn, Jade. You sent me a text. You didn't even call, or give me a chance."

"I know…" Jade said, unable to look Rachel in the eyes.

"Where'd you go when you left for that week?" asked Rachel, hoping to buy some time to process her feelings.

"After I dropped Brianna off I went to the cabin that Amy and I used to rent every summer. I talked to her. I thought about you…I replayed that last night over and over in my head. I missed you. After two days at the cabin I couldn't take it. I needed to do something to make me feel closer to you so I looked up several hiking trails and I went and walked those."

"Jade! You should not have done that alone," exclaimed Rachel.

"Yeah, Kristel said, well actually she yelled, the same thing. She added that I could have been murdered and nobody would know."

"She's right."

"I just wanted to feel closer to you and that was

the best way I knew how to do it. I walked the one that you said was your favorite to go on with Emily. I also walked the one that she was hurt on."

"I don't know what to say…"

"I'm not looking for you to say anything, Rachel. I'm just glad that I was able to get some of your time and the chance to tell you. The past couple of weeks have been a torturous hell. I've had two meetings at Scott's gallery. Every time we went to his office we passed your photograph. I wanted to call you, but I couldn't. I didn't deserve the right to speak to you. I still don't."

"I would have been okay with a call," said Rachel, her eyes meeting Jade's for the first time since Jade started her story.

"I'm a better, happier, person with you in my life, Jade. I don't want to lose you completely, but you hurt me deeply. I understand now or have a better understanding, but you are going to have to earn my trust back."

"A second chance is more than I ever thought I would get. I don't deserve it, but I'll take it," Jade said, giving Rachel a lopsided smile.

"We should go check on Brianna and wake her up," said Rachel.

❧❧❧❧

Jade led Rachel up to Brianna's room. She opened the door and saw her daughter lying just how they had left her. Jade sat down on the edge of the bed and rubbed her daughter's back.

"Bri, baby," Jade said softly, leaning over her daughter as she started to stir.

"Mama?" Brianna said, her voice full of sleep.

"I'm right here, sweetie."

"My head hurts," whimpered Brianna.

"I know, baby. You got a pretty bad boo-boo on your head. Do you want some medicine?"

Brianna nodded and as Jade started to move to get up to get the medicine, Rachel entered the room holding the medicine and a glass of water. Jade smiled at her as she took the items from her hands.

"R-Rachel?"

"Hi, munchkin. I know you don't feel good now, but it will get better."

"Here, sit up and take this to help with your arm and head," Jade said, helping Brianna sit up and giving her the syrup to drink and then the water to chase the bad taste away.

"I'm tired," said Brianna.

"Well, you go back to sleep. Mama and I will wake you up again in two hours."

"You're staying? Did you two make up?"

"Yes, I am staying. Mama and I talked, but…"

"I hurt her feelings and I have to earn her trust back."

"So, she doesn't love us anymore?" Brianna sniffled.

"I never said that. I wouldn't be here if I didn't still care deeply about you and your Mama. You know when your friends hurt your feelings it takes a while to stop hurting?" Rachel saw Brianna nod. "Well, it is a lot like that. It is going to take time, but Mama and I are willing to try."

"I'm sorry I was mean and naughty," said Brianna, yawning.

"Get some sleep. I love you, sweetie." Jade leaned

down and kissed Brianna's head.

Once Brianna settled down, Jade opened the closet and pulled out an old baby monitor and plugged it in.

Rachel and Jade left the bedroom and went back downstairs. Jade set the monitor on the coffee table and leaned back on the couch, taking a shaky breath.

"I can't imagine how hard this is, but she is going to be fine," Rachel said, placing a hand on Jade's leg.

"As bad as it is to say, I think it is worse than watching Amy when she first got sick. She understood or at least had the capability of understanding what was going on. Brianna doesn't. She's just a little kid," said Jade, wiping a tear away.

"Come here." Rachel pulled Jade into her arms.

"But..."

"We still have a lot to work through, but I'm not going to sit here and watch the woman I love cry. Like it or not, I am still in love with you. You're a very hard woman to get over," said Rachel as Jade relaxed into the embrace.

Rachel and Jade woke Brianna up every two hours as instructed by the hospital. As late morning arrived, Brianna's headache had subsided enough to where Rachel told Jade she could let Brianna sleep in peace. Hearing that, Jade pulled them into her room where they fell asleep on top of the covers. After a long nap, the three spent a quiet afternoon and evening together.

✻✻✻✻

Jade woke up the following morning on her side and found that she had been covered up. She knew she hadn't done it, as she had spent the previous evening and night checking on Brianna and making sure she was okay. It was late when she and Rachel collapsed on the bed and fell asleep. Now, she was covered up and she thought maybe Rachel had done it. She started to panic thinking that maybe Rachel had woken up and left without saying good-bye. Cautiously she turned over and saw Rachel and Brianna curled up together. Rachel had her arm wrapped around Brianna, holding her close while Brianna had her arm draped across Rachel's chest and her head on Rachel's shoulder. Jade wished she could get a picture of how content and peaceful they looked together.

"And just what are you staring at?" mumbled Rachel.

"You two look so cute together," smiled Jade. "Do you want me to move her?"

"No, we're good. I wonder when she came in here. Did you cover us up?"

"No, I was afraid you had done it and then left without saying good-bye," admitted Jade.

"I would never do that to you, no matter how peaceful you looked sleeping."

"Mama?" said Brianna as she started to stir. She opened her eyes and saw she was cuddled with Rachel instead.

"Morning, Bri, how are you feeling?" asked Rachel, smiling at the little girl in her arms.

"Morning, Rachel. You're nice to cuddle with."

"I agree, she is, isn't she. Morning, Baby Girl," Jade said, moving closer to both Brianna and Rachel.

"Morning, Mama," said Brianna, burrowing into Rachel, allowing Jade the opportunity to get closer as well.

Jade realized that this was the first time in two years it felt like a family was cuddled up in her bed. She and Amy used to cuddle with Bri in bed all the time, but when she got sick they weren't able to. Now, lying with Brianna and Rachel, she felt that family connection again and it made her smile.

After a while Brianna asked if she could go watch TV. Jade told her she could and that she would make them something to eat shortly. Brianna slipped out of bed and they heard her go downstairs and turn the TV on.

"You know, the last time we were in this bed together was the best and worst day I've had in years," said Rachel.

"Yep, I remember that day very well. It was one of the best and worst days I've had, as well. I'd like to work at making more great days." Jade moved closer to Rachel.

"I wouldn't object to that," Rachel said softly.

"Good," said Jade, her lips only millimeters away from Rachel's. Jade felt Rachel lick her own lips. Jade couldn't take it any longer and leaned forward and kissed Rachel tentatively. She felt the surge and connection she had almost destroyed between them. Both women groaned, but both were content where they were, and with just their lips together.

❧❧❧❧

Jade made breakfast for the three of them, and then they got comfortable in the living room and watched movies. Rachel and Brianna knew all the words to the first two they put in. Brianna fell asleep during the third movie. Rachel carried her upstairs and then joined Jade back in the living room.

"Did you have patients today?" asked Jade, realizing that it was Wednesday and not the weekend.

"I cancelled stuff for today and tomorrow. I wanted to be here if you or Brianna needed anything." Rachel smiled reassuringly at Jade.

"Even before you knew what I did?"

"Yeah, even before I knew what happened. It was presumptuous, but I just wanted to be here for you both."

"Thank you," Jade said, lowering her head in guilt. All she could think about was how amazing this woman sitting next to her was, and how horrible she had been to her.

"Hey," said Rachel, raising Jade's head with her finger. "We're working on it and moving forward."

"That doesn't make the fact that I hurt you any less true."

"I want to move forward, baby," Rachel said, taking Jade's hand in her own and kissing it. "If Brianna can accept us as a couple, I don't want to hide it."

"I don't either, Rach," said Jade.

"Good, so, you'll talk to Bri?"

"No." Rachel looked at her in confusion. "We'll talk to her."

"I like that idea," Rachel said, smiling and leaning forward to kiss Jade softly.

The two women were sitting close together, laughing, when Brianna came down the stairs.

"Mama, my head hurts again."

Jade glanced at Rachel, slightly panicked. Rachel gave her a reassuring smile.

"Come here, sweetie." Rachel motioned to her

lap. Brianna climbed onto Rachel's lap and leaned her head against Rachel's shoulder. "Does it hurt anywhere else?"

"No, just my head hurts."

"Is it worse than yesterday?"

"It hurts like it did yesterday, before you and Mama gave me my medicine."

Rachel asked Jade to go get Brianna's medicine and some juice.

"Rach?" asked Jade, entering the room again.

"She's fine. I checked Brianna's stability, strength, and motor skills to make sure that nothing is being hindered. We'll just keep a closer eye on her for a little bit. I'm not worried." Rachel helped Brianna take her medicine and then get her straw into the juice box. "Bri, honey, let Mama and me know if the headache gets better or worse, okay?"

Brianna nodded as she drank her juice and leaned her head against Rachel's shoulder. Jade sat down next to them and rested Brianna's legs across her own. Brianna drifted to sleep in Rachel's arms. They tried to wake her up a little while later, and she started to wake up, but she had a hard time of it. Rachel told Jade she thought they should take her to the ER just as a precaution, as one of the signs to watch out for was trouble waking up or staying awake.

⁂

Rachel drove them to the ER and was relieved to see that the same duty nurse was on. She was talking to the nurse when Jade came in with Brianna. The nurse directed them to one of the private rooms and told them that Dr. Ashe would be in shortly. Both Rachel and Jade were relieved to hear that it was Dr. Ashe who was currently covering the ER. The duty nurse took Brianna's vitals and started a chart. She was just about to leave when the doctor entered.

"Hi, I'm Dr. Ashe...and you already know that," said the doctor, recognizing Jade and smiling as she saw Rachel holding Jade's hand. "Ms. Donovan, Dr. Cassidy."

"Hi," Jade said softly, and Rachel smiled.

"So, I see that Brianna was in two days ago for a concussion and broken arm. What's going on today?"

Rachel proceeded to tell the doctor what had transpired over the past few hours and about the neurological test she had done while Jade was getting Brianna's medicine. The doctor took notes and then did a couple tests of her own. She requested that they start an IV to get some extra fluids and electrolytes in Brianna's system, and then she requested another CAT scan to make sure that there was nothing new going on. Jade started to protest because of how scared Brianna was of the machine, but Rachel stopped her and told her that it needed to be done, and that she would see if they could get her bumped up to the front since she was still asleep. Dr. Ashe said she would make sure that Brianna was next. A nurse came in and took Brianna for the scan. Rachel and Jade were told that they couldn't go with her this time. Jade was on the edge of hysterics when Rachel pulled her into a hug and held her close.

"She's going to be all right Jade. This is one of the best hospitals in the country for kids. Why don't you call Kristel, and Amy's parents, and update them. I'm going to go see if I can find out what Dr. Ashe is thinking."

"Thank you," Jade said before kissing the side of Rachel's head and then pulling out her phone.

✿✿✿✿

Dr. Ashe smiled when she saw Rachel round the corner.

"I wondered how long it would take for you to make it out here to grill me," said the doctor, laughing. "And don't tell me she is just someone from your group. You were just as scared as Jade was."

"You're right, Maria. She is so much more than what she was the last time we were in here."

"You make a cute family. But back to business. I suspect that we're going to see a little swelling, maybe a little bleeding, but nothing to worry about. Brianna is young, and her body doesn't know how to handle trauma. Do you know if she has a history of getting hurt or being sick?"

"In the year and a half I've known them, the two times we've seen you and the other day are the only times she's been sick or injured," said Rachel, rubbing her temples.

"How long have you and Jade been dating?"

"We haven't even been together for two months yet," said Rachel, letting out a long breath.

"Brianna is going to be fine. Go take care of your girlfriend. Brianna should be back in a few minutes and then I'll be in to talk about what the scans show."

"Thanks, Maria," Rachel said, smiling at the woman before heading back to Brianna's room.

✿✿✿✿

"Hey, Jade! How's Brianna?" asked Kristel.

"We're back in the ER," Jade said, on the verge of tears.

"Is Rachel there?"

"Yeah, she's out trying to get more information from the doctor."

"What happened?"

Jade told Kristel about the morning. Kristel asked if Jade wanted her to come down to the hospital. Jade told her that it wasn't necessary, but she promised to keep Kristel updated.

Jade then called Bo and Alice and told them what was going on. They insisted on coming down. Jade told them the room number and was just hanging up when Rachel came back in.

"How'd it go?" asked Rachel, walking over and holding Jade close.

"Kristel wanted to come down, but I told her we'd keep her updated. Bo and Alice are on their way," Jade said with a shudder. "What were you able to find out?"

"Well, I found out that Maria, um, Dr. Ashe, thinks we make a cute family," said Rachel, clearly trying to lighten the moment and calm Jade a bit. Jade chuckled. "Maria said she doesn't expect anything serious. There may be some swelling or some bleeding, but Bri is young and her body doesn't know how to handle trauma. Maria said she should be back soon, and that she would be in shortly after that to discuss the results."

"Thank you," Jade said as Rachel squeezed her closer.

They separated as they heard them wheeling Brianna back into the room. The orderlies said that she didn't wake up at all. Jade wasn't sure if she should be relieved or not. She sat on the edge of the bed and took Brianna's hand. Rachel placed her hands on Jade's shoulders and kissed the top of her head.

Dr. Ashe brought Amy's parents in with her. Jade could see the knowing smile on the doctor's face and the surprised look on Amy's parents' faces at the physical closeness of Rachel and Jade.

"I found them in the hallway," said the doctor.

"Thank you," Jade said, smiling in that direction and feeling Rachel press a little tighter to her back.

"So, the scan is back and there is a little swelling. It's nothing more than I would expect given the fall she took the other day. The body heals faster when you are asleep. My theory is her body knows it needs time to heal and is making her sleepy so that she can do so. I'm glad you were cautious and brought her in. I'd like to finish this IV and get another one going just to make sure she has ample fluids in her. I can keep her overnight, but honestly, as long as you're willing to watch her, I think she'd be more comfortable at home. Are there any questions?"

"Is the swelling going to cause any damage?" asked Bo.

"No, none at all, here, let me show you," said Dr. Ashe as she turned on the computer screen and pulled up the CAT scans from the previous day and compared them to today. "Right here is the swelling from today. And if you look at the original scan…honestly it is just a fraction more. She'll be fine in a few days. Jade, would you like her to stay or go home?"

"If you believe it is safe, I'd feel better with her at home in her own bed…or next to me in mine," Jade said, looking down at her daughter.

"I think Bri would be more comfortable there as well. I'll get the orders written and then when she gets done with the second batch of fluids, you'll be free to go."

"Thank you, Dr. Ashe," said Jade.

"Thanks, Maria," Rachel said, smiling at the doctor.

"My pleasure. Rachel, can I talk to you briefly about that case you attended to over the weekend? I know the timing is bad."

"Go, really," said Jade, looking back at Rachel and smiling.

"Sure." Rachel followed the doctor out of the room.

※ ※ ※ ※

"What's up, Maria?" asked Rachel when they got to the hall.

"The girl you were treating. I'm going to release her to the foster care system tomorrow late. I needed to make sure you were okay with that."

"Yep. I talked with her two days ago and she understood what was going to happen and what it meant. She is as ready as she can be. I spoke with the police and her parents are still in jail, so she can be moved and kept under protection without interference."

"Thank you for being so thorough. Working with you makes things a whole lot easier."

"I'm glad I can help."

"I won't keep you. That older couple didn't seem pleased you were so close to your girlfriend."

"Yeah, I'm not their favorite. Their daughter

was Jade's wife, who passed away. They're seeing me as a threat right now and are taking it out on her."

"Good luck!"

With that, Rachel made her way back to the hospital room.

❧❧❧❧

"You two seem close," said Alice, her eyes narrowing at Jade.

"Not here and not now Alice." Jade glanced over at her mother-in-law before looking back at Brianna.

"Mama?"

"I'm right here, Baby Girl," Jade said, squeezing Brianna's hand.

"W-where are w-we?"

"Rachel and I brought you back to the hospital. We couldn't wake you up. You're going to be okay, though. Grandma and Grandpa are here to see you, too."

Brianna looked to the other side of the bed and saw the older couple. Brianna smiled at them and then frowned.

"What's wrong?" asked Bo.

"Where's Rachel?" asked Brianna, her voice a little panicked.

"I'm right here," she said as she entered the room. "I had to talk to the doctor about one of my patients from over the weekend."

"You have a patient here?" asked Brianna as Rachel sat down at the foot of the bed and rested her hand on Brianna's leg.

"Yep, but she is getting better and is going to be leaving late tomorrow. How are you feeling?"

"My head doesn't hurt as much."

"I'm glad. Mama and I were worried about you."

"Is that why you brought me here?"

"Exactly," said Rachel.

"Mama, can I talk to Grandma and Grandpa alone?" asked Brianna.

"Sure," Jade said, and she and Rachel stepped out of the room.

"What's up, Bri?" asked Alice.

"Stop giving Mama and Rachel mean looks. Mama is happy and it doesn't mean that Mommy loves me any less or that anyone is replacing Mommy."

"Is that what they told you?" asked Bo.

"Yes, and so did Aunt Kristel, and she doesn't lie to me."

"Do you like Rachel?" asked Alice.

"She's nice and she cares about Mama and me."

"Okay, we'll try to be nicer," said Bo.

They motioned for Rachel and Jade to come back in. After a couple of hours they were told that they could leave. Jade told Bo and Alice she would call them in the morning to let them know how Brianna was doing. They thanked her and Rachel, and left. Brianna told Rachel and Jade that she talked to Bo and Alice and they weren't going to be mean to Rachel anymore. After that the three set out for Jade's house.

Chapter Thirty-one

Out and Proud

Rachel drove Jade and Brianna home. Once they were home, Jade settled Brianna in her bed, knowing that the medicine she had been given would allow her to sleep through the night. Jade went to the kitchen trying to find something to make for dinner.

"We could just order something so that you can finally rest and relax," said Rachel, wrapping her arms around Jade from behind and resting her chin on Jade's shoulder.

"Mmmmm, and what would you like for dinner?" asked Jade, leaning into Rachel's embrace.

"Anything that doesn't involve you cooking," said Rachel, smiling.

"Subs?"

"Perfect."

The two women pulled up the menu and ordered their dinner. They retreated to the living room to wait for dinner to arrive. They stretched out on the couch, their legs entwined together. Jade brushed a stray lock of hair behind Rachel's ear.

"You are so beautiful," Jade said. "I can't believe that I'm here with you. The past few days have been heaven and hell combined."

"I've been afraid that I'm dreaming," admitted

Rachel. "That I am going to wake up alone in my bed."

"It's real, sweetheart. You're really here with me. I don't know that I would or could have survived the past few days without you. Thank you for giving me a second chance," Jade said.

"You know, I normally don't give people second chances, but I want...no...I need you in my life," said Rachel.

"I promise you won't regret it," Jade said before kissing Rachel softly.

After their dinner arrived and they ate, they went up and checked on Brianna again. Jade was happy to see Brianna still sleeping so soundly. She and Rachel went into her room and changed for bed. Rachel wore one of Jade's old T-shirts and a pair of boxers. Jade wore her favorite thin T-shirt and boxers. Neither left much to the imagination, and that was why she had chosen them. They got into bed and lay facing one another.

"What time do you have to get up tomorrow for work?" asked Jade.

"I'm not going to work tomorrow. I'm actually thinking about cancelling group or getting someone to look after it tomorrow so that I can be here with you."

"Rach, you have patients and group, and they need you," said Jade.

"Work is covered. I have my critical patients seeing my colleagues, and those that I can reschedule, I have. As for group, I had two weeks without you there and I don't know that I can do a third. On top of that Carmen was back last week, and it was really uncomfortable."

"I'm sorry, sweetie. Please don't cancel group.

If Bri is doing better, I can have Kristel come and stay with her while we go to group, or she can go over there."

"That would be great, but only if Brianna is doing better."

The two women lay there, lost in the other's eyes. They had been on an emotional roller coaster the past couple of days, but they were together and that was what they both needed.

"I don't want to hide our relationship anymore," Jade said, breaking the silence.

"Are you sure?"

"Yes, I'm sure that I want a relationship with you, and I don't care who knows about us," said Jade confidently. "The only reason it was a secret before was because of Brianna. Well, she knows about us, and is okay with us now that she understands that you aren't trying to replace Amy, and that we don't expect her to forget about Amy."

"You are an amazing woman, you know that?"

The two women cuddled together and drifted off to sleep. The day had taken its toll on them and they needed sleep.

❧❧❧❧

When Brianna woke in the morning, she seemed to be feeling a lot better. She helped Rachel make Jade breakfast in bed. After they ate breakfast, Rachel insisted on cleaning up the kitchen while Jade and Brianna had some time alone. Jade asked Brianna how she felt about her going to group and if Brianna would like to hang out with Kristel and Jake. Brianna said she thought it sounded like fun. Jade also talked to Brianna about her dating Rachel to make sure that they didn't have another blowout. Brianna stated that she understood more now, and told Jade she was okay with the relationship, and that she liked seeing her Mama smile the past couple of days. When Rachel finally came back upstairs Brianna told them she was going to go watch a movie in her room.

"She really seems to be back to her old self," said Rachel.

"Yeah, and we talked about group tonight and she is excited about going to visit Kristel and Jake while we go. And I took the opportunity to talk to her about us," said Jade.

"What about us?" Rachel asked, unable to hide her grin.

"I wanted to make sure she knew and understood that we were a couple. She may see us kissing and holding hands. I just didn't want another blowout like we had the last time she saw us kiss," said Jade.

"And how do you feel about us kissing?," Rachel said coyly.

"I feel like it has been too long," Jade said in a sultry tone.

Rachel leaned in, kissing Jade lightly, then deeply. Jade groaned at the feel of the soft lips pressed against her own.

After kissing for longer than they had time for, Rachel told Jade that she had to get home to get some paperwork done, but that she would be by later to pick her and Brianna up. They had called Kristel and were going to drop Brianna off on their way to group and then they would pick her up afterward. Jade had offered to drive herself, but Rachel said she wanted to spend the time together.

"Rachel Danielle Cassidy," yelled the voice when Rachel answered her phone.

"Geez, what the hell, Skye?" snapped Rachel.

"What the hell? Where the hell have you been? Would it have killed you to send a text or call?"

"You were the one that told me to go back to check on Bri. That's what I did, and I have been with her and Jade ever since. I'm going home now to get some work done before group."

"You've been with Jade and Brianna?"

"Yes. We had to take Bri back to the ER yesterday," said Rachel.

"Is she okay?" Skye said, her voice laced with concern.

"Yeah, she is. There was a little brain swelling, but nothing serious."

"Soooo, what's the status of you and Jade?"

"We're dating and not hiding it. We've talked with Brianna about it and she understands that I'm not here to take Amy's place or to have her forget about Amy."

"That's fantastic, Rachel. I'm happy for you, but I am still going to give Jade a piece of my mind."

"Please don't. We're past it."

"Fine, but she better not hurt you again…"

"If that happens, you have permission to let her have it. I gotta get some work done. I'll talk to you later," said Rachel.

"Fine! I'm glad you two worked it out. Love ya, Rach," said Skye.

"Love ya, too, Skye."

❧❧❧❧

Jade and Brianna spent the remainder of the day coloring and watching movies. Jade made sure that Brianna took a bath and kept her cast dry. Jade showered and got dressed in an old pair of very faded jeans and a low-cut V-neck shirt. She hadn't consciously chosen the revealing shirt, but when she realized it, she smiled and hoped it pleased Rachel.

"Mama, is Rachel staying over again tonight?" asked Brianna as they sat in the living room.

"I don't know. Is it okay if she does?"

"Yeah. I like seeing you smile."

"I like smiling. I love you, Bri. I need to know that you are really okay with this and that you aren't going to get upset like you did before."

"I love you, too, Mama. I like Rachel. She's helped us lots and she cares. I like that she makes you happy."

"Thank you," said Jade, wrapping her daughter into a hug.

❧❧❧❧

After dropping Brianna off at Kristel's, Jade and Rachel headed to the Community Center for their group meeting. Once Rachel parked the car she leaned over and kissed Jade soundly on the lips.

"Are you ready for this?" Rachel asked.

"As long as you're with me, I'm ready for anything."

The couple got out of Rachel's car and walked inside holding hands. As they entered the room,

Rachel saw that several of the regulars were already there setting up, noticing the intimacy between the two of them. She suspected that everyone knew that Carmen had a crush on her, and they all saw Carmen's demeanor change as she locked eyes with Jade.

"So, what's up with you two?" asked Doug.

"What are you talking about?" Jade asked.

"She's been moping through the last two weeks because you weren't here. Now you're holding hands and she's smiling."

"We found an attraction and we enjoy spending time together. Brianna has formed a strong connection to Rachel, and Bri was in the hospital twice this week, Rachel was there for us."

"You two are so cute together," said Doug.

"Is Brianna okay?" Sharon asked.

"She will be. She has a broken arm and a concussion."

"Rachel, what about your professional rules and ethics?" the woman who stood next to Carmen asked.

"Jade isn't a patient of mine. I do not see her professionally, so there are no professional rules and ethics being compromised. This group is something I do on my own time. I don't get paid for it. I'm sorry some of you may have an issue with me dating Jade, but you are welcome to find another group if it is that big of an issue."

"Rach, sweetie," Jade said softly.

"I'm sorry," Rachel said, looking lovingly at Jade.

They started group and although it started tense, they managed to settle it down. When group ended Doug and Sharon helped Rachel and Jade clean up. When the four walked out to the parking lot, Carmen was leaning up against Rachel's car.

"What can we do for you Carmen?" asked Rachel.

"I just wanted to remind Jade that she'd better not hurt you. By the way you were acting last week, I know she already has, but if it happens again, she'd better watch herself." Carmen locked her eyes with Jade's.

"It was a misunderstanding." Rachel stepped between the two women. Jade wrapped her arms around Rachel's waist and pulled her body close.

"Watch yourself, blondie." Carmen walked past the group, got in her car, and left.

"Well, that was intense," said Doug.

"Are you okay?" said Rachel, turning in Jade's arms.

"I'm fine," Jade said before she softly kissed Rachel's lips. Both of them forgot that Doug and Sharon were standing there as well.

"All right, break up the mushiness," teased Doug, causing the two women to part.

"Thanks for helping clean up, and for sticking around while the craziness happened," said Rachel.

"I'm glad you two found one another." Sharon hugged the two women before heading to her car.

"I'm glad you two found one another, too. You are so cute together." Doug hugged Rachel and then Jade.

"Thank you," both women said.

Rachel and Jade got in the car and headed to pick up Brianna before going back to Jade's house.

✥ ✥ ✥ ✥

Jade put Brianna in bed and as she turned around to leave, she saw Rachel standing in the doorway smiling at her.

"What are you smiling at?" asked Jade, closing Brianna's door and taking Rachel by the hand, and leading her down the hall to her room.

"Do you realize how low cut that shirt is? How teasingly mean it was to wear such a thing when I had to keep my hands to myself?" asked Rachel, allowing herself to be led by Jade.

"Did you think that I may have planned it that way? Planned…" said Jade, closing her bedroom door and pushing Rachel back against it and then pressing her body into Rachel's. "Planned, to make you want me as much as I want you."

Jade said the last part as a whisper before kissing Rachel firmly while pressing her thigh against her lover's heated core. Jade felt Rachel pressing into her leg and then she felt hands cupping her breasts. Jade too let out a loud moan as Rachel started to massage her breasts. Jade broke the kiss and arched into Rachel's hands.

"Mmmm, Rachel," said Jade, feeling Rachel drop her head and start to kiss the exposed parts of Jade's breasts while her hands continued massaging them.

Rachel walked Jade backward. Jade sat down when the back of her legs hit the edge of the bed and pulled Rachel to stand between her legs. Rachel looked deep into Jade's eyes. Rachel audibly gulped as she felt Jade start to unbutton and unzip her pants. Jade slid her hands around Rachel's hips and then pushed the pants and panties down. The scent of arousal was intoxicating. Jade raised the hem of Rachel's shirt and placed several wet kisses on her soft skin. Rachel ran her hands through Jade's hair. Jade's hands worked their way up Rachel's firm body to unhook the front clasp of Rachel's bra. Jade stood and removed her lover's shirt and bra. Rachel stepped out of the clothes pooled at her feet.

"You are so beautiful," Jade said, gazing at the body before her.

"You make me believe that," Rachel said softly as she started to remove Jade's shirt and bra. Rachel dipped her head and kissed Jade's breasts. Jade leaned her head backward and let out a sensual moan as Rachel helped her get out of her jeans and panties.

They lay in the middle of the bed, Rachel covering Jade's body with her own. Jade pulled Rachel into a heated kiss. Their lips were moving together. Their bodies started to move together, hips rocking. Rachel pulled back from the kiss grudgingly. She pressed their foreheads together trying to keep as much of their bodies in contact with the other. Jade ran her hands up and down Rachel's body and each time she passed, she teased Rachel's breasts and squeezed her ass.

"Jade...that feels so good," moaned Rachel, arching into her lover's touch.

Jade leaned up and pressed her lips to Rachel's neck. Feeling Jade latch onto her neck, Rachel pressed her leg harder between Jade's heated center. Jade let out a gasp and moan, feeling Rachel pressing against her. Jade adjusted her leg so that Rachel was pressed tightly against her. Both women groaned at the increased pressure.

Rachel leaned down and kissed Jade softly on the lips before trailing kisses along her jaw and down her neck. Jade tilted her head to one side allowing Rachel better access. As Rachel sucked on Jade's neck, Jade threaded fingers into her hair, holding her tightly against Jade's neck.

"Oh yes," said Jade, the words coming out as a barely audible moan.

Rachel moved down Jade's collarbone to kiss her way down to the valley between Jade's breasts. She kissed around each breast and was extra careful not to touch the hypersensitive areas. Jade was in heaven and being tortured with wanton desire.

"Rachel, please," begged Jade.

"Soon, baby," Rachel said while kissing and teasing Jade's body. Jade felt that Rachel had to know her body was aching with need right now.

"Oooohh, Rachel," groaned Jade.

"Mmmm, yes."

"Oh yes," moaned Jade. "Rachel...come up here...I want...mmmm...us to...come together."

Rachel moaned and the vibrations surged through Jade's body. They were both moving closer to their climax.

"Jade...so close..." Rachel panted.

"Me, too, baby."

It wasn't long before Rachel sent Jade over the edge, and she called out Rachel's name. Rachel followed, screaming Jade's name in return. They rode out the orgasms as long as they could. Rachel collapsed on top of Jade before being pulled into a deep kiss.

"Was that what you had in mind when you put that shirt on, my little vixen?" asked Rachel, still lying on top of Jade.

"I planned on seducing you. However, I had no idea it was going to be so mind blowing. I think we get better every time."

"I think we do, too. As for mind blowing...yeah, definitely." Rachel smiled. "I will get off of you as soon as I regain control of my limbs."

"No rush," said Jade, wrapping her arms around Rachel.

When the afterglow subsided and with their limbs finally responding, the two women decided to shower together. Being naked and wet ignited their primal urges and they took each other again in the shower. When they were done with their shower they got dressed in their pajamas to make sure that they were decent in case Brianna came in the room.

"You are an amazing woman, Rachel," Jade said as they started to drift off to sleep.

"So are you, my love. So are you," responded Rachel.

Chapter Thirty-two

Living Life

Rachel and Jade woke early. They lay in bed kissing for a long time before deciding to get up and go downstairs. Jade was making coffee and Rachel was checking her schedule on her phone when Brianna walked in.

"Morning, Mama. Morning, Rachel," said Brianna around a yawn.

"Good morning, Bri," said Rachel.

"Morning, Baby Girl," Jade said, picking her daughter up and hugging her close before setting her on the chair next to Rachel.

"Can I go to school today?" asked Brianna.

"No, but you will be able to go back on Monday."

"What am I going to do today then?" pouted Brianna.

"Well, you and I can hang out and play a board game, watch movies, color, and maybe even draw me a new picture for work."

"Are you going to be here too, Rachel?"

"Sorry, Bri. I have to go to work today."

"But I didn't get to spend time with you when I wasn't hurt or sleeping," whined the little girl.

"Whining isn't the way to get that either," Jade said, giving her daughter a knowing look.

"Yes, Mama," mumbled Brianna.

"How about this," started Rachel. "If you are a good girl today, and there is no more whining, you, me, and your Mama can hang out tomorrow. I know of a perfect place where we will all have fun. How does that sound?"

"Can we, Mama?" Brianna asked softly.

"If you are good today and you still feel good tomorrow, we can go hang out with Rachel."

"Thank you, Rachel." Brianna hugged Rachel. "Mama? Can I go watch TV before breakfast?"

"Sure, sweetie."

"Can I have a hug quick? I have to head to work in a couple of minutes," said Rachel.

"I promise to be good," Brianna said into Rachel's ear.

"Thank you," whispered Rachel.

When they broke the hug, Brianna smiled and skipped into the living room.

"I'm going to miss you today," Jade said, wrapping her arms around Rachel's waist.

"I'm going to miss you, too. I hope what I offered was okay. I didn't mean to put you on the spot or anything."

"I want us to spend time together, the three of us. I need her comfortable with our relationship. I care very deeply for you."

"I want her comfortable with us as well. I love you both and I want us to work," Rachel said, looking deep into her lover's eyes.

"You are such an amazing woman," Jade said before pulling Rachel close and kissing her gently.

Rachel poked her head in the living room and said good-bye to Brianna again. After Rachel left, Jade and Brianna had some cereal for breakfast and then they pulled out the crayons and coloring books.

✠ ✠ ✠ ✠

After leaving Jade's house, Rachel drove home and changed before going to work. She arrived at work and was headed into the building when she heard a male voice call her name. Rachel turned to see one of her colleagues.

"Good morning, Mark," said Rachel as the man caught up to her.

"Good morning. Is everything all right? You've been gone for a couple of days," asked Mark as they entered the elevator.

"Yes. My girlfriend's daughter was in the hospital and I just needed to be there for them."

"I'm glad everything is all right. So, girlfriend? This is the first I've heard of this."

"It's a new relationship," said Rachel, giggling. "You are as bad as Skye."

"What? Skye knows? And I thought we had something special," teased Mark.

"Well, if you're nice, I may introduce you to Jade and Brianna."

"So, tell me about her."

"I met Jade in the grief counseling group I run on Thursday nights. She lost her wife two years ago. Brianna, her daughter, is five and a mini version of Jade."

"What does Jade do for a living?"

"Jade is an art agent. She helps artist get shows, spots in galleries, even sponsored on some of the art circuits."

"Wow, that sounds interesting. You seem happy.

That's what is important. Have a good day and I expect to meet her soon," Mark said as he turned to go to his office.

Rachel saw that her assistant wasn't at her desk yet, but it was still early. Rachel went into her office and sat down to prep for her first patient.

❧ ❧ ❧ ❧

"Mama, can I draw Rachel a picture?" asked Brianna as they were cleaning up after coloring.

"I bet she would love that," Jade said, smiling.

"Can we take her lunch?"

"Bri, is this your way of getting us out of the house?" Jade asked, seeing her daughter smile.

"Um, no?"

"I'll send Rachel a message to see if she has time for lunch or not. Does that work?"

"Thank you, Mama!"

Jade picked up her phone and sent a text to Rachel. She was surprised when she received a reply almost immediately saying that she would love to have lunch with them. Rachel suggested they do the in-office picnic again. Jade agreed that sounded like a good idea. Rachel said she'd have her assistant order them lunch and they just had to show up at noon.

"You better get drawing if you are going to take her a picture when we meet her at noon for lunch." Jade laughed as Brianna giggled and quickly started to draw a picture for Rachel.

❧ ❧ ❧ ❧

Brianna and Jade rode up in the elevator to

Rachel's office. The doors opened and Brianna smiled when she saw Rachel's name on the door in front of them. They entered and saw that the main receptionist and Rachel's assistant were both away from their desks. Jade was about to go sit by Rachel's office when a man in his lower thirties came out of one of the offices.

"Hello. May I help you?" he asked Jade.

"We're here to see Dr. Cassidy," she replied.

"Well, it appears that the receptionist and her assistant have stepped away. Let me see if Rachel is available."

The man went and knocked on Rachel's door before popping his head in. Jade couldn't hear what was said, but she smiled when she saw Rachel coming out.

"Mark, this beautiful blonde is my girlfriend Jade, and this is her daughter Brianna. This is Mark. He's one of the guys I work with," said Rachel, walking over to them.

"Hi," said Brianna, smiling and holding her hand out.

"It's nice to meet you," said Mark, shaking Brianna's hand.

"It's nice to meet you, Mark," Jade said, shaking Mark's hand as well.

"And you as well. I won't keep you," said Mark as he bowed out of the conversation and headed out of the main door.

"Come on in, my assistant is picking up lunch now. She should be back any minute, though."

Jade and Brianna followed Rachel into her office. Rachel had placed a blanket on the floor for them to sit on.

"Um, Rachel?" said Brianna softly.

"What's up Bri?"

"I made you a picture." Brianna held out the creation.

Rachel looked at the picture and smiled. The picture was of the three of them on top of a rock looking over a bunch of trees and animals.

"This is beautiful, Brianna. Thank you," Rachel said, hugging Brianna. "Where should we hang it?"

Just as Brianna was about to answer Rachel's office door opened and her assistant walked in carrying a bag containing their food.

"I'm sorry it took so long. The line was outrageous today," said her assistant as she set the food down next to the blanket before exiting the room.

"So, where do you think we should put the picture?" Rachel asked Brianna again.

"How about right here?" said Brianna, pointing to a cabinet door behind Rachel's desk.

"Perfect," said Rachel, taking two pieces of tape and put the picture up.

The two joined Jade on the blanket and ate their lunch. Brianna told Rachel about their morning and asked her what they were doing the next day. Rachel told Brianna it was a surprise, but it was something that would be a lot of fun for them all. After lunch Jade and Brianna helped Rachel clean up her office before they had to leave. Rachel hugged Brianna and then Jade, who gave her a soft kiss.

As they were leaving they saw Mark again, and he waved to them before following Rachel back into her office.

"She's quite attractive, Dr. Cassidy," said Mark.

"Yep, gorgeous, brains, and an amazing mother."

"That little girl was just adorable. What happened

to her arm?"

"Some older kids were fighting on the playground. One of them got knocked into Bri and she fell. She hit her head, giving her a nice concussion, and broke her arm as well. That's why I've been out the past few days."

"Good reason. I'm glad she's okay. You seem happy," said Mark.

"I am. I love them both," Rachel admitted to him.

"Wow, love. I don't know that I have heard you say that word since Emily died."

"I haven't…"

"Well, does she feel the same way?"

"I think she's getting there. Jade is more cautious because it's only been two years since Amy died, and because she doesn't want Brianna to get hurt."

"That is a good plan. I guess you were right, she is hot and smart," said Mark, grinning and wiggling his eyebrows.

"Jackass! Get out of my office. I have a patient due in a couple of minutes."

"Fine, be that way," Mark said as he left the office.

❧ ❧ ❧ ❧

Jade was up and dressed in a semi low-cut shirt and a pair of jean shorts. She had dressed Brianna in a pair of cargo shorts and a Minion T-shirt. They were waiting for Rachel to arrive. Just as Brianna was starting to get impatient she saw the car she had been waiting for pull into the driveway. Rachel got out of her car and she was met at the door by her two favorite people.

"Good morning," Rachel said, smiling at Brianna.

As she entered, Rachel noticed the cut of Jade's shirt and smiled.

"Morning, Rachel," Brianna said before running to the bathroom down the hall.

"Good morning." Jade pulled Rachel into a hug and kissed her slowly.

"You look beautiful as always," said Rachel. "That T-shirt is going to be very distracting today."

"Do you want me to change it?"

"No, I don't *want* you to change it, but you may want to. We're going to a small amusement park. They have a couple of roller coasters, some water rides, a train ride, and mini golf."

"Bri, go put your shoes on. Rachel said my shirt won't be good to wear today, so she's going to pick one out for me. When we get back down we'll be ready to go."

"Yes, Mama," said Brianna, going to get her shoes. Rachel and Jade made their way up to Jade's room.

Once inside Jade's room, Rachel turned to face her and placed her lips on Jade's neck as her hands cupped Jade's breasts.

"Mmmm, Rachel," groaned Jade, feeling the lips on her neck and Rachel's hands on her breasts.

"I have never known anyone that can get me so turned on," Rachel said into Jade's neck.

"You do the same thing to me," said Jade, pulling Rachel up to a searing kiss.

"Mmmm, not to ruin the mood, but you make me feel like a horny teenager."

"Trust me, what you do with your hands, no teenager would be skilled enough to do," Jade said. They came together in another powerful kiss.

When they broke apart, they both calmed

themselves and Rachel chose a different shirt for Jade before heading back downstairs just as Brianna had finished pulling her shoes on with her one good hand and waited for Jade to tie them.

"Are we ready?" asked Rachel.

"YES!" said Jade and Brianna together.

"Then let's go," said Rachel, leading them out of the house and over to her car.

Once they were in the car Brianna asked how far they had to go and Rachel told her only about thirty minutes. Jade looked at her questioningly, Rachel just smiled and after about twenty minutes on the highway she pulled off. After a few corners and hills they came upon a sign in bright lights that read "Family Park." The tag line below made Jade smile. "Come as a family, Grow as a family."

"I've lived in this area for years and I had no idea this place existed," Jade said.

"You've never been here before Mama?"

"Nope, I've never been here."

"I brought Connor and Lacey here a few times after Emily died. It was a lot of fun," Rachel said, smiling at them.

"Can they come with us another time?" asked Brianna.

"I think they would love that," said Rachel. "Let's go have some fun."

Jade couldn't help but smile when she saw Brianna take Rachel's hand as they walked in the park entrance. It wasn't a big park and it wasn't very crowded. Jade really liked the feel of the place. They paid the entrance fee and got their bracelets. Brianna got a special bag decorated with zoo animals to protect her cast in case they went on a water ride. Jade put that in her handbag so they didn't lose it. They walked around the full park to its offerings. After they had a good idea of what was there, Jade sat back and let Rachel and Brianna make the game plan. She was amazed at how comfortable Brianna seemed with Rachel. It stunned her how much had changed over the past week.

"Mama? Why are you smiling?" Brianna asked, crawling on Jade's lap.

"Because I'm happy. So, do we have a plan?"

"Yep! Brianna and I worked out a plan. We're going to start at the back of the park and work our way forward going down this side," said Rachel, pointing to the map they had found of the park. "Then we'll have lunch and continue up the middle section, then go back down this side and we'll end up by the exit to go home."

"That sounds like a great plan to me. Lead the way," said Jade as they got up and headed toward the first stop on their day together.

❧ ❧ ❧ ❧

"That was the best ride yet!" Brianna shouted as they came off the corkscrew roller coaster.

"I have to agree," said Jade, smiling. "What did you think, sweetie?"

Rachel laughed. "I think we need to go on that ride again!"

They went on the ride again, then made their way to the last ride before their planned stop for lunch. Brianna chose to ride the bumper cars with Jade. Brianna told Jade which direction to turn and Jade followed her instructions. They bumped into several people before they caught up to Rachel. When they bumped Rachel, Brianna squealed, causing the two adults to laugh. After the ride they hit the snack bar for lunch, before making their way to the back of the park. The rides in the middle section were very tame and allowed their food to settle. When they reached the back of the park Brianna asked if she could go on the kids' train ride. They told her she could, and she hugged them both before getting in line.

"This place is amazing." Jade and Rachel waved to Brianna and the train pulled away.

"Yeah, it is a cool place. Come with me," said Rachel, taking, Jade's hand and pulling her along.

They walked for a couple of minutes on a path until it led them to a small wooden bridge over a little stream.

"We'll be able to see Bri from here," said Rachel, leaning against the railing.

Jade put her hands on the railing on either side of Rachel and smiled.

"I haven't seen Bri this happy in a long time. Thank you for bringing us today."

"She isn't the only one having a good time and happy. I never knew this place could be like this." Rachel rested her hands on Jade's hips and pulled their bodies closer.

Jade leaned forward and kissed Rachel. The kiss was a slow and deep one.

"Rach, tell me this is real and not a dream. Tell me that the feelings I have inside are real and that I can trust them," Jade said, almost in a whisper.

"I love you, Jade. I'm not going anywhere and whatever happens, we'll work it out. I know what I feel for you is real. Trust your heart, baby," replied Rachel, kissing Jade softly. "What does your heart tell you?"

"It tells me that I'm falling in love with you…" said Jade kissing Rachel softly. "It tells me…" Jade brushed her lips against Rachel's. "to trust in you…to trust in us."

Rachel pulled Jade as close as she could and kissed her with all the emotion she could put into a kiss.

The women pulled apart when they heard the train whistle. Rachel turned in Jade's arms to look and wave at Brianna. Brianna was laughing and she waved when she saw them. After Brianna passed Rachel turned to face Jade again and smiled.

"What are you smiling at?" asked Jade.

"You. You make me so happy," said Rachel.

The couple shared a quick kiss before going to meet Brianna where the train ride ended.

❧❧❧❧

"That was fun," said Brianna.

"What'd you see?" Jade asked.

"I saw deer, and pigs, and goats. We went under a waterfall, too," Brianna said excitedly.

"That sounds awesome. Are you ready for more rides?" asked Rachel.

"Yeah!"

The remainder of the rides were either water rides or go karts, and Brianna took turns sitting with Rachel and Jade. By the time they made it to the exit they were all exhausted.

"Who's tired?" asked Jade, raising her hand.

"Too much effort to raise my hand," Rachel said.

"I got you covered," said Brianna, raising both of her hands.

"Thank you."

By the time they made it back to Jade's house, Brianna was dozing off. Jade carried her up to bed, put her pajamas on, and tucked her in. Jade went back downstairs and saw Rachel lying on her back on the couch, lost in thought. Jade smiled to herself before quietly walking over to the couch and sitting down at the end where Rachel's feet were. She pulled Rachel's legs onto her lap and started to massage her feet and calves.

"That feels amazing," said Rachel, glancing down at Jade.

"Thank you for today. I still can't believe that place is so close and I never knew it existed."

"We'll have to go back again."

"We'll definitely have to," Jade said. "Maybe next time we can take Connor and Lacey."

"I'd like that. You have the most incredible heart of anyone I've ever met," Rachel said, sitting up and cupping Jade's face with one hand before kissing her.

"Why's that?"

"You just met them and you are already thinking of including them in stuff we're doing."

"They're important to you. That makes them important to me."

"Are you tired?" asked Rachel, her green eyes a bit darker.

"No," replied Jade, her blue eyes turning a darker shade. "Rachel?"

"Yeah, baby?"

"Take me upstairs and make love to me."

Rachel growled with desire, pulling Jade up and leading her to Jade's bedroom. After locking the door behind them, the couple made love for most of the night.

Chapter Thirty-three

A New Lease

It had been two months since their adventure at Family Park, since Jade had told Rachel she was indeed falling in love with her. Things between them had gotten more intense. Brianna had noticed the change in Rachel and Jade's relationship as well. She enjoyed seeing her Mama happy and she really liked that Rachel made her so happy. Tonight Jade was having Kristel, Jake, Rachel, Skye, Lacey, and Connor over for dinner.

"Mama, you have a phone call," said Brianna, handing Jade her cell phone. Jade had been out on the deck getting the grill started when her phone rang.

"Thanks, sweetie. Do you want to go keep an eye out for Rachel?" She saw Brianna nod her head as she smiled and then put the phone to her ear. "Jade Donovan here."

Brianna went back in the house to keep an eye out for the others. When she saw Rachel's car pull in she ran to the door. Her excitement rose when she saw Connor and Lacey get out of the car. The three were walking to the door when Kristel and Jake pulled in, followed by Skye.

"Everyone's here," said Brianna as they all walked up to the door.

"Where's Mama?" asked Rachel, knowing it was

unusual that Brianna would be answering the door alone.

"She had a phone call and is outside," said Brianna.

Still finding this unusual, Rachel made her way outside to find her girlfriend sitting with her head in her hands.

"Baby?" Rachel cautiously closed the door behind her.

Jade looked up and had tears in her eyes. Rachel raced over and wrapped her arms around her as she felt Jade hug her close.

"What's wrong?"

"My d-dad's attorney called to tell me that my dad and brother were in a car crash. My brother is dead, and my father is in critical condition and they don't expect him to make it. He wants to see me before he dies."

"I'm so sorry. I know you said you have nothing to do with them, but I'm still sorry. When are you leaving?"

"I told the attorney that I would try to drive up there early tomorrow, but I had some obligations that I needed to take care of here first. They don't know about Bri, and I intend on keeping it that way," said Jade, pulling back from the hug so that she could look at her girlfriend. "You can say no if you don't feel comfortable, but would you be okay with maybe Bri staying with you while I'm gone?"

"Baby, of course she can stay with me."

"Bo and Alice are off on a cruise and…"

"Jade, I would love to have Brianna stay with me. We can even stay here if she is more comfortable."

"How did I get so lucky to find you?" Jade said,

kissing Rachel softly.

"Fate, my love. Everyone is here. Do you need a few minutes or do you want to cancel tonight?"

"Just don't go too far and I'll be okay." Jade took Rachel's hand and squeezed it.

The two entered the house and Jade smiled when she saw that her guests playing video games in the living room. Jade hugged Jake, Connor, and Lacey, and told them and Bri to continue playing games while she, Rachel, Skye, and Kristel moved to the kitchen to finish the prep for dinner.

"What's going on? Why the red eyes?" Kristel asked the moment they were in the kitchen and out of earshot of the kids.

"Duane and my dad were in a car accident. Duane died and my dad isn't going to make it, but he wants to see me."

"Serves the rotten bastards right," said Kristel before she could stop herself. "Sorry."

"No, I have to admit that was my first thought, too." Jade offered her friend a reassuring smile. Jade then noticed the confused look on both Rachel and Skye's faces. "I haven't had contact with my family since I came out in high school. My mom sent me to live with her parents when I was fourteen. My dad and brother used to verbally and physically abuse me." Jade felt Rachel wrap her arms around her from behind. Jade took solace in this and continued. "When I was fourteen I knew that I was gay. I told my mom, not realizing my father was in the next room and he heard me. He went to hit me...to 'beat the gayness out of me,' as he put it. My mom stopped him and the next day she took me to live with her parents. When my mom died, my brother told me it was my fault for being a horrible daughter. The last time I saw them was when my grandparents died. It was right after Amy and I got married. Needless to say, bringing my wife to the funeral wasn't received well by my brother and father. They were cruel at best. I have no idea why he wants to see me now."

"Are you going to go?" asked Skye.

"Yeah. I told the attorney I had some things to take care of but that I would head out tomorrow afterward. I'm going to have Bri stay with Rachel. My father doesn't know about her, and I am very happy to keep it that way."

After the shock wore off, Jade told them she wasn't going to dwell on the subject or ruin their enjoyment of the evening together,

The rest of the night was full of food, laughter, and fun. They played badminton in the back yard. The teams were Jade, Brianna, Lacey, and Skye versus Rachel, Kristel, Jake, and Connor. Rachel's team called it unfair when Jade's team beat them.

As the night came to an end, Kristel and Jake were the first to leave. Kristel told Jade to call if she needed anything. Skye was the next to leave, citing an early morning and a need for beauty sleep. Rachel started to comment, but was stopped by a glare from her sister-in-law. Rachel told Jade she was going to take Connor and Lacey home and then she would be back. Jade smiled and told her she'd be waiting.

※ ※ ※ ※

"Is everything okay with Jade?" asked Connor as they pulled out of the driveway.

"Yeah," said Rachel, smiling at him. "She got

some bad news just before we got there that dampened her mood a bit."

"I hope it wasn't too bad," Lacey said. "She's such a fun person to be around."

"She is. Her brother and dad were in a car accident. She doesn't see them anymore, but it was still upsetting to her."

"Why doesn't she see them?" Connor asked.

"They were a lot like your dad growing up."

"Well, they suck," said Lacey.

"Is she going to see them?"

"Jade is going to go see her father for the last time. Her brother died in the accident."

"What about Bri?" asked Lacey.

"She's going to stay with me."

"You and Jade are really serious aren't you?"

"Yeah, we are. We're in love," admitted Rachel.

"It's about time," Connor and Lacey said together.

"HEY!" Rachel laughed, pulling up outside the apartment complex that both kids lived in.

"Thanks for taking us," said Lacey, hugging Rachel.

"I love you guys. You two are my older kids," Rachel said, smiling at them.

"We love you, too," Connor said, hugging Rachel tight.

Rachel watched the kids enter the building and they each stepped out on their balcony, waving to her let her know they made it inside. Once she knew they were safe she headed back over to Jade's.

❧❧❧❧

"Can we talk for a minute?" Jade asked Bri after

everyone left.

"Am I in trouble?" asked Brianna hesitantly.

"No, not at all," said Jade, hugging Brianna as they sat down on the couch together. "It has to do with the phone call I got before everyone arrived."

"Oh."

"Bri, I have to go out of town for maybe a couple of days. Would you feel okay staying with Rachel? If you aren't I'm sure I can talk to Kristel."

"Is it for work?"

"No, it isn't, sweetie. My dad and brother were in a car accident and I have to go say good-bye to them because they were hurt really bad."

"You have a daddy and a brother?"

"They aren't nice people. They were very mean to me when I was a kid and when Mommy and I went to my grandparents' funeral."

"Then why do you have to go back?"

"It is the last chance I get to show them how wrong they were about me," Jade said confidently. "So, would you be okay with staying with Rachel? She said you two can even stay here at the house."

"Okay, I don't mind staying with Rachel."

"I love you, Bri."

Brianna climbed on her lap and hugged her tight. Rachel found them like this when she got back to Jade's house. Jade told Brianna to get ready for bed, and that she'd be up to tuck her in soon. Brianna headed upstairs while Rachel sat down next to Jade and held her close in her arms.

❧❧❧❧

After tucking Brianna in, Jade led Rachel into

her room where they lay down on the bed, Rachel holding Jade in her arms.

"What's going on inside that beautiful head?" asked Rachel.

"A lot."

"How can I help?"

"I don't know. I haven't thought about that part of my life in a really long time."

"Baby, I love you and am here to listen if you want to tell me about what it was like or what you are feeling."

"I love you, too. I know, I just started saying it within the last few weeks, but I feel like I've loved you forever," Jade said before kissing Rachel softly.

"I know that feeling."

"I guess what is mostly going through my head is that I keep replaying my mom's funeral and then my grandparents' funeral. I was seventeen when my mom died from cancer. I found out that she had fought it for several years, but I didn't find out until about a year before she died. My grandma used to sneak me into the hospital so that my dad and brother didn't know I was visiting. I saw her the night before she died. I remember when Amy got sick I felt the same fear and loneliness that I did when my Mom was sick and then died."

"That would explain why it hit you even harder. I wish I would have known you then so I could have helped you," said Rachel, kissing the side of Jade's head and pulling her close.

"I know, sweetie. I love it that you are here now," said Jade, kissing Rachel softly on the lips. "The day my grandma came into my room to tell me about my mom passing away was one of the worst days I'd ever had."

"*Jade.*"

"*What's wrong, Grandma?*" Jade saw the sadness in the older woman's eyes.

"*Jade, your mom passed away this morning.*"

Jade stared at her grandmother for several agonizing seconds before collapsing into her arms and crying.

"*I should have been there with her. She wasn't alone was she?*" asked Jade, panicked.

"*No, Grandpa was there with her. He held her hand and told her how much we all loved her.*"

"I had nightmares for months that my mom died alone, and not knowing how much I loved her. My grandma told me it was my own guilt messing with my mind, and I agreed she was right, but it didn't make it any easier. The funeral was three days later. My grandparents didn't want me to go because Duane and my dad were going to be there, and they didn't know what they would do to me. They offered to take me to the grave later, but I felt I needed to be there."

"*I don't care if Dad and Duane are going to be there. She was my mom, too. I deserve the right to be there...to say good-bye properly,*" cried Jade as her grandfather held her.

"*I know, sweetie. I just don't want you any more upset. This is harder on you than those heartless bastards,*" said her grandfather, receiving a disapproving look from his wife.

"*I don't care if it is harder. Please, let me go...*" pleaded Jade.

"*I wouldn't stop you, honey. We just want you safe.*"

"*We should be going soon,*" said her grandmother.

They drove in silence to the church. Jade's grandparents escorted her to the front to pay her last respects. Her grandparents flanked her, ensuring that Jade was protected. After the service they went out for the burial and Duane was able to catch Jade alone while her grandparents spoke to the grounds crew about the headstone.

"You know that Mom got sick because of you, right?" said Duane in a menacing tone.

"She did not!" said Jade.

"Yeah, she got sick because you were a rotten daughter. You are so bad that a good woman like Mom had to die. I hope you can live with yourself. I know I wouldn't be able to if it were me."

"That isn't why this happened, Duane."

"Dad said it is. I believe it is. Hell, I bet Mom was cursing your name when she died. You ruined the family dynamic when you were born. You know the real reason that Mom sent you away was because you're gay and she couldn't bear to look at you anymore. You were such a disappointment."

Jade felt her heart clench at her brother's words. She knew they weren't true, but they still cut deep. Just as Jade was about to respond, her grandparents came back and Duane walked away.

"I didn't tell them what he said for months. When I did, I thought for certain one of them was going to take his head off," said Jade.

"It would have been justified in my book. I'm so sorry you had to go through that. Kristel knows these stories doesn't she?"

"She was around when my grandparents died. She knows how things went at their funeral with Duane and dad."

"I understand her reaction now," said Rachel, pulling Jade's body tighter to her body. "I wish I could have met your grandparents."

"Me, too. They would have loved you."

"Did they meet Amy and Brianna?"

"They met Amy, but they died shortly after we got married. They were on their way home from visiting my mom's grave when a car crossed the center line and hit them head on. I'm only grateful that they died instantly and didn't suffer."

"That is horrible."

"Hello?" said Jade, answering her cell phone.

"Is this Jade Donovan?"

"Yes, who is this?"

"This is Officer Howard from the State Highway Patrol. Do you know a Tim and Sherry Jones?"

"Yes, they are my grandparents," Jade said, her voice shaking.

"I'm sorry to inform you that there has been a car accident involving your grandparents."

"A-a-are they o-okay?"

"I'm truly sorry ma'am, but your grandparents were hit head-on and were killed in the accident."

"I'm sorry, can you r-repeat that?" asked Jade, hoping that she had heard the man wrong.

"I'm sorry for your loss ma'am. Your grandparents are being taken to Memorial Hospital. We need for you to come down and make a positive ID."

"O-okay," Jade said, trying not to puke.

After Jade hung up the phone, Amy came bouncing into the room with Kristel on her heals.

"Jade, you gotta hear thi—Jade? What's wrong?" asked Amy, seeing her wife paler than she had ever seen her before and shaking uncontrollably.

"Jade?" asked Kristel.

"T-they're...oh god...no," whispered Jade as the emotion started to overcome her. "No..."

"Jade? What's going on?" asked Amy.

"I n-need to go t-to Memorial Hospital."

"Honey? Are you okay?"

"M-my grandparents are there..."

"What? Why are they there? Are they okay?" asked Kristel.

"They were in an accident...they're um...they didn't..." it was then that Jade lost it and started to cry uncontrollably.

"Oh, honey," said Amy, wrapping her wife tightly in her arms.

"Jade, I'm so sorry," said Kristel.

"It was a while before I was able to function. They took me to identify the bodies. I was such a wreck," said Jade, shuddering.

"I think everyone is when they have to do that."

"To this day I don't know how my dad and Duane found out about the funeral. We intentionally didn't put anything in the paper or have it known at the funeral home. Somehow they found out and showed up."

"Well, well, if it isn't the family disgrace," said Duane as he and his father walked up to Jade and Amy.

"What are you doing here?" asked Jade with venom in her voice.

"Hey, they were my grandparents, too, bitch."

"Duane, watch your tone," said the older man under his breath. "It would have been nice for you to have notified us of their passing. Who is this?"

"I'm Amy," said the woman standing next to Jade. Jade raised her left hand and rubbed the bridge

of her nose.

"Can we not do this now?" asked Jade, looking at the three people standing around her.

"I'm sorry, honey," Amy said softly, her hand going to Jade's lower back.

"Honey? Oh is THIS what you are dating if you can even call it that?" scoffed Duane.

"No, she isn't who I'm dating. We are married. She is who I am married to," said Jade, knowing that she just made a huge mistake.

"No daughter of mine is going to violate the sanctity of marriage. You will not use the word 'married' unless you are referring to a man and a woman," snapped her father.

"Good thing I'm not a daughter of yours," said Jade. "I recall you telling me you had only one child before Mom moved me out. And the state recognizes us as married, so therefore I am using the term accurately. I'm not doing this with the two of you here. This is a funeral. It would be nice if you two would respect them enough to just go away."

"I'll go when I am damn well good and ready," said Duane, glaring at Jade and Amy. "I'm not the one desecrating their memory by showing up with THAT."

"She's my wife, Duane. That state recognizes her as that, I recognize her as that, and Grandma and Grandpa were at our wedding. The only two having an issue or making it an issue is you and Dad. It isn't about us today, it's about them," said Jade, looking at her grandparent's coffins.

"They backed off for the service and burial, which should have been a clue that something was up. After we finished and were getting ready to head to the gathering, my dad grabbed my arm and pulled me into another room. He stated that he and Duane were going 'fix' me," said Jade, stiffening. "Amy saw him grab me and quickly came over to us. We were the only ones in the room."

"Listen, bitch, this is family business. You aren't family," sneered Duane at Amy.

"Legally, I am. Now get your hands off my wife," Amy said in a tone that shocked both of the men in the room.

The elder Donovan shoved Jade down into a chair before heading toward the smaller woman and his son. Amy saw this and tried to prepare herself for anything. Seeing Jade's brother and father coming her way, Amy sidestepped the two men and quickly rushed to her wife's side.

"Are you okay?" asked Amy.

"Yeah, I'm fine," replied Jade

Duane lunged at the two women, knocking Jade from the seat she was in, but missing Amy. Duane hit Jade in the side, knocking the air out of her. Amy saw this and moved towards her wife but was stopped by a large hand grabbing her wrist and whipping her away from Jade and Duane.

Jade watched as her wife stumbled and fell. She saw the menacing look on her father's face. Jade managed to knee Duane between the legs and roll him off her. She scrambled up and hurried over make sure Amy was okay.

"Don't you ever put your hands on my wife again," Jade said in a cold tone. "Now, get the hell out of here before I call the police and have you both arrested for assault."

"You don't have the balls to do that," said Duane.

"You're right, I have the ovaries to do it," said

Jade, taking her phone out and dialing 911.

The police arrived shortly after the call, Mr. Donovan and Duane smug enough to think that Jade would cave.

"What is the issue here ma'am?" asked the officer.

Amy and Jade explained what had happened and Jade showed the bruise on her ribs that was already starting to form. Duane had a proud smile on his face the whole time they were telling the story. The police believed the two women and arrested the two men. Charges were filed and the Donovan men spent two nights in jail and were fined $5000 each.

"Until tonight, that was the last contact I had with them. Now, my brother is dead and my dad isn't going to live much longer."

"Wow, that is a hell of a story."

"Is it too much?" asked Jade, afraid that she may have scared Rachel off.

"Never, my love," Rachel said, placing a soft kiss on Jade's lips. "I have to admit that I'm not thrilled about the idea of you going there alone."

"I'll be fine. They can't hurt me anymore. I love you for being concerned."

Jade brushed her lips against Rachel's. They barely touched at first, but the need to be close and to feel something overcame them, and they pressed their bodies together.

Chapter Thirty-four

Closing Doors

As Jade drove up the highway she smiled and thought about the morning. She had woken up in Rachel's arms. They had showered together before making breakfast with Brianna. She loved how her life was working out. This trip would finally close the door on her past, a past to which she no longer had ties.

Driving through the city to the hospital, Jade was amazed at how much hadn't changed. She was grateful that she had. She didn't let this place keep her down. She didn't let it hold her back or ruin who she was. Jade pulled into the hospital ramp and parked her car.

She made her way to the ICU and asked at the nurses' desk where her father was. The nurse escorted her to the room. Before Jade was allowed in, a man dressed in an expensive suit came out of the room.

"Ms. Donovan?" said the balding man.

"Yes," said Jade.

"Thank you for coming. I know that this is probably the last place you want to be, but he isn't going to be with us much longer."

"I'm really not sure why I'm here. The last time I saw him, I had him arrested."

"Well, I will give you two a few minutes," said the man, reaching in the room to get his coat and walking off.

Jade entered the room and saw her father hooked up to several machines. Some were beeping, some were helping him breathe. He had an IV that had Morphine written on the bag.

"Who's there?" asked her father, Scott Donovan.

"Jade," she said as she walked farther into the room.

"I didn't think you would come."

"I'm still not sure why I'm here. Why you had to see me?"

The man adjusted and Jade saw him wince in pain. She realized that she felt some satisfaction in his pain.

"Did you come alone?"

"I don't know anyone I would subject to one of our confrontations."

"I know your wife died. I'm sorry."

"How do you know that? And did you hit your head? I am a disgrace, remember?" snapped Jade.

"I saw her obituary."

"How?"

"I search on Donovan obituaries regularly."

"Hoping to see mine?" Jade said bitterly.

"No, I was hoping not to. I know that I've been a horrible father to you. I asked you here to ask for your forgiveness."

"That's not going to happen. You were never a father to me. You and Duane abused me until Mom took me out of the situation. Then at the funeral of the people who helped raise me, you assaulted myself and my wife. Why the hell would you think that I would consider granting you forgiveness?"

"I was hoping because you are a bigger and

better person than I am. And that you might do it to set an example for your daughter."

"I'm a bigger and better person than you are without giving you forgiveness. As for the example I set for my daughter, that's my business, not yours. She is aware that I was coming here and that it was to say good-bye to my past so that I can focus on her and my new love."

"You found someone new? That's good. I appreciate you coming here. I know you didn't owe me the kindness. Since Duane is gone, the family inheritance falls to you. My attorney has drawn up the papers and set up the trust accounts for both you and your daughter."

"What inheritance? I don't want anything from you," said Jade, disgusted by the thought of having a connection to this man.

"This isn't from me. This is from your mother. It was supposed to go to you when she died, but Duane and I hid it away," said Scott, his voice getting weaker.

"I see."

"I hope you find happiness."

"I have. I have an amazing life, no thanks to you."

A nurse came in and told them that Jade would need to leave as it was time for them to move Scott. Jade's father asked for another minute. He apologized again and said his good-byes. Jade wasn't sure what to say so she just left. When Jade left, she saw the attorney sitting outside the room. He explained to Jade that they had set up a trust account for her to give regular distributions, and one for her daughter for the future. Jade was still skeptical. The attorney gave her the papers and told her to have her own attorney look them over and then call him. She told him she would. After she finished at the hospital, she called Rachel to find out how things were going with them and to see if they minded her coming home that night. Rachel told Jade that she couldn't wait to see her.

❧ ❧ ❧ ❧

It was late when Jade pulled into the driveway. There had been a car accident on her way home that delayed her by a couple of hours. Jade smiled as she got out of the car and saw that Rachel was waiting in the doorway for her.

"Hey, sweetie." Jade tiredly walked up to the door and Rachel pulled her into a hug.

"Welcome home," said Rachel, kissing the side of Jade's head.

Rachel took Jade's bag from her as they went inside. Rachel offered to make something for Jade to eat, but she declined stating that she just wanted to be held. The couple settled in the living room and Rachel wrapped her arms around her girlfriend.

Jade told Rachel about her conversation with her father and the subsequent conversation with the attorney. Rachel told Jade that she had a friend that was an attorney and if she wanted, she could have him look over the documents. Jade seemed glad that it was one less thing that she was going to have to deal with.

"Rachel?" said the little voice coming down the stairs.

"Yeah, honey," responded Rachel.

"I had a bad dream."

"Come here and snuggle with Mama and me," said Rachel, opening her arms for Brianna to join them.

"Mama? When did you get home?"

"Just a few minutes ago. Come snuggle with us," Jade said, pulling Brianna into her arms and then feeling Rachel close her arms around the two.

"Do you want to tell us about your dream?" Rachel asked Brianna.

"I dreamed that a bad man hurt you and Mama."

"Well, that isn't going to happen," said Jade, pulling her daughter closer to her. Jade kissed the side of her daughter's head. "I love you, Brianna."

"I love you, too, Mama. I love you, too, Rachel."

"I love you, and your Mama," said Rachel.

The three lay there for a while. Rachel felt the breathing pattern of both Brianna and Jade change. She smiled down at the two sleeping in her arms and realized how perfect everything was at this moment.

☙❧☙❧

Everyone was in their morning routine when Jade's phone rang. It was the attorney telling her that her father had passed. Jade thanked him for the call and said she would be in touch after her attorney looked over the documents.

"What are you feeling?" asked Rachel, wrapping her arms around Jade's waist from behind and rested her chin on her shoulder.

"Relief he won't be able to hurt anyone I care about again. I feel like I got the closure that I needed yesterday," Jade said, leaning back into Rachel's embrace.

"I'm glad you got the closure that you needed," Rachel said before kissing the side of Jade's head. "I'll call my attorney friend and see if he can look over the documents or if he can refer us to someone."

"Thank you."

"I love you, Jade."

"I love you, too."

Jade turned in Rachel's arms and kissed her gently. Their lips were moving together for several minutes before they heard Brianna coming down the stairs.

Everyone finished getting ready. Rachel took Brianna to school as she had started doing every Monday and Tuesday. Dawn was happy to see the connection growing between Rachel and Brianna. She had known Amy and Jade, but she saw a different light in Jade's eyes when Rachel was around. She smiled and told Rachel that she would see her after school.

After dropping Brianna off at school Rachel went to work and called her friend. He stated that he would definitely take a look at the papers, but it was going to cost Rachel dinner. She knew that he was looking for her to make her signature steak. She hadn't had a chance to make this for Jade yet, but she figured that tonight was going to be the night. Rachel called and told Jade that she was being blackmailed into making steaks. Jade told Rachel that she was okay with her cooking because she had a pretty busy schedule lined up.

After work, Rachel picked up Brianna from school and they went grocery shopping before heading over to Jade's house. Rachel and Brianna prepped dinner and then waited for Jade to arrive.

"Mama," squealed Brianna as Jade entered the house.

"Hi, Baby Girl! How was your day?" asked Jade.

"It was good. I got to help Rachel prep dinner tonight. She said I was the best helper she ever had," boasted Brianna.

"She's right, she was the best helper," said Rachel, finishing the last of the prep work.

"It smells fantastic." Jade kissed Rachel.

"It tastes better than it smells," promised Rachel. "You have time to relax. Greg won't be here for another half hour. He was in court today."

Jade was thankful for the time to relax. She had been on the go with various clients and museum curators all day. She had even skipped lunch to fit in a new client that she knew had promise.

"Great. I'm going to go get changed into something more comfortable."

❧❦❧❦❧

Greg arrived and Rachel introduced him to Jade and Brianna. Greg could see the love and happiness in the couple. He was grateful that his friend had finally found someone.

"So, how did you two meet?" asked Jade, taking a glass of wine from Rachel's hand.

Rachel handed Greg a beer and received a smile as she moved back near Jade.

"Greg was my attorney after Emily died. He made sure I just had to deal with the critical stuff. Her estate, her life insurance, the house, all that stuff—he took care of for me."

"I took care of it, I got to know Rachel and we formed a friendship after that. I have referred a few of my clients to her and she has done the same with her clients. What do you do, Jade? I mean Rachel has kept you quite the secret," said Greg.

"I have not, you just never returned my calls," said Rachel, sticking her tongue out.

"I own my own business. I'm an art agent."

"Wow, that is fantastic," said Greg. "Rach, you finally found someone who knows more about that artsy fartsy stuff than you do."

"Shut up," Rachel said, laughing. "Why don't you two go over the documents while Bri and I go cook dinner?"

"Sounds good. Thanks, sweetie," said Jade as Rachel leaned down and they kissed.

❧❧❧❧

"Bri? Are you ready to help me cook that amazing dinner you helped prep?" asked Rachel as she went into the playroom.

"Yep. I'm ready," said Brianna, turning off the TV and putting her toys away.

The two went into the kitchen to get the meat and veggie tents they had prepared. Rachel carried the meat and Brianna carried the veggie tents. When they got outside to the grill, Brianna crawled up in a chair so she could see what Rachel was doing, but not be close enough to the heat to get hurt. Rachel opened the preheated grill and put the meat on. The meat made a sizzling sound, and then she added the veggie tents to the top rack and closed the lid.

"We'll let it cook for a few minutes and then we'll flip the steaks."

"Rachel, is Mama in trouble?" asked Brianna questioningly.

"No, why would you think that, honey?"

"Because I heard you say that man was a lawyer. In school, we talked about lawyers helping people who are naughty."

"Honey," said Rachel, picking Brianna up and placing her on her lap. "Lawyers help with all sorts of stuff. They do help when people are in trouble, but they also help people like Mama understand what her options are and they make sure that someone isn't breaking the law and trying to sneak something by. Greg is looking over some papers that your Mama got yesterday."

"When she went to visit the bad man?"

"Yep."

"Is the bad man going to hurt Mama?" asked Brianna, her voice cracking.

"No, he is never going to hurt her. Is that why you had the bad dream last night? You were afraid the bad man was going to hurt Mama?" asked Rachel. Rachel wrapped her arms around Brianna and felt her nod her answer to Rachel's question. "I promise you that I will never let anyone hurt you or your Mama. Not if I can help it."

They sat there for several minutes before Rachel had to flip the steaks. Once she tended to the grill, she picked Brianna up and held the little girl hoping, that she was calming her fears.

❧ ❧ ❧ ❧

"So, Jade, what have you been given?" asked Greg.

"I have no idea. My father told me that when my mother died she left me some money and that he and my brother hid it. They both passed away. My brother died Saturday and my father today.”

“I’m sorry for your loss.”

“Really, I haven’t seen them in years and the last time I did I had them arrested for assaulting my wife and me.”

“Wow, are you still married or separated?”

“No, Amy died two years ago. I met Rachel in the grief counseling group she runs.”

“I’m sorry for your loss.”

“Thank you.”

“All right, let’s look at these papers,” said Greg, grabbing the stack that Jade had been given.

Greg read through the papers, and read through some sections again. Jade watched and realized that he had to be a good lawyer because she could not read a damn thing he was thinking about.

“Well, these are very cut-and-dried. Your father established two trust funds. One for Brianna, although he doesn’t have her name—she is just listed as your daughter. That one is set to start dispersing money to her at age eighteen or when she graduates high school, whichever is later. And then he set one up for you to be dispersed in increments every two years following his death.”

“How were they able to hide this money? And really, how much is it?” asked Jade.

“Well, I can only guess, but I’m certain they were able to hide it because your father was still married to your mother when she died. He, in dirty technicalities, had first dibs even if her will stated otherwise. And to your second question...a lot. You and Brianna each have upward of $5 million dollars.”

“I’m sorry; did you say $5 million? Each?”

“Yep, and the accounts will continue to grow as

they are being invested and are set to never go below the current balance. So, essentially, if you don't like what you were doing for a living, you could quit and not have to work again for a long time if ever."

"Wow," said Jade, shocked. "So, what do we do?"

"Well, if you want me to represent you I can call your father's attorney tomorrow and get the transition of the accounts to you and your daughter finalized."

"That would be fantastic. I really appreciate your help on this. And I guess it is safe to say, bill me for your time." Jade laughed.

"Well, tonight Rachel is paying with steak. Tomorrow, we'll talk." Greg grinned.

"Sounds good. Should we go see how those steaks are coming along?"

"Definitely."

Jade and Greg walked over to the patio door heading outside to where Rachel and Brianna were cooking. Jade saw the two talking, and then saw Brianna hug Rachel tightly. Jade and Greg exchanged a look before opening the patio door and stepping outside.

"Rachel? Brianna?" asked Jade.

"Hi, baby. Did you two get everything ironed out?" asked Rachel, still holding Brianna close.

"Yes, we did. Well, for what we can tonight. I'm going to take care of some stuff for her tomorrow," replied Greg.

Rachel noticed the concerned look in Jade's eyes as she sat down next to them.

"We were talking about her dream last night. She was scared because she thought your dad might still be able to hurt you. I explained that he wouldn't be able to, but she needed a hug for reassurance."

Brianna lifted her head and moved over to cuddle with Jade while Rachel got up and tended to the steaks.

❧❧❧❧

After dinner Greg said his good-byes and told Jade that he'd give her a call the following day. Jade thanked him again for his help, then she went into the living room to join Rachel and Brianna.

"Bri, Baby Girl, you don't need to worry about anyone hurting me," Jade said, trying to reassure her daughter.

"But the bad man…" started Brianna as Jade scooped her up and wrapped her in her arms.

"The bad man can never hurt me again. He died today."

"Can he hurt Mommy?"

"No, he isn't going to the same place where Mommy is. I promise," said Jade, kissing Brianna on the head.

"Good."

"All right, bath time," said Jade.

Brianna said she could do it herself, but she would call if she needed help. Rachel and Jade watched Brianna ascend the stairs before Rachel pulled her girlfriend close.

"How are you doing?" asked Rachel.

"I'm here, in your arms. That makes it perfect. Thank you for bringing Greg by. He's really nice and was very helpful."

"I'm glad he was able to help. He's one of the few lawyers I've worked with over the years that I actually liked. I'm sorry if Bri and I scared you earlier."

"I am glad that she felt comfortable talking to you and allowed you to comfort her. We've come a long way in the past couple of months," said Jade, kissing Rachel's neck.

"Yes, we have," said Rachel, tilting Jade's head up and pressing their lips together in a loving kiss. The kiss started slow, but grew more passionate as their lips moved together. As the kiss progressed Rachel threaded her fingers in Jade's hair, holding their lips together.

"I need to go check on Bri. Come read a story with us."

"I'd love to," smiled Rachel.

The two women made their way upstairs where Brianna was just finishing her bath and getting her pajamas on.

"Mama, you sit here," said Brianna, patting one side of the bed and then patted the other side of the bed looking at Rachel. "Rachel, you sit here."

"What story are we reading tonight?" Jade asked.

"Can we read 'Bunnicula' together?"

"We sure can," said Rachel.

"We'll start reading two chapters per night," said Jade, grabbing the book off Brianna's bookshelf.

Jade started reading, and then Rachel took over. They each read a page, but the end of the second chapter Brianna was fighting to keep her eyes open.

"Go to sleep, Baby Girl," said Jade, kissing her daughter's cheek.

"I love you, Mama," mumbled the little girl.

"I love you, too."

Rachel bent over and kissed the top of Brianna's head.

"Good night, sweet girl," Rachel said.

"I love you, Rachel," mumbled Brianna.

"I love you, too, Brianna," said Rachel, choked up by the girl's words.

Jade led them to her room and they lay down on the bed. Jade had her arms wrapped around Rachel who was resting her head on her shoulder.

"You know she meant it when she said she loves you, right?"

"I love her, too," said Rachel.

"Do you have to leave tonight?"

"Not if you want me to stay," Rachel said.

"Good, I want to spend all night with us wrapped together," said Jade, rolling on her side.

"I love that idea almost as much as I love you," said Rachel, brushing their lips together.

Chapter Thirty-five

Planning the Future

It had been two weeks since Jade had seen her father and his attorney. Greg had taken over the contact and the setting up of the accounts. Jade was still hesitant about the money and the accounts, but she had to admit that the security they offered for her and Brianna was nice.

Jade had invited Bo and Alice over for dinner to ask a favor of them and to tell them officially about her and Rachel.

"Mama, I got my room cleaned and I cleaned up the living room. Now what can I help with?"

"Thank you, sweetie. Do you want to help with dinner? I know you are usually Rachel's special helper, but do you want to be mine today since she is at work?"

"YAY!"

Jade helped Brianna get situated at the island. She gave Brianna the ingredients to make the cake with and told her in what order to dump them into the bowl, and then she gave her a whisk to stir the mixture with. After Brianna mixed the ingredients together, Jade poured it into a cake pan and put it in the oven. Just as she was getting ready to give Brianna her next task there was a knock at the door.

"Can I get it, Mama?"

"We'll go together, but you can get the door."

The two walked to the door and saw Bo and Alice standing on the other side.

"Grandma! Grandpa! You're here," squealed Brianna as she threw the door open.

"Hey there, beautiful," said Bo, scooping Brianna up into his arms.

"Hello," smiled Jade as she hugged both of them. Jade was just about to close the door when she saw Rachel coming up the walkway.

"Great timing," said Jade, noting that Bo and Alice were occupied with Brianna.

"I'm sorry I ran late," said Rachel, kissing Jade quickly.

"They just got here."

"Rachel," said Brianna, running and throwing herself into Rachel's outstretched arms.

"How was your day?" Rachel asked, hugging Brianna as she stood up.

"I got my math test back and because of your help, I got them all right!"

"I'm so proud of you! That is fantastic," Rachel said, hugging Brianna again.

Jade's heart warmed at the contact between Rachel and Brianna. Bo and Alice watched the interaction and shared a look that told the other that the relationship between Rachel and Jade had definitely grown beyond friendship.

Rachel set Brianna down, and then said hi and shook hands with Bo and Alice. Jade seeing, the older couple hesitate in their interaction with Rachel, knew they had picked up on the relationship change. Jade asked Brianna to go check the timer in the kitchen for her.

"Is your relationship why we are here tonight?"

asked Alice, a hint of hurt in her voice.

"It is part of the reason, but the bigger part is because I want Brianna to see us all together," said Jade, taking Rachel's hand in her own.

"So, this is something serious?" asked Bo.

"Yes, it is," answered Rachel confidently.

"Mama, it says you have fifteen minutes until it is done," said Brianna, entering the room again.

"Thank you, sweetie!"

"Can I show Grandma and Grandpa the project we've been working on, Rachel?"

"Yep, but you have to make sure they promise not to tell Mama," Rachel smiled.

"We promise," said Bo and Alice as they were led out of the room by Brianna and up the stairs.

"What are you two up to?" asked Jade, wrapping her arms around Rachel's waist and pulling their bodies together tightly.

"You'll have to wait and see," Rachel said, wrapping her arms around Jade's neck and kissing her softly. "I love you."

"Mmmm, I love you, too. Now come help me finish dinner," said Jade, dragging Rachel into the kitchen with her.

❧❧❧❧

Brianna led Bo and Alice up to her room and then she crawled under her bed to get something. She came out with a box and a folder.

"Rachel and I are making this for Mama," said Brianna, handing Bo and Alice the folder.

The older couple opened the folder and saw it was several pages of what looked to be a memory book.

As they paged through it, tears filled both their eyes. The early pages were pictures of Amy and Jade when they were kids, then teens, and then when they started dating. There were pictures of their life together, and pictures of Brianna as a baby and as she had grown up.

"Brianna, when was this taken?" asked Bo, holding a picture of Amy and Brianna together.

"Aunt Kristel took it right before Mommy went into the yucky hospital."

"So, you and Rachel have been working on this?"

"Yep," Brianna said proudly.

Bo and Alice handed the stuff back to Brianna and she put it away back under her bed. They went back downstairs and joined Rachel and Jade in the kitchen.

"So, now that EVERYONE but me knows what's going on, I am going to go put this stuff on the grill," teased Jade. "You wanna help, Bri?"

Brianna nodded and carried the plate that contained the veggie packs Rachel had just put together while Jade took the meat.

"Thank you," Alice said, wiping a tear from her eye as soon as Jade and Brianna had left the room. She looked pointedly at Rachel. "Why?"

"I thought it would be a nice way for Brianna to see Amy and Jade as they grew up and started their life together. Then I thought Jade might appreciate something that their daughter put together regarding their life. Brianna has been the main designer of the book, I just helped her get the pictures copied and with some of the words and such."

"I don't know what to make of you, Rachel. Part of me wants to hate you for being here with them because Amy can't be, but then part of me is grateful that you are because you do such an amazing job of making sure Amy isn't forgotten. I don't know that I could do what you are doing. I think I'd be too selfish and want the other woman to be forgotten," said Alice.

"I love Jade and Brianna. I know that Brianna is only here because of the love that Jade and Amy shared. I choose to celebrate that."

"Well, thank you for honoring our daughter," said Bo, hugging Rachel.

Just as the embrace ended Jade and Brianna came back in. Jade caught sight of the hug and gave a questioning look to Rachel.

Dinner was lighthearted. Bo and Alice were trying hard to get to know Rachel better, and Jade was encouraged by their interaction. Jade asked if they would mind watching Brianna the following weekend so that she and Rachel could go out of town. The older couple said they would be delighted. As they said their goodnights, Bo pulled Jade aside.

"She's a good one. If you can't be with my daughter, I definitely approve of your choice," said Bo.

"Thank you," Jade said, hugging her father-in-law.

"I know you don't need our approval, but thank you for keeping us in Brianna's life and for tonight. It was nice to spend the evening as a family."

"I appreciate you giving Rachel a chance. She is a big part of my and Brianna's life."

"She loves you a lot and I can see you love her, too. Embrace it, grow it, and don't waste time. We all know you never know how much time you have."

"Thank you," said Jade as they hugged again and then joined her lover and daughter.

Rachel wrapped an arm around Jade's waist as

they waved good-bye to the older couple. Once they were gone, they cleaned up after dinner and dessert, and Brianna went and took her bath and got ready for bed.

⚜ ⚜ ⚜ ⚜

After getting Brianna to bed, Rachel and Jade made their way to the living room where they cuddled together on the couch. Jade lay between Rachel's legs with her head resting on her chest.

"Tonight went surprisingly well," said Rachel, absently running her fingers through Jade's hair.

"I agree. I thought us dating would have caused an uproar. Whatever you and Bri are up to seemed to win them over."

"Yeah, I'm still not telling you what it is," said Rachel, laughing and poking Jade in the side, causing her to squirm.

"Fine, be that way," teased Jade.

⚜ ⚜ ⚜ ⚜

Jade and Rachel were loading the car to go to the cabin for their weekend away. Brianna was excited to be staying with Amy's parents. They had promised to take her to the park, which meant she was getting ice cream.

"Bri, are you ready to go?" asked Jade.

"Yep, I am all packed and I have my best buddies going with me," she answered, picking up her two favorite stuffed animals.

"Great, why don't you take your bag out and put it in the backseat next to you and then get in your booster and we'll be out in a second."

"Okay," said Brianna, grabbing her stuff and racing out the door.

"You ready, sexy?" asked Jade.

"Am I ready to have you to myself in a clothing-optional weekend? Hell yes," Rachel said, coming up behind her girlfriend, wrapping her arms around Jade's waist and kissing her neck.

"Then let's go...because if we don't I'm going to rip your clothes off and have my way with you here and now."

"Not seeing a downside," giggled Rachel before kissing Jade deeply.

"We really need to get going. I need you," said Jade in a sultry voice.

"Yeah, definitely time to get going," Rachel said, kissing the side of Jade's head as they headed out the door.

❧❧❧❧

Jade drove to Bo and Alice's house to drop Brianna off.

"You be good for Grandma and Grandpa. Rachel and I will pick you up on Sunday night," Jade said, hugging her daughter. "I love you! If you need me, call. I promise that we will call you nightly."

"I love you, too, Mama."

"Have a great weekend, Bri," said Rachel, hugging Brianna tightly. "As Mama said, we'll call and check on you. I love you."

"I love you, too, Rachel. You and Mama have fun."

"I'm sure they will, sweetie" said Alice, seeing

Jade wrap her arms around Rachel.

"Thank you again for watching her this weekend," Jade said to Alice.

"I love Brianna and I love you. Rachel makes you happy and that is important to me as well. Now go away and let me bond with my granddaughter."

"Yes ma'am," Jade and Rachel got in the car and drove up to the cabins that Jade had booked for their weekend getaway.

⚜ ⚜ ⚜ ⚜

Rachel grabbed their bag while Jade unlocked the cabin. As they entered they both smiled at the champagne and strawberries that had been left. Rachel read the card and blushed.

"Rachel and Jade, we thought you could use some extra nourishment this weekend. We love seeing you happy. Love, Bo & Alice."

"Oh my." Jade let out a nervous giggle before she wrapped her arms around Rachel and kissed her with all the passion she could.

"Mmmm, Jade," moaned Rachel.

Rachel took Jade's hand and led her to the bedroom. She pushed Jade back on the bed and quickly covered her body with her own and Rachel sucked on Jade's lower lip.

Jade ran her hands along the sides of her lover's body. Their tongues dueled for dominance. There were moans and groans from each woman.

"Too many clothes," groaned Jade as she started to pull Rachel's clothes off.

After removing Rachel's clothes, Jade stood and removed her own as Rachel watched with lust in her eyes. After she was naked, Jade crawled up the bed and hovered over Rachel's upper body as her lower body pressed between Rachel's legs. Looking Rachel in the eyes, she leaned down and slowly kissed her, allowing the passion that she was feeling to transfer to Rachel. She heard Rachel moan into the kiss. Rachel threaded her fingers into Jade's hair, pulling her deeper into the kiss. Her hand slid down Jade's back and encouraged her down so that their bodies were pressed tightly together. Jade ground her hips into her lover's center and they both groaned at the feeling. Jade pulled back from the kiss and worked her way along Rachel's jawline. When she reached her ear, she ran her tongue around the edge of it and when she reached the earlobe, she sucked on it before whispering into Rachel's ear.

"Lie back, relax, and enjoy while I worship you," whispered Jade before taking Rachel's earlobe between her teeth.

"Yes...please..." Rachel managed to breathe out in a whisper.

The room was filled with grunts and moans as the two women loved and moved one another toward their climax. Jade could feel how close Rachel was and she knew she was just as close. Moving faster, Jade sent Rachel over the edge, and as she screamed her lover's name, she sent Jade into ecstasy calling out Rachel's name. Both women rode out their climaxes as long as they could prolong them. Both spent, Jade collapsed panting on top of Rachel.

"T-that was...incredible," panted Rachel.

"M-mind blowing," panted Jade. "As soon as my body responds...I'll move."

"Don't, I want you again," Rachel said with a mischievous smile.

Both women came together again. Jade rolled off Rachel and they stared into the other's eyes while regaining their breath and allowing their racing hearts to slow.

"I love you so much," said Rachel, brushing the hair off Jade's face and running her fingers down the side of her face.

"I love you, too," Jade said before kissing Rachel softly.

The two women curled up together and drifted off to sleep.

᪐᪐᪐᪐

When Jade woke up, she looked at the clock and saw that they had been asleep for about three hours. She softly pressed her lips to her sleeping lover's to wake her up. After a few seconds, she felt Rachel start to respond.

"Hello, my love," Jade said, pulling back from the kiss.

"That is an incredible way to wake up. How long did we sleep?"

"About three hours."

"I guess I wore you out a bit," said Rachel, laughing.

"I think it was a mutual wearing out."

"I think you are right."

"I often am, you should remember that." Jade smiled and Rachel rolled her eyes playfully. "Can we talk about something important that I don't know how to talk about?"

"Cryptic much, baby? Not to mention, kinda scary phrasing."

"Sorry," said Jade, adjusting so that she and Rachel were lying on their side facing each other. "I have been trying to find words for this for a while now."

"Baby, just say it however it is easiest for you and we'll work from there," Rachel said, cupping Jade's face with one hand and running the pad of her thumb along her cheek. "Communication is key for us working."

"I want to come home to you, nightly, I want your arms wrapped around me at night when I fall asleep. I want to wake up in your arms. I don't do well without you," Jade said, looking deep into Rachel's emerald green eyes. "Not at all."

"Baby, are you trying to ask me to move in and live with you and Bri?" Rachel said, smiling softly.

"Yes, I am." Jade let out a defeated sigh as a pink hue formed in her cheeks.

"I love you and Brianna. I don't do well without you, either. I'd love for the three of us to live together."

"Really?" asked Jade, and Rachel nodded. "I love you so much!"

"I had actually been toying with the idea of asking you the same thing, but um, what do you think about us getting a house together? A place of our own. A place where we can build our own life together."

"I hadn't thought about that. I would need to make sure Bri was okay with it."

"Of course. She needs to be a part of that decision too."

꙳꙳꙳꙳

Rachel and Jade got dressed and went to watch

the sunset over the nearby lake. Jade found a large boulder for them to sit on. She pulled Rachel up into her arms and they watched the sun descend behind the mountains in the distance and over the treetops. The sky was a fiery orange and red with hues of purple meshed in. The sun slowly dipped out of sight, but the sky was still full of color and light. Jade pulled Rachel close, kissing her deeply. The couple sat there kissing as the light from the sunset dissipated and the moon and stars took over lighting the night. As they naturally broke apart, Rachel got down off the boulder and extended her hand to help Jade. Once they were on solid ground, Jade wrapped her arms around Rachel's waist from behind and rested her chin on her shoulder. The couple stood together watching the moonlight dance off the waves of the lake before heading back to the cabin.

"It's so quiet up here. Did you come here often? With Amy, that is."

"Amy, Bri, and I used to go to some cabins nearby. I didn't want to go to the same ones with you. I wanted some that were ours. I just love the lake here," said Jade, making them dinner in the cabin's rustic kitchen.

"It's gorgeous. Not quite as gorgeous as you are, though," said Rachel, wrapping her arms around Jade and pressing her back against the counter.

"You're biased," said Jade, brushing their lips together several times, teasing one another.

The couple spent the weekend walking along the shoreline, making love, enjoying their private time together, and increasing their connection and commitment to their relationship.

Chapter Thirty-six

Building a Family

Rachel and Jade picked Brianna up late on Sunday night from Amy's parents. Having had such a good time with her grandparents, Brianna rapidly told them all about her weekend on the drive home. Rachel kept stealing glances at Jade, who couldn't help stealing glances back.

"Did you two have a good weekend?" Brianna asked when they pulled into the driveway of Jade's house.

"We had a fantastic weekend," Rachel said happily.

"What did you do?"

"Why don't you go put your clothes away and then come back down and we'll tell you about our weekend?" said Jade as they entered the house.

Once they heard Brianna upstairs the couple wrapped their arms around one another and Jade kissed Rachel softly.

"I love you," whispered Jade.

"I love you, too," Rachel whispered back. "I had an amazing weekend."

When they heard Brianna coming down the stairs, they moved to the living room and Jade sat at one end of the couch, leaning up against the armrest. She pulled Rachel to sit between her legs and Brianna sat at the end opposite the two women.

"What did you do over the weekend?" asked Brianna as soon as everyone was situated.

"Well, we went to a cabin and we watched some sunsets, a very beautiful sunrise, we took walks along the beach, we..." smiled Jade.

"Did you kiss?" interrupted Brianna.

"Yes, we, um did," said Jade, seeing Rachel blush.

"Seeing you and Rachel kiss is okay, but seeing Grandma and Grandpa kiss is yucky."

"I'm glad you're okay with us kissing now," said Rachel. She still remembered all too well what happened when Brianna wasn't okay with their kissing.

"I think I am used to it now, but I still don't like seeing Grandma and Grandpa kiss."

"Why is that, baby girl?"

"They're old," Brianna said matter-of-factly, causing Jade and Rachel to laugh.

"Well, let's not tell them that." Jade was amused by her daughter's observation and reasoning. "There is one thing we want to talk to you about, Bri. Rachel and I talked about the possibility of the three of us living together."

"You mean her moving in here?"

"Not exactly. We were thinking that Rachel would sell her house, and we would sell our house and the three of us would pick a new house to live in."

"But, but, but, what about Mommy?" asked Brianna as her voice started to quiver.

"What about her? Tell Mama or me what you are thinking and feeling," said Rachel, moving closer to Brianna and Jade moved with her.

"This was where Mommy lived..." said Brianna, her eyes starting to fill with tears.

"Bri, baby, you will always have the memories of Mommy here. If we move to a new house, you will still have these memories. We aren't moving to take them away from you or make you forget them."

"Then why move?"

"We would move to have a place that gives us all a fresh start. If we lived here, there's the reminder that this was Mommy's and my house, our life together. Rachel's house is her life with Emily."

"And the baby...the baby that is up with Emily and Mommy."

"Yep. We want to get a place that will be Mama's, yours, and mine," interjected Rachel. "We will take pictures and video of everything here so that you will always have those to look back on to remember."

"We can?"

"Of course," said Jade, hugging her daughter closer. "We agreed that we won't do anything unless you are okay with it."

"Do I get to help pick out the new house?"

"Yes, you do. You're going to be living there and we need to make sure that you like it too," said Rachel.

"Can I think about it?"

"Of course," said both Jade and Rachel.

"Thank you," Brianna said, yawning.

"Why don't you go get ready for bed and we'll come up and read more of your book."

"Okay, Mama." With that, Brianna headed upstairs.

"That went better than I anticipated," said Jade.

"I agree."

The two sat there lost in their thoughts for several minutes before getting up and going to read Brianna her story.

It took Brianna a week before she was able to tell Rachel and Jade that she was okay with the idea of the three of them getting a new house together. Rachel and Jade were thrilled that she was on board. Rachel called Nicole, a friend of hers that was a real estate agent, and they scheduled a meeting with her to discuss the selling of the two homes and the subsequent buying of a new one.

"Hi, Rachel," said Nicole as they shook hands.

"Hi, Nicole. This is my girlfriend Jade and her daughter Brianna."

"It's nice to meet you," said Jade, shaking Nicole's hand.

"You, too."

"Hi," said Brianna, holding her hand out too.

After the introductions were through, they sat down in Nicole's office and she explained her process to buying and selling a house. After she explained things she asked them what they were looking for in a house.

"At least four bedrooms, two or more bathrooms, garage…" started Jade. "I'm not sure what else to say."

"Do you want a new house, a newer build, or an older one? Pool? Neighborhood?"

"Preferably a newer house, a pool would be nice, but isn't required," added Rachel.

"Neighborhood isn't a big deal as long as it is nice, safe, and has parks nearby."

"If it has a big tree can I have a tree house?" asked Brianna.

"Yes, you can. If there is a big enough backyard

we'll get that swing set you and I were looking at yesterday," said Rachel, receiving a raised eyebrow from Jade.

"Rachel, you weren't supposed to tell anyone that...remember? It was our secret," whispered Brianna loudly, causing everyone in the room to laugh.

Nicole started to plug the details of what they were looking for into her computer, and she found several places that met the criteria. They made an appointment to go out looking the following day. They then discussed the selling of their current houses.

After they finished with Nicole, the three went to get ice cream and then headed home to formulate a plan for packing.

Jade and Brianna took pictures and video of the house before they started packing or going through things to find out what they could get rid of.

They started to pack as they looked with Nicole for houses. Rachel's house sold within days of listing for more than the listing price. She put her stuff in storage and moved in with Jade and Brianna. On their fourth outing with Nicole, they found their dream house. They put in an offer that was quickly accepted. The following day Jade's house sold.

❧❧❧❧

They had finished moving in and unpacking in three days. They were seated outside on the deck overlooking their pool when Brianna came out with something in her hands. Rachel caught a glimpse of it and smiled.

"Mama, Rachel and I made this for you," said Brianna, handing Jade the picture book they had been working on and then sat on Rachel's lap.

Jade opened the book and flipped through the pages carefully seeing pictures and labels of her as a child and teenager, Amy as a child and teenager, and then the pages that showed her life with Amy. Jade had tears streaming down her face as she saw the pictures from her first date with Amy, their first apartment together, and other early memories. She saw pictures of Amy pregnant with Brianna. She glanced up at Rachel and Brianna, her heart so filled with love that they had done this for her. Continuing, she saw Brianna as a baby and their life with her. There were pictures of them as a family as Amy got sick and her health deteriorated. There were a few blank pages at the end with a Post-It that read "Rachel will explain later."

"Y-you t-two m-made this?" asked Jade through the tears as both Rachel and Brianna moved to hug her.

"Yes, we did," Rachel said proudly.

"Baby Girl, is this what you showed Grandma and Grandpa when they came for dinner that one night?"

"Yeah, but it wasn't done yet."

"I now understand their reaction. I love you both so much," said Jade, hugging them close again.

"We love you, too, Mama."

"We do. Very, very much," Rachel said, kissing the side of Jade's head.

Brianna jumped out of Jade's lap and ran inside and got something and came back out and stood in front of Rachel.

"I made you a picture," Brianna said, holding out the picture she had drawn for Rachel.

Rachel knelt down to Brianna's level and looked at the picture. She was shocked and amazed by what she saw. A tear rolled down her face before she hugged the amazing girl standing in front of her and whispered thank you.

"Baby, did you see this?" asked Rachel.

"No, she said it was for you and that you were the one to see it first."

Rachel handed Jade the picture and she was also shocked by the picture. It showed her, Rachel, and Brianna in front of a house. Two women and a baby looking down on them. In the middle of the picture were the words "My Family" neatly printed.

About the Author

BL Clark lives in Southern Wisconsin with her partner, their very opinionated cat, and occasionally, their now college bound daughter. When not being distracted by her day job, she can be found working on various story ideas, or playing with some form of technology, be it her computer, phone, tablet, or any other piece of technology she can get her hands on.

You can follow BL Clark at:
Twitter: bl_clarks
Facebook: blclark.author
Website: blc.bkclark.net

www.ingramcontent.com/pod-product-compliance
Lightning Source LLC
Chambersburg PA
CBHW050955210726
48287CB00004B/1237